EXORSISTERS

IMAGE COMICS, INC.

Robert Kirkman—Chief Operating Officer
Erik Larsen—Chief Financial Officer
Todd McFarlane—President
Marc Silvestri—Chief Executive Officer
Jim Valentino—Vice President

Eric Stephenson—Publisher/Chief Creative Officer
Corey Hart—Director of Sales
Jeff Boison—Director of Publishing Planning
& Book Trade Sales
Chris Ross—Director of Digital Sales
Jeff Stang—Director of Specialty Sales
Kat Salazar—Director of PR & Marketing
Drew Gill—Art Director
Heather Doornink—Production Director
Nicole Lapalme—Controller
IMAGECOMICS.COM

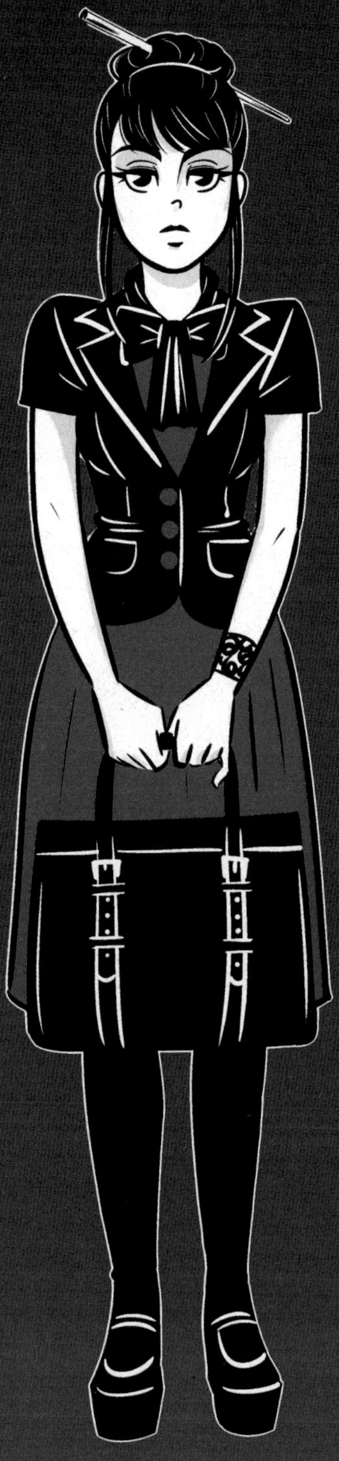

WRITER
IAN BOOTHBY

ARTIST
GISÈLE LAGACÉ

COLORIST
PETE PANTAZIS

LETTERER
TAYLOR ESPOSITO

EDITOR
BRANWYN BIGGLESTONE

PRODUCTION
CAREY HALL

COVER ART
GISÈLE LAGACÉ
& PETE PANTAZIS (COLORS)

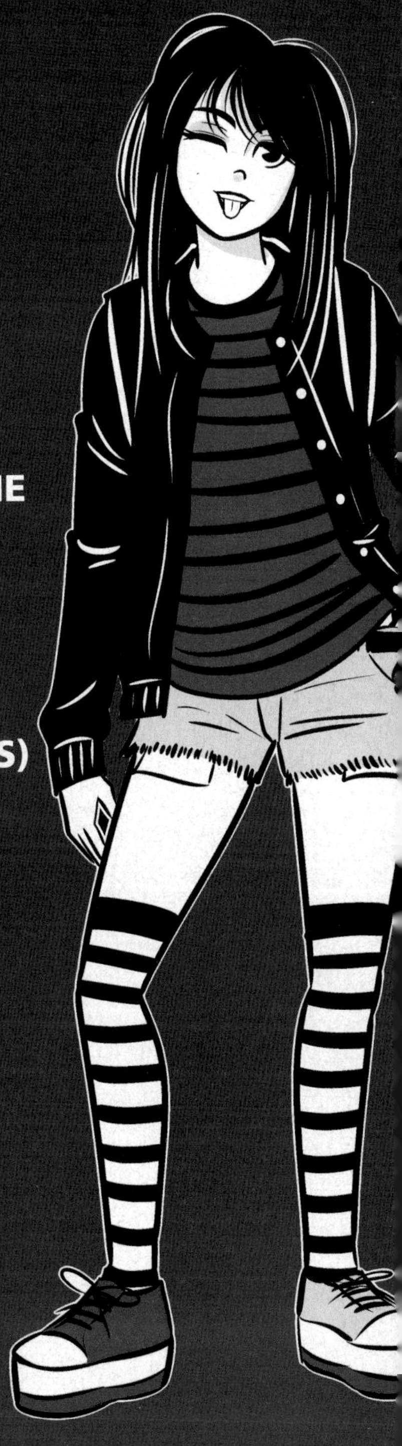

CHAPTER ONE

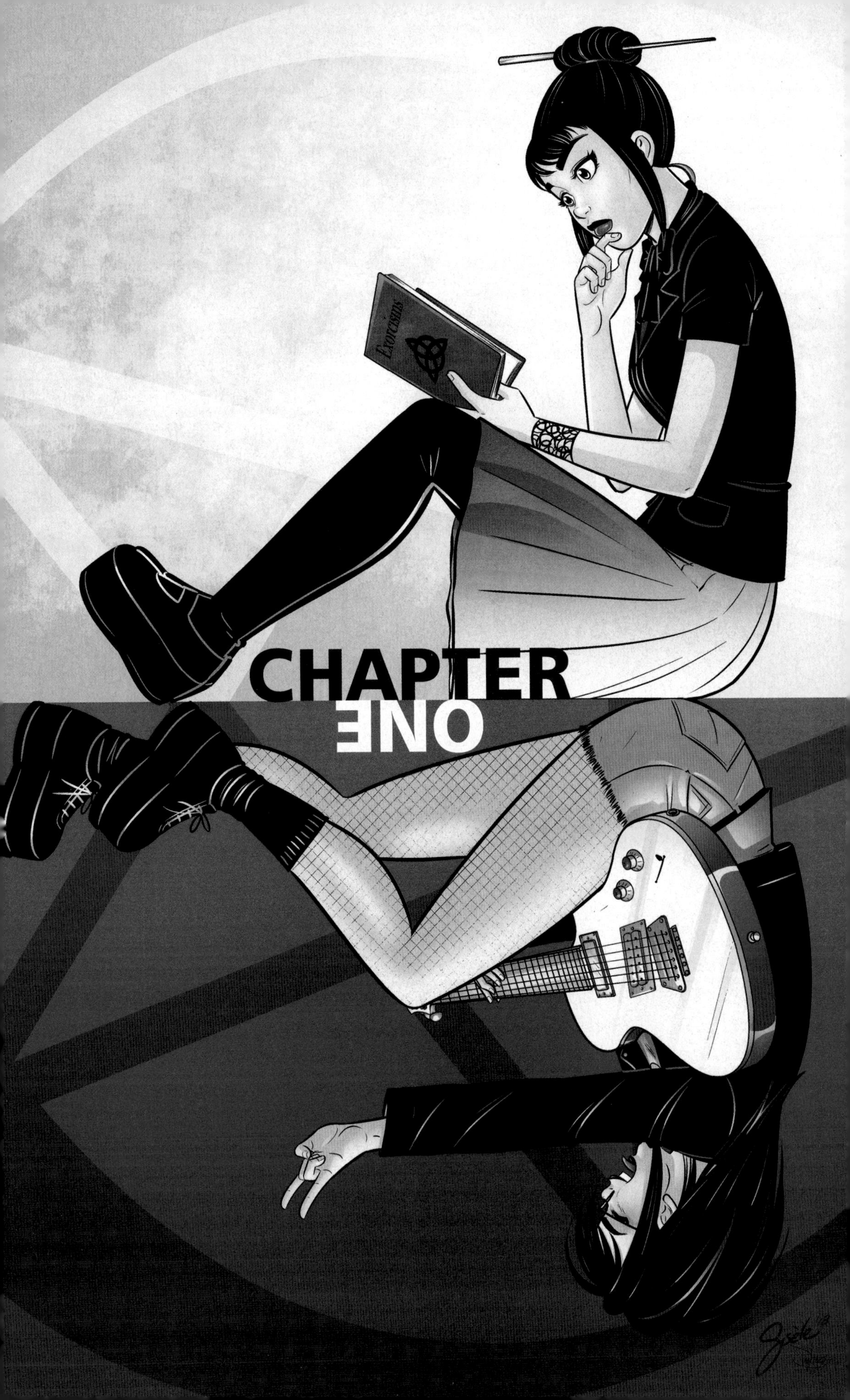
Exorcisms

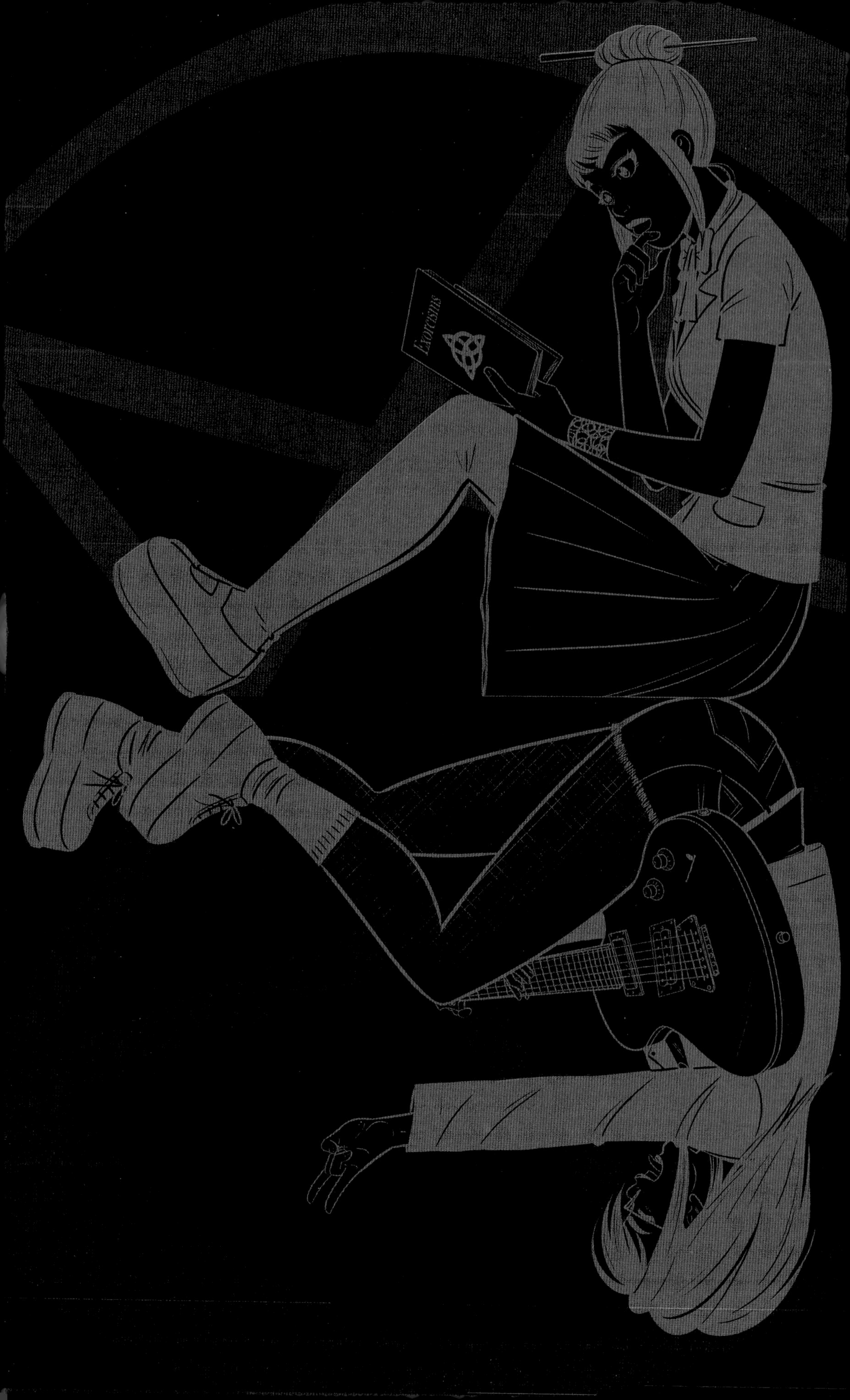
Exorcisms

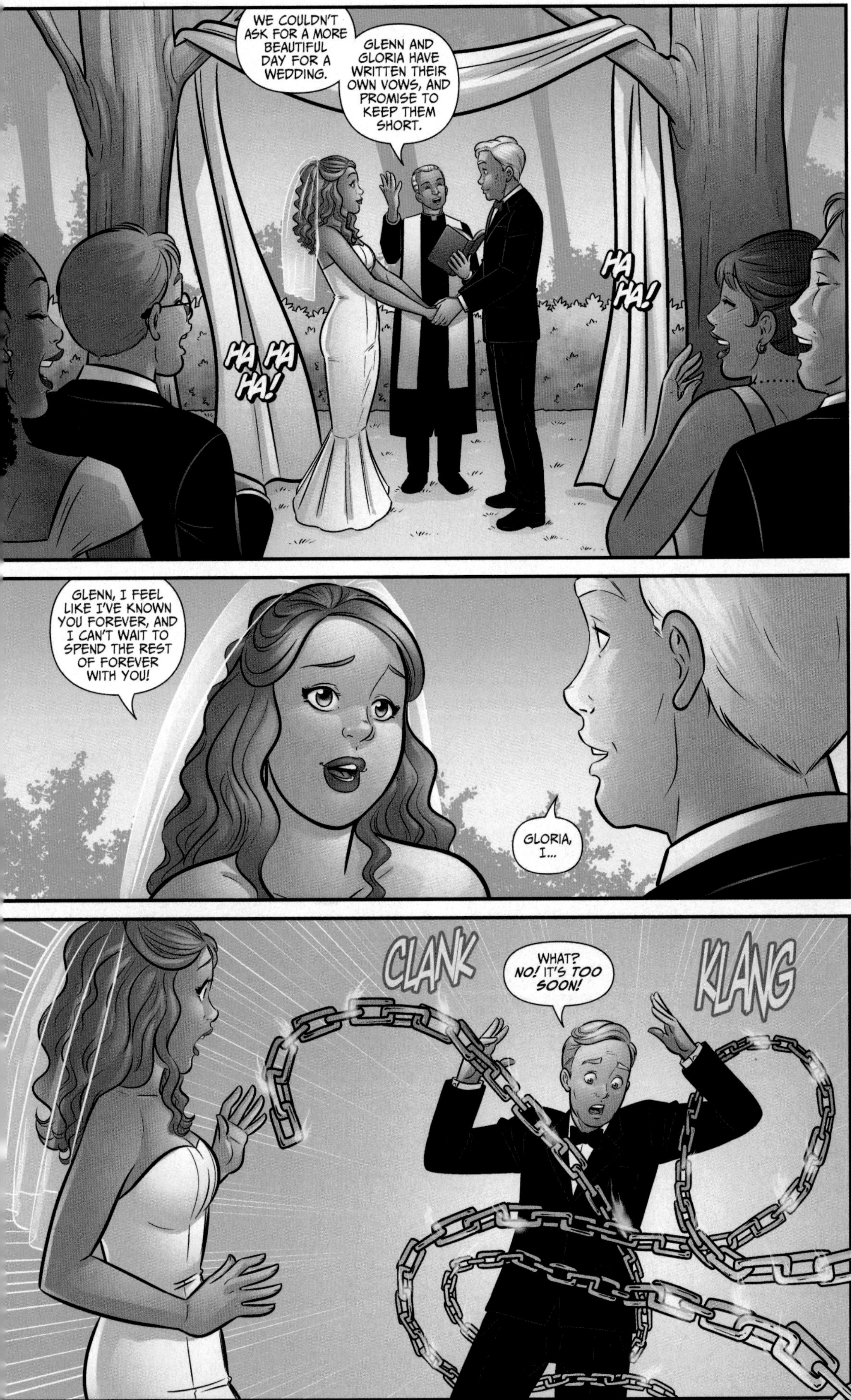
WE COULDN'T ASK FOR A MORE BEAUTIFUL DAY FOR A WEDDING.
GLENN AND GLORIA HAVE WRITTEN THEIR OWN VOWS, AND PROMISE TO KEEP THEM SHORT.
HA HA HA!
HA HA!
GLENN, I FEEL LIKE I'VE KNOWN YOU FOREVER, AND I CAN'T WAIT TO SPEND THE REST OF FOREVER WITH YOU!
GLORIA, I...
CLANK
WHAT? NO! IT'S TOO SOON!
KLANG

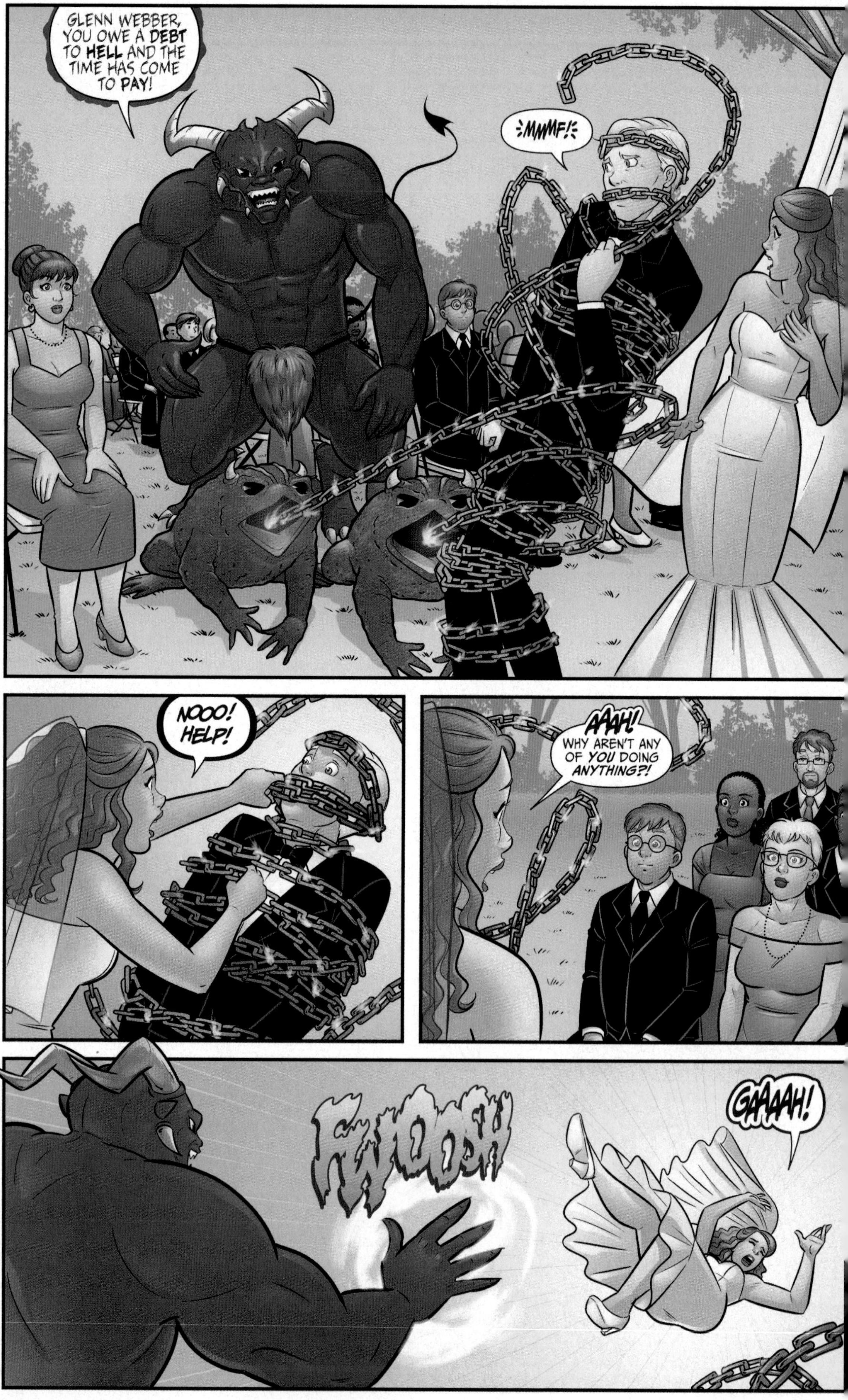
GLENN WEBBER, YOU OWE A DEBT TO HELL AND THE TIME HAS COME TO PAY!
MMMF!
NOOO! HELP!
AAAH! WHY AREN'T ANY OF YOU DOING ANYTHING?!
FWOOSH
GAAAAH!

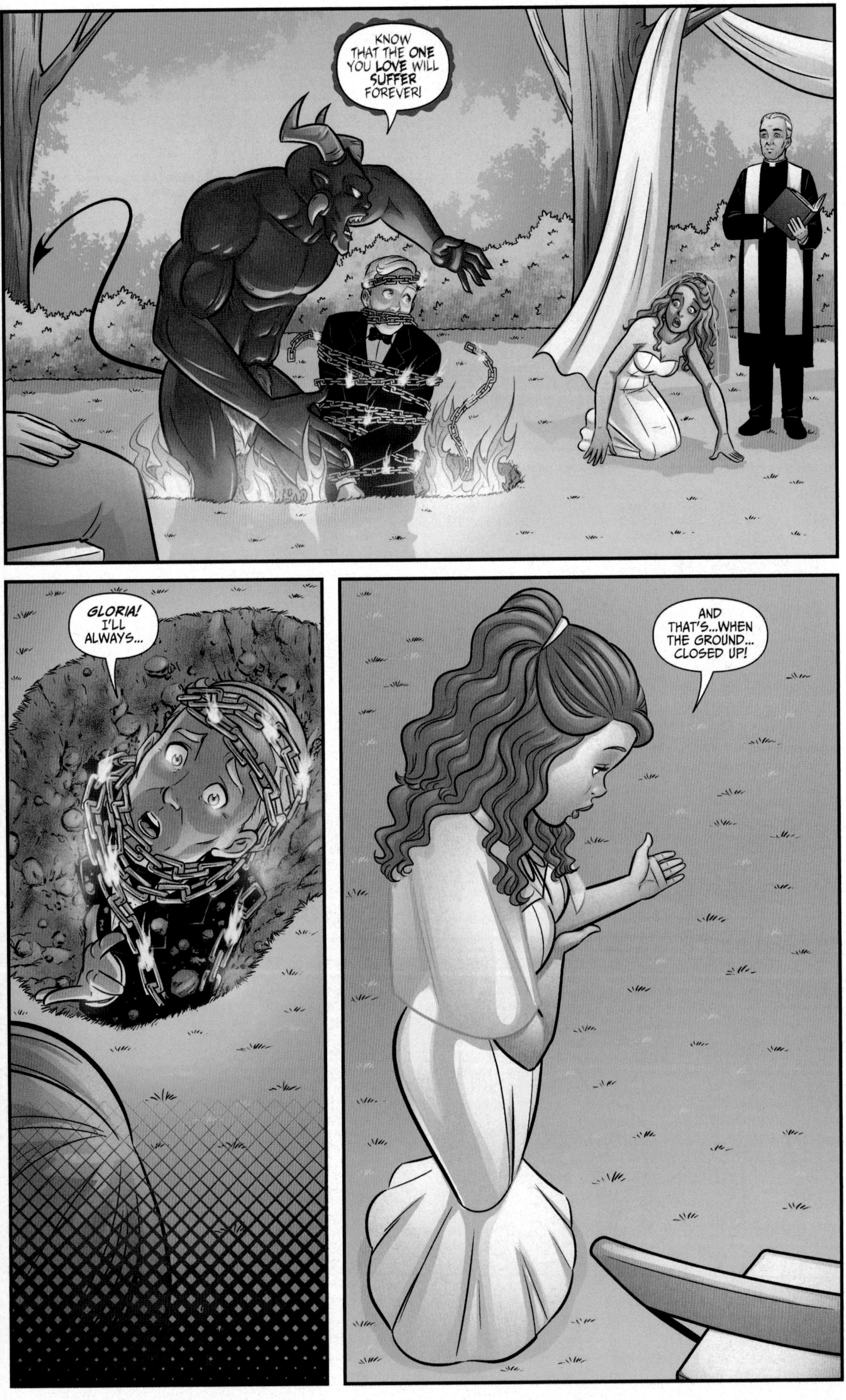
KNOW THAT THE ONE YOU LOVE WILL SUFFER FOREVER!
GLORIA! I'LL ALWAYS...
AND THAT'S...WHEN THE GROUND... CLOSED UP!

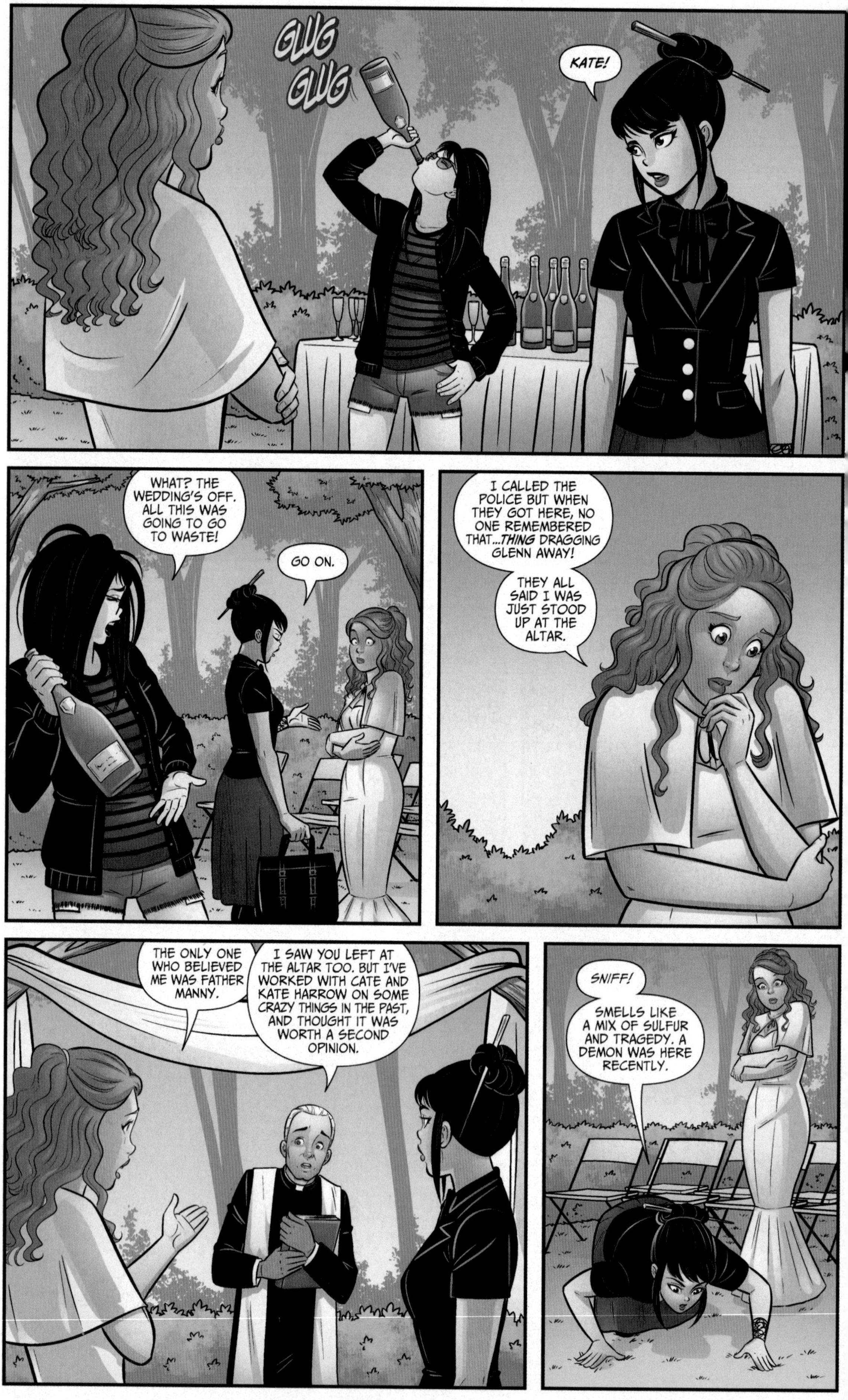

GLUG GLUG
KATE!
WHAT? THE WEDDING'S OFF. ALL THIS WAS GOING TO GO TO WASTE!
GO ON.
I CALLED THE POLICE BUT WHEN THEY GOT HERE, NO ONE REMEMBERED THAT...THING DRAGGING GLENN AWAY!
THEY ALL SAID I WAS JUST STOOD UP AT THE ALTAR.
THE ONLY ONE WHO BELIEVED ME WAS FATHER MANNY.
I SAW YOU LEFT AT THE ALTAR TOO. BUT I'VE WORKED WITH CATE AND KATE HARROW ON SOME CRAZY THINGS IN THE PAST, AND THOUGHT IT WAS WORTH A SECOND OPINION.
SNIFF!
SMELLS LIKE A MIX OF SULFUR AND TRAGEDY. A DEMON WAS HERE RECENTLY.

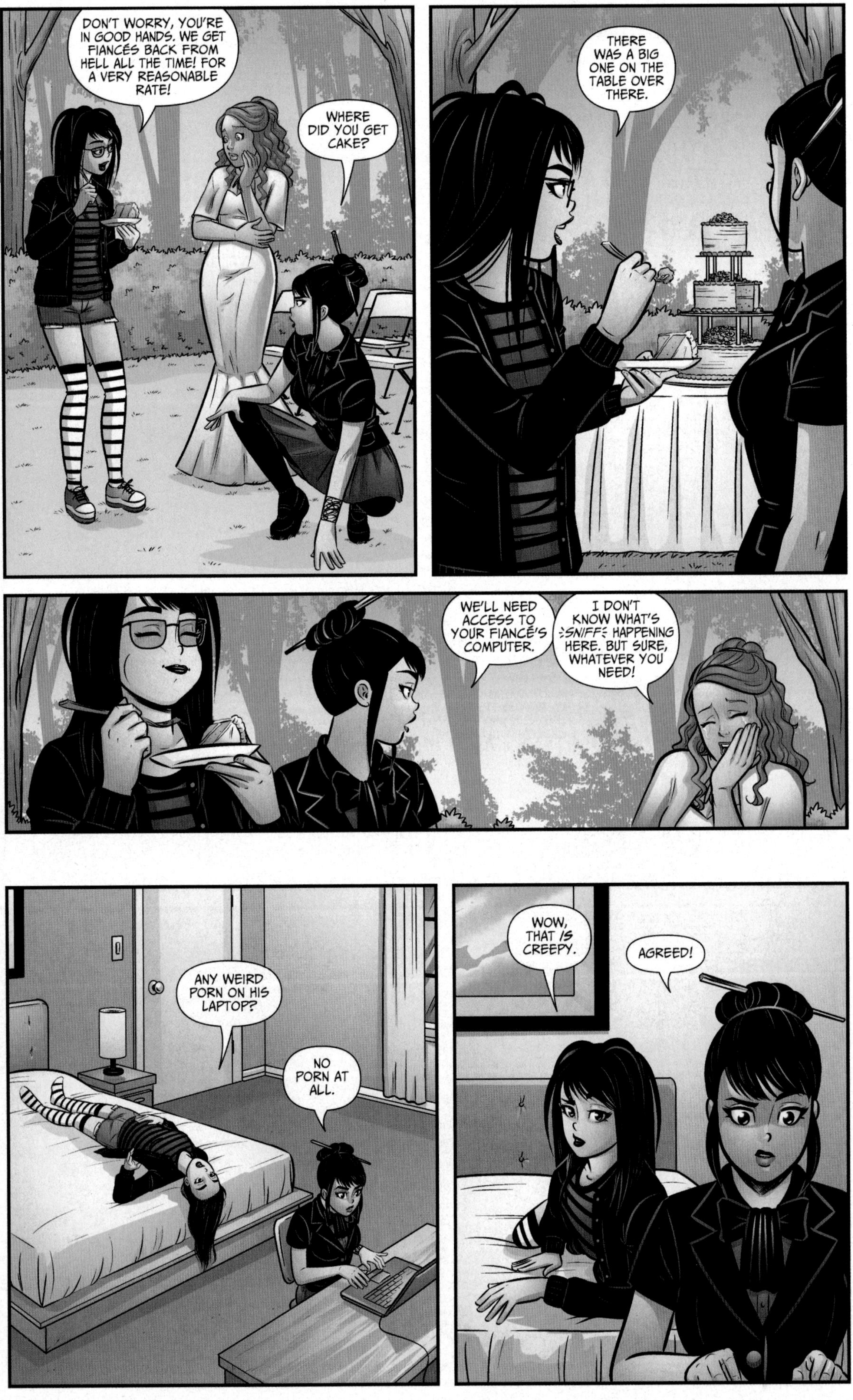
DON'T WORRY, YOU'RE IN GOOD HANDS. WE GET FIANCÉS BACK FROM HELL ALL THE TIME! FOR A VERY REASONABLE RATE!
WHERE DID YOU GET CAKE?
THERE WAS A BIG ONE ON THE TABLE OVER THERE.
WE'LL NEED ACCESS TO YOUR FIANCÉ'S COMPUTER.
I DON'T KNOW WHAT'S *SNIFF* HAPPENING HERE. BUT SURE, WHATEVER YOU NEED!
ANY WEIRD PORN ON HIS LAPTOP?
NO PORN AT ALL.
WOW, THAT *IS* CREEPY.
AGREED!

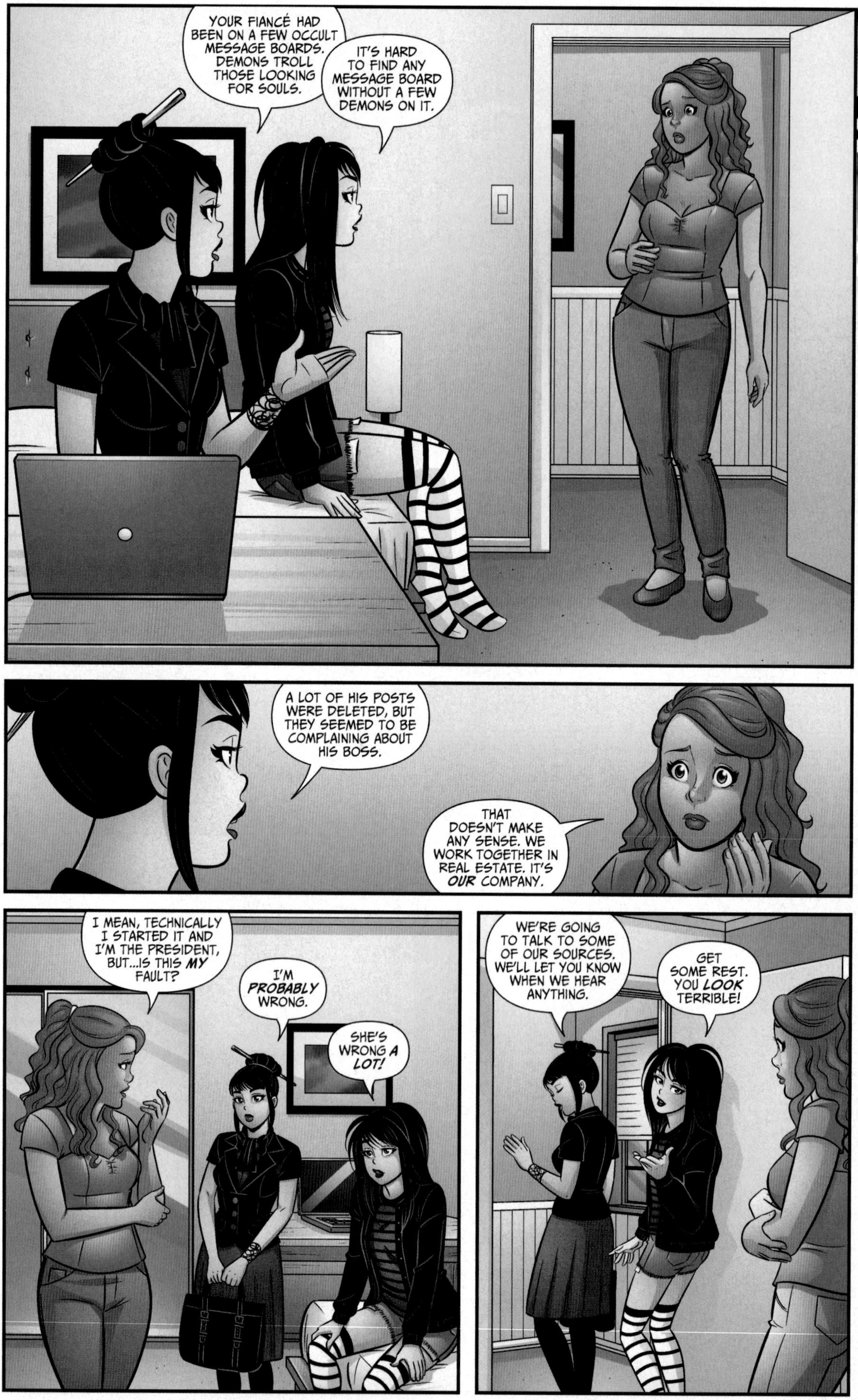

YOUR FIANCÉ HAD BEEN ON A FEW OCCULT MESSAGE BOARDS. DEMONS TROLL THOSE LOOKING FOR SOULS.
IT'S HARD TO FIND ANY MESSAGE BOARD WITHOUT A FEW DEMONS ON IT.
A LOT OF HIS POSTS WERE DELETED, BUT THEY SEEMED TO BE COMPLAINING ABOUT HIS BOSS.
THAT DOESN'T MAKE ANY SENSE. WE WORK TOGETHER IN REAL ESTATE. IT'S ***OUR*** COMPANY.
I MEAN, TECHNICALLY I STARTED IT AND I'M THE PRESIDENT, BUT...IS THIS ***MY*** FAULT?
I'M ***PROBABLY*** WRONG.
SHE'S WRONG ***A LOT!***
WE'RE GOING TO TALK TO SOME OF OUR SOURCES. WE'LL LET YOU KNOW WHEN WE HEAR ANYTHING.
GET SOME REST. YOU ***LOOK*** TERRIBLE!

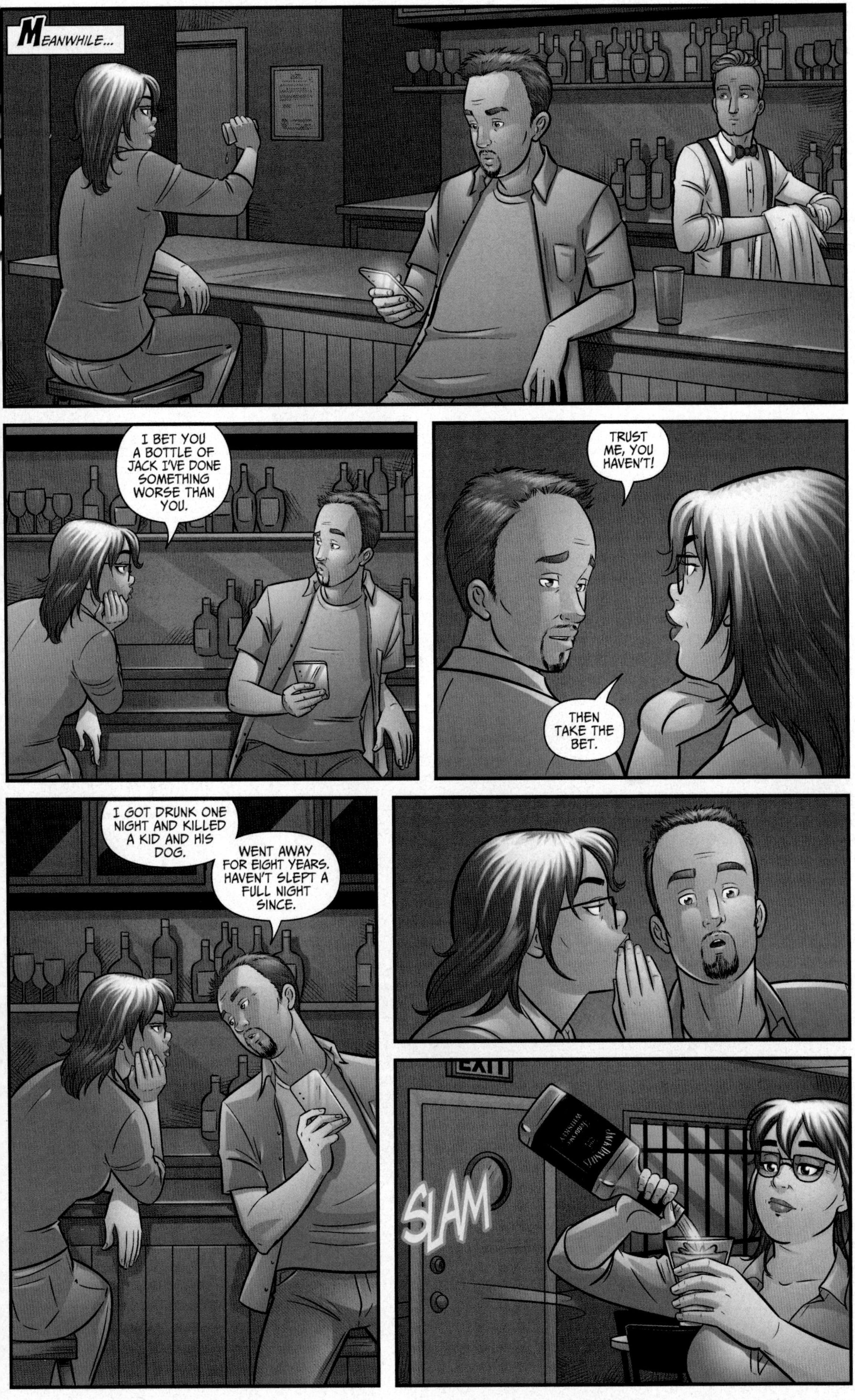
MEANWHILE...
I BET YOU A BOTTLE OF JACK I'VE DONE SOMETHING WORSE THAN YOU.
TRUST ME, YOU HAVEN'T!
THEN TAKE THE BET.
I GOT DRUNK ONE NIGHT AND KILLED A KID AND HIS DOG.
WENT AWAY FOR EIGHT YEARS. HAVEN'T SLEPT A FULL NIGHT SINCE.
EXIT
SLAM

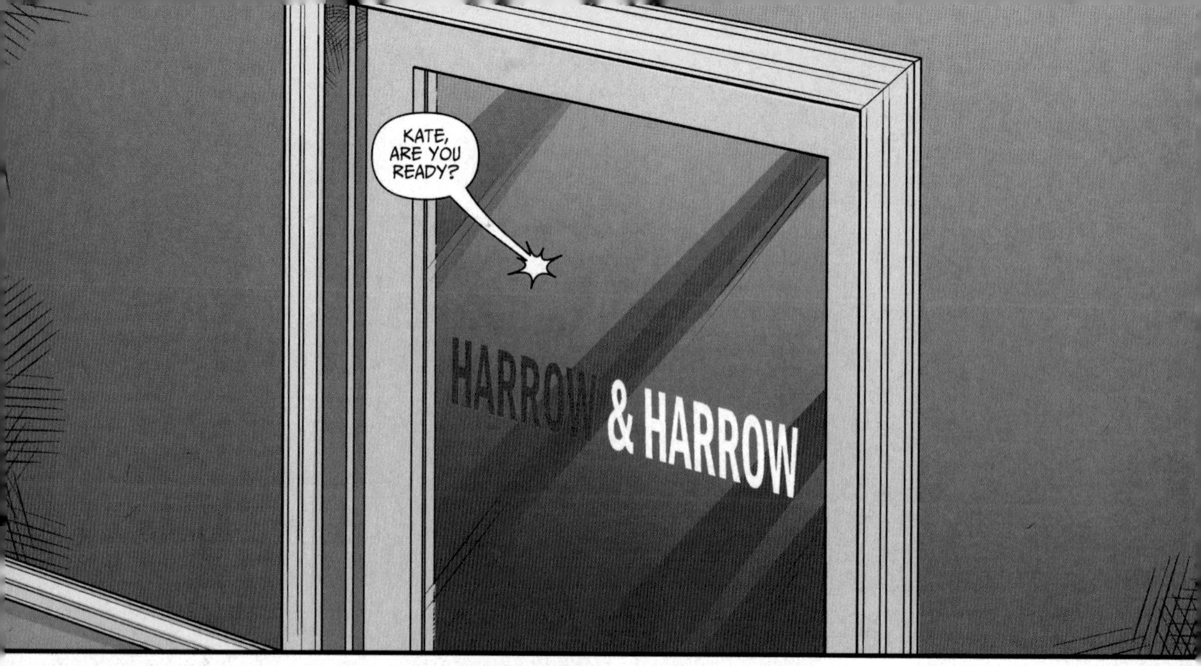
KATE, ARE YOU READY?
HARROW & HARROW

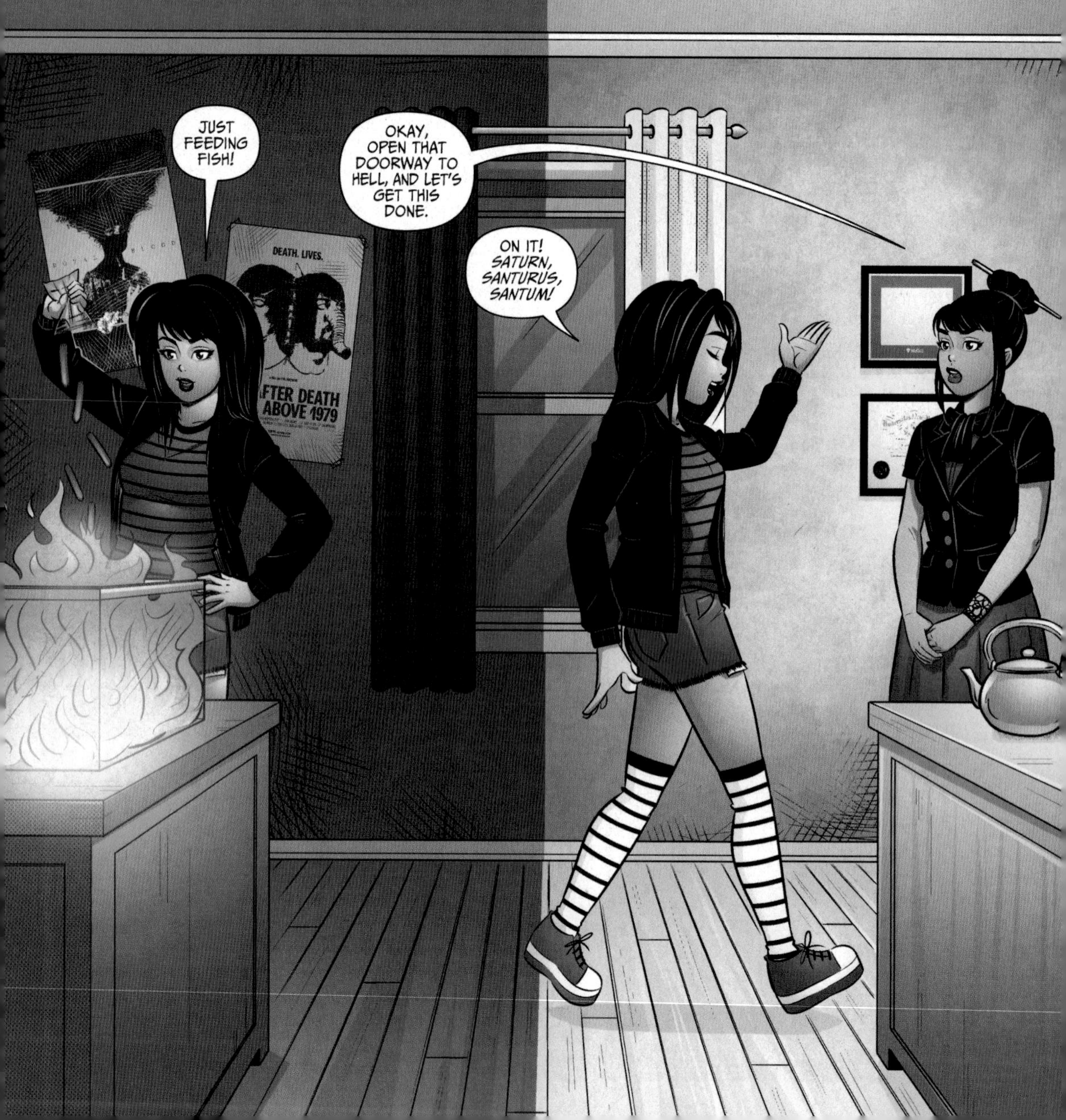
JUST FEEDING FISH!
OKAY, OPEN THAT DOORWAY TO HELL, AND LET'S GET THIS DONE.
ON IT! *SATURN, SANTURUS, SANTUM!*
DEATH. LIVES.

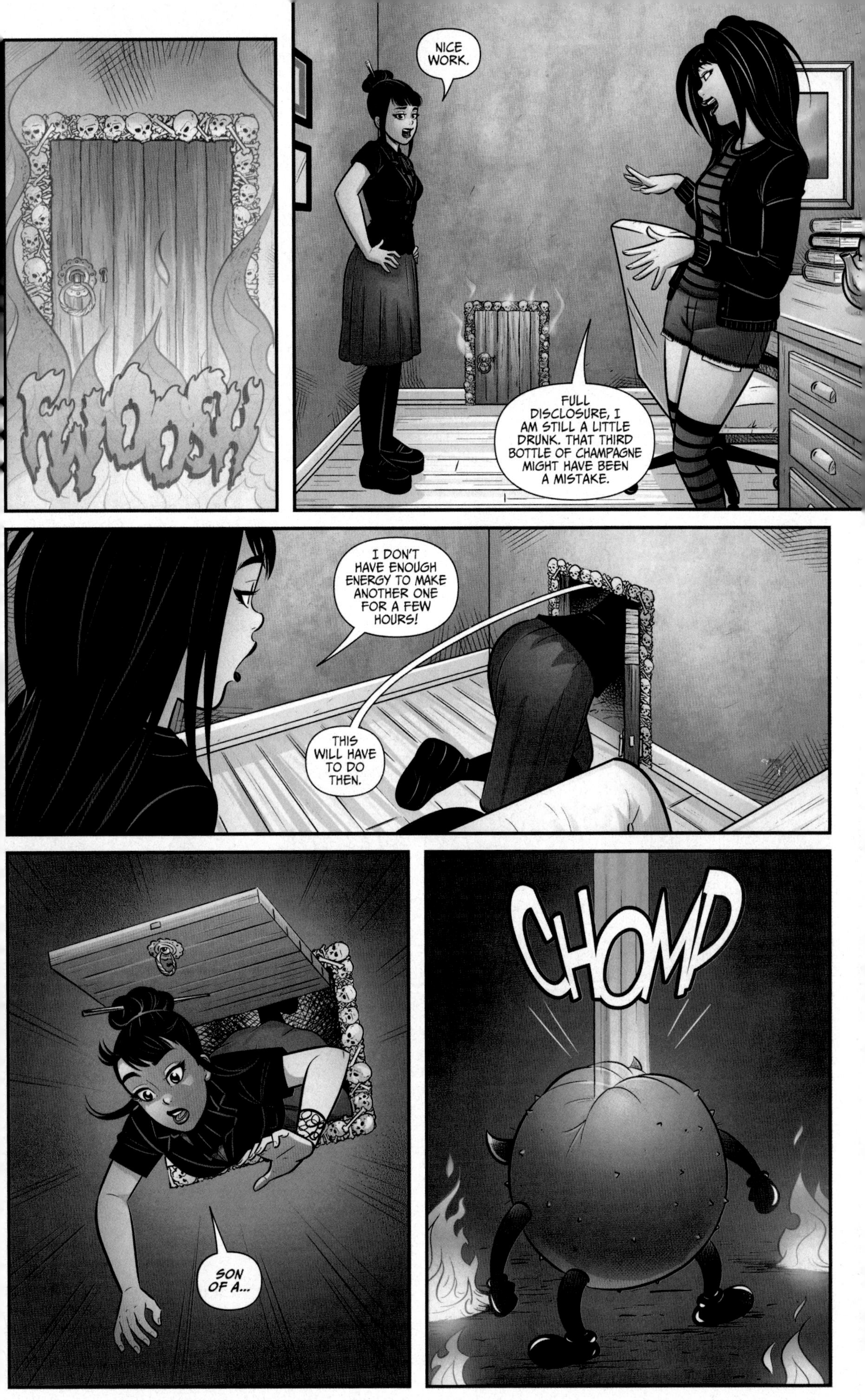
FWOOSH
NICE WORK.
FULL DISCLOSURE, I AM STILL A LITTLE DRUNK. THAT THIRD BOTTLE OF CHAMPAGNE MIGHT HAVE BEEN A MISTAKE.
I DON'T HAVE ENOUGH ENERGY TO MAKE ANOTHER ONE FOR A FEW HOURS!
THIS WILL HAVE TO DO THEN.
SON OF A...
CHOMP

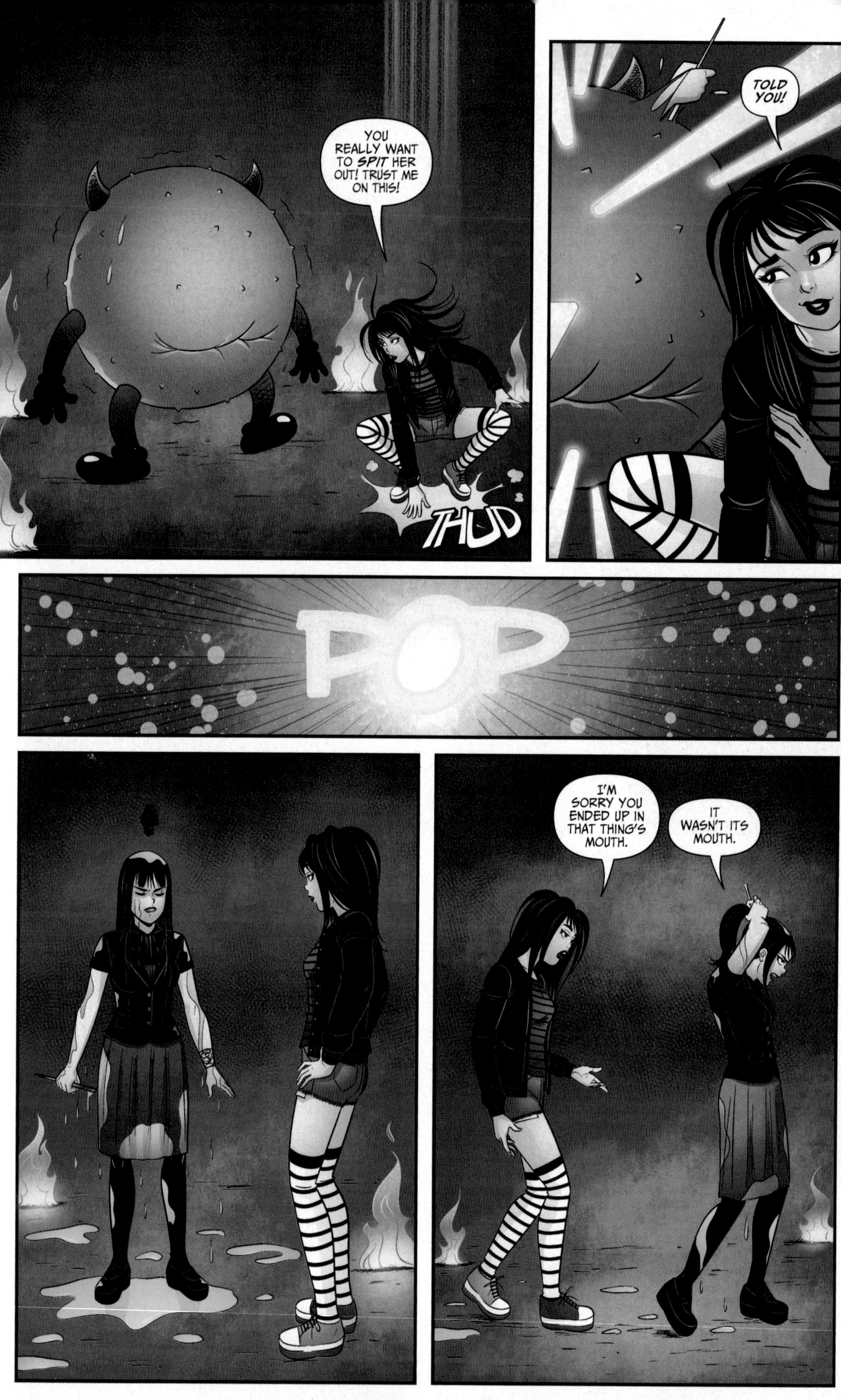
YOU REALLY WANT TO SPIT HER OUT! TRUST ME ON THIS!
THUD
TOLD YOU!
POP
I'M SORRY YOU ENDED UP IN THAT THING'S MOUTH.
IT WASN'T ITS MOUTH.

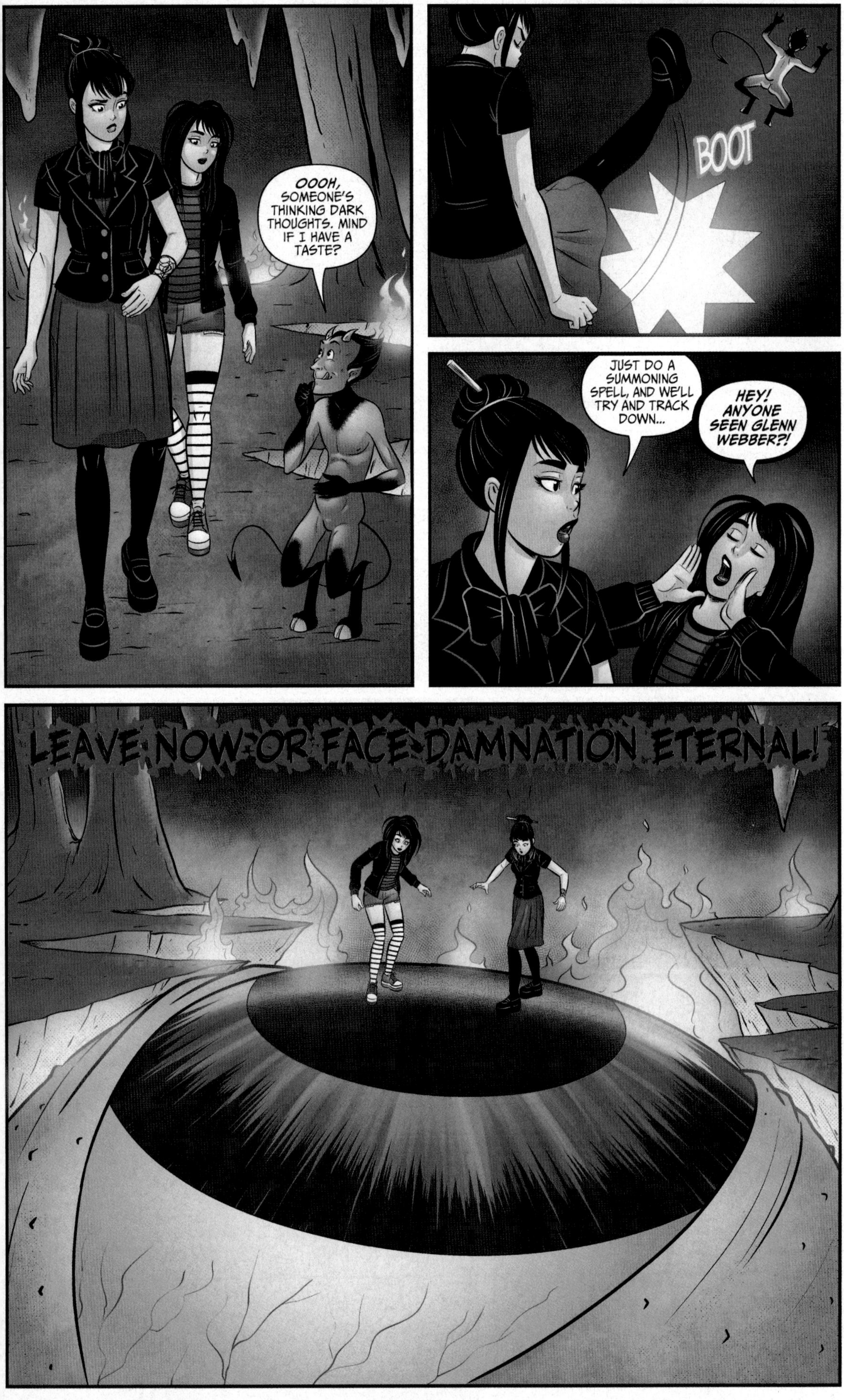
OOOH, SOMEONE'S THINKING DARK THOUGHTS. MIND IF I HAVE A TASTE?
BOOT
JUST DO A SUMMONING SPELL, AND WE'LL TRY AND TRACK DOWN...
HEY! ANYONE SEEN GLENN WEBBER?!
LEAVE NOW OR FACE DAMNATION ETERNAL!

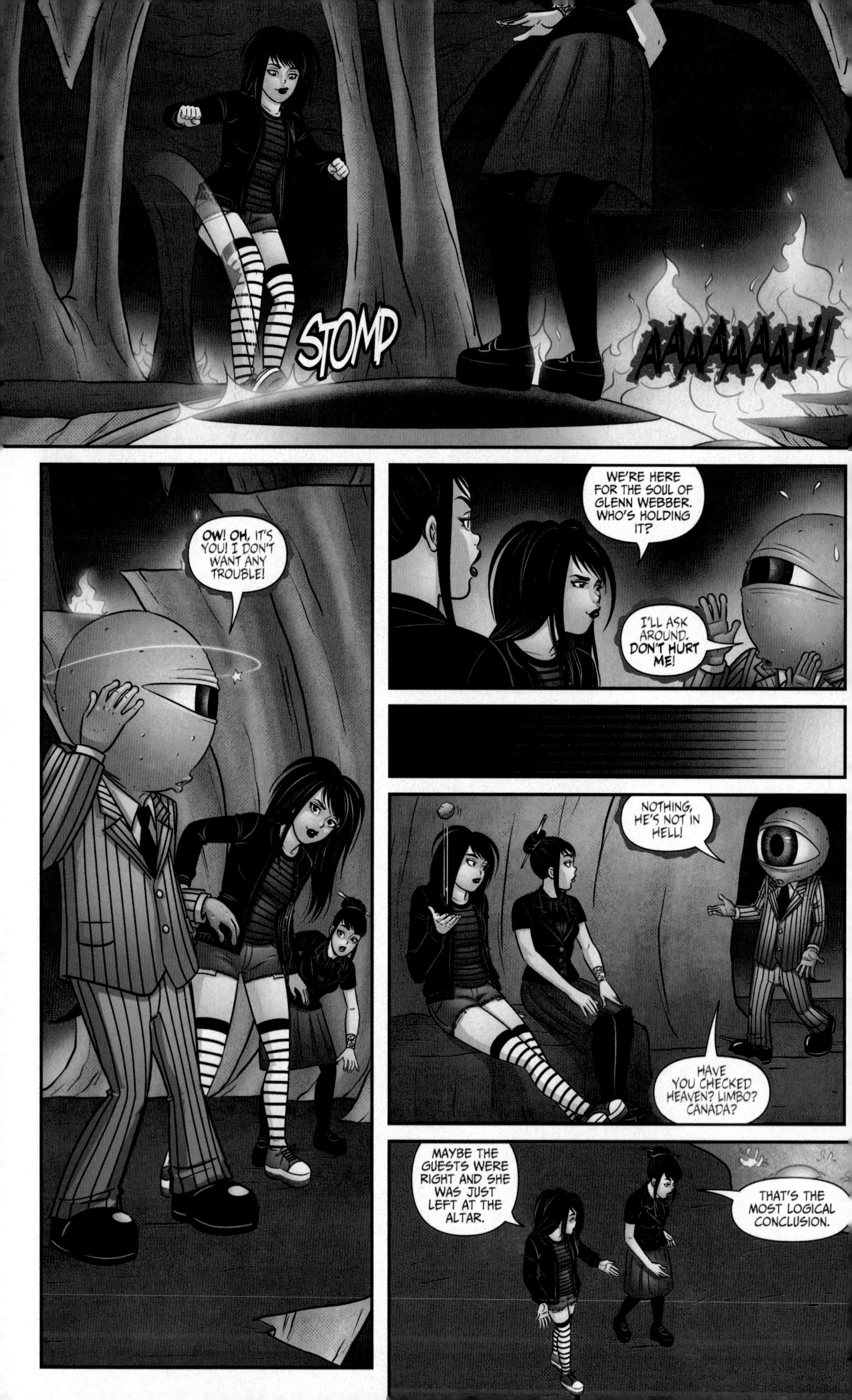
STOMP
AAAAAAAAH!
OW! OH, IT'S YOU! I DON'T WANT ANY TROUBLE!
WE'RE HERE FOR THE SOUL OF GLENN WEBBER. WHO'S HOLDING IT?
I'LL ASK AROUND. DON'T HURT ME!
NOTHING, HE'S NOT IN HELL!
HAVE YOU CHECKED HEAVEN? LIMBO? CANADA?
MAYBE THE GUESTS WERE RIGHT AND SHE WAS JUST LEFT AT THE ALTAR.
THAT'S THE MOST LOGICAL CONCLUSION.

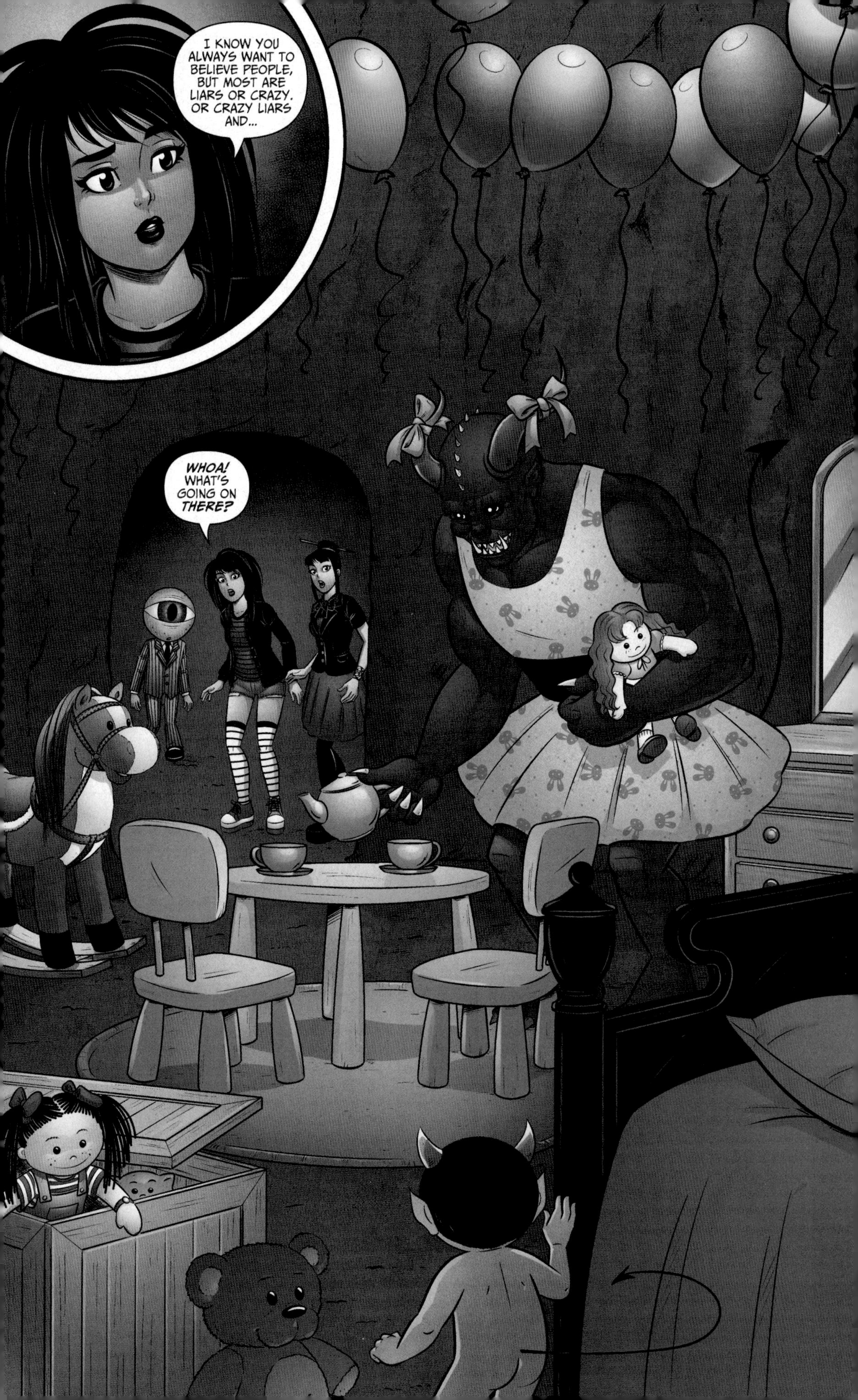
I KNOW YOU ALWAYS WANT TO BELIEVE PEOPLE, BUT MOST ARE LIARS OR CRAZY. OR CRAZY LIARS AND...
WHOA! WHAT'S GOING ON *THERE?*

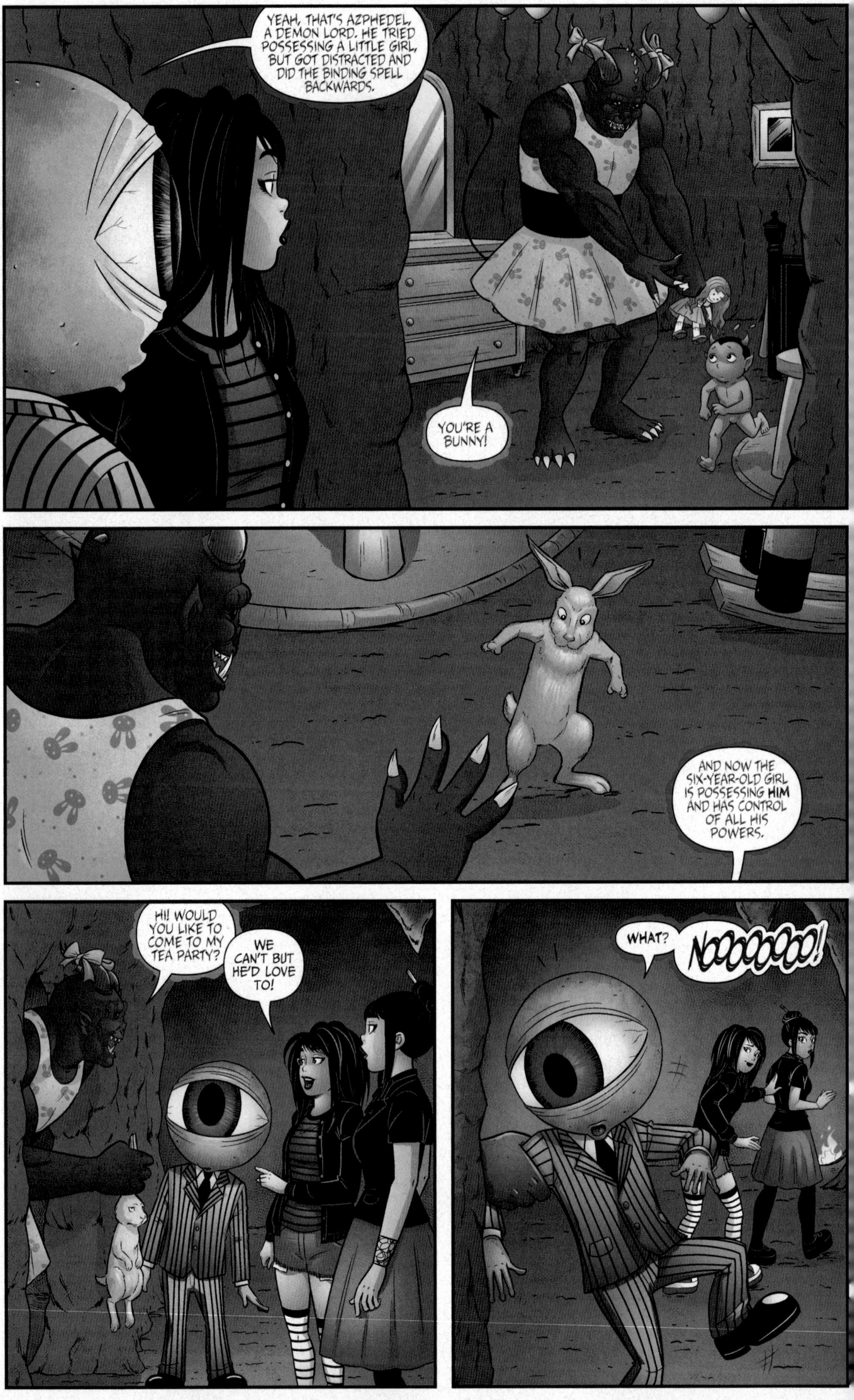
YEAH, THAT'S AZPHEDEL, A DEMON LORD. HE TRIED POSSESSING A LITTLE GIRL, BUT GOT DISTRACTED AND DID THE BINDING SPELL BACKWARDS.
YOU'RE A BUNNY!
AND NOW THE SIX-YEAR-OLD GIRL IS POSSESSING HIM AND HAS CONTROL OF ALL HIS POWERS.
HI! WOULD YOU LIKE TO COME TO MY TEA PARTY?
WE CAN'T BUT HE'D LOVE TO!
WHAT?
NOOOOOOOO!

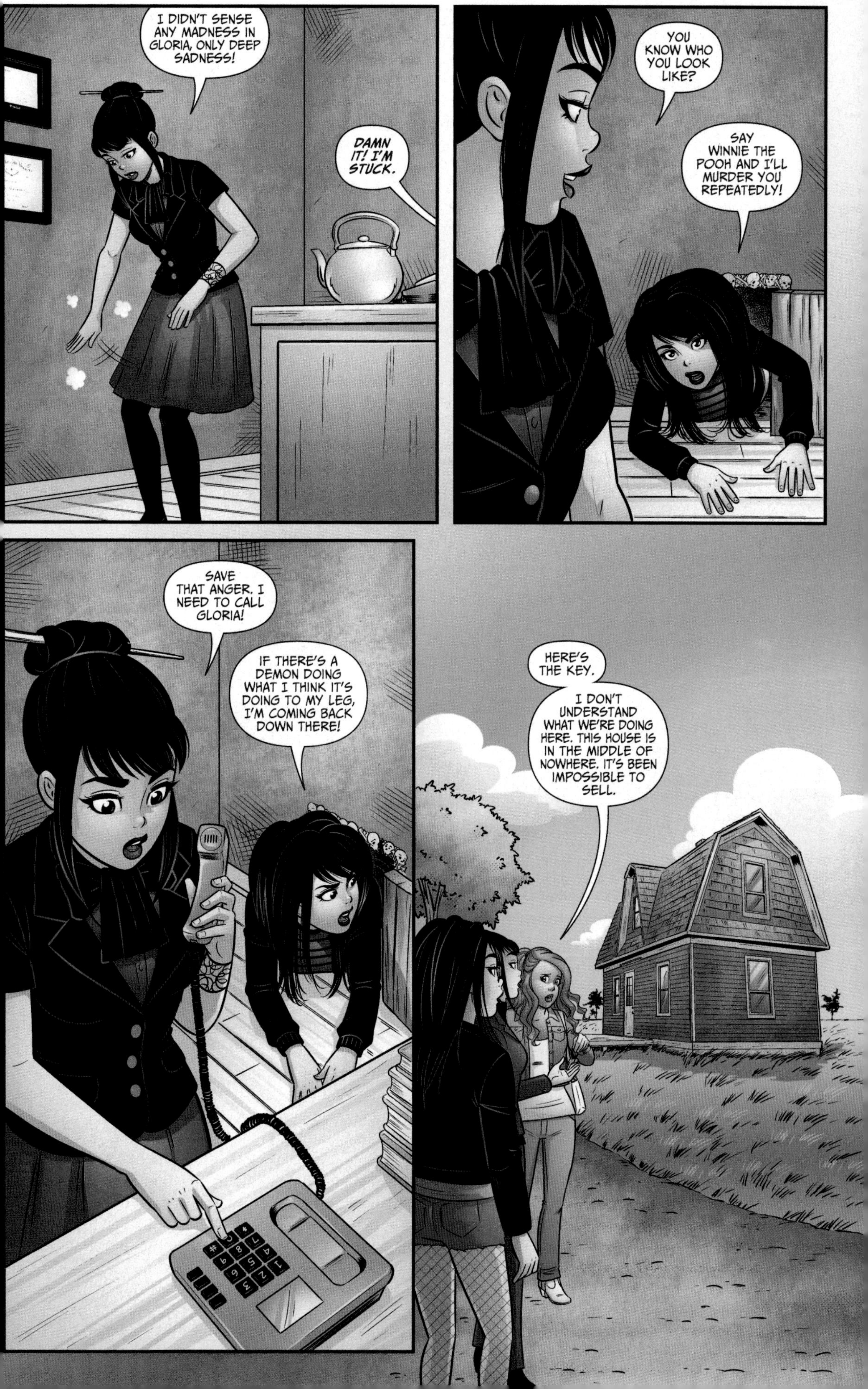
I DIDN'T SENSE ANY MADNESS IN GLORIA, ONLY DEEP SADNESS!
DAMN IT! I'M STUCK.
YOU KNOW WHO YOU LOOK LIKE?
SAY WINNIE THE POOH AND I'LL MURDER YOU REPEATEDLY!
SAVE THAT ANGER. I NEED TO CALL GLORIA!
IF THERE'S A DEMON DOING WHAT I THINK IT'S DOING TO MY LEG, I'M COMING BACK DOWN THERE!
HERE'S THE KEY.
I DON'T UNDERSTAND WHAT WE'RE DOING HERE. THIS HOUSE IS IN THE MIDDLE OF NOWHERE. IT'S BEEN IMPOSSIBLE TO SELL.

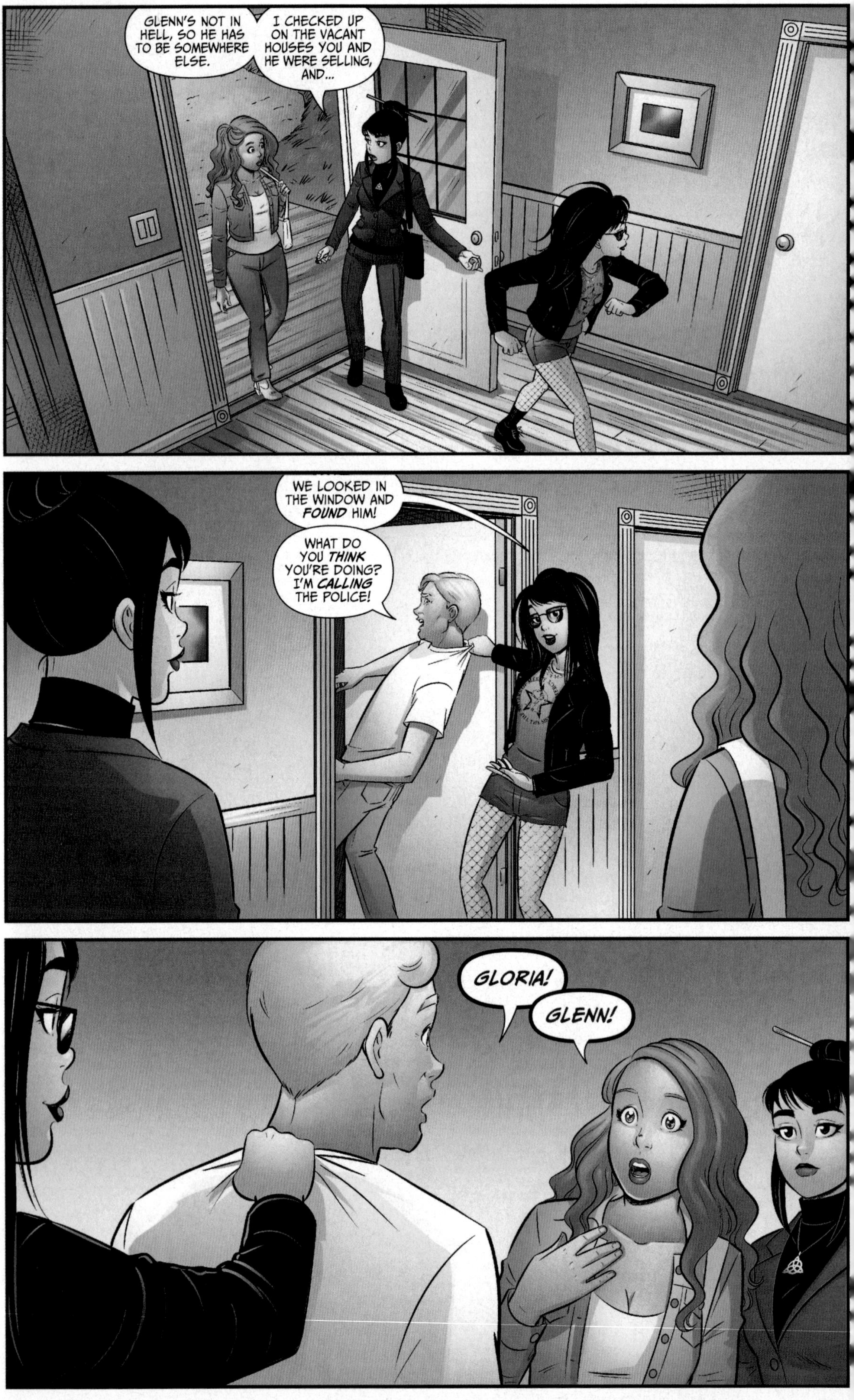
GLENN'S NOT IN HELL, SO HE HAS TO BE SOMEWHERE ELSE.
I CHECKED UP ON THE VACANT HOUSES YOU AND HE WERE SELLING, AND...
WE LOOKED IN THE WINDOW AND FOUND HIM!
WHAT DO YOU THINK YOU'RE DOING? I'M CALLING THE POLICE!
GLORIA!
GLENN!

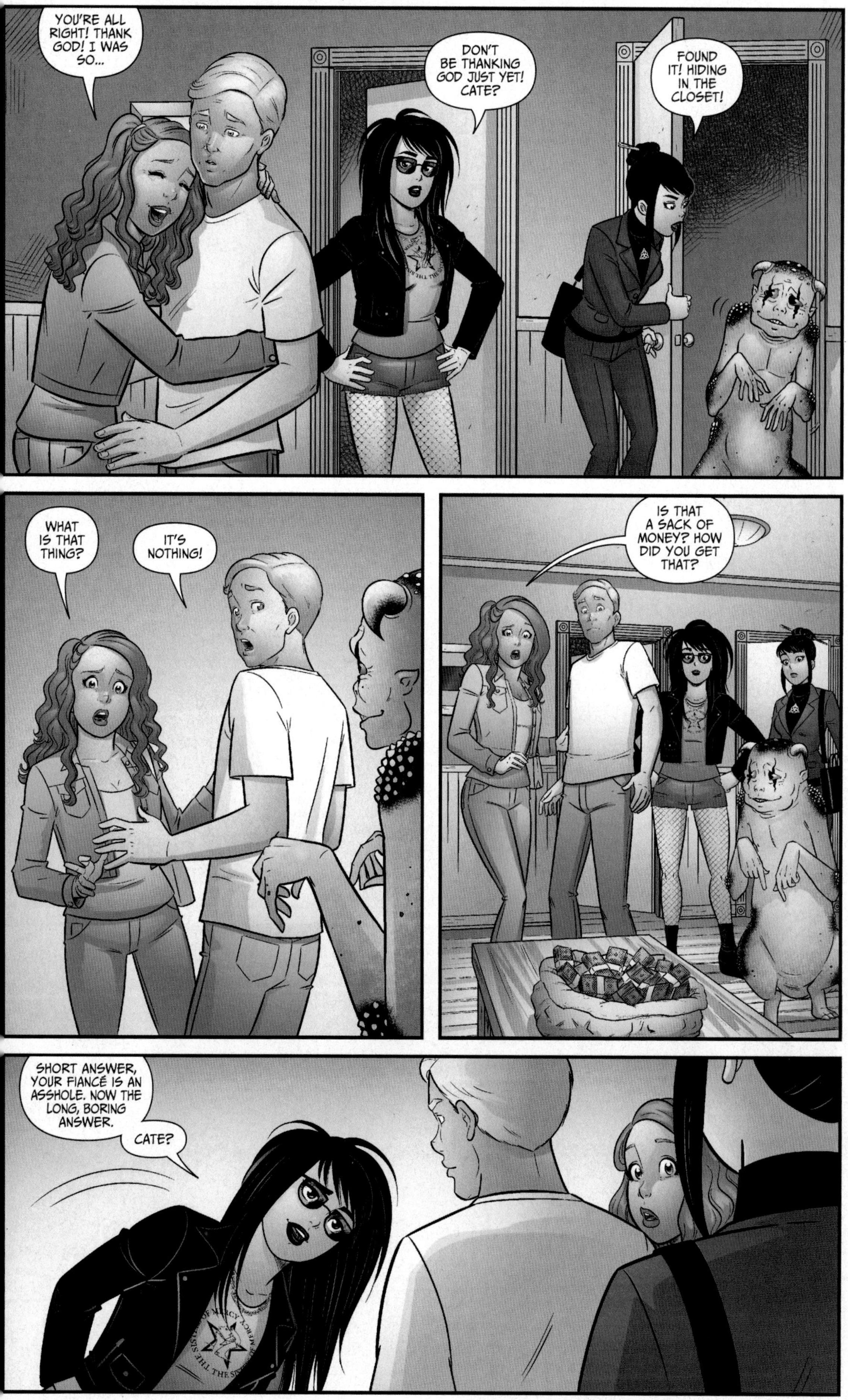
YOU'RE ALL RIGHT! THANK GOD! I WAS SO...
DON'T BE THANKING GOD JUST YET! CATE?
FOUND IT! HIDING IN THE CLOSET!
WHAT IS THAT THING?
IT'S NOTHING!
IS THAT A SACK OF MONEY? HOW DID YOU GET THAT?
SHORT ANSWER, YOUR FIANCÉ IS AN ASSHOLE. NOW THE LONG, BORING ANSWER.
CATE?

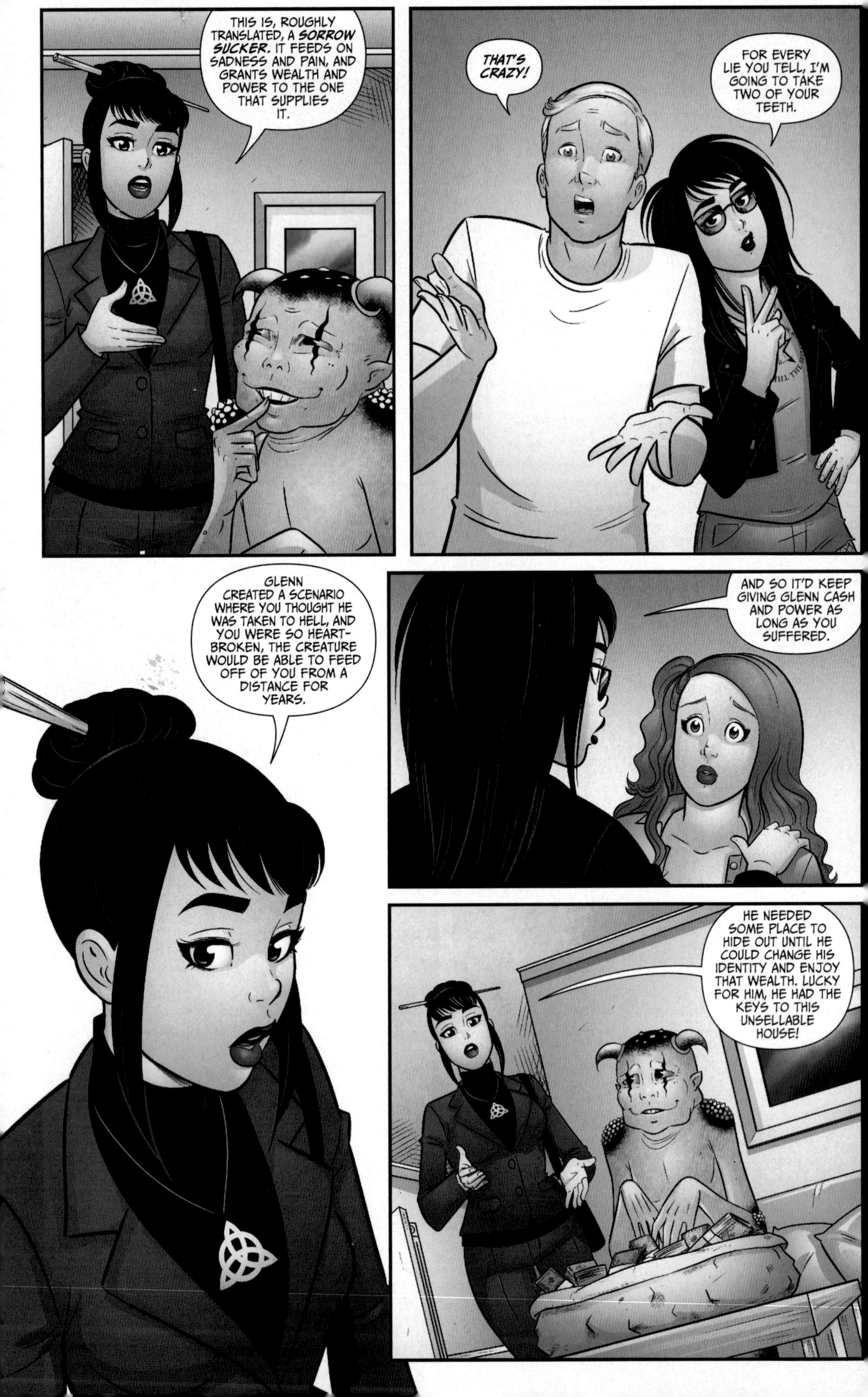
THIS IS, ROUGHLY TRANSLATED, A SORROW SUCKER. IT FEEDS ON SADNESS AND PAIN, AND GRANTS WEALTH AND POWER TO THE ONE THAT SUPPLIES IT.
THAT'S CRAZY!
FOR EVERY LIE YOU TELL, I'M GOING TO TAKE TWO OF YOUR TEETH.
GLENN CREATED A SCENARIO WHERE YOU THOUGHT HE WAS TAKEN TO HELL, AND YOU WERE SO HEART-BROKEN, THE CREATURE WOULD BE ABLE TO FEED OFF OF YOU FROM A DISTANCE FOR YEARS.
AND SO IT'D KEEP GIVING GLENN CASH AND POWER AS LONG AS YOU SUFFERED.
HE NEEDED SOME PLACE TO HIDE OUT UNTIL HE COULD CHANGE HIS IDENTITY AND ENJOY THAT WEALTH. LUCKY FOR HIM, HE HAD THE KEYS TO THIS UNSELLABLE HOUSE!

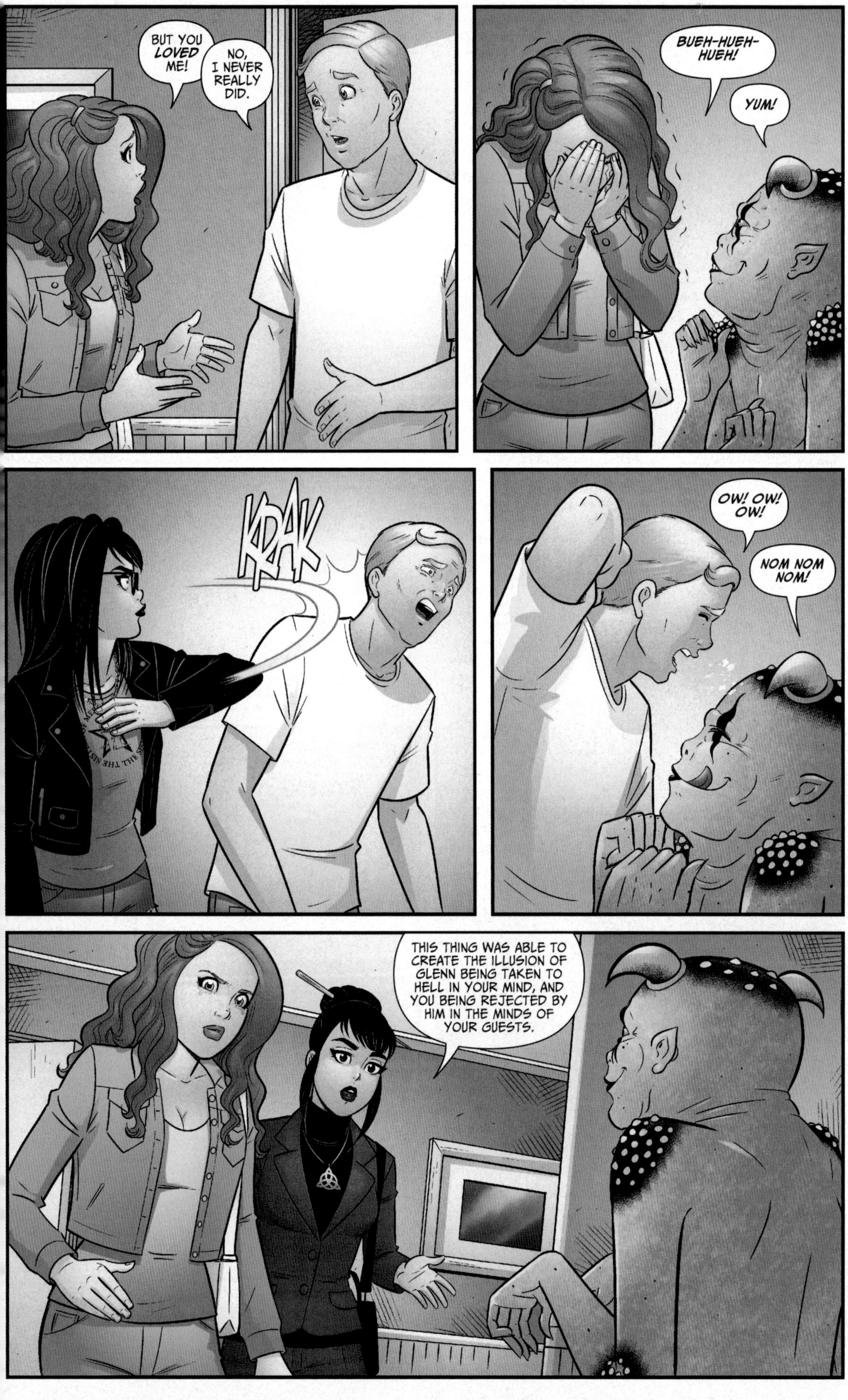
BUT YOU LOVED ME!
NO, I NEVER REALLY DID.
BUEH-HUEH-HUEH!
YUM!
KRAK
OW! OW! OW!
NOM NOM NOM!
THIS THING WAS ABLE TO CREATE THE ILLUSION OF GLENN BEING TAKEN TO HELL IN YOUR MIND, AND YOU BEING REJECTED BY HIM IN THE MINDS OF YOUR GUESTS.

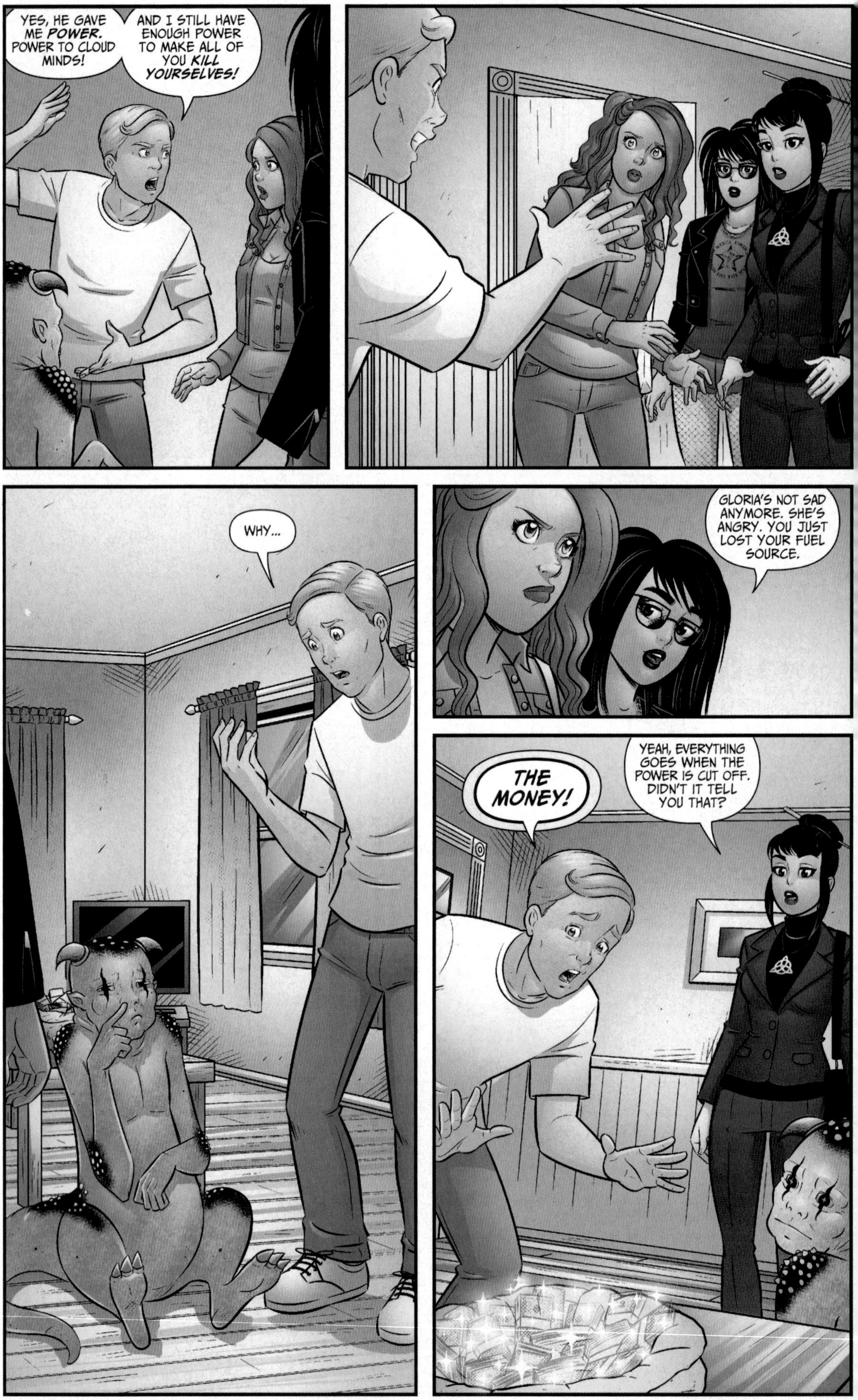
YES, HE GAVE ME POWER. POWER TO CLOUD MINDS!
AND I STILL HAVE ENOUGH POWER TO MAKE ALL OF YOU KILL YOURSELVES!
WHY...
GLORIA'S NOT SAD ANYMORE. SHE'S ANGRY. YOU JUST LOST YOUR FUEL SOURCE.
THE MONEY!
YEAH, EVERYTHING GOES WHEN THE POWER IS CUT OFF. DIDN'T IT TELL YOU THAT?

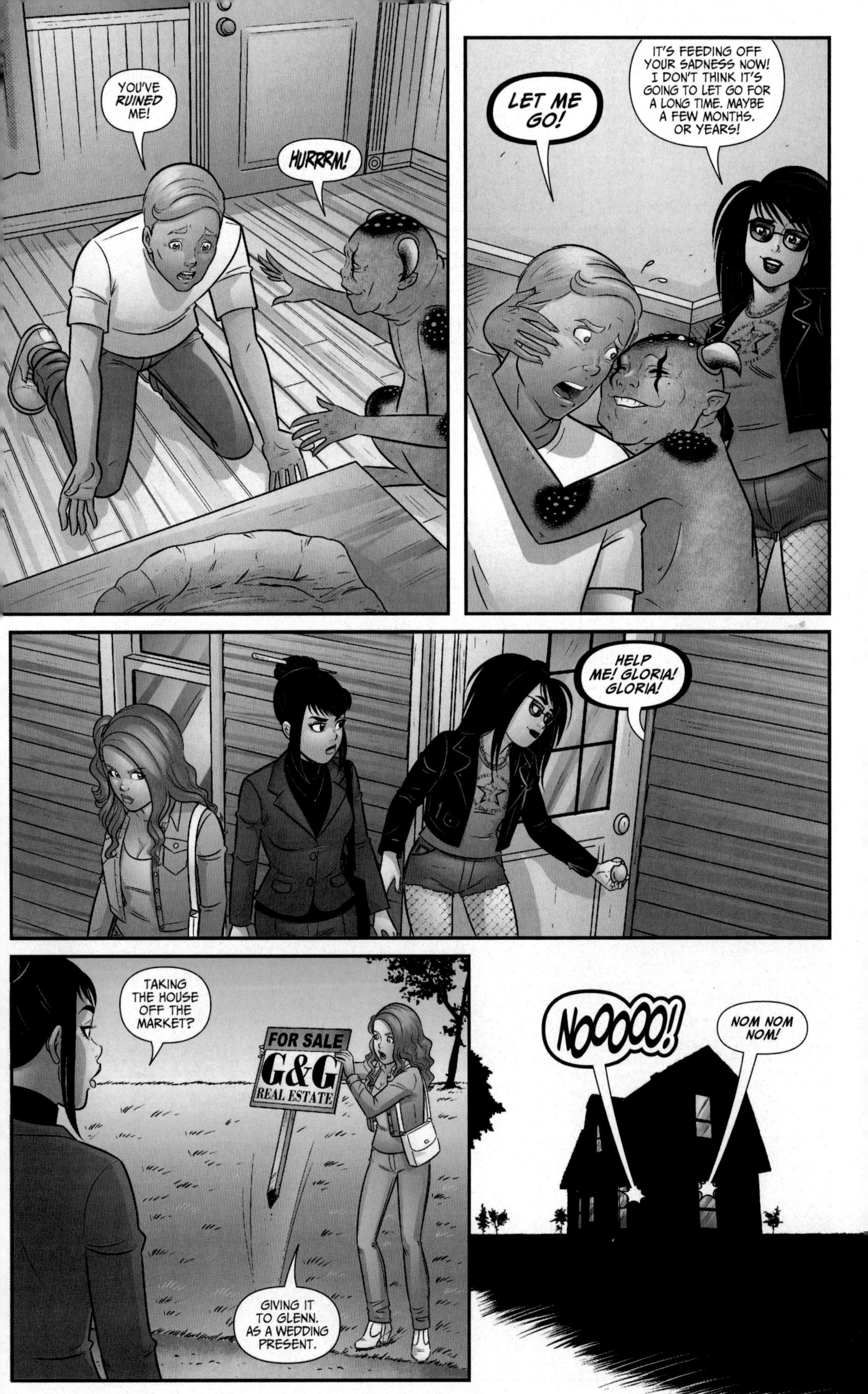
YOU'VE RUINED ME!
HURRRM!
LET ME GO!
IT'S FEEDING OFF YOUR SADNESS NOW! I DON'T THINK IT'S GOING TO LET GO FOR A LONG TIME. MAYBE A FEW MONTHS. OR YEARS!
HELP ME! GLORIA! GLORIA!
TAKING THE HOUSE OFF THE MARKET?
FOR SALE
G&G
REAL ESTATE
GIVING IT TO GLENN. AS A WEDDING PRESENT.
NOOOOO!
NOM NOM NOM!

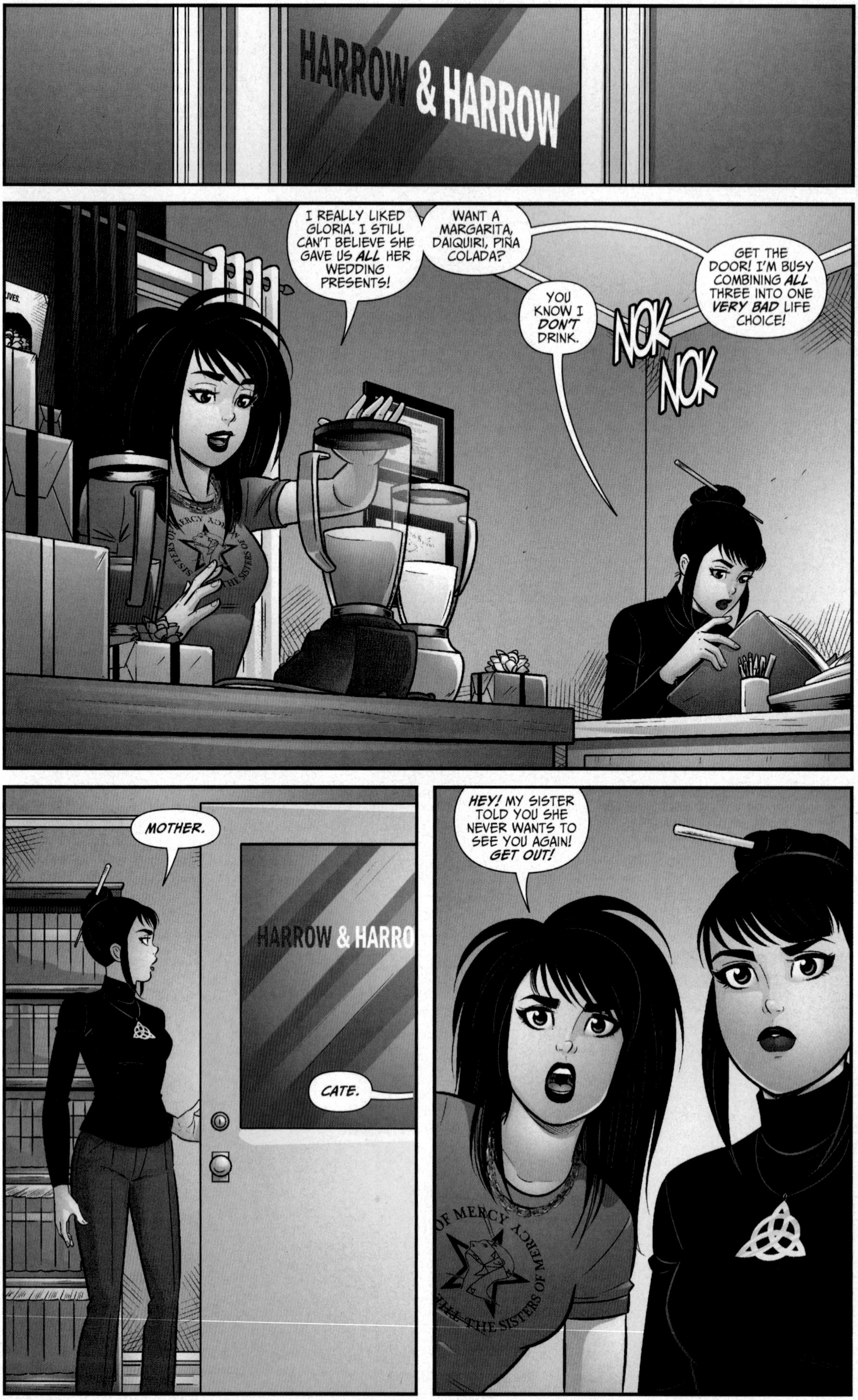
HARROW & HARROW
I REALLY LIKED GLORIA. I STILL CAN'T BELIEVE SHE GAVE US ALL HER WEDDING PRESENTS!
WANT A MARGARITA, DAIQUIRI, PIÑA COLADA?
YOU KNOW I DON'T DRINK.
GET THE DOOR! I'M BUSY COMBINING ALL THREE INTO ONE VERY BAD LIFE CHOICE!
NOK NOK
MOTHER.
HARROW & HARRO
CATE.
HEY! MY SISTER TOLD YOU SHE NEVER WANTS TO SEE YOU AGAIN! GET OUT!

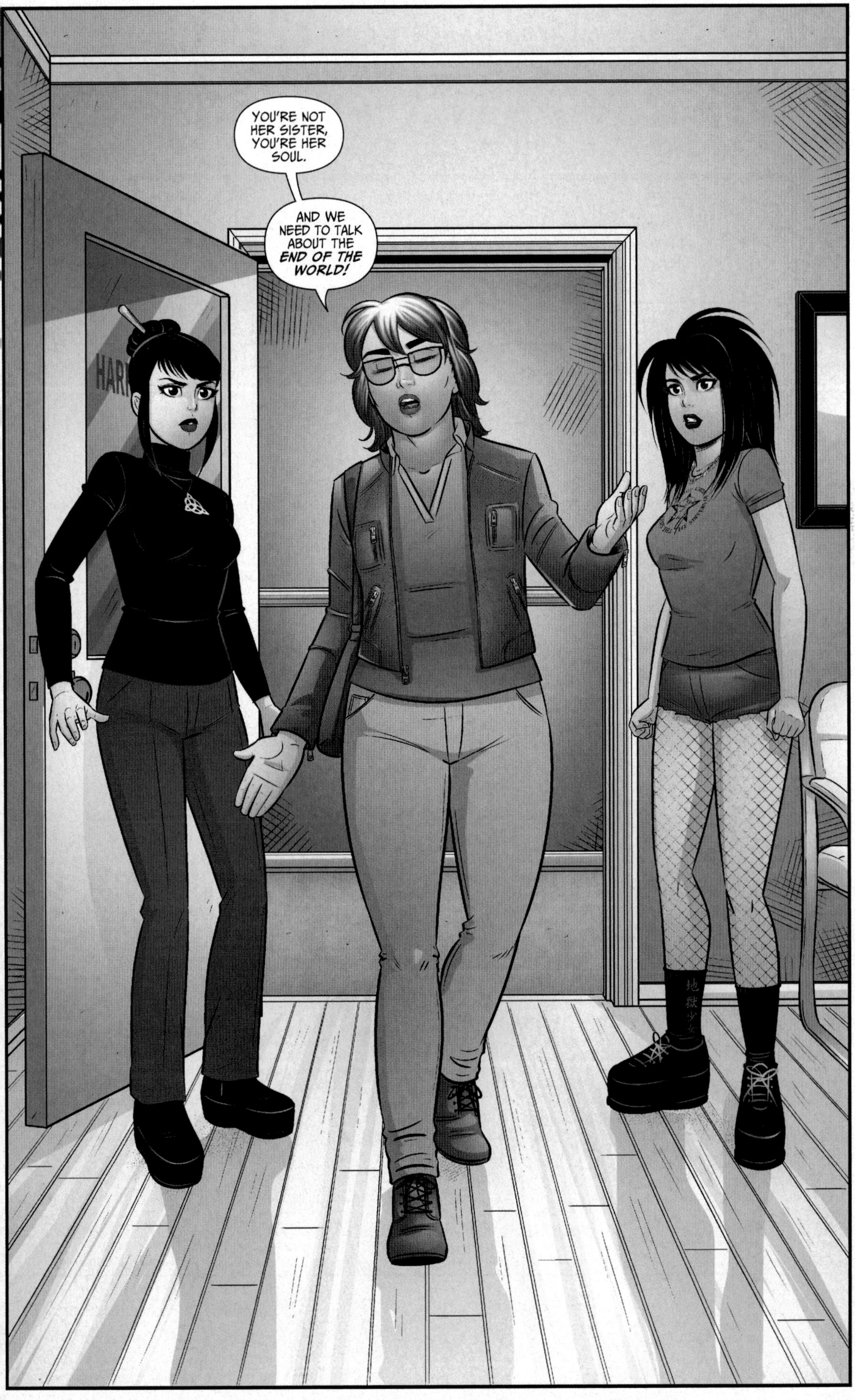
YOU'RE NOT HER SISTER, YOU'RE HER SOUL.
AND WE NEED TO TALK ABOUT THE ***END OF THE WORLD!***

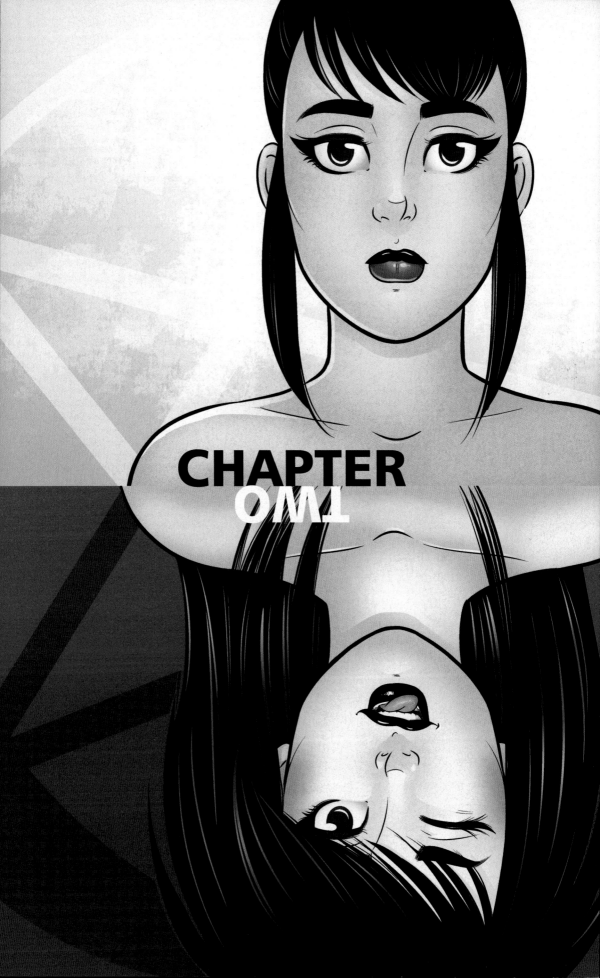

CHAPTER
TWO

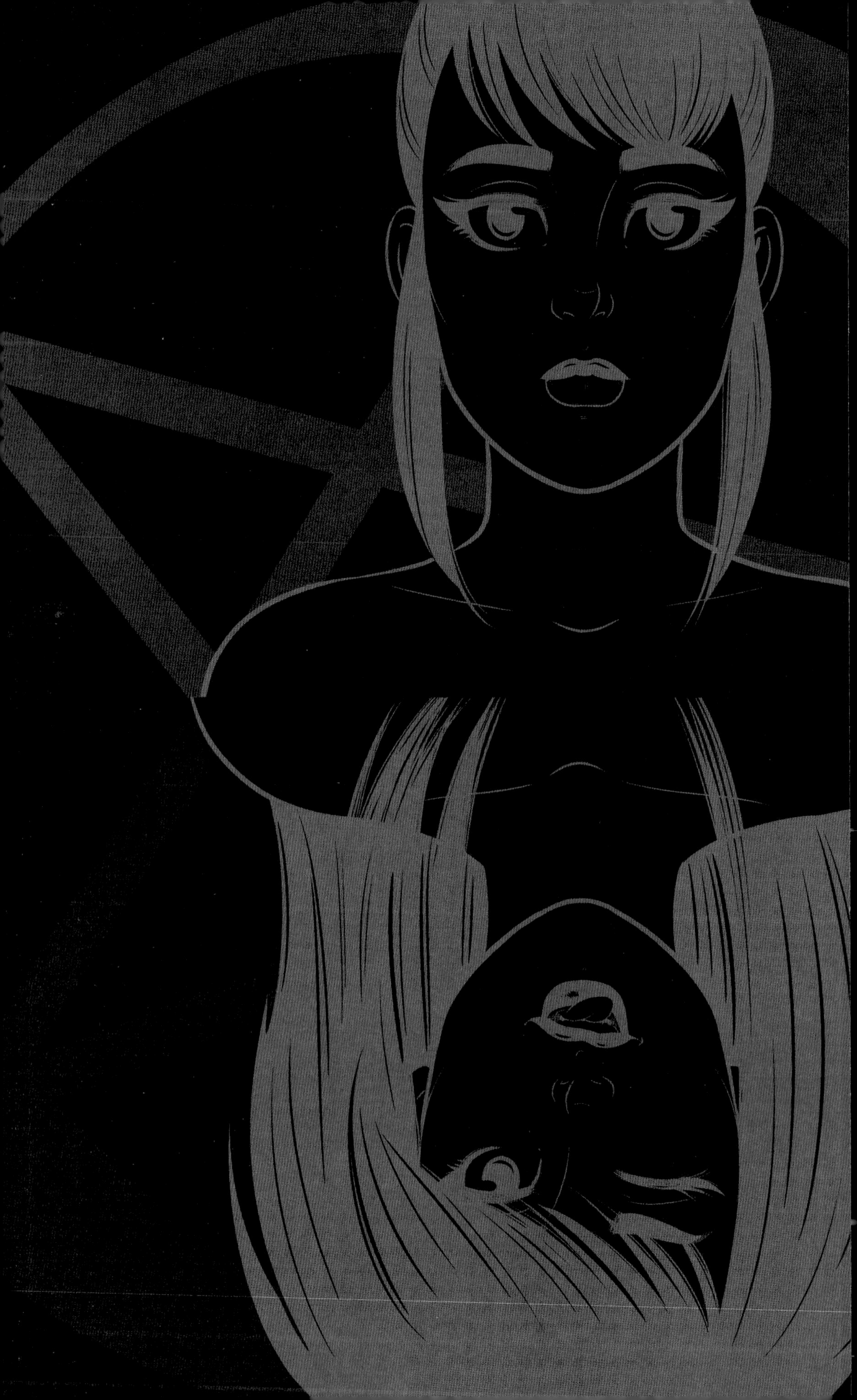

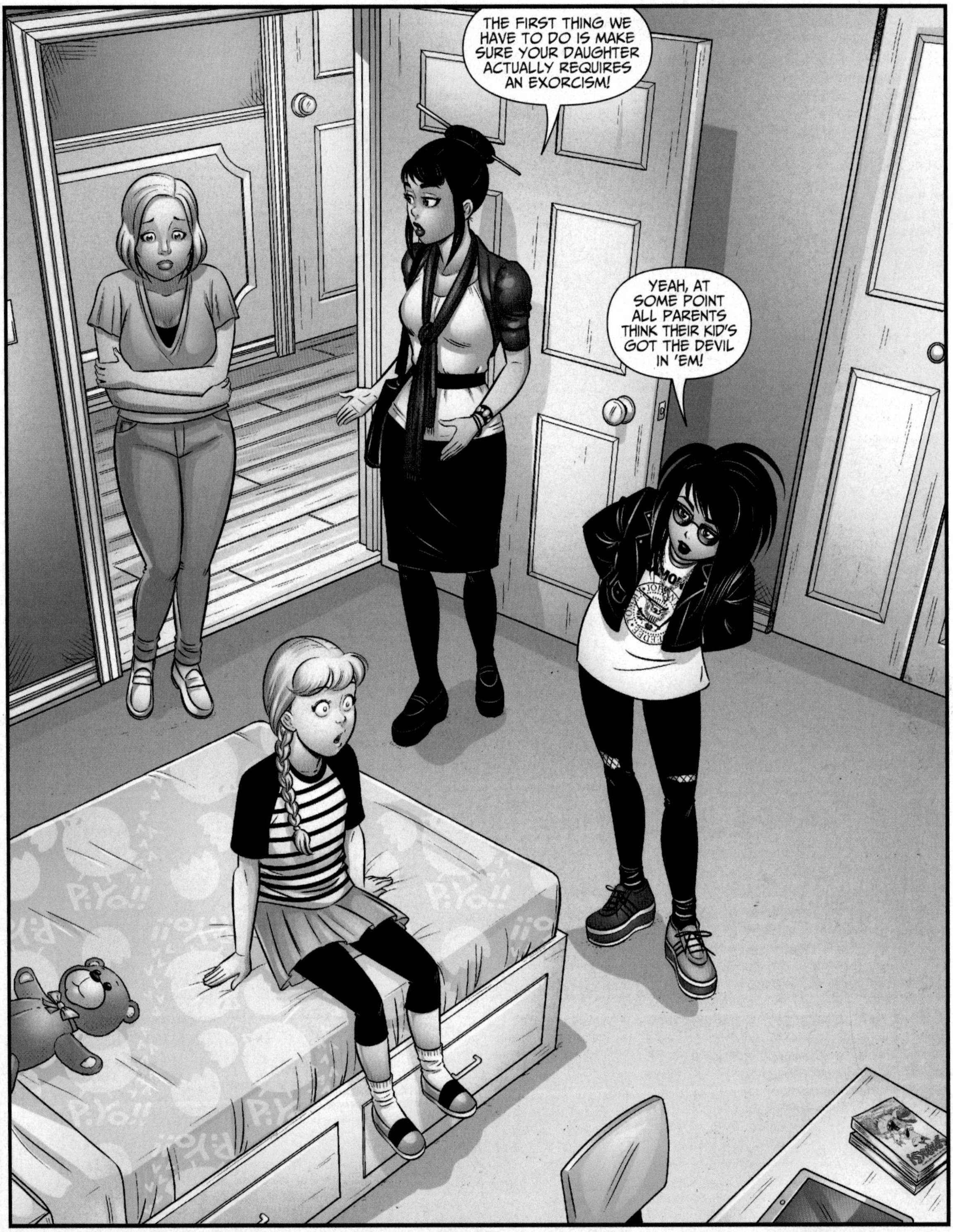
THE FIRST THING WE HAVE TO DO IS MAKE SURE YOUR DAUGHTER ACTUALLY REQUIRES AN EXORCISM!
YEAH, AT SOME POINT ALL PARENTS THINK THEIR KID'S GOT THE DEVIL IN 'EM!
P-Yo!!

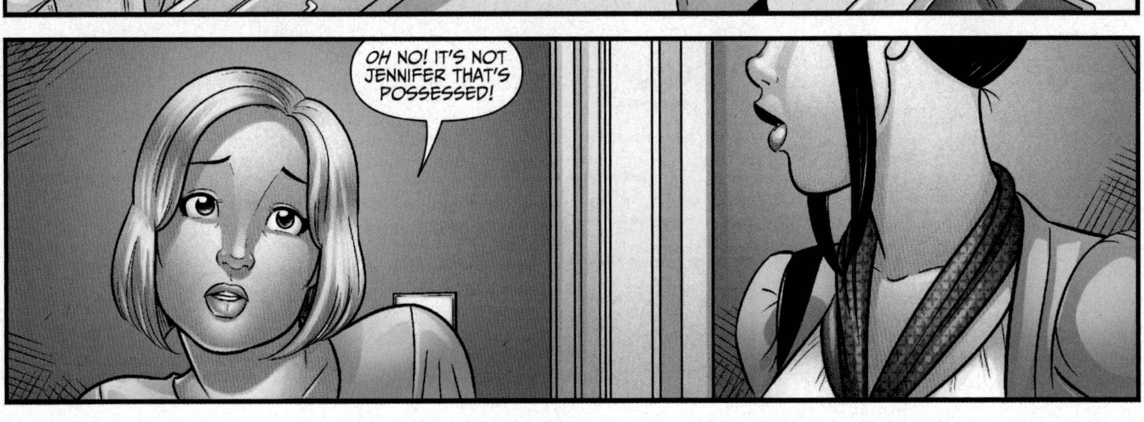
OH NO! IT'S NOT JENNIFER THAT'S POSSESSED!

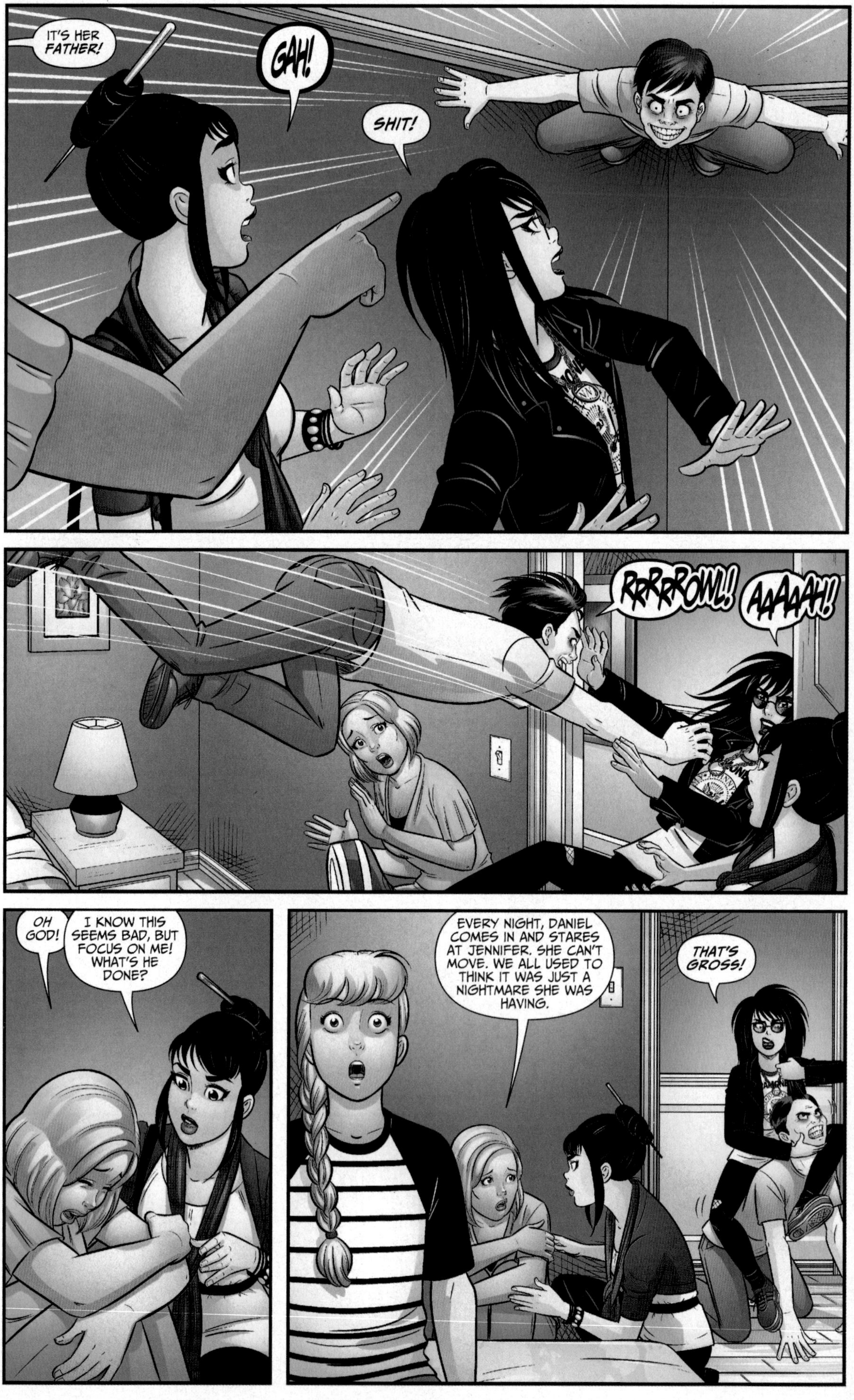
IT'S HER FATHER!
GAH!
SHIT!
RRRRROWL!!
AAAAAH!!
OH GOD!
I KNOW THIS SEEMS BAD, BUT FOCUS ON ME! WHAT'S HE DONE?
EVERY NIGHT, DANIEL COMES IN AND STARES AT JENNIFER. SHE CAN'T MOVE. WE ALL USED TO THINK IT WAS JUST A NIGHTMARE SHE WAS HAVING.
THAT'S GROSS!

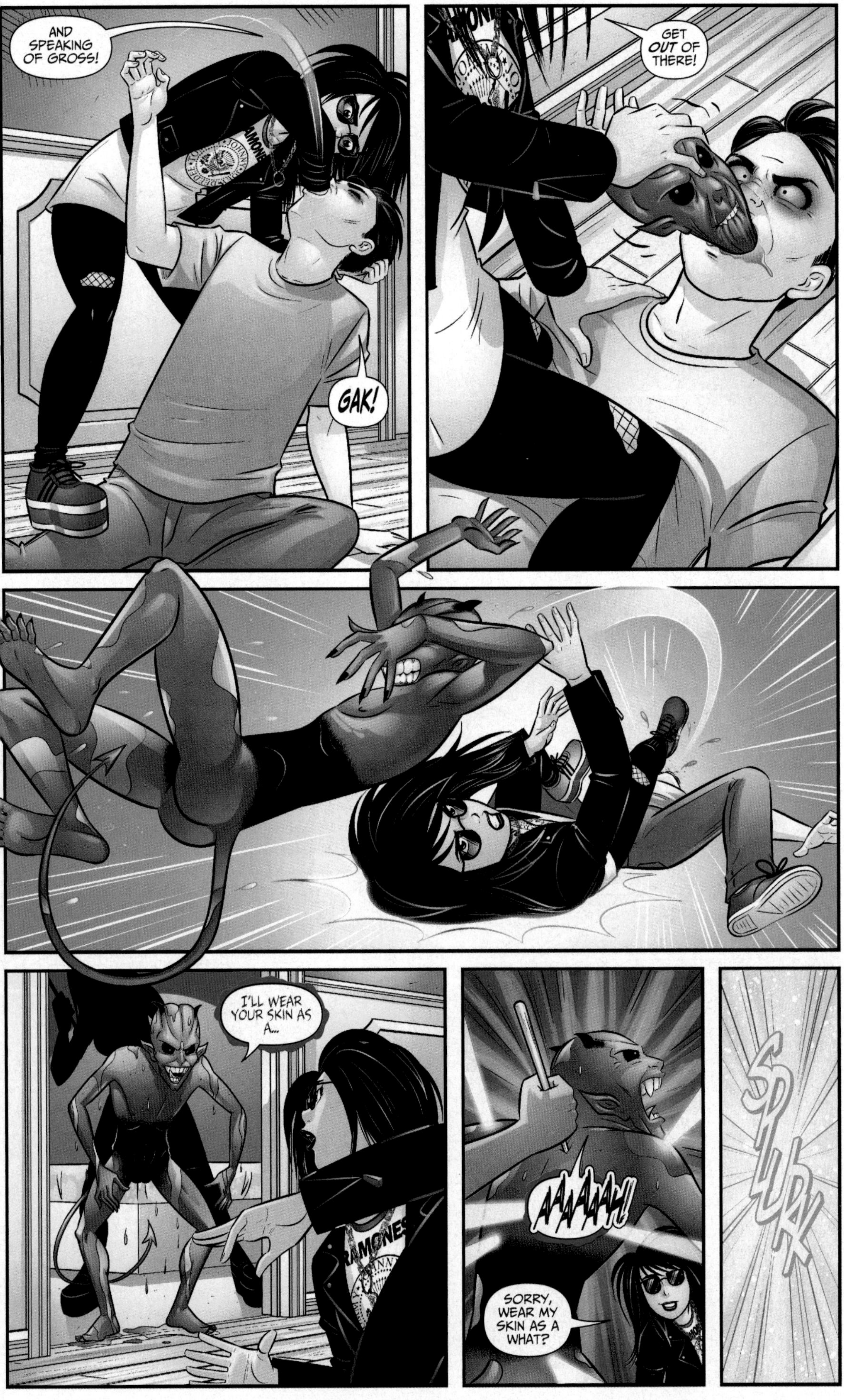
AND SPEAKING OF GROSS!
GAK!
GET OUT OF THERE!
I'LL WEAR YOUR SKIN AS A...
AAAAAAH!
SORRY, WEAR MY SKIN AS A WHAT?
SPLUK!

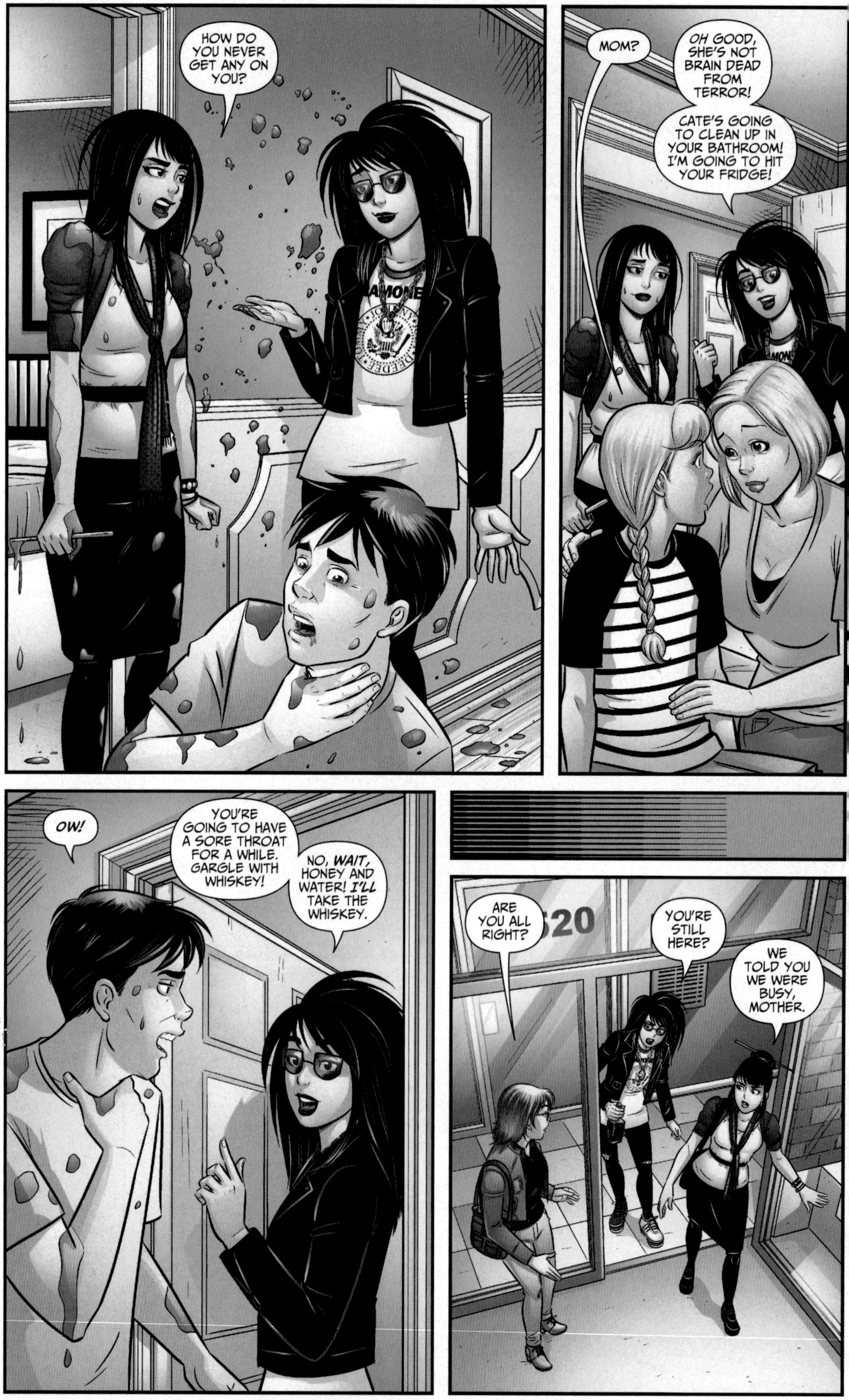
HOW DO YOU NEVER GET ANY ON YOU?
MOM?
OH GOOD, SHE'S NOT BRAIN DEAD FROM TERROR!
CATE'S GOING TO CLEAN UP IN YOUR BATHROOM! I'M GOING TO HIT YOUR FRIDGE!
OW!
YOU'RE GOING TO HAVE A SORE THROAT FOR A WHILE. GARGLE WITH WHISKEY!
NO, WAIT, HONEY AND WATER! I'LL TAKE THE WHISKEY.
ARE YOU ALL RIGHT?
YOU'RE STILL HERE?
WE TOLD YOU WE WERE BUSY, MOTHER.

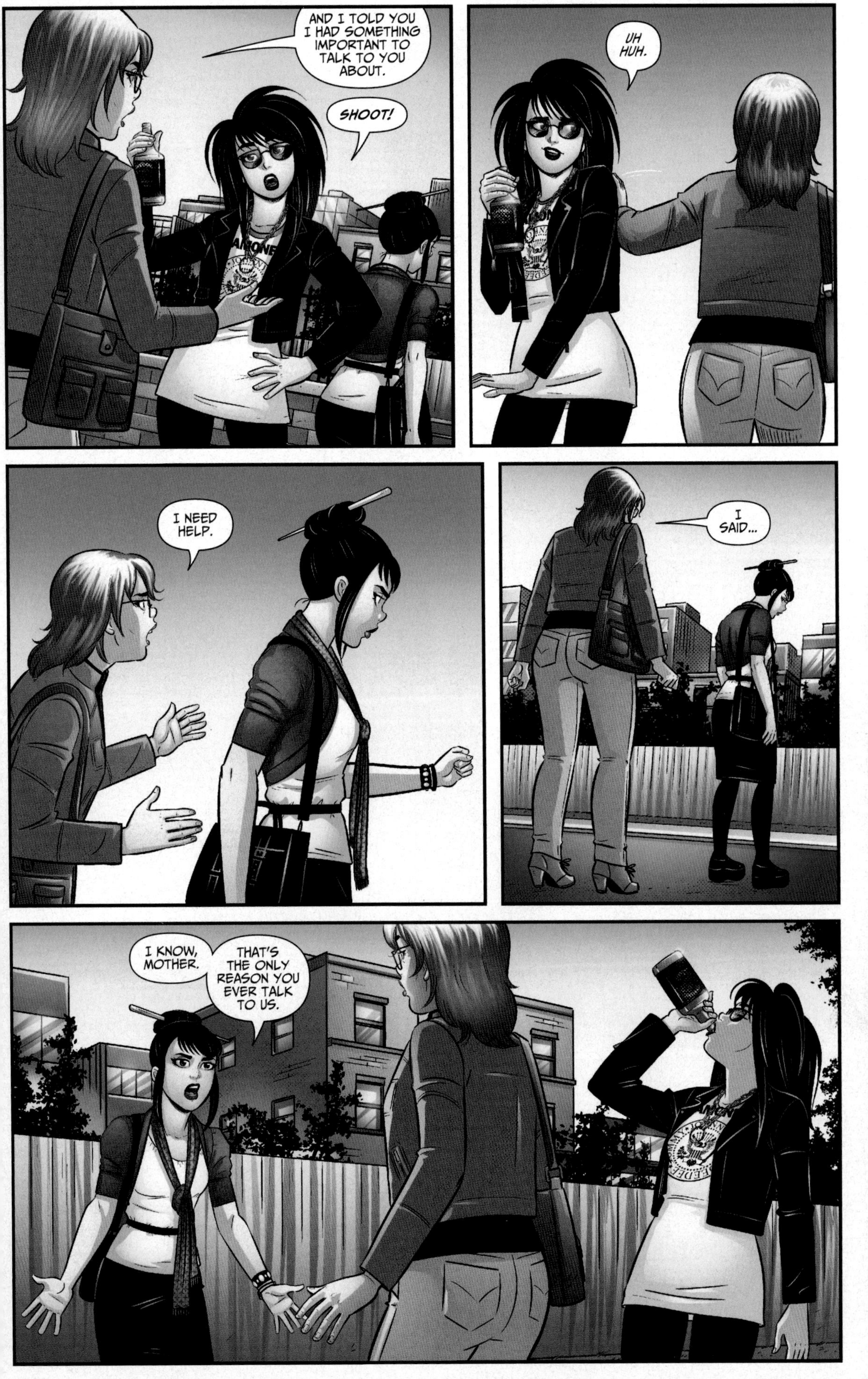
AND I TOLD YOU I HAD SOMETHING IMPORTANT TO TALK TO YOU ABOUT.
SHOOT!
UH HUH.
I NEED HELP.
I SAID...
I KNOW, MOTHER.
THAT'S THE ONLY REASON YOU EVER TALK TO US.

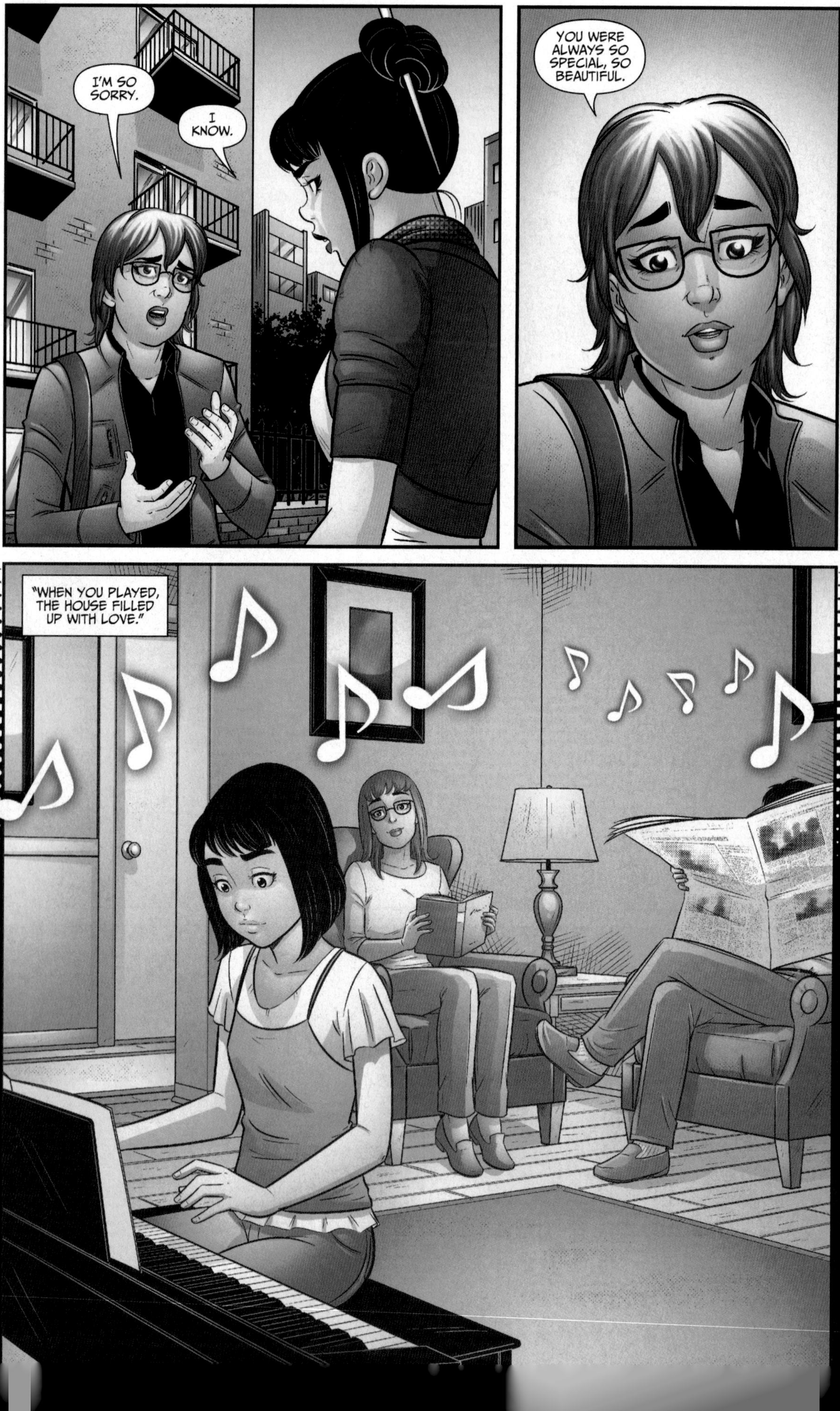

I'M SO SORRY.
I KNOW.
YOU WERE ALWAYS SO SPECIAL, SO BEAUTIFUL.
"WHEN YOU PLAYED, THE HOUSE FILLED UP WITH LOVE."

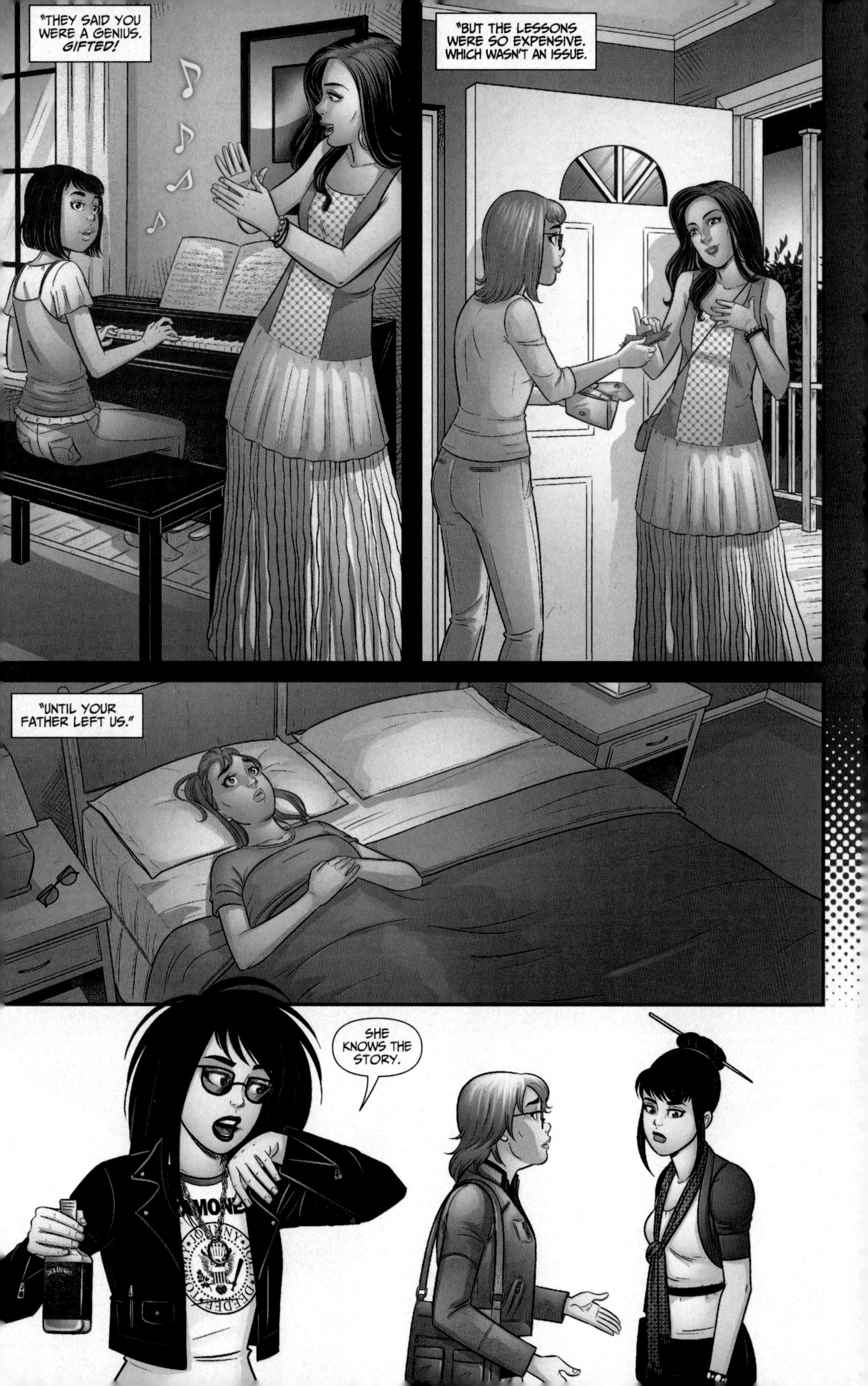
"THEY SAID YOU WERE A GENIUS. *GIFTED!*
"BUT THE LESSONS WERE SO EXPENSIVE. WHICH WASN'T AN ISSUE.
"UNTIL YOUR FATHER LEFT US."
SHE KNOWS THE STORY.

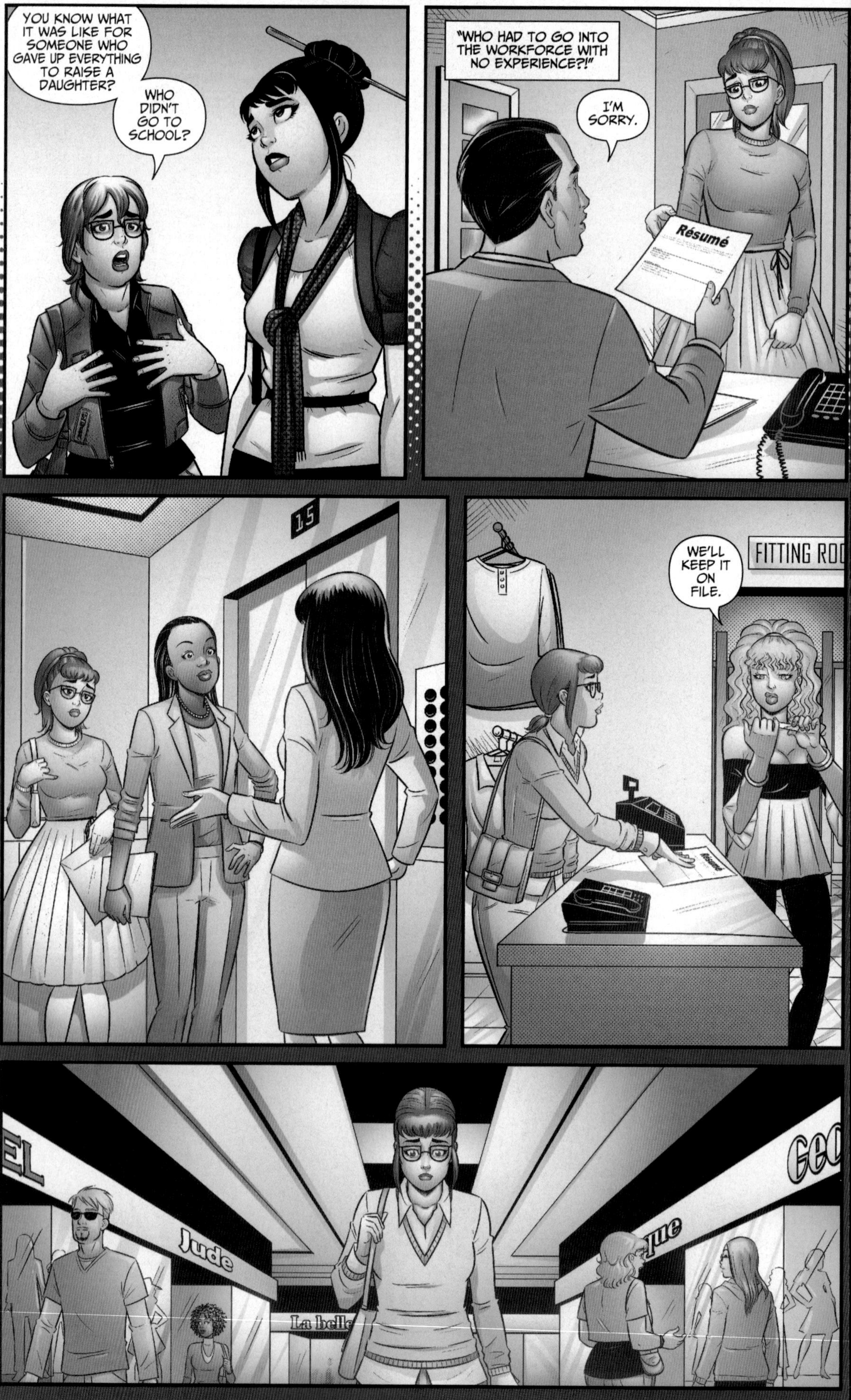
YOU KNOW WHAT IT WAS LIKE FOR SOMEONE WHO GAVE UP EVERYTHING TO RAISE A DAUGHTER?
WHO DIDN'T GO TO SCHOOL?
"WHO HAD TO GO INTO THE WORKFORCE WITH NO EXPERIENCE?!"
I'M SORRY.
Résumé
15
FITTING ROO
WE'LL KEEP IT ON FILE.
Résumé
EL
Jude
La belle
que
Geo

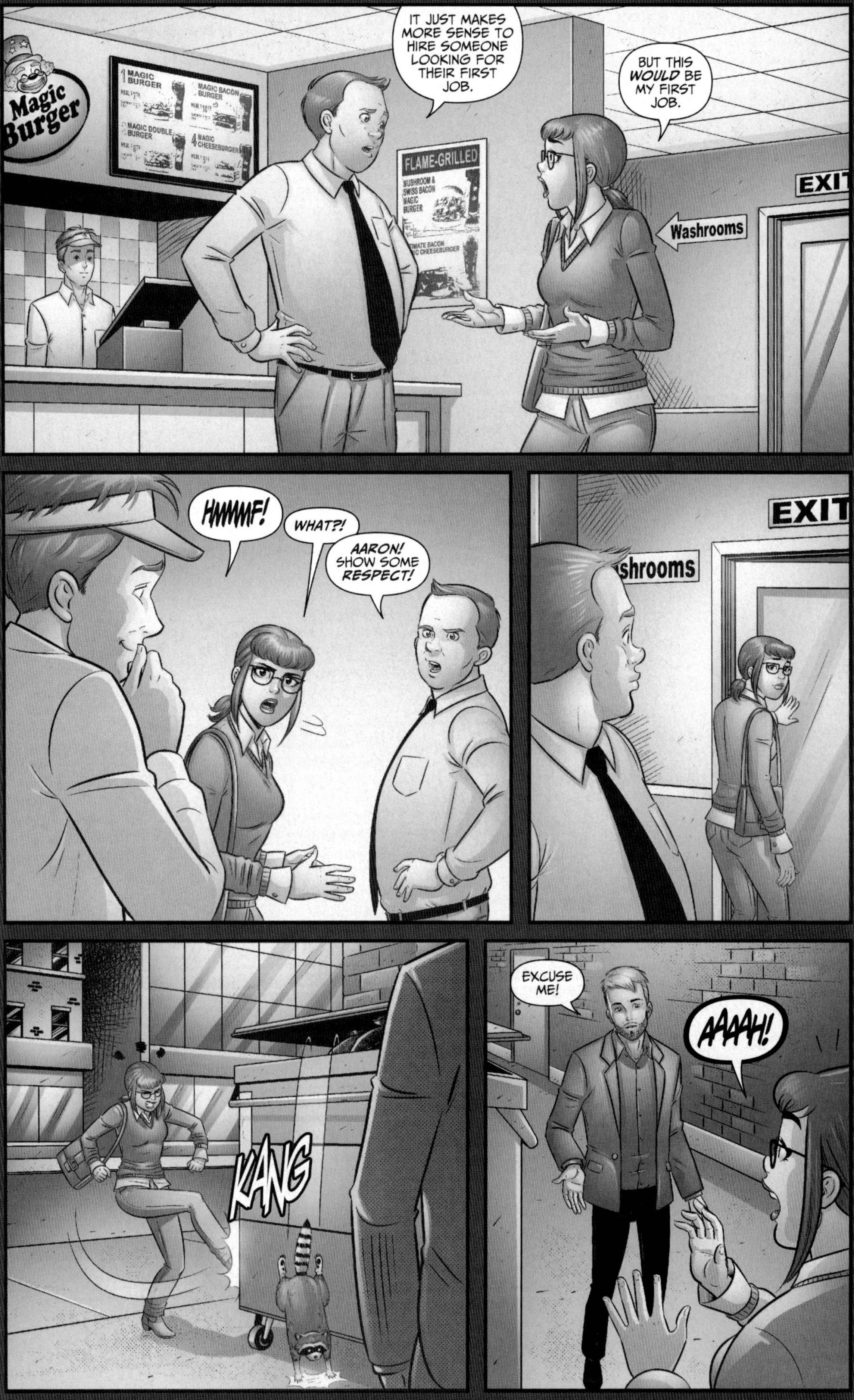
Magic Burger
1 MAGIC BURGER
2 MAGIC BACON BURGER
3 MAGIC DOUBLE BURGER
4 MAGIC CHEESEBURGER
FLAME-GRILLED
MUSHROOM & SWISS BACON MAGIC BURGER
IT JUST MAKES MORE SENSE TO HIRE SOMEONE LOOKING FOR THEIR FIRST JOB.
BUT THIS *WOULD* BE MY FIRST JOB.
EXIT
Washrooms
HMMMF!
WHAT?!
AARON! SHOW SOME *RESPECT!*
EXIT
KANG
EXCUSE ME!
AAAAH!

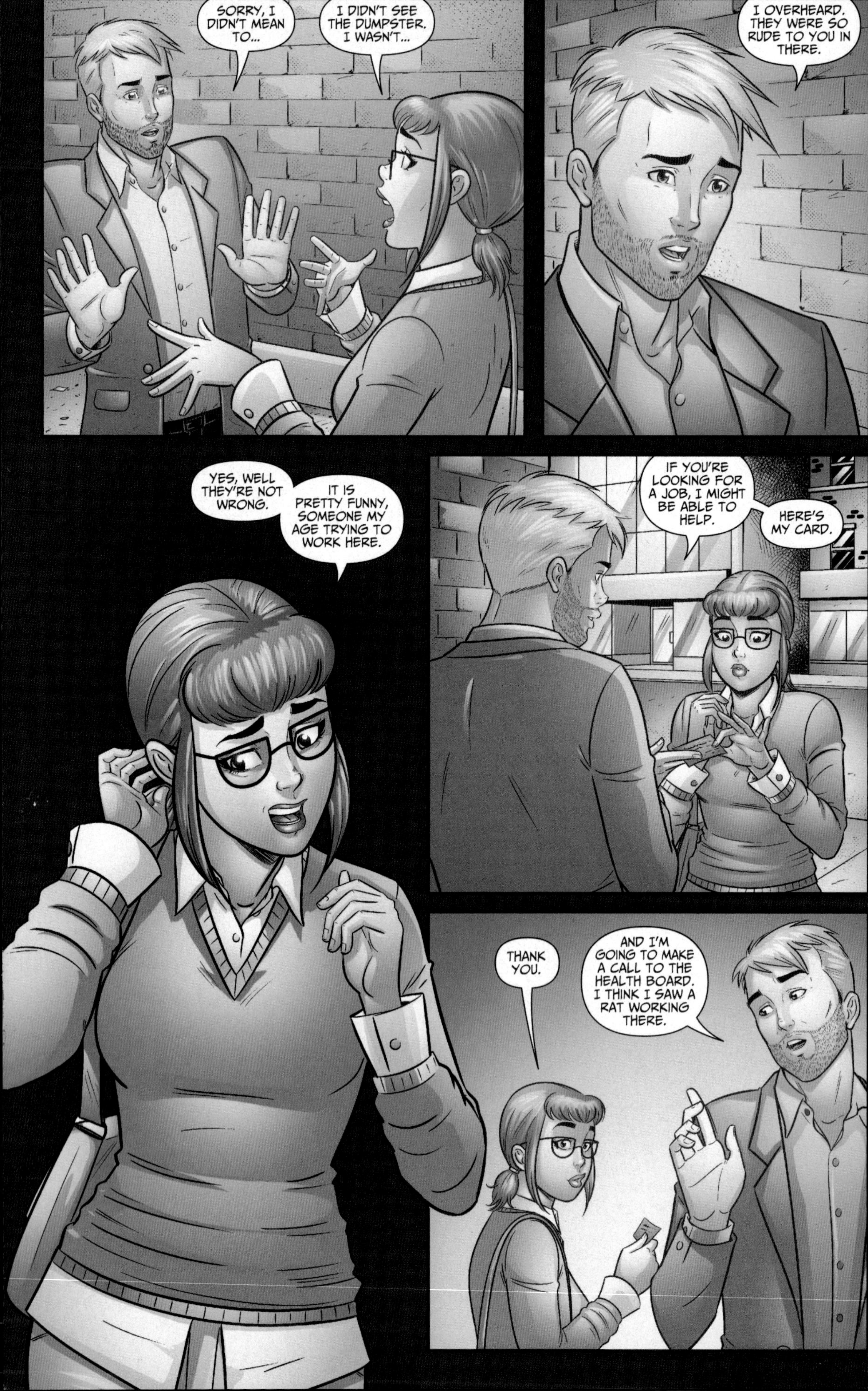
SORRY, I DIDN'T MEAN TO...
I DIDN'T SEE THE DUMPSTER. I WASN'T...
I OVERHEARD. THEY WERE SO RUDE TO YOU IN THERE.
YES, WELL THEY'RE NOT WRONG.
IT IS PRETTY FUNNY, SOMEONE MY AGE TRYING TO WORK HERE.
IF YOU'RE LOOKING FOR A JOB, I MIGHT BE ABLE TO HELP.
HERE'S MY CARD.
THANK YOU.
AND I'M GOING TO MAKE A CALL TO THE HEALTH BOARD. I THINK I SAW A RAT WORKING THERE.

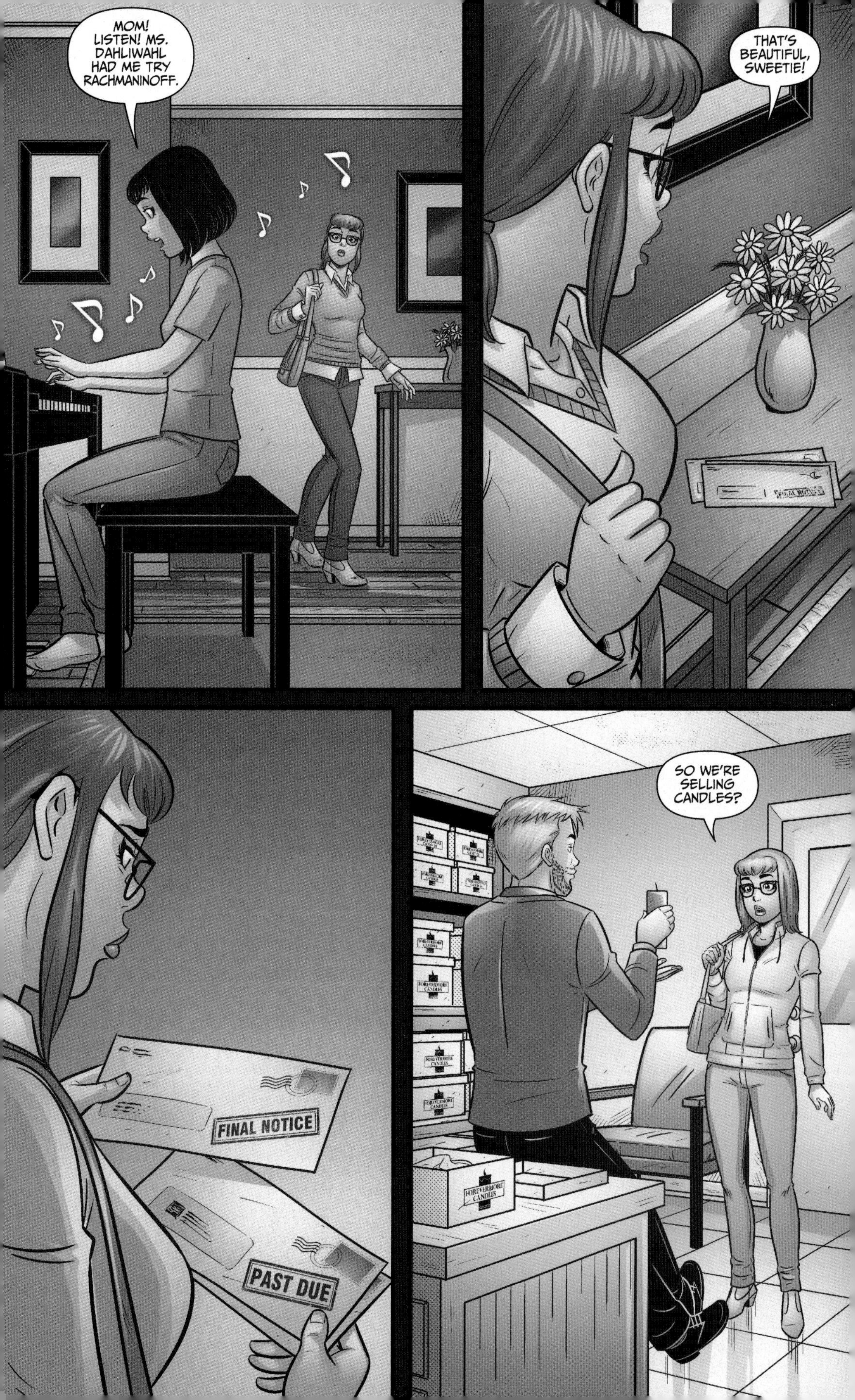
MOM! LISTEN! MS. DAHLIWAHL HAD ME TRY RACHMANINOFF.
THAT'S BEAUTIFUL, SWEETIE!
FINAL NOTICE
PAST DUE
SO WE'RE SELLING CANDLES?
FOREVERMORE CANDLES

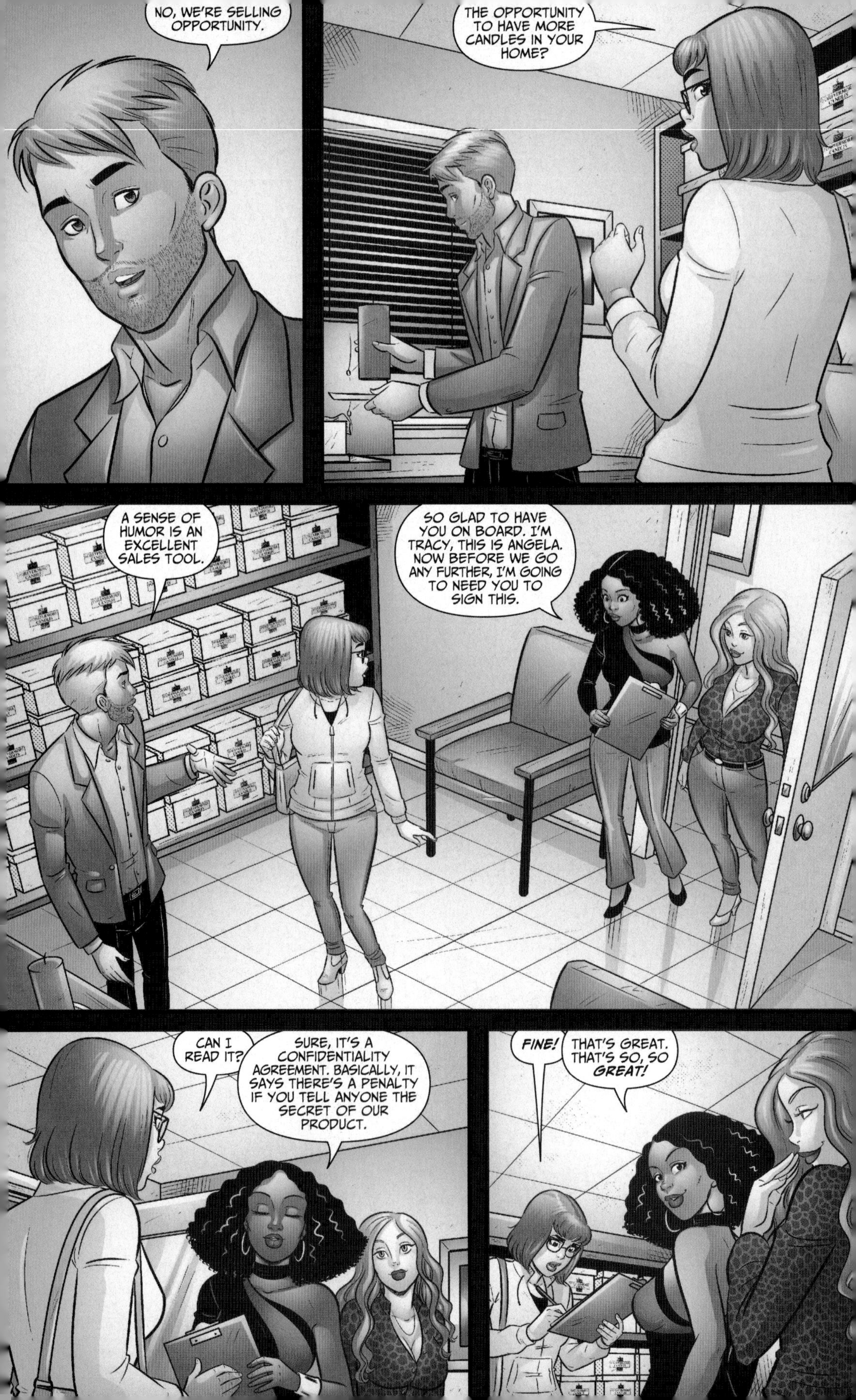
NO, WE'RE SELLING OPPORTUNITY.
THE OPPORTUNITY TO HAVE MORE CANDLES IN YOUR HOME?
A SENSE OF HUMOR IS AN EXCELLENT SALES TOOL.
SO GLAD TO HAVE YOU ON BOARD. I'M TRACY, THIS IS ANGELA. NOW BEFORE WE GO ANY FURTHER, I'M GOING TO NEED YOU TO SIGN THIS.
CAN I READ IT?
SURE, IT'S A CONFIDENTIALITY AGREEMENT. BASICALLY, IT SAYS THERE'S A PENALTY IF YOU TELL ANYONE THE SECRET OF OUR PRODUCT.
FINE!
THAT'S GREAT. THAT'S SO, SO GREAT!

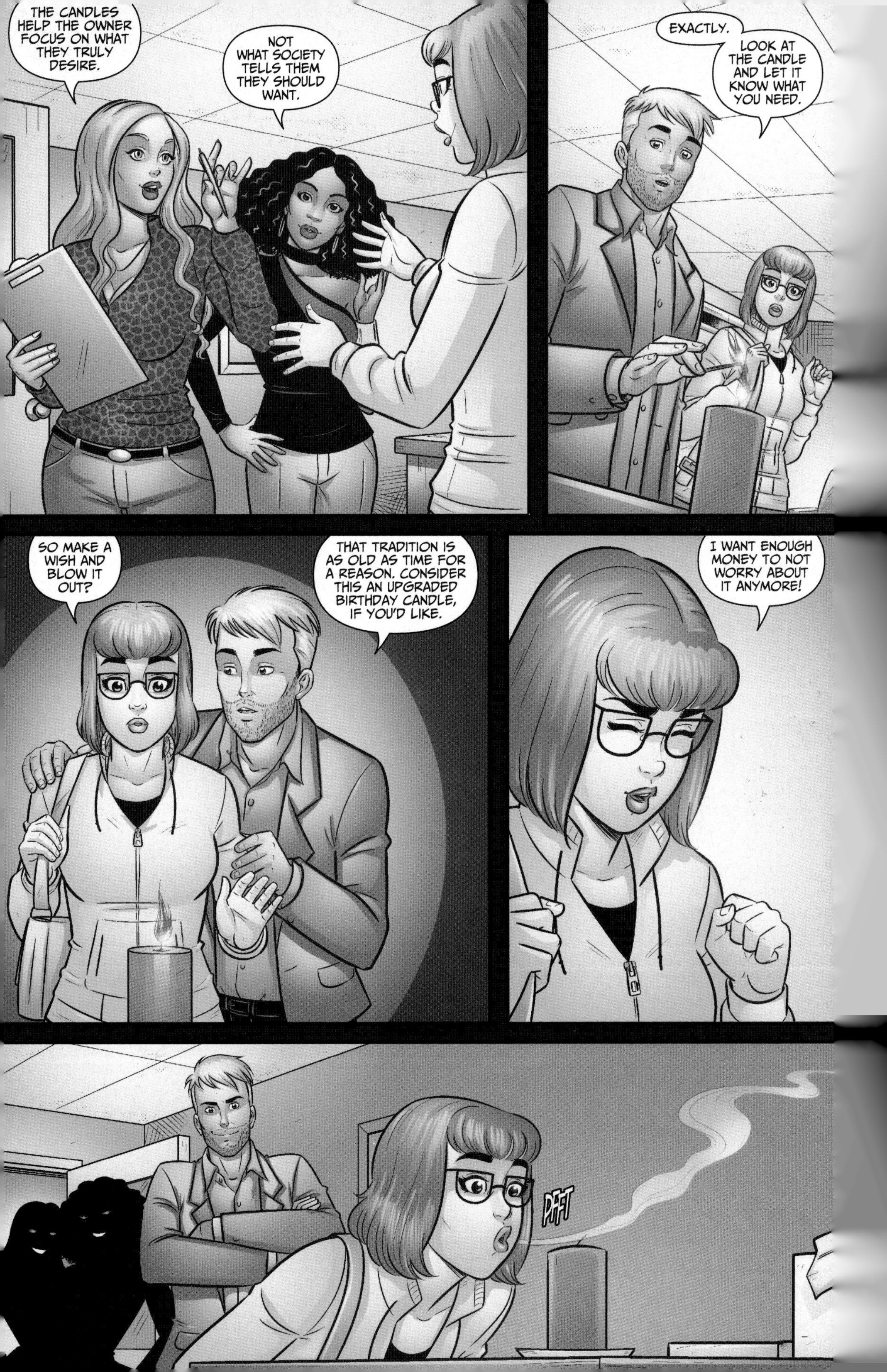
THE CANDLES HELP THE OWNER FOCUS ON WHAT THEY TRULY DESIRE.
NOT WHAT SOCIETY TELLS THEM THEY SHOULD WANT.
EXACTLY.
LOOK AT THE CANDLE AND LET IT KNOW WHAT YOU NEED.
SO MAKE A WISH AND BLOW IT OUT?
THAT TRADITION IS AS OLD AS TIME FOR A REASON. CONSIDER THIS AN UPGRADED BIRTHDAY CANDLE, IF YOU'D LIKE.
I WANT ENOUGH MONEY TO NOT WORRY ABOUT IT ANYMORE!
PFFT

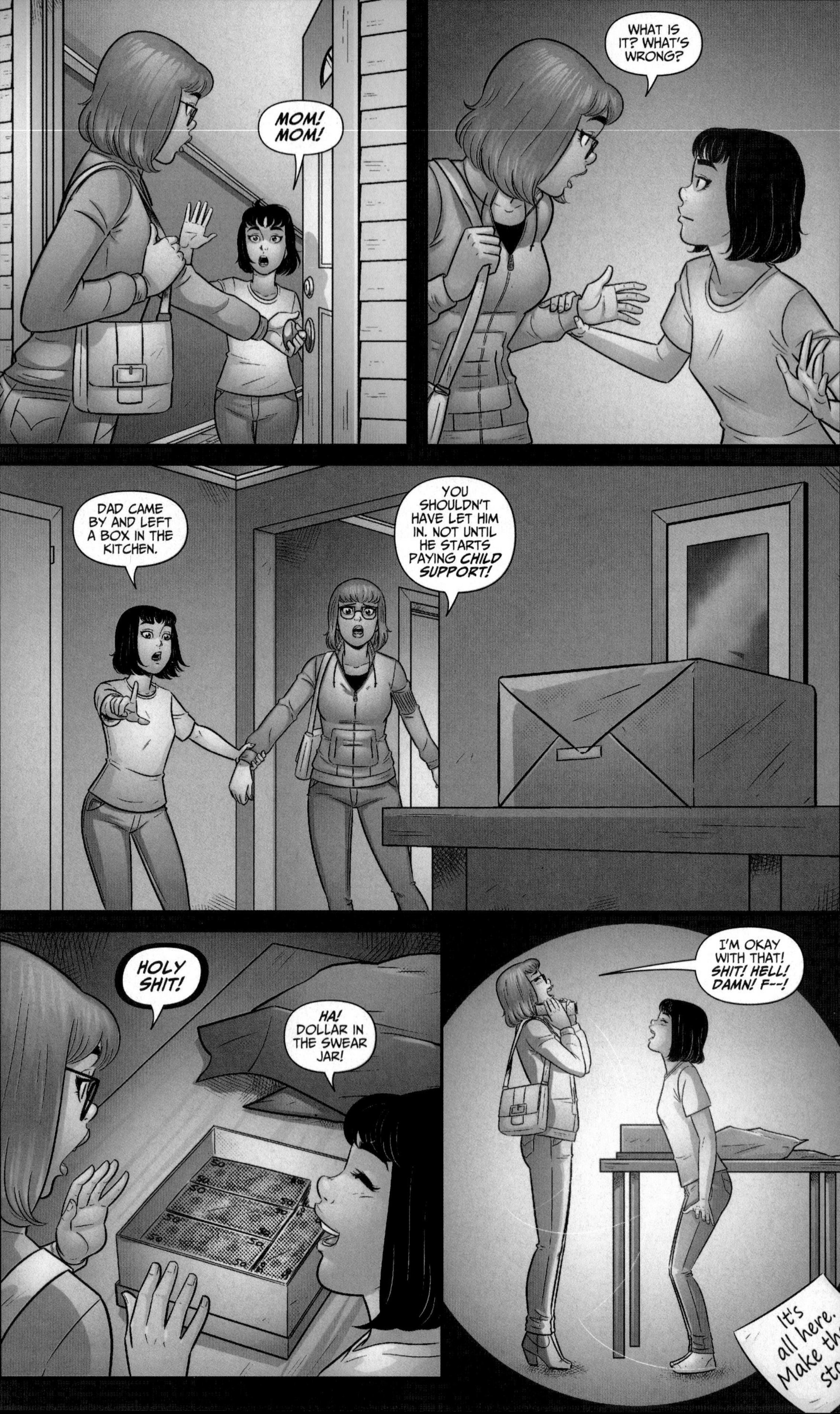
MOM! MOM!
WHAT IS IT? WHAT'S WRONG?
DAD CAME BY AND LEFT A BOX IN THE KITCHEN.
YOU SHOULDN'T HAVE LET HIM IN. NOT UNTIL HE STARTS PAYING *CHILD SUPPORT!*
HOLY SHIT!
HA! DOLLAR IN THE SWEAR JAR!
I'M OKAY WITH THAT! *SHIT! HELL! DAMN! F--!*
It's all here. Make th

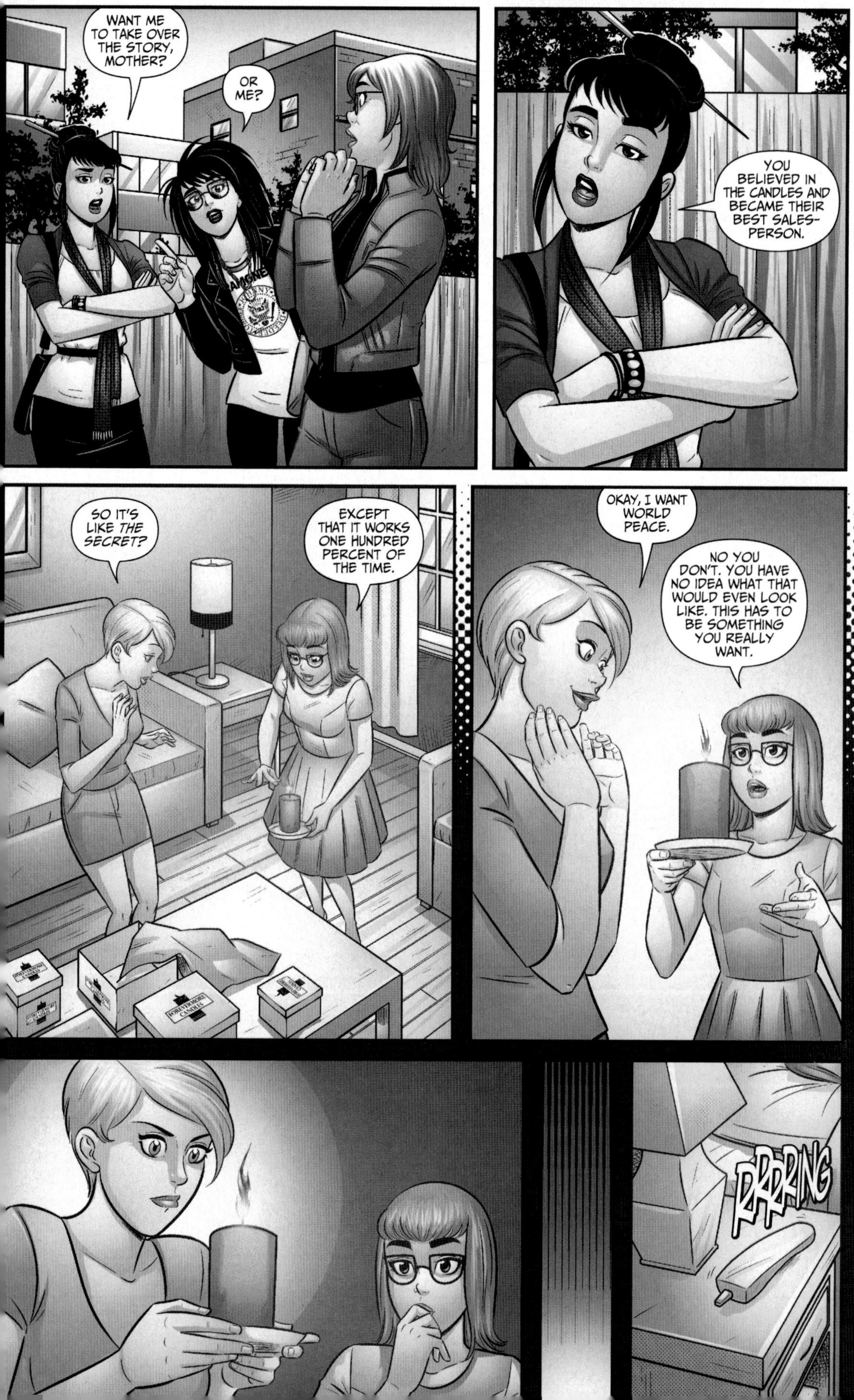
WANT ME TO TAKE OVER THE STORY, MOTHER?
OR ME?
YOU BELIEVED IN THE CANDLES AND BECAME THEIR BEST SALES-PERSON.
SO IT'S LIKE *THE SECRET*?
EXCEPT THAT IT WORKS ONE HUNDRED PERCENT OF THE TIME.
OKAY, I WANT WORLD PEACE.
NO YOU DON'T. YOU HAVE NO IDEA WHAT THAT WOULD EVEN LOOK LIKE. THIS HAS TO BE SOMETHING YOU REALLY WANT.
RRRRING

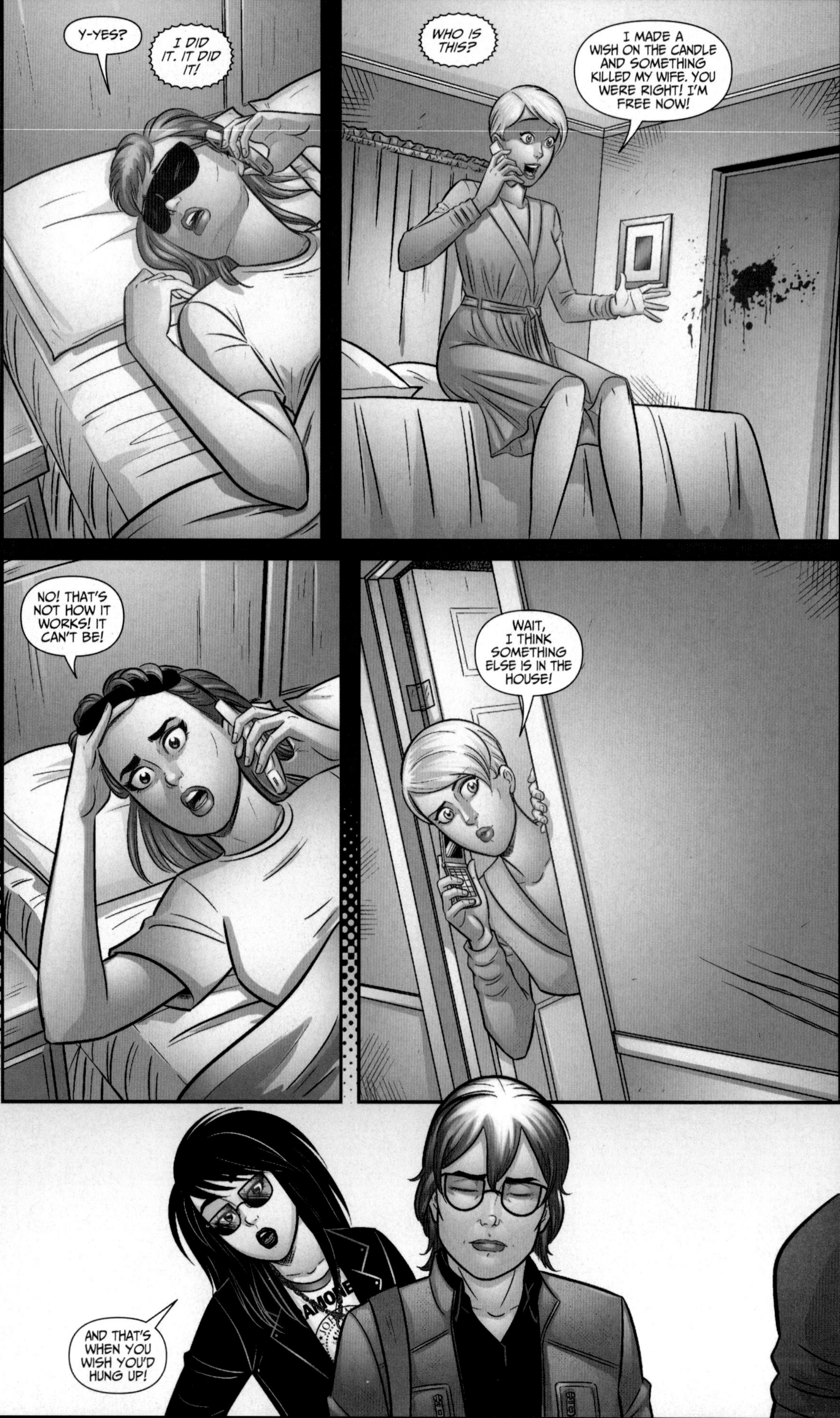
Y-YES?
I DID IT. IT DID IT!
WHO IS THIS?
I MADE A WISH ON THE CANDLE AND SOMETHING KILLED MY WIFE. YOU WERE RIGHT! I'M FREE NOW!
NO! THAT'S NOT HOW IT WORKS! IT CAN'T BE!
WAIT, I THINK SOMETHING ELSE IS IN THE HOUSE!
AND THAT'S WHEN YOU WISH YOU'D HUNG UP!

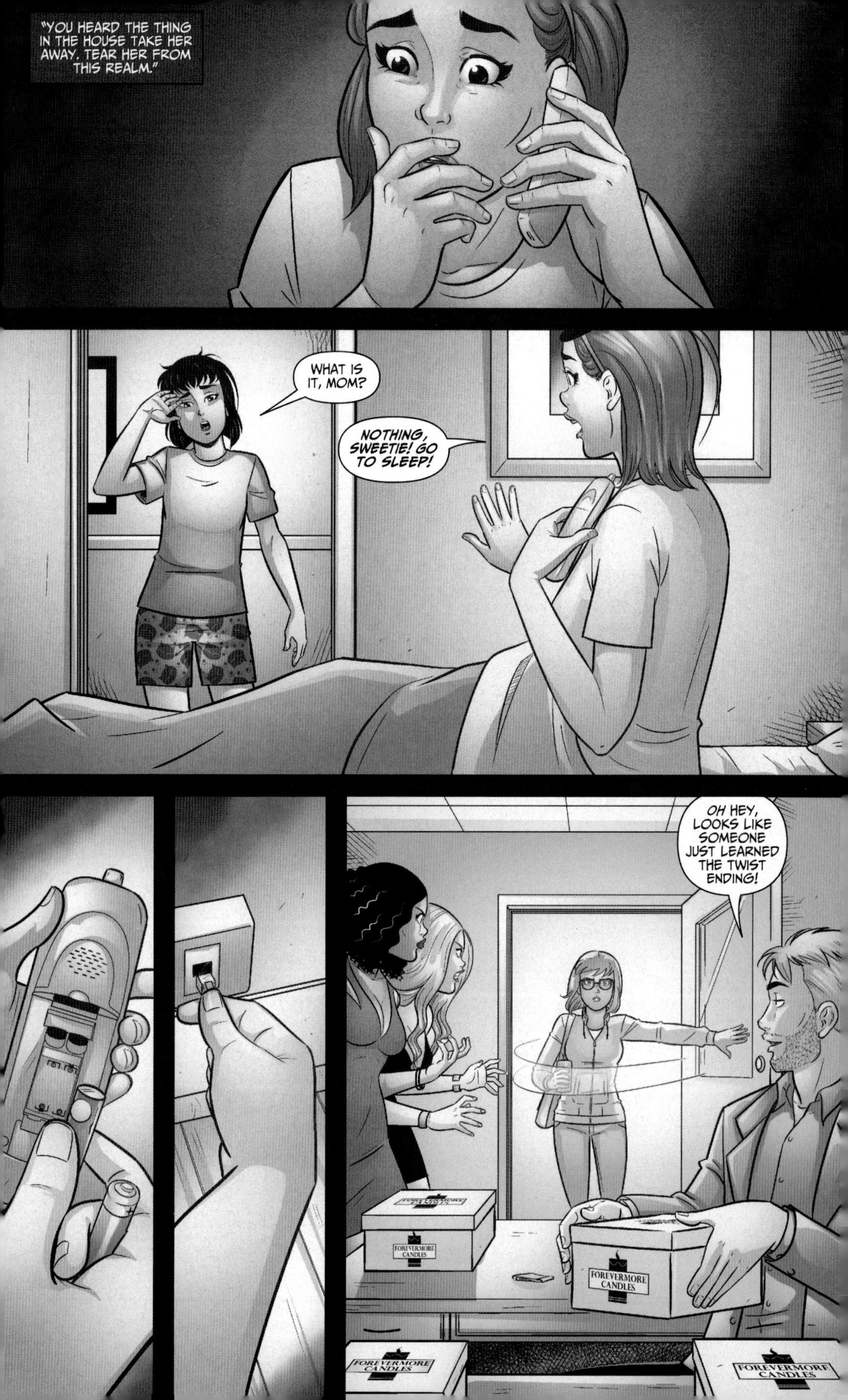
"YOU HEARD THE THING IN THE HOUSE TAKE HER AWAY. TEAR HER FROM THIS REALM."
WHAT IS IT, MOM?
NOTHING, SWEETIE! GO TO SLEEP!
OH HEY, LOOKS LIKE SOMEONE JUST LEARNED THE TWIST ENDING!
FOREVERMORE CANDLES
FOREVERMORE CANDLES
FOREVERMORE CANDLES
FOREVERMORE CANDLES

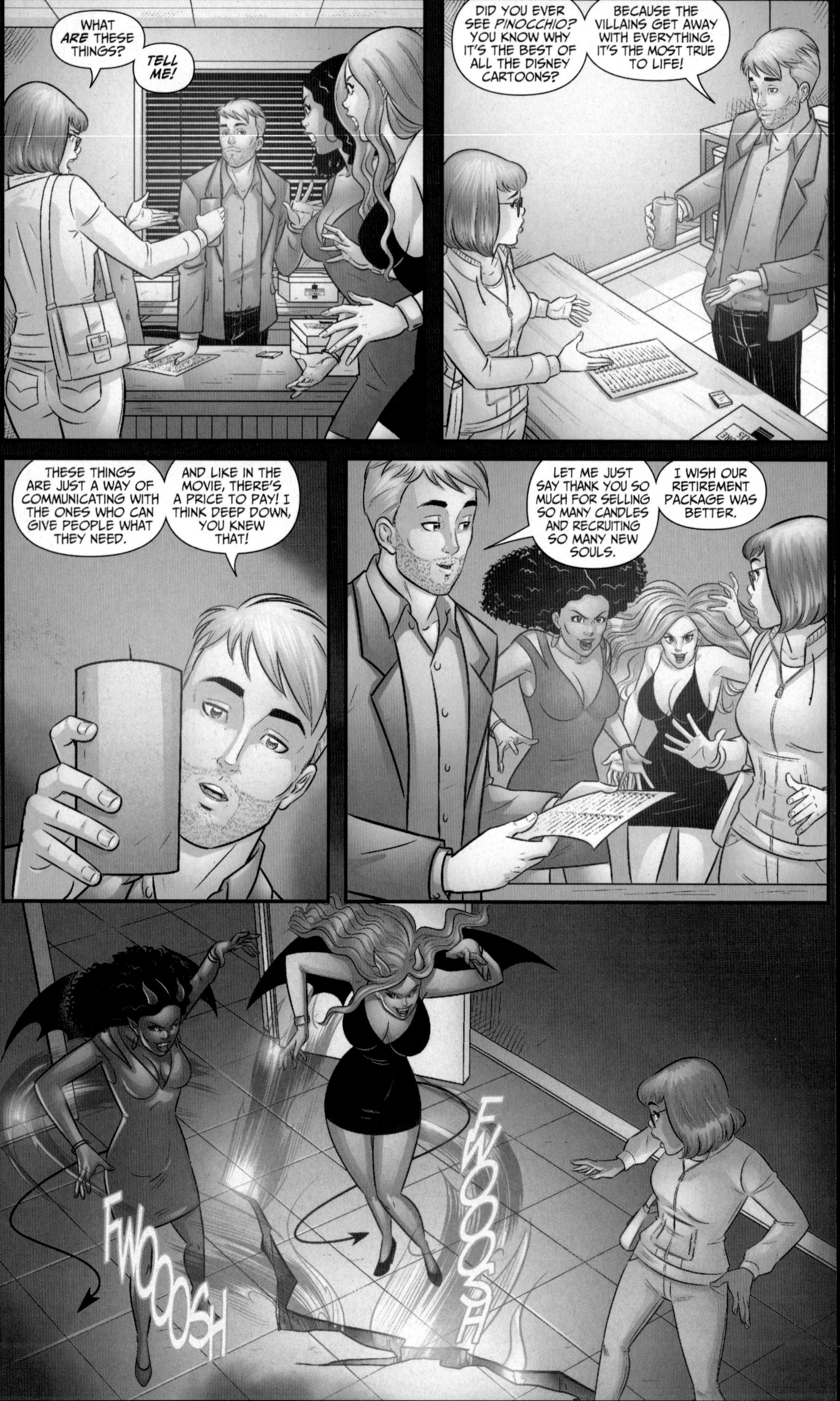
WHAT ARE THESE THINGS?
TELL ME!
DID YOU EVER SEE PINOCCHIO? YOU KNOW WHY IT'S THE BEST OF ALL THE DISNEY CARTOONS?
BECAUSE THE VILLAINS GET AWAY WITH EVERYTHING. IT'S THE MOST TRUE TO LIFE!
THESE THINGS ARE JUST A WAY OF COMMUNICATING WITH THE ONES WHO CAN GIVE PEOPLE WHAT THEY NEED.
AND LIKE IN THE MOVIE, THERE'S A PRICE TO PAY! I THINK DEEP DOWN, YOU KNEW THAT!
LET ME JUST SAY THANK YOU SO MUCH FOR SELLING SO MANY CANDLES AND RECRUITING SO MANY NEW SOULS.
I WISH OUR RETIREMENT PACKAGE WAS BETTER.
FWOOOSH
FWOOOSH

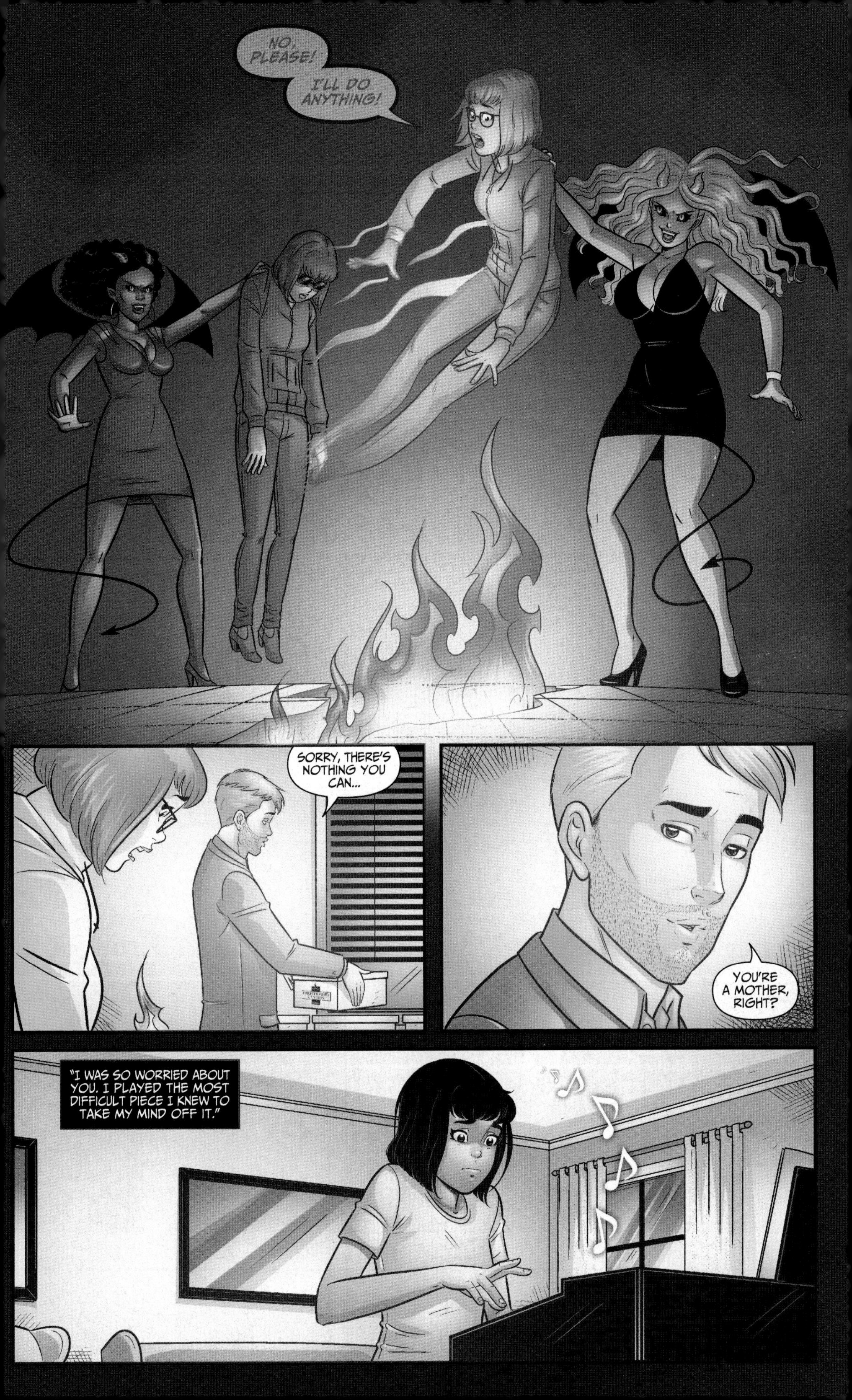
NO, PLEASE!
I'LL DO ANYTHING!
SORRY, THERE'S NOTHING YOU CAN...
YOU'RE A MOTHER, RIGHT?
"I WAS SO WORRIED ABOUT YOU. I PLAYED THE MOST DIFFICULT PIECE I KNEW TO TAKE MY MIND OFF IT."

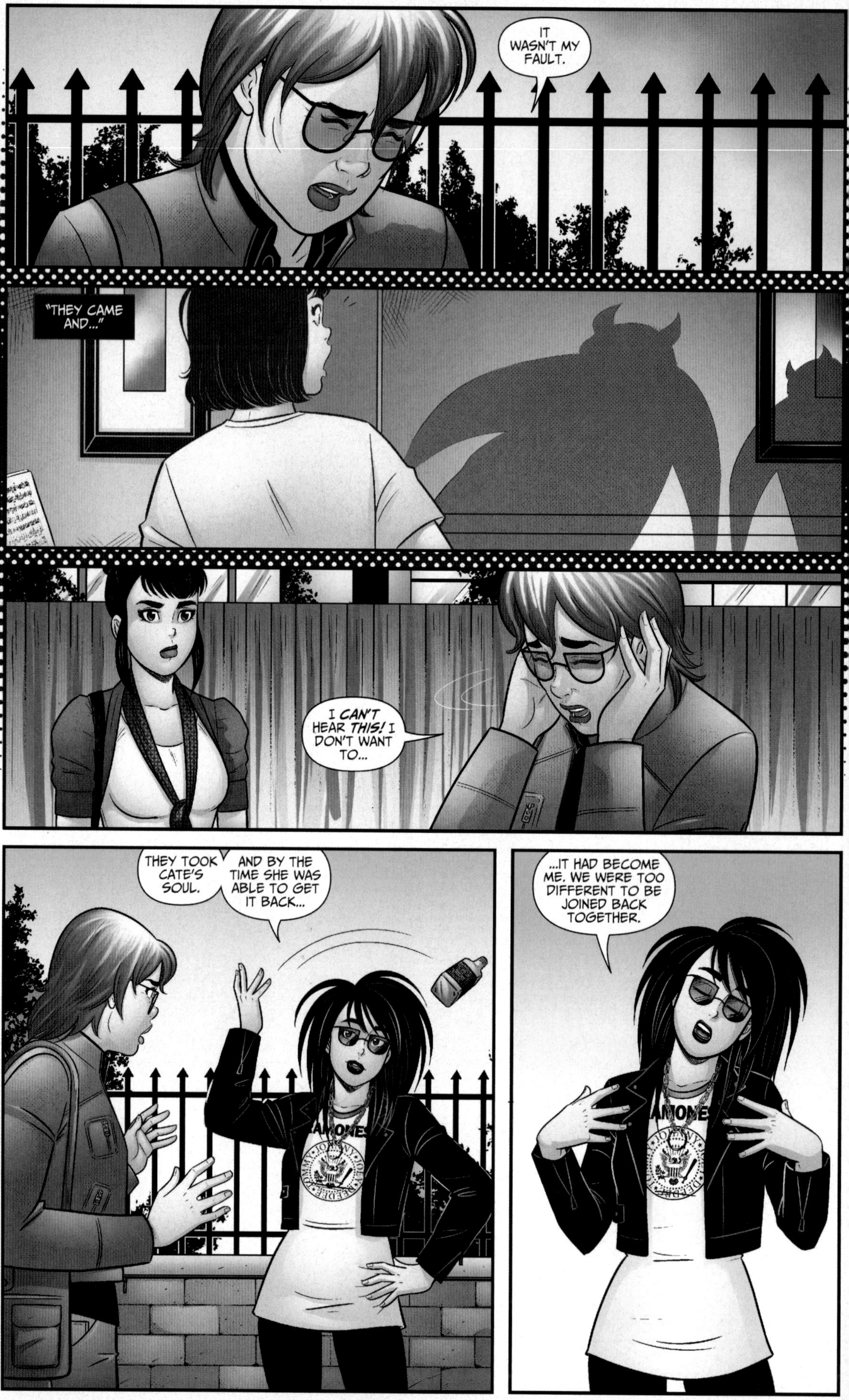
IT WASN'T MY FAULT.
"THEY CAME AND..."
I CAN'T HEAR THIS! I DON'T WANT TO...
THEY TOOK CATE'S SOUL.
AND BY THE TIME SHE WAS ABLE TO GET IT BACK...
...IT HAD BECOME ME. WE WERE TOO DIFFERENT TO BE JOINED BACK TOGETHER.
RAMONES

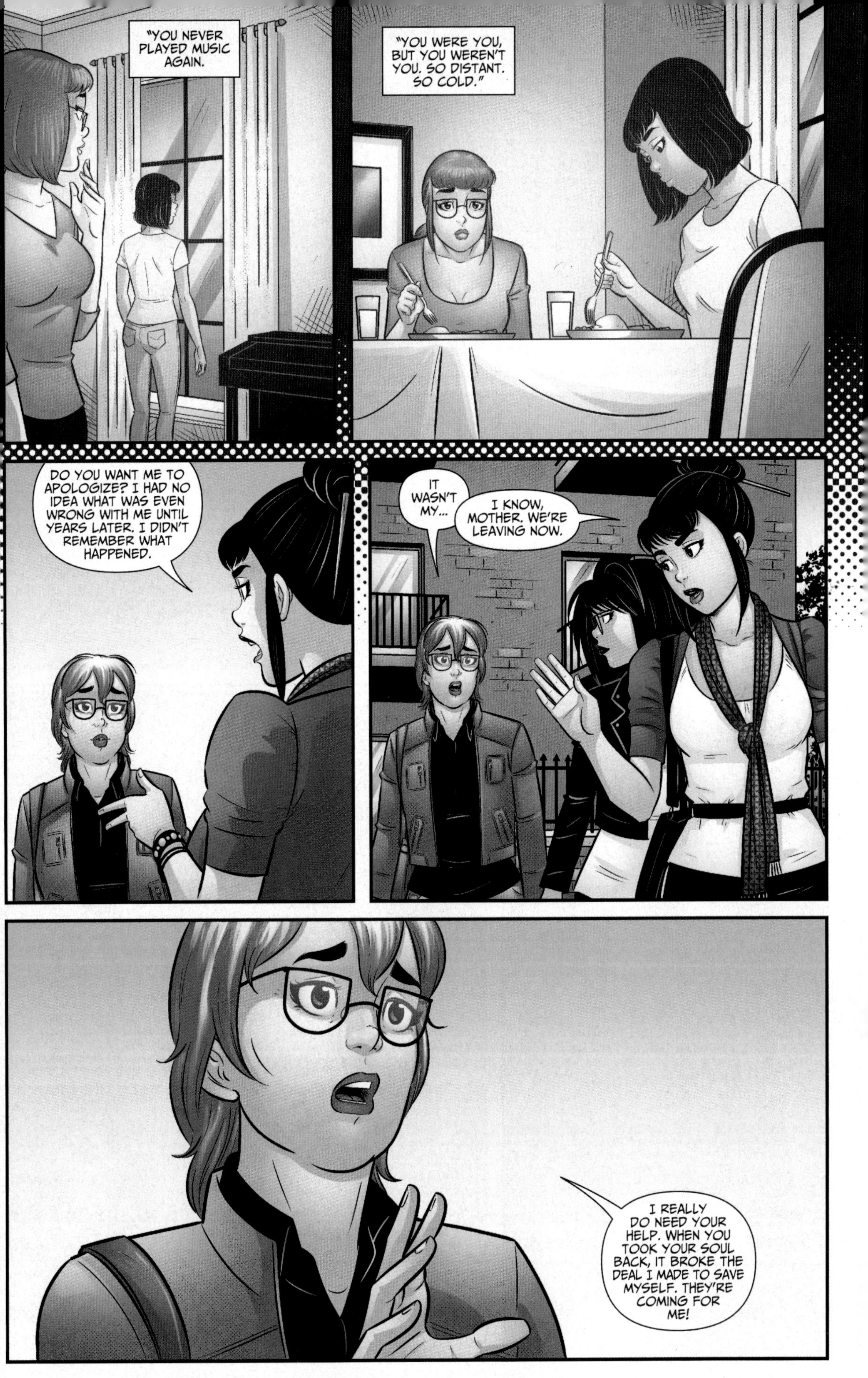
"YOU NEVER PLAYED MUSIC AGAIN.
"YOU WERE YOU, BUT YOU WEREN'T YOU. SO DISTANT. SO COLD."
DO YOU WANT ME TO APOLOGIZE? I HAD NO IDEA WHAT WAS EVEN WRONG WITH ME UNTIL YEARS LATER. I DIDN'T REMEMBER WHAT HAPPENED.
IT WASN'T MY...
I KNOW, MOTHER. WE'RE LEAVING NOW.
I REALLY DO NEED YOUR HELP. WHEN YOU TOOK YOUR SOUL BACK, IT BROKE THE DEAL I MADE TO SAVE MYSELF. THEY'RE COMING FOR ME!

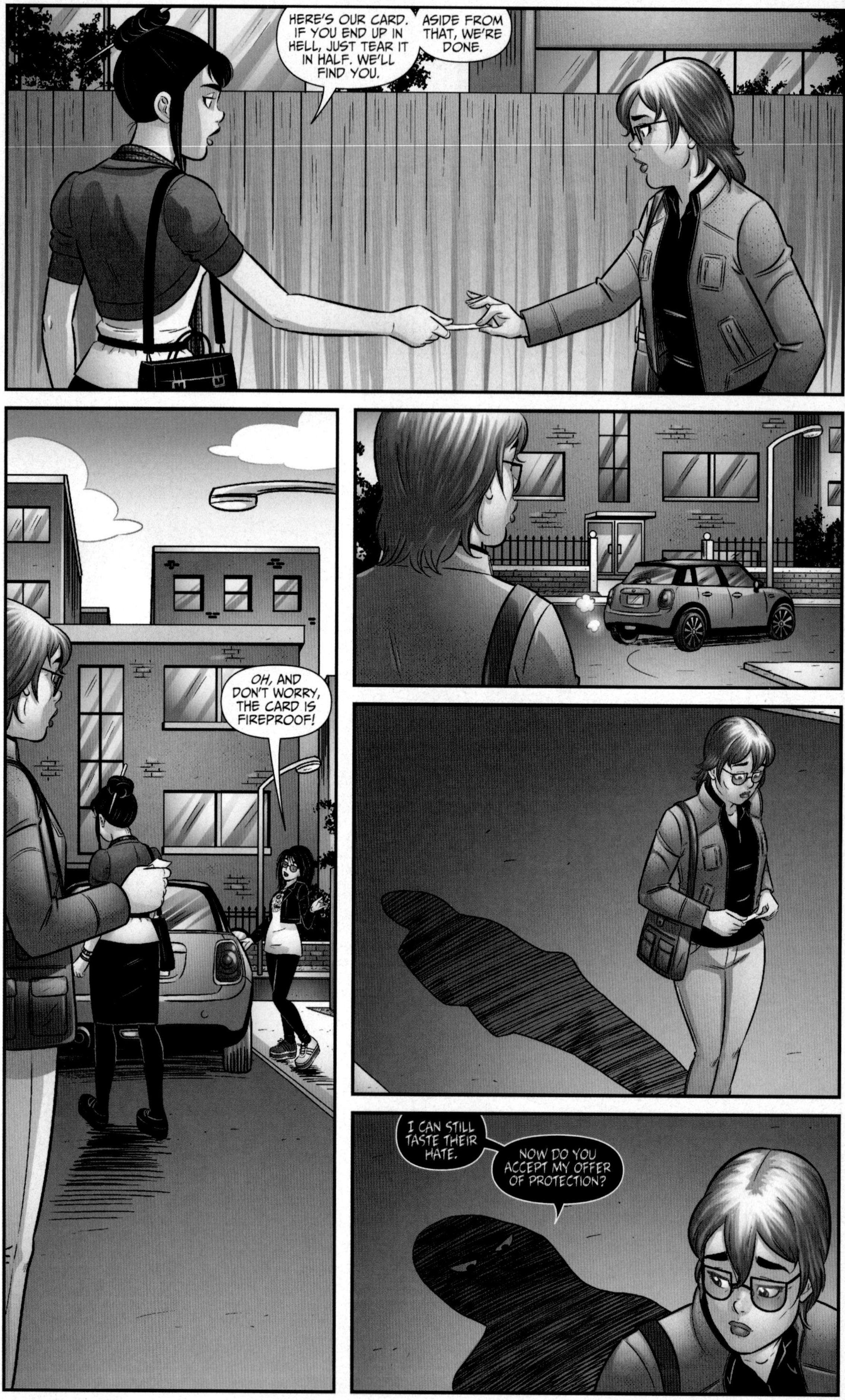
HERE'S OUR CARD. IF YOU END UP IN HELL, JUST TEAR IT IN HALF. WE'LL FIND YOU.
ASIDE FROM THAT, WE'RE DONE.
OH, AND DON'T WORRY, THE CARD IS FIREPROOF!
I CAN STILL TASTE THEIR HATE.
NOW DO YOU ACCEPT MY OFFER OF PROTECTION?

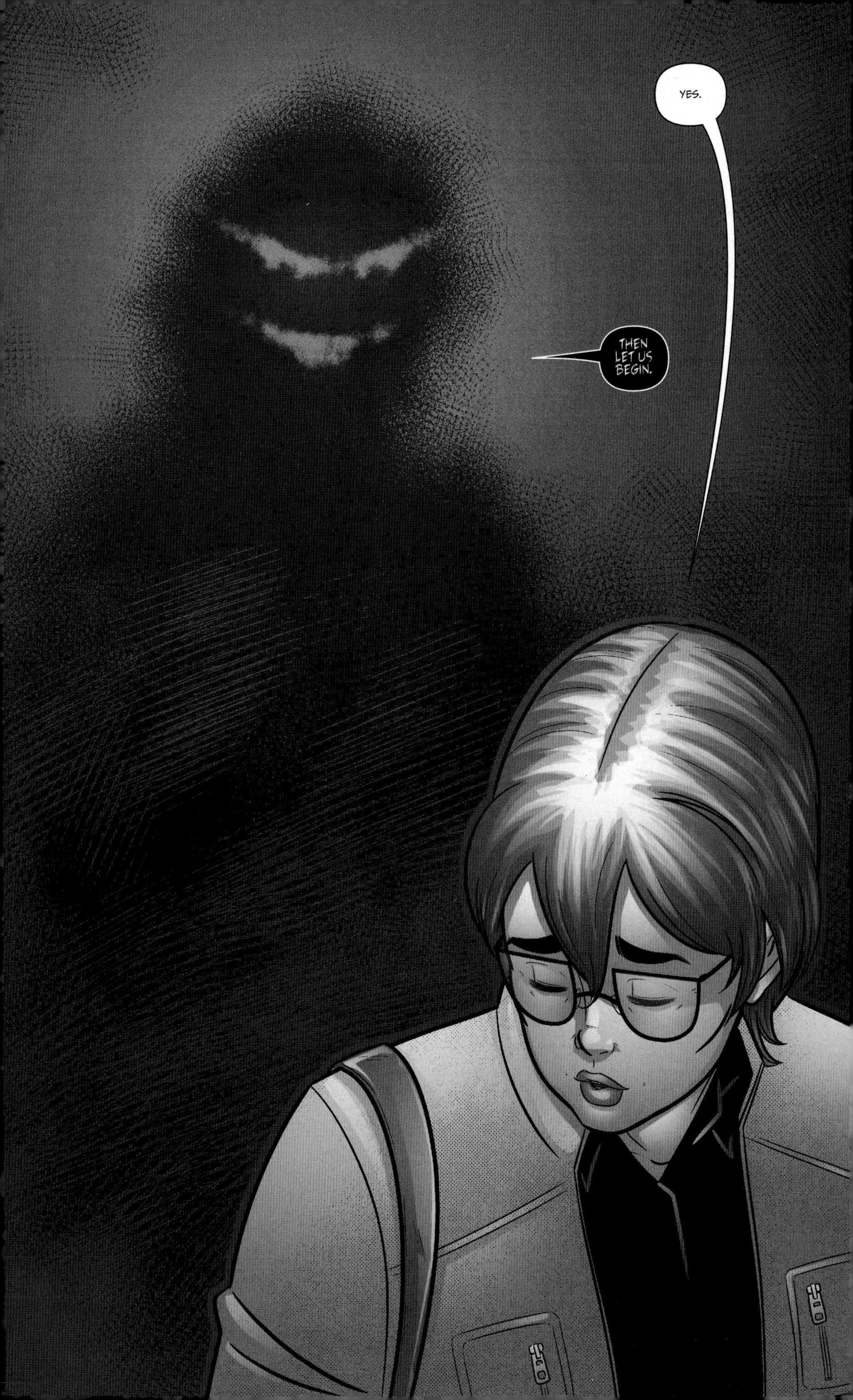
YES.
THEN LET US BEGIN.

CHAPTER THREE

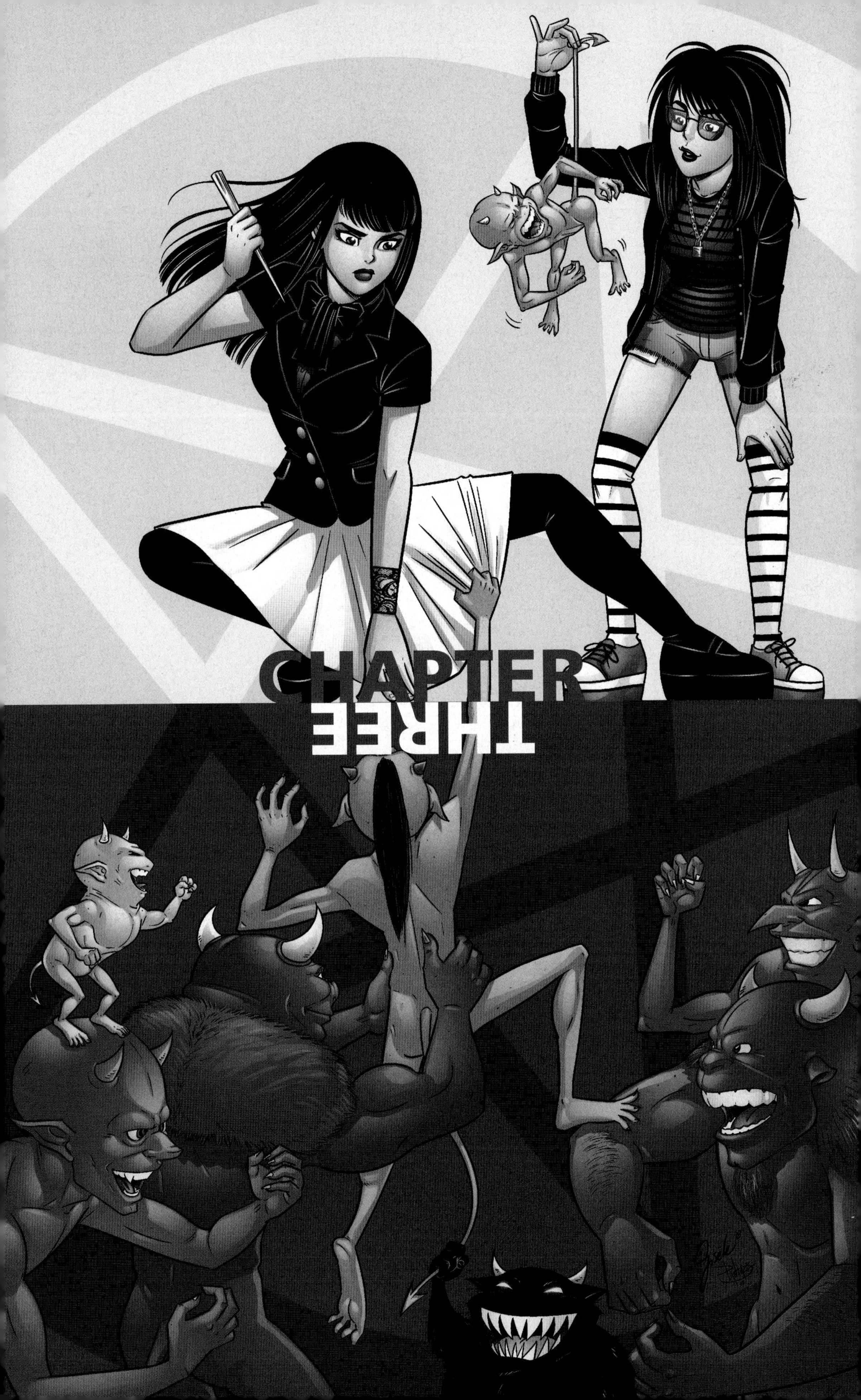

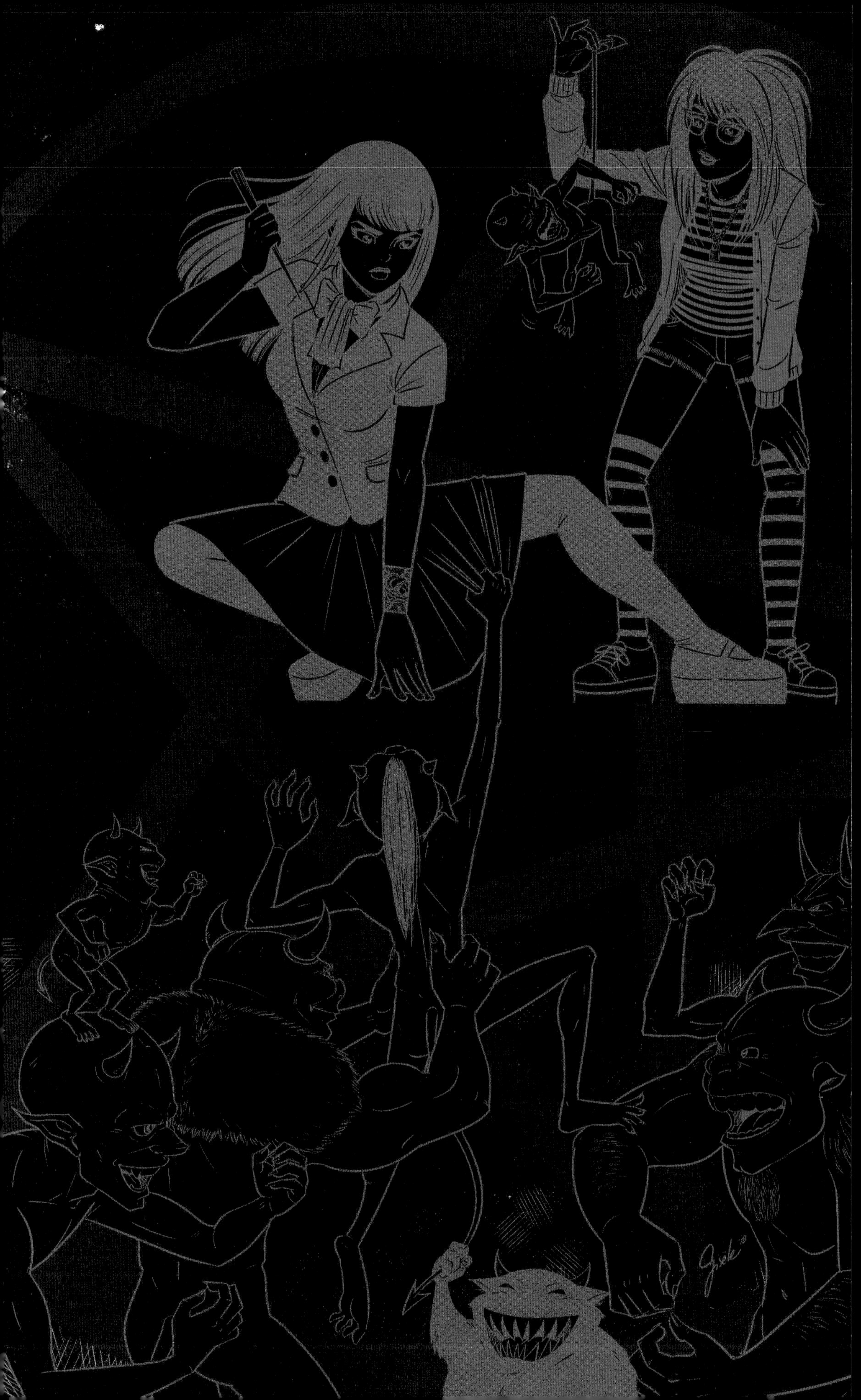

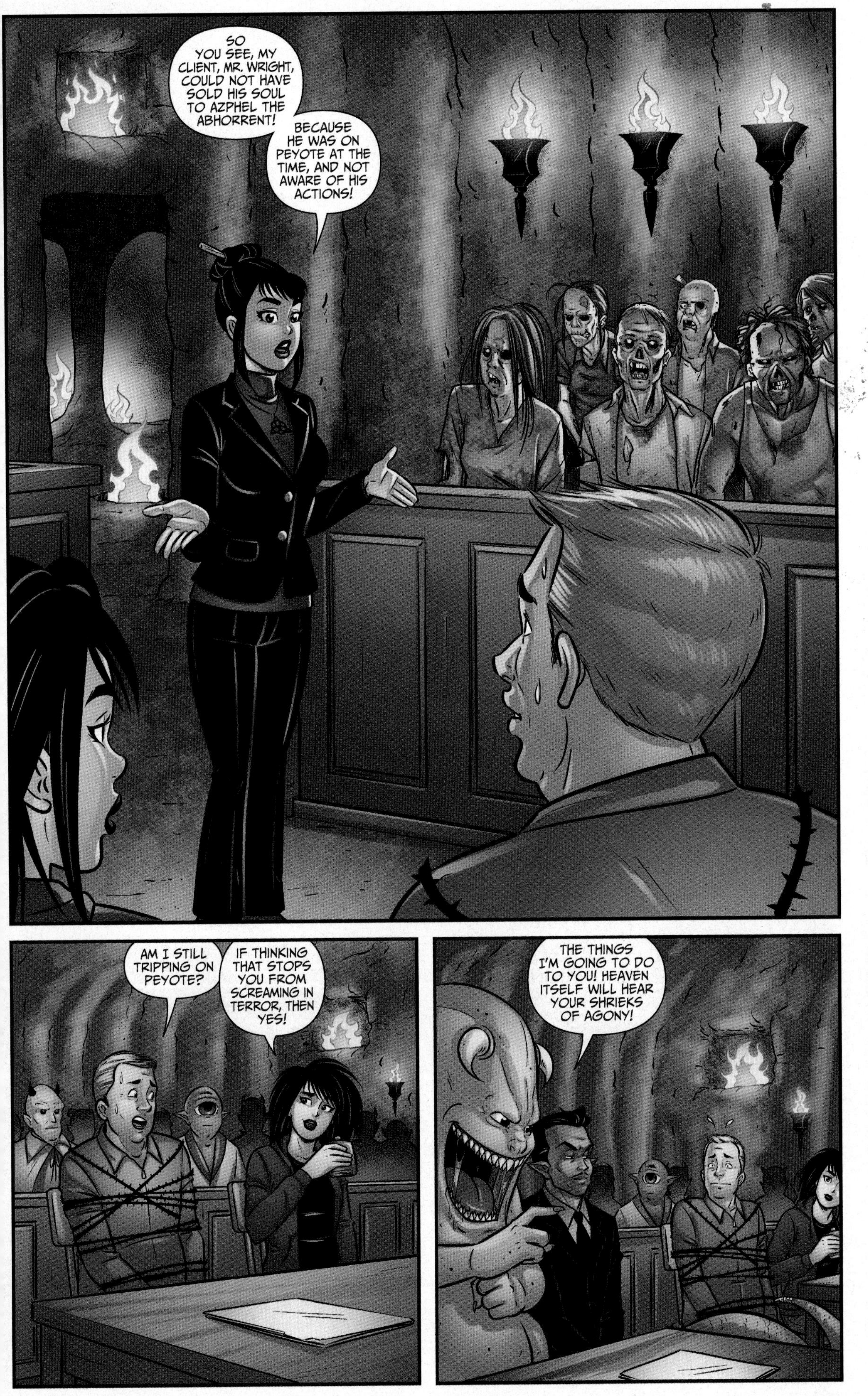
SO YOU SEE, MY CLIENT, MR. WRIGHT, COULD NOT HAVE SOLD HIS SOUL TO AZPHEL THE ABHORRENT!
BECAUSE HE WAS ON PEYOTE AT THE TIME, AND NOT AWARE OF HIS ACTIONS!
AM I STILL TRIPPING ON PEYOTE?
IF THINKING THAT STOPS YOU FROM SCREAMING IN TERROR, THEN YES!
THE THINGS I'M GOING TO DO TO YOU! HEAVEN ITSELF WILL HEAR YOUR SHRIEKS OF AGONY!

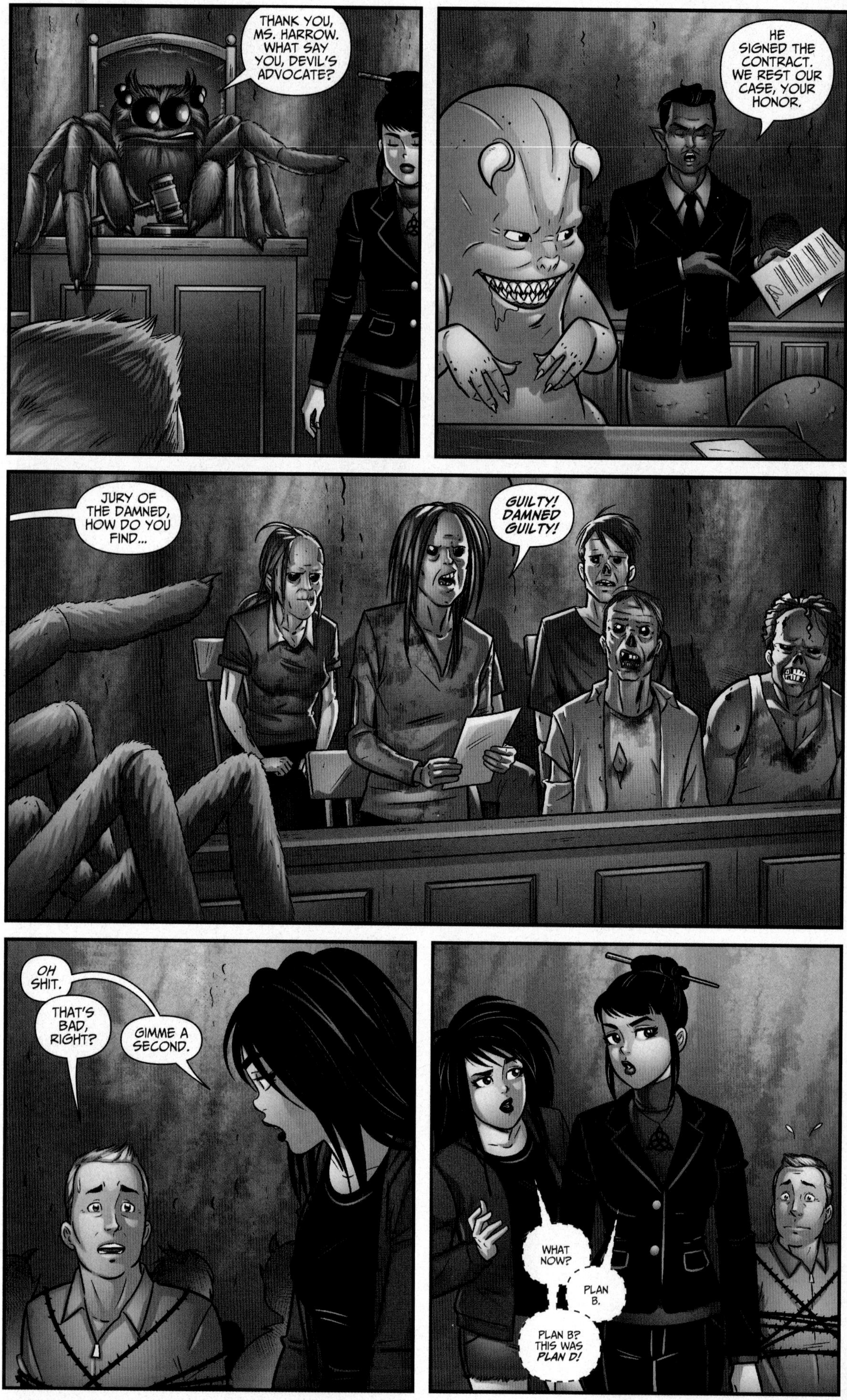
THANK YOU, MS. HARROW. WHAT SAY YOU, DEVIL'S ADVOCATE?
HE SIGNED THE CONTRACT. WE REST OUR CASE, YOUR HONOR.
JURY OF THE DAMNED, HOW DO YOU FIND...
GUILTY! DAMNED GUILTY!
OH SHIT.
THAT'S BAD, RIGHT?
GIMME A SECOND.
WHAT NOW?
PLAN B.
PLAN B? THIS WAS PLAN D!

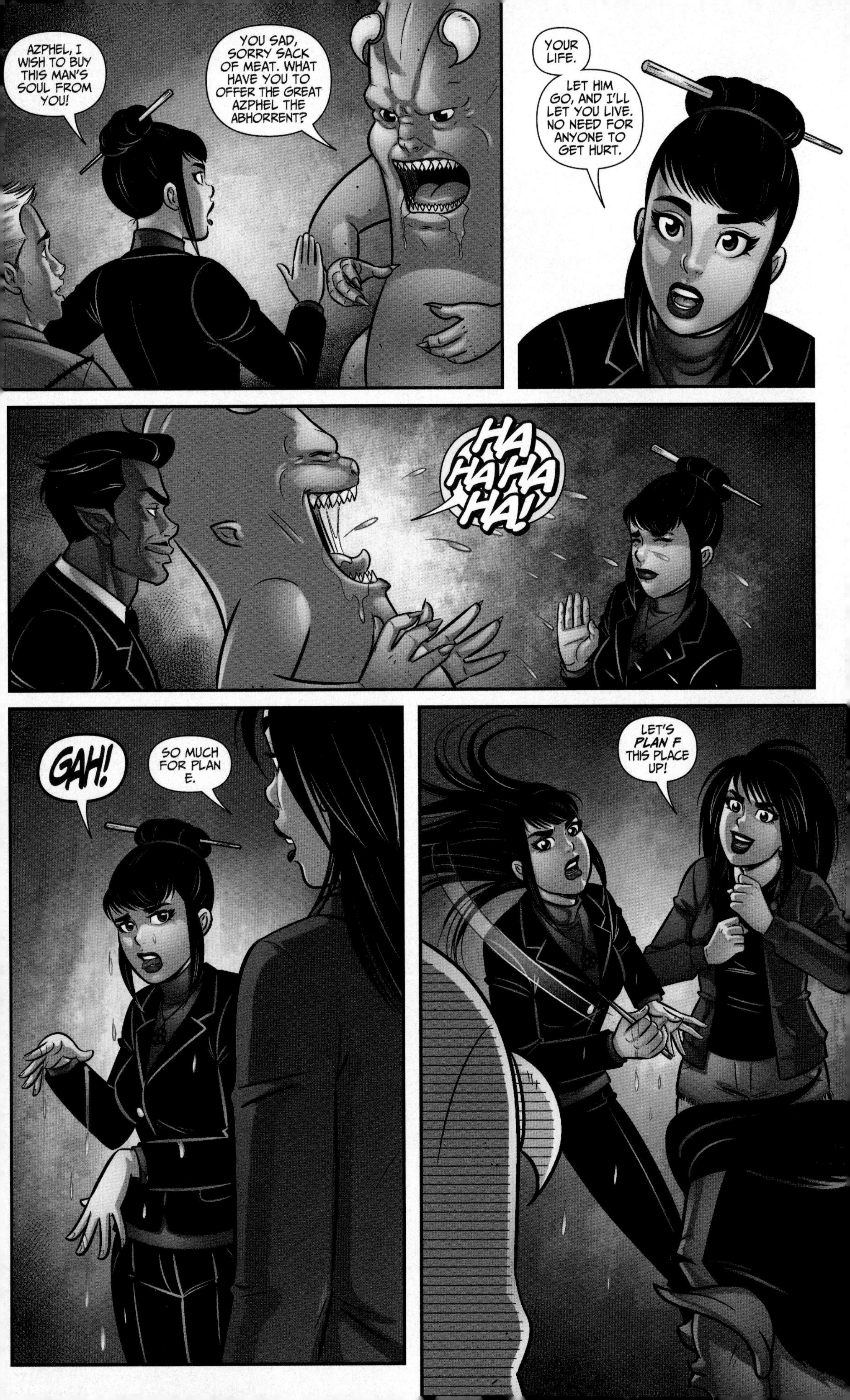

AZPHEL, I WISH TO BUY THIS MAN'S SOUL FROM YOU!
YOU SAD, SORRY SACK OF MEAT. WHAT HAVE YOU TO OFFER THE GREAT AZPHEL THE ABHORRENT?
YOUR LIFE.
LET HIM GO, AND I'LL LET YOU LIVE. NO NEED FOR ANYONE TO GET HURT.
HA HA HA HA!
GAH!
SO MUCH FOR PLAN E.
LET'S PLAN F THIS PLACE UP!

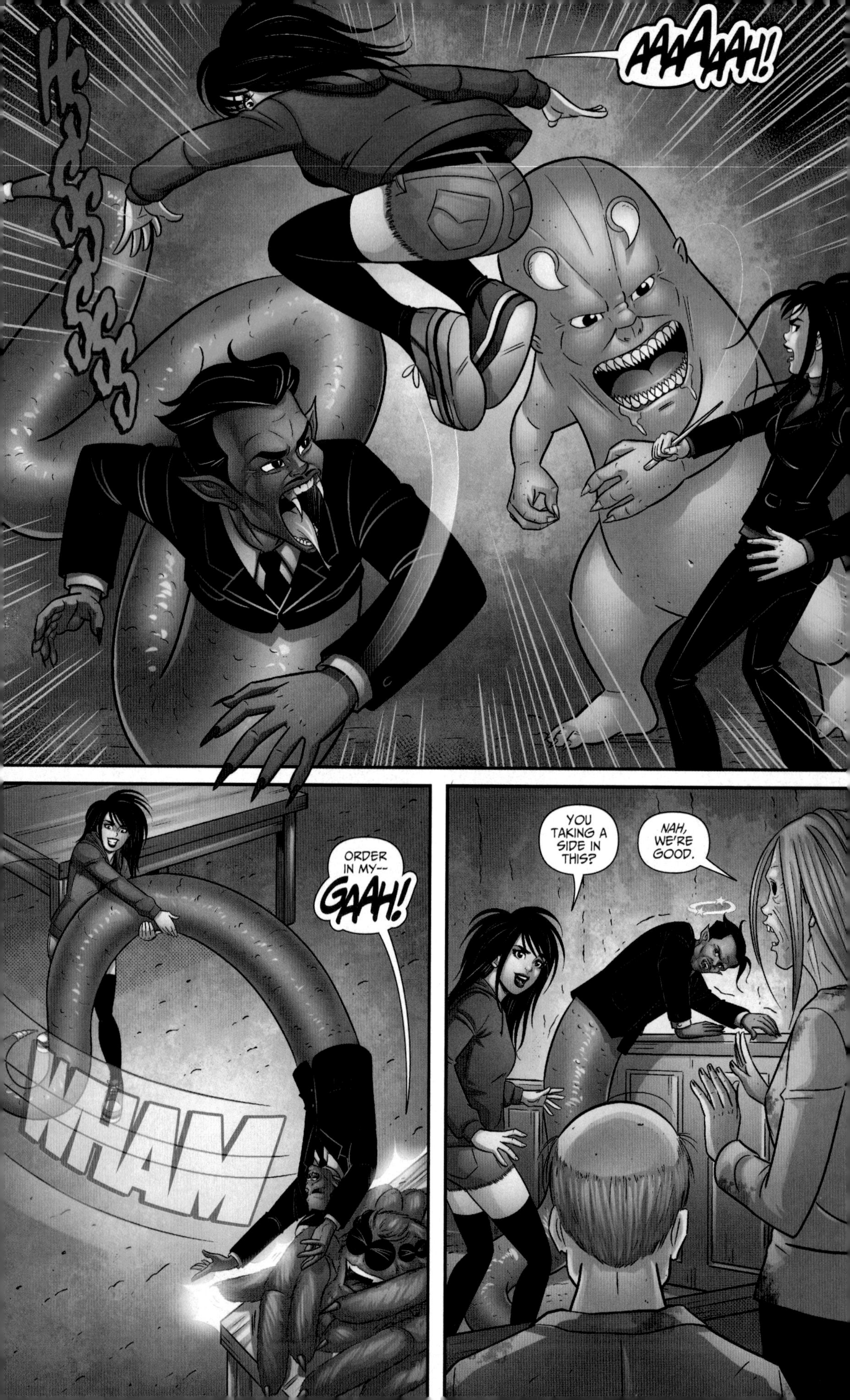
HSSSSSS
AAAAAAH!
ORDER IN MY--
GAAH!
WHAM
YOU TAKING A SIDE IN THIS?
NAH, WE'RE GOOD.

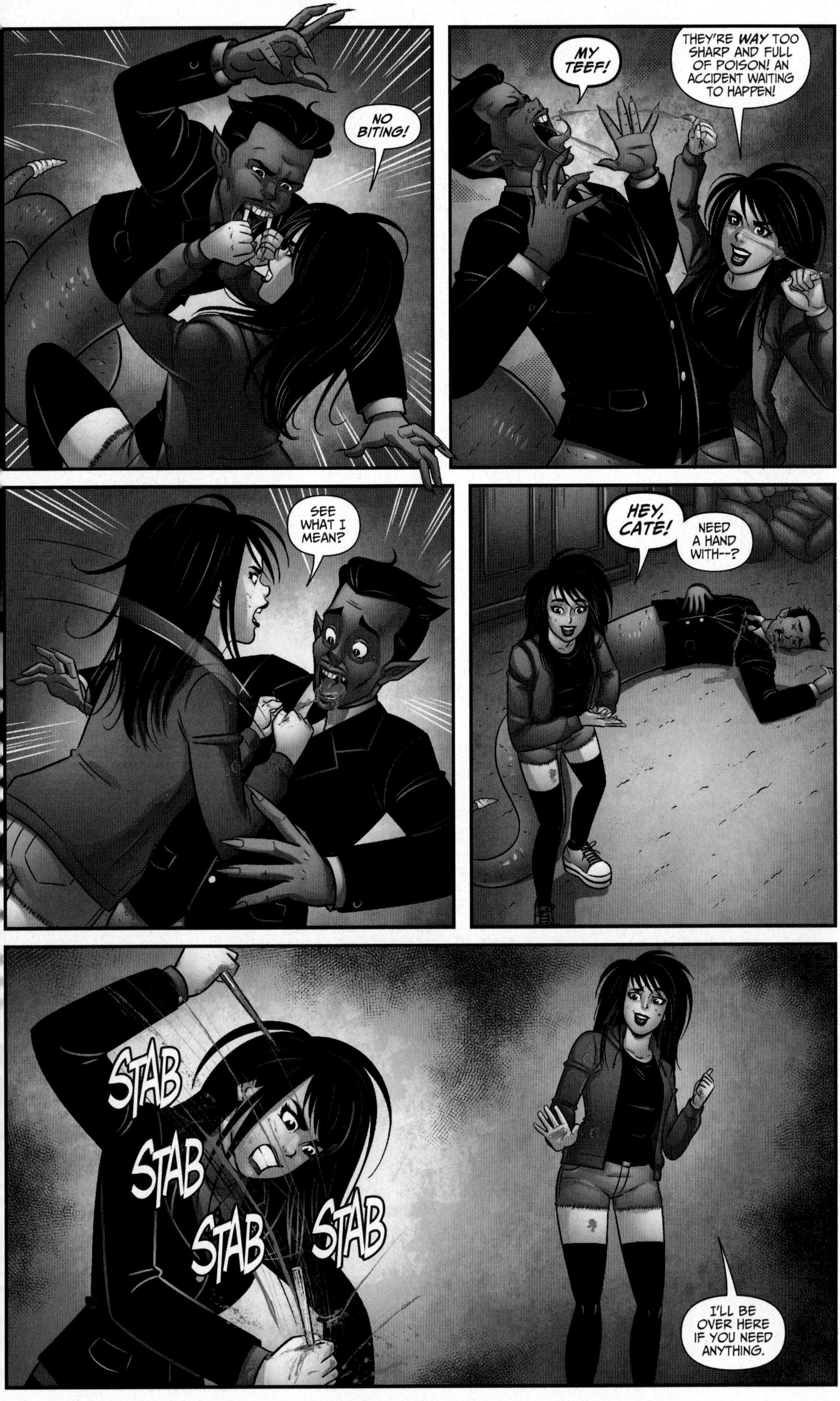
NO BITING!
MY TEEF!
THEY'RE WAY TOO SHARP AND FULL OF POISON! AN ACCIDENT WAITING TO HAPPEN!
SEE WHAT I MEAN?
HEY, CATE!
NEED A HAND WITH--?
STAB
STAB
STAB
STAB
I'LL BE OVER HERE IF YOU NEED ANYTHING.

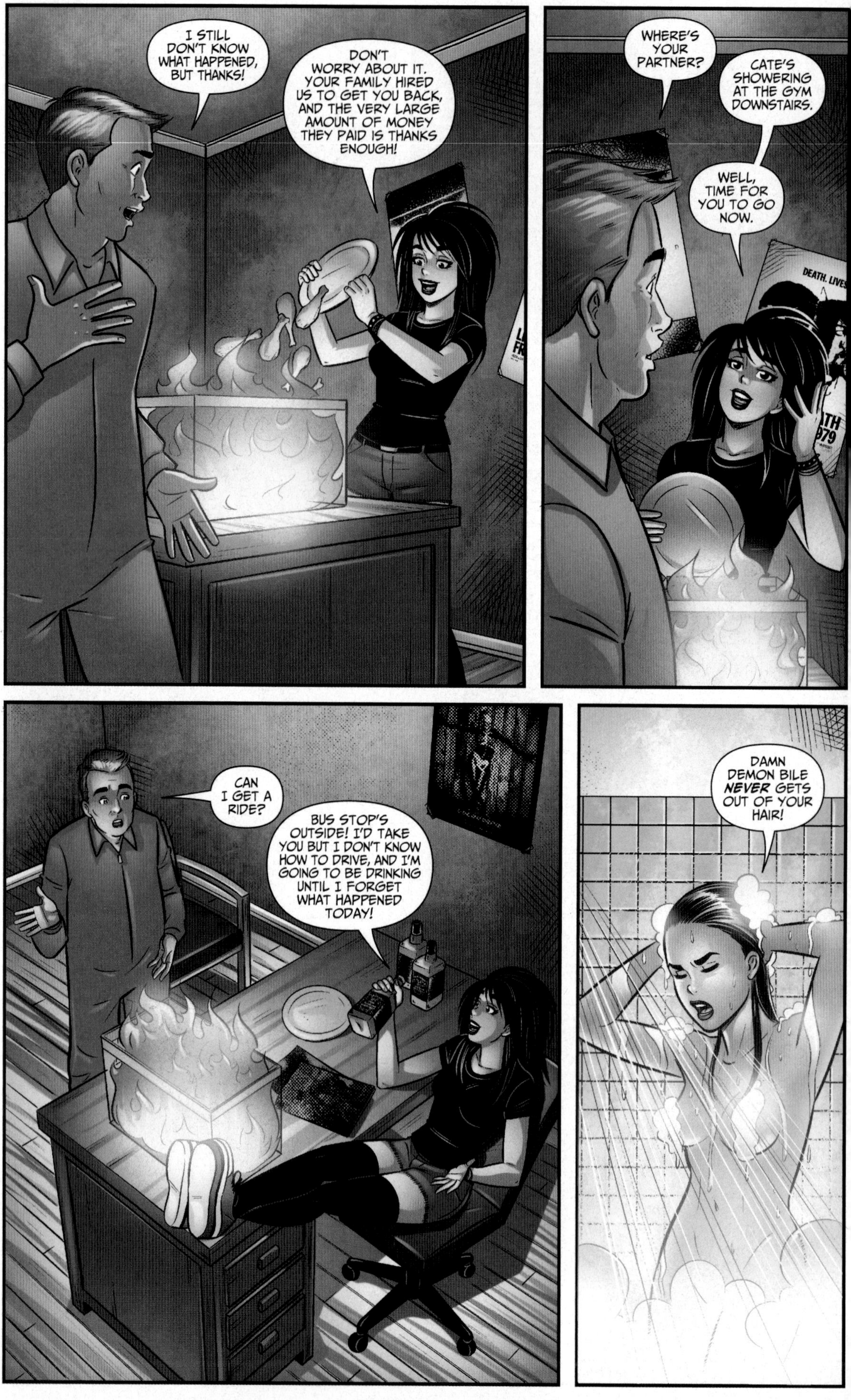
I STILL DON'T KNOW WHAT HAPPENED, BUT THANKS!
DON'T WORRY ABOUT IT. YOUR FAMILY HIRED US TO GET YOU BACK, AND THE VERY LARGE AMOUNT OF MONEY THEY PAID IS THANKS ENOUGH!
WHERE'S YOUR PARTNER?
CATE'S SHOWERING AT THE GYM DOWNSTAIRS.
WELL, TIME FOR YOU TO GO NOW.
DEATH. LIVES
CAN I GET A RIDE?
BUS STOP'S OUTSIDE! I'D TAKE YOU BUT I DON'T KNOW HOW TO DRIVE, AND I'M GOING TO BE DRINKING UNTIL I FORGET WHAT HAPPENED TODAY!
DAMN DEMON BILE ***NEVER*** GETS OUT OF YOUR HAIR!

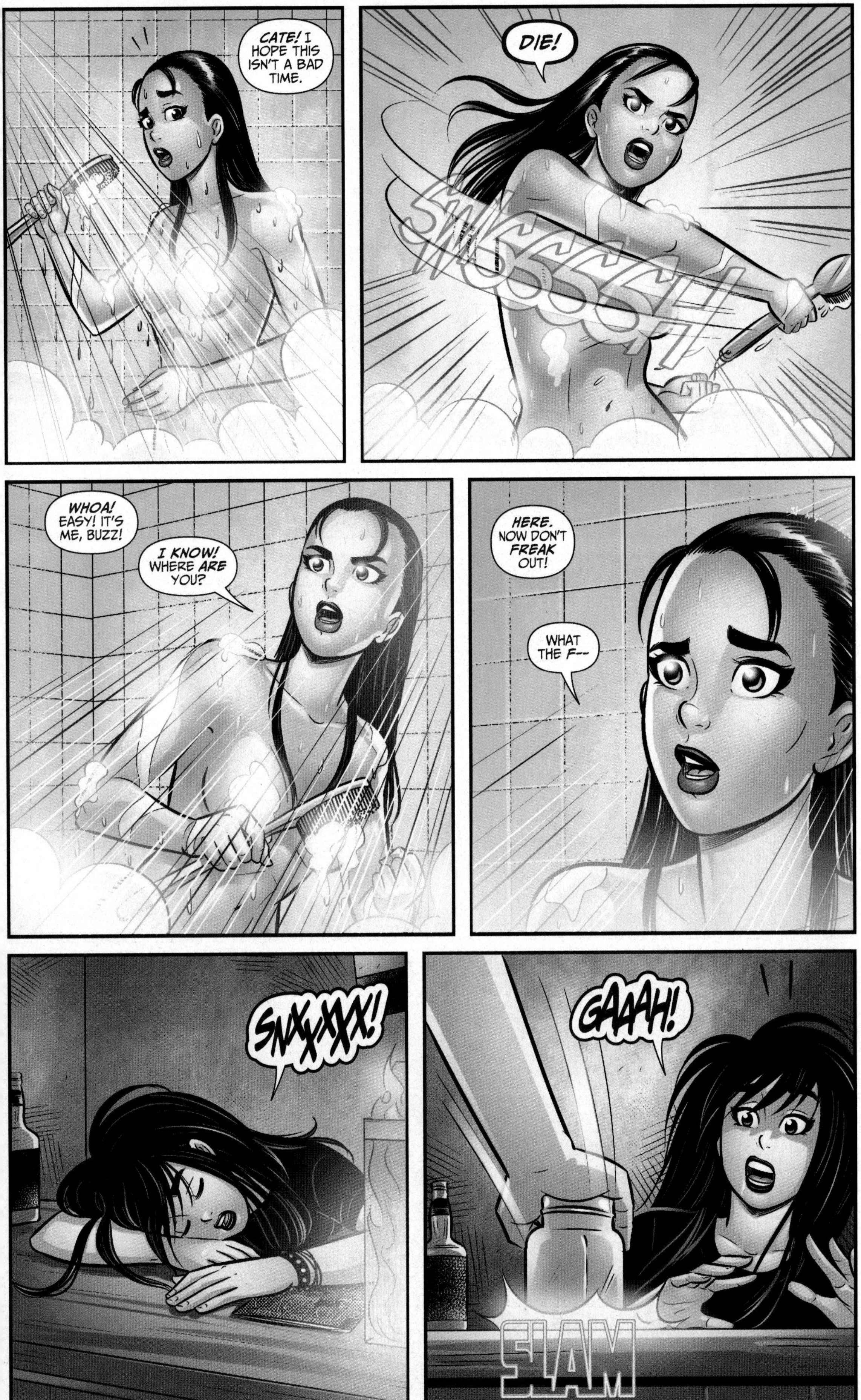
CATE! I HOPE THIS ISN'T A BAD TIME.
DIE!
SWOOSSSH
WHOA! EASY! IT'S ME, BUZZ!
I KNOW! WHERE ARE YOU?
HERE. NOW DON'T FREAK OUT!
WHAT THE F--
SNXXXXX!
GAAAH!
SLAM

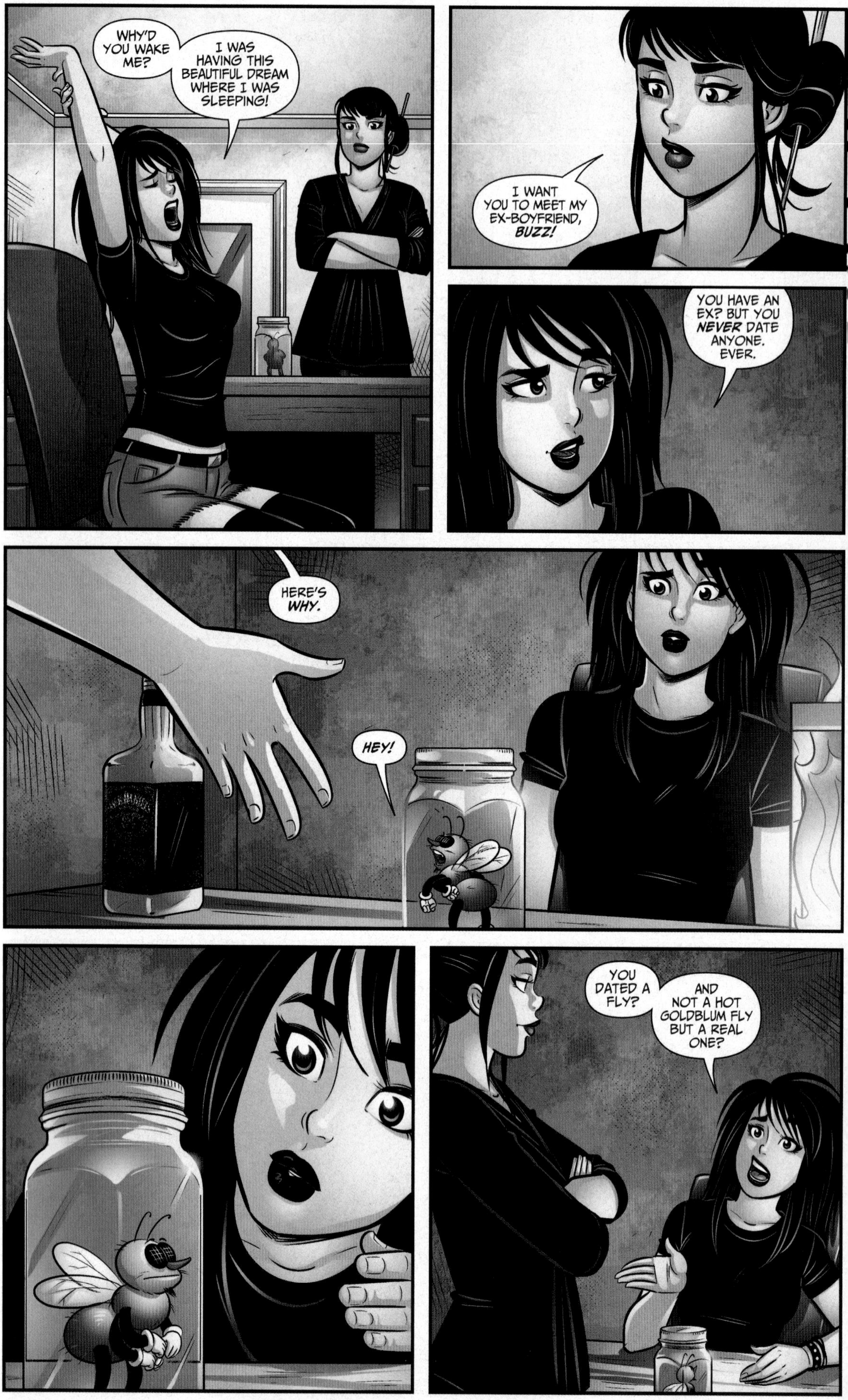
WHY'D YOU WAKE ME?
I WAS HAVING THIS BEAUTIFUL DREAM WHERE I WAS SLEEPING!
I WANT YOU TO MEET MY EX-BOYFRIEND, BUZZ!
YOU HAVE AN EX? BUT YOU NEVER DATE ANYONE. EVER.
HERE'S WHY.
HEY!
YOU DATED A FLY?
AND NOT A HOT GOLDBLUM FLY BUT A REAL ONE?

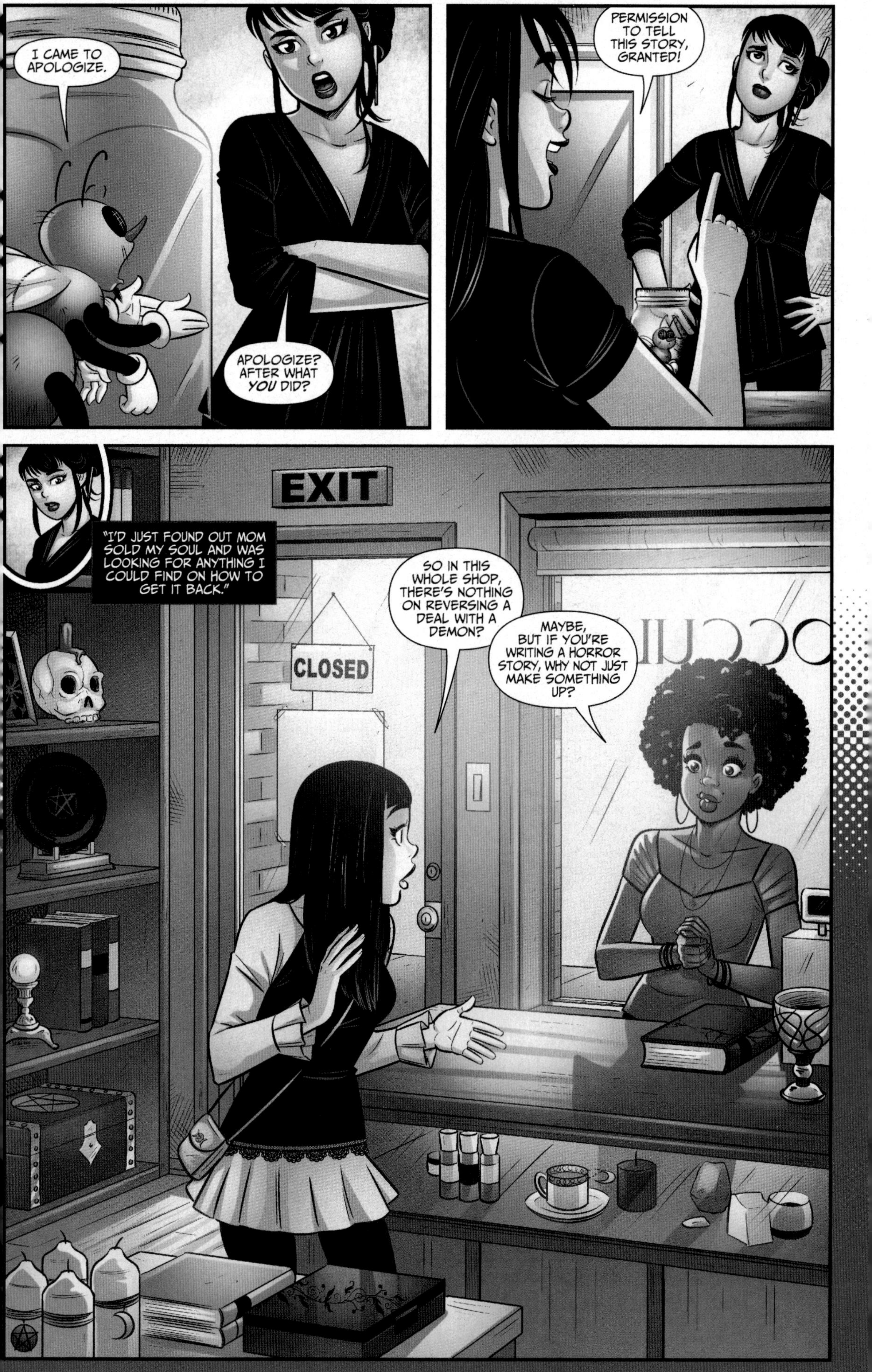
I CAME TO APOLOGIZE.
APOLOGIZE? AFTER WHAT *YOU* DID?
PERMISSION TO TELL THIS STORY, GRANTED!
"I'D JUST FOUND OUT MOM SOLD MY SOUL AND WAS LOOKING FOR ANYTHING I COULD FIND ON HOW TO GET IT BACK."
EXIT
CLOSED
SO IN THIS WHOLE SHOP, THERE'S NOTHING ON REVERSING A DEAL WITH A DEMON?
MAYBE, BUT IF YOU'RE WRITING A HORROR STORY, WHY NOT JUST MAKE SOMETHING UP?

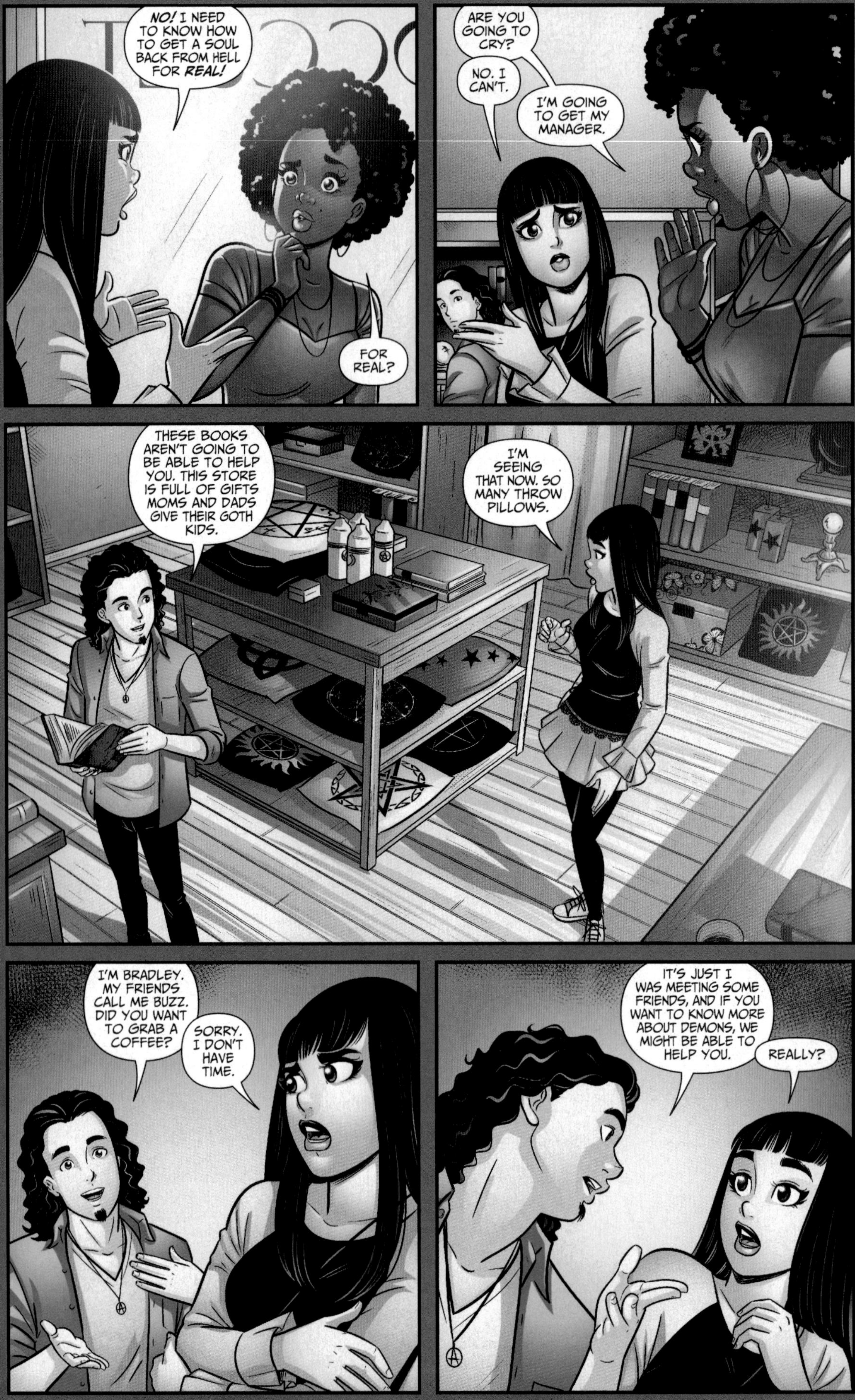
NO! I NEED TO KNOW HOW TO GET A SOUL BACK FROM HELL FOR REAL!
FOR REAL?
ARE YOU GOING TO CRY?
NO. I CAN'T.
I'M GOING TO GET MY MANAGER.
THESE BOOKS AREN'T GOING TO BE ABLE TO HELP YOU. THIS STORE IS FULL OF GIFTS MOMS AND DADS GIVE THEIR GOTH KIDS.
I'M SEEING THAT NOW. SO MANY THROW PILLOWS.
I'M BRADLEY. MY FRIENDS CALL ME BUZZ. DID YOU WANT TO GRAB A COFFEE?
SORRY. I DON'T HAVE TIME.
IT'S JUST I WAS MEETING SOME FRIENDS, AND IF YOU WANT TO KNOW MORE ABOUT DEMONS, WE MIGHT BE ABLE TO HELP YOU.
REALLY?

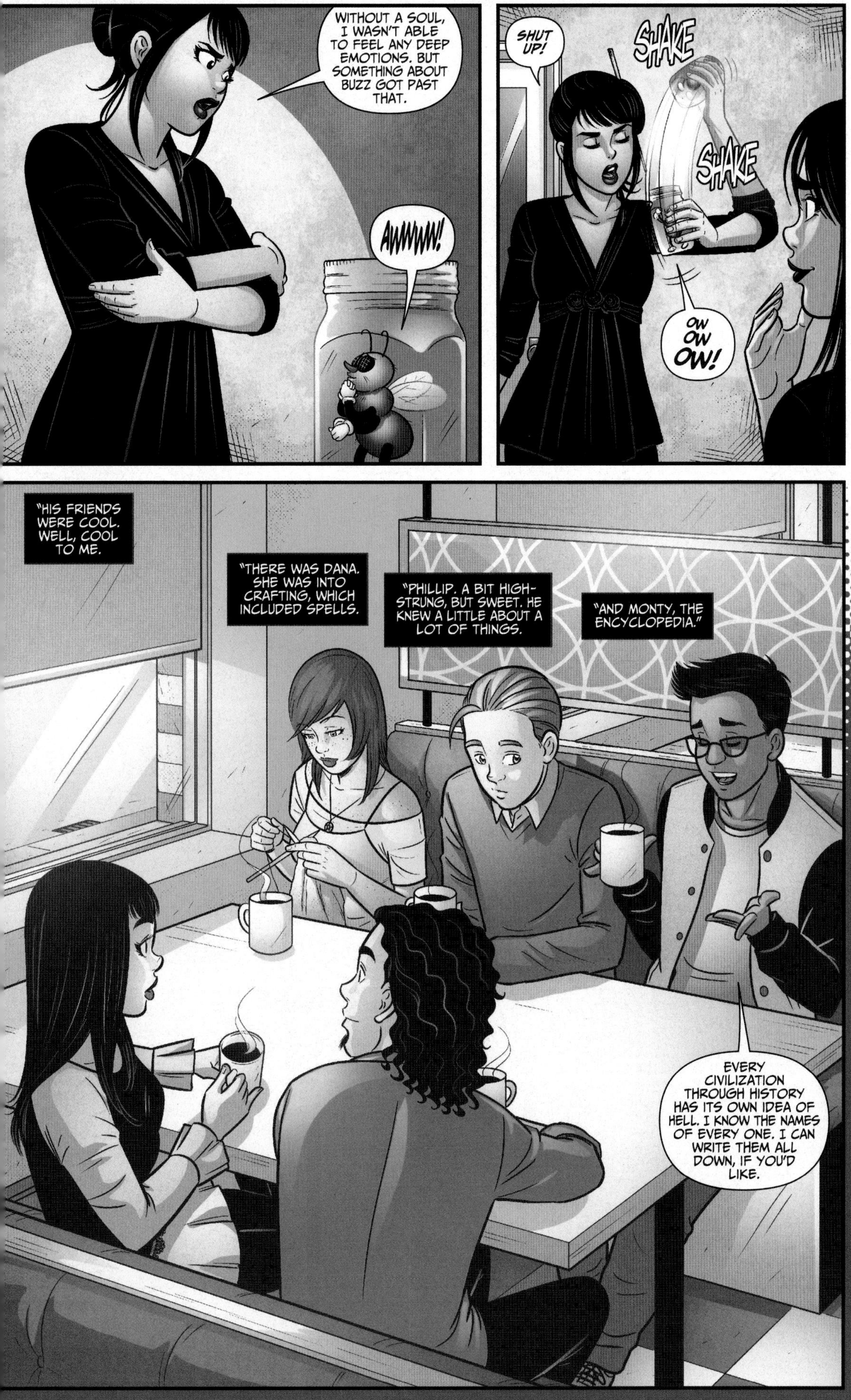
WITHOUT A SOUL, I WASN'T ABLE TO FEEL ANY DEEP EMOTIONS. BUT SOMETHING ABOUT BUZZ GOT PAST THAT.
AWWWW!
SHUT UP!
SHAKE
SHAKE
OW OW OW!
"HIS FRIENDS WERE COOL. WELL, COOL TO ME.
"THERE WAS DANA. SHE WAS INTO CRAFTING, WHICH INCLUDED SPELLS.
"PHILLIP. A BIT HIGH-STRUNG, BUT SWEET. HE KNEW A LITTLE ABOUT A LOT OF THINGS.
"AND MONTY, THE ENCYCLOPEDIA."
EVERY CIVILIZATION THROUGH HISTORY HAS ITS OWN IDEA OF HELL. I KNOW THE NAMES OF EVERY ONE. I CAN WRITE THEM ALL DOWN, IF YOU'D LIKE.

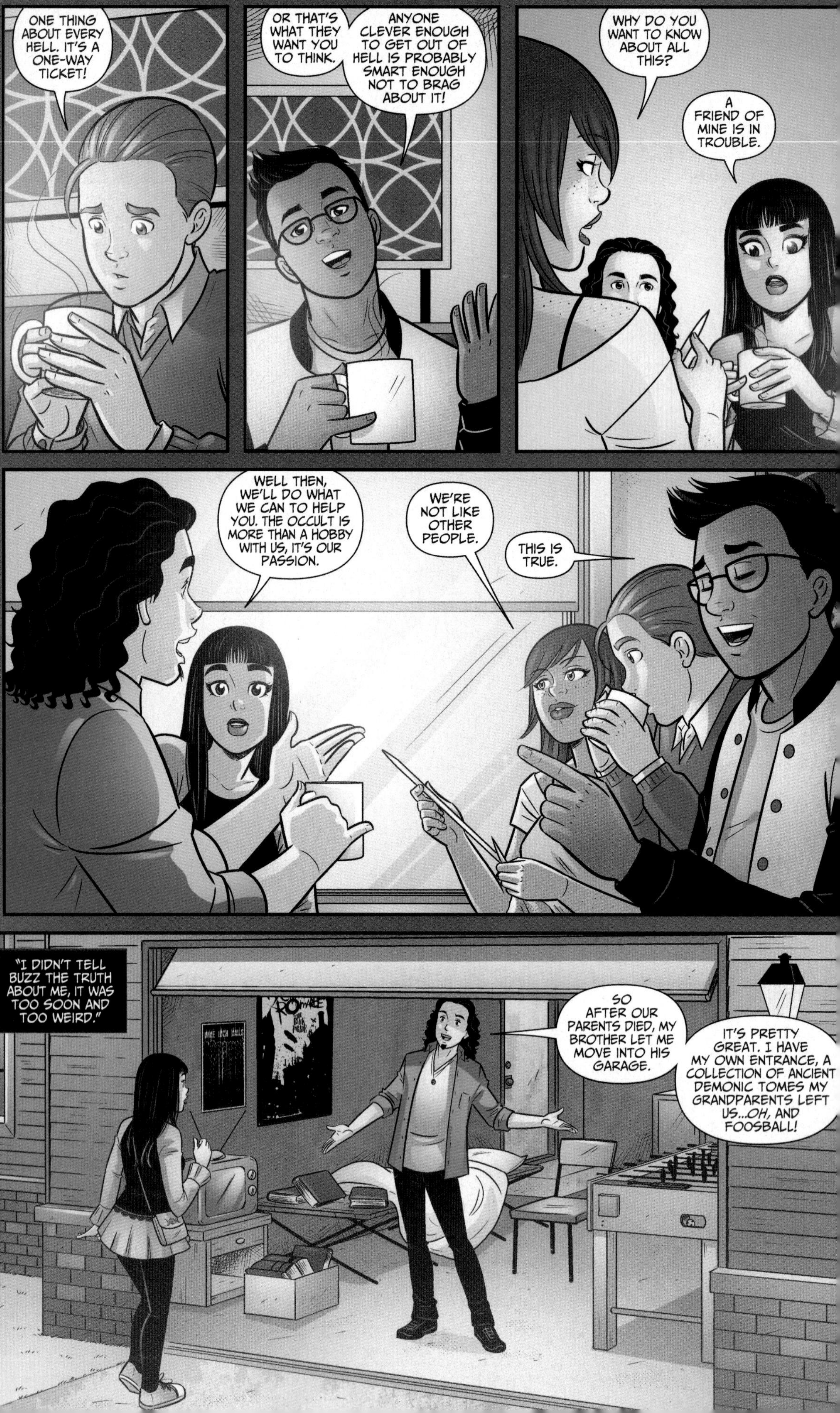

ONE THING ABOUT EVERY HELL. IT'S A ONE-WAY TICKET!
OR THAT'S WHAT THEY WANT YOU TO THINK.
ANYONE CLEVER ENOUGH TO GET OUT OF HELL IS PROBABLY SMART ENOUGH NOT TO BRAG ABOUT IT!
WHY DO YOU WANT TO KNOW ABOUT ALL THIS?
A FRIEND OF MINE IS IN TROUBLE.
WELL THEN, WE'LL DO WHAT WE CAN TO HELP YOU. THE OCCULT IS MORE THAN A HOBBY WITH US, IT'S OUR PASSION.
WE'RE NOT LIKE OTHER PEOPLE.
THIS IS TRUE.
"I DIDN'T TELL BUZZ THE TRUTH ABOUT ME, IT WAS TOO SOON AND TOO WEIRD."
SO AFTER OUR PARENTS DIED, MY BROTHER LET ME MOVE INTO HIS GARAGE.
IT'S PRETTY GREAT. I HAVE MY OWN ENTRANCE, A COLLECTION OF ANCIENT DEMONIC TOMES MY GRANDPARENTS LEFT US...*OH*, AND FOOSBALL!

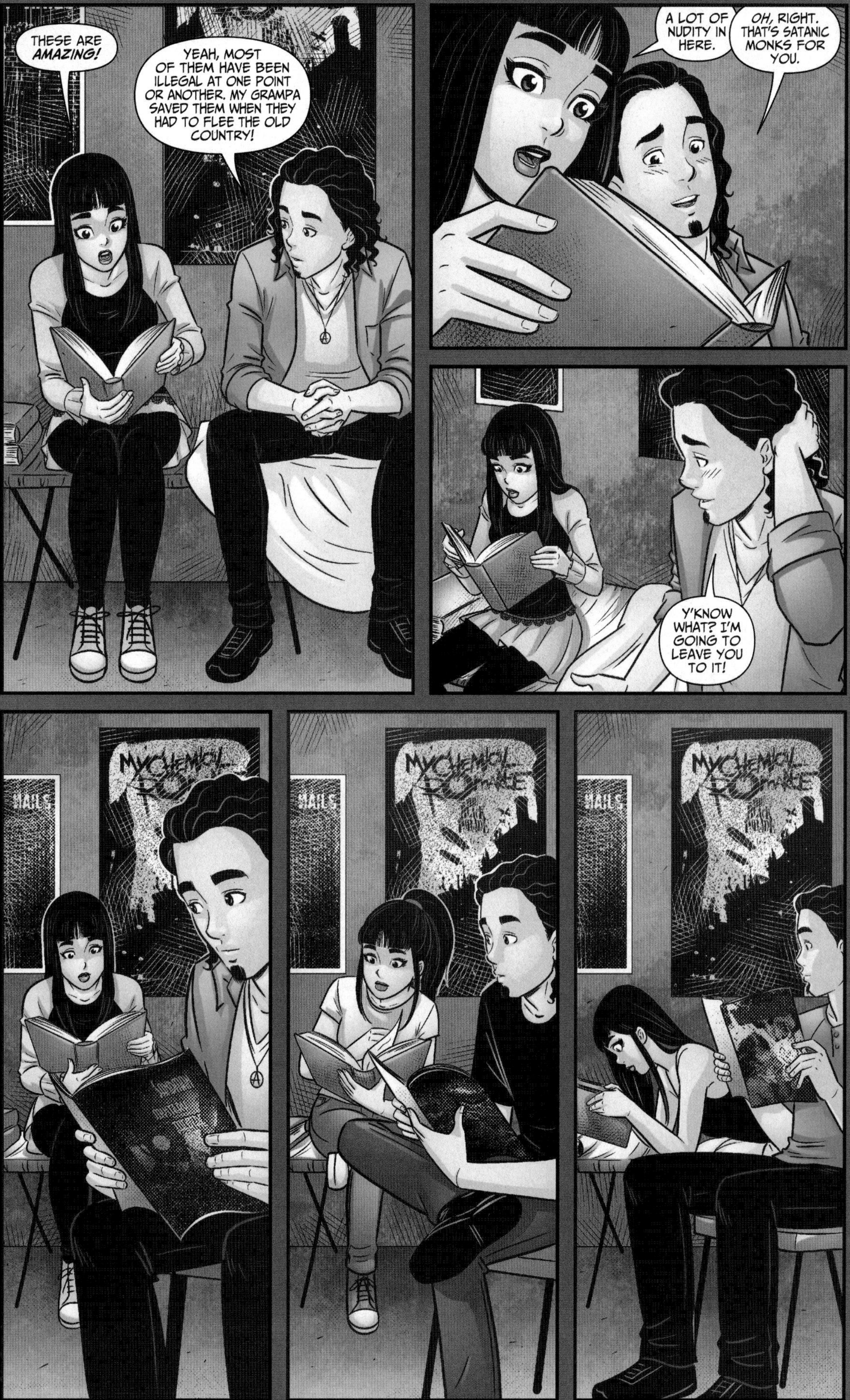
THESE ARE *AMAZING!*
YEAH, MOST OF THEM HAVE BEEN ILLEGAL AT ONE POINT OR ANOTHER. MY GRAMPA SAVED THEM WHEN THEY HAD TO FLEE THE OLD COUNTRY!
A LOT OF NUDITY IN HERE.
OH, RIGHT. THAT'S SATANIC MONKS FOR YOU.
Y'KNOW WHAT? I'M GOING TO LEAVE YOU TO IT!

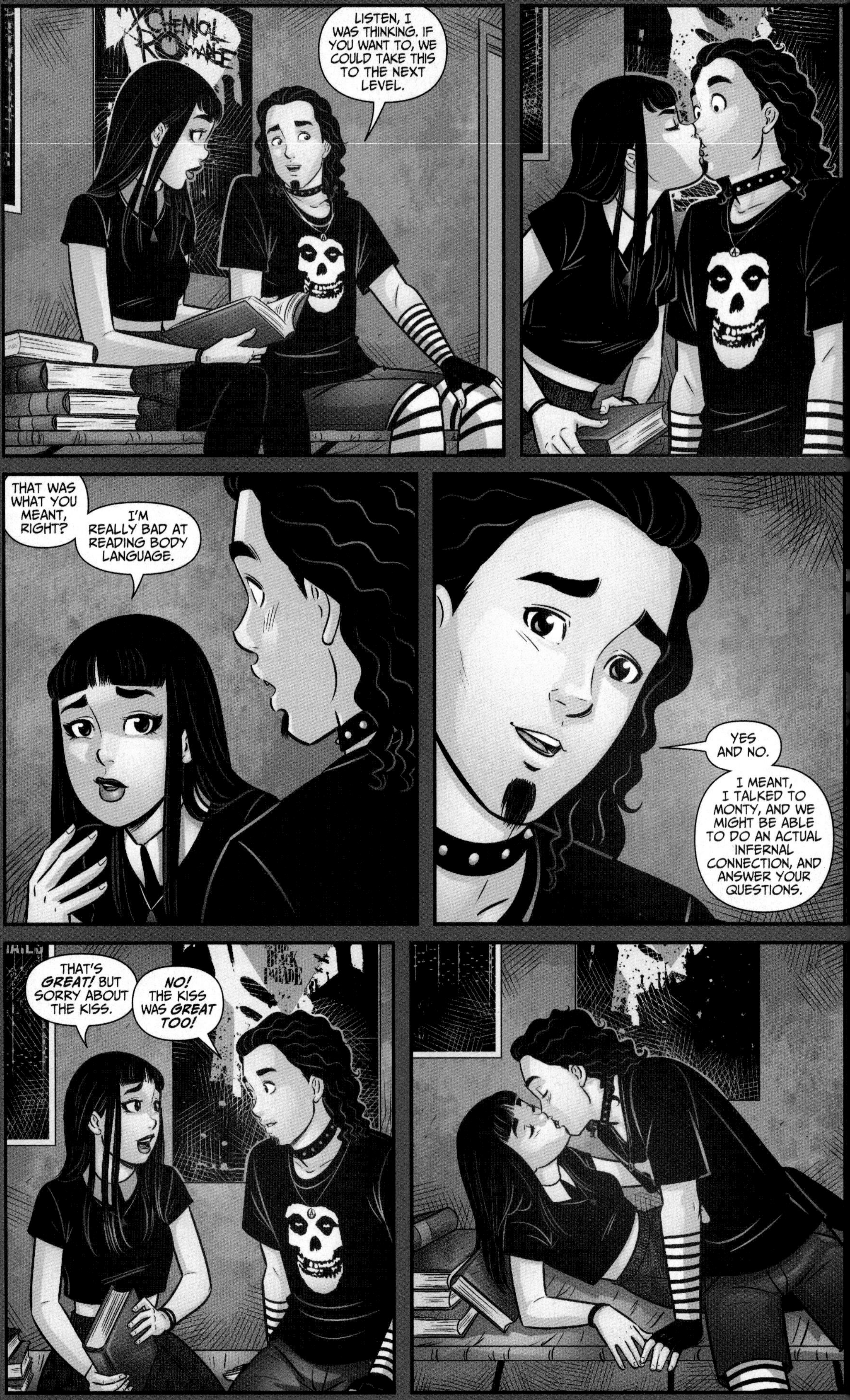

MY CHEMICAL ROMANCE
LISTEN, I WAS THINKING. IF YOU WANT TO, WE COULD TAKE THIS TO THE NEXT LEVEL.
THAT WAS WHAT YOU MEANT, RIGHT?
I'M REALLY BAD AT READING BODY LANGUAGE.
YES AND NO.
I MEANT, I TALKED TO MONTY, AND WE MIGHT BE ABLE TO DO AN ACTUAL INFERNAL CONNECTION, AND ANSWER YOUR QUESTIONS.
THAT'S *GREAT!* BUT SORRY ABOUT THE KISS.
NO! THE KISS WAS *GREAT TOO!*
THE BLACK PARADE

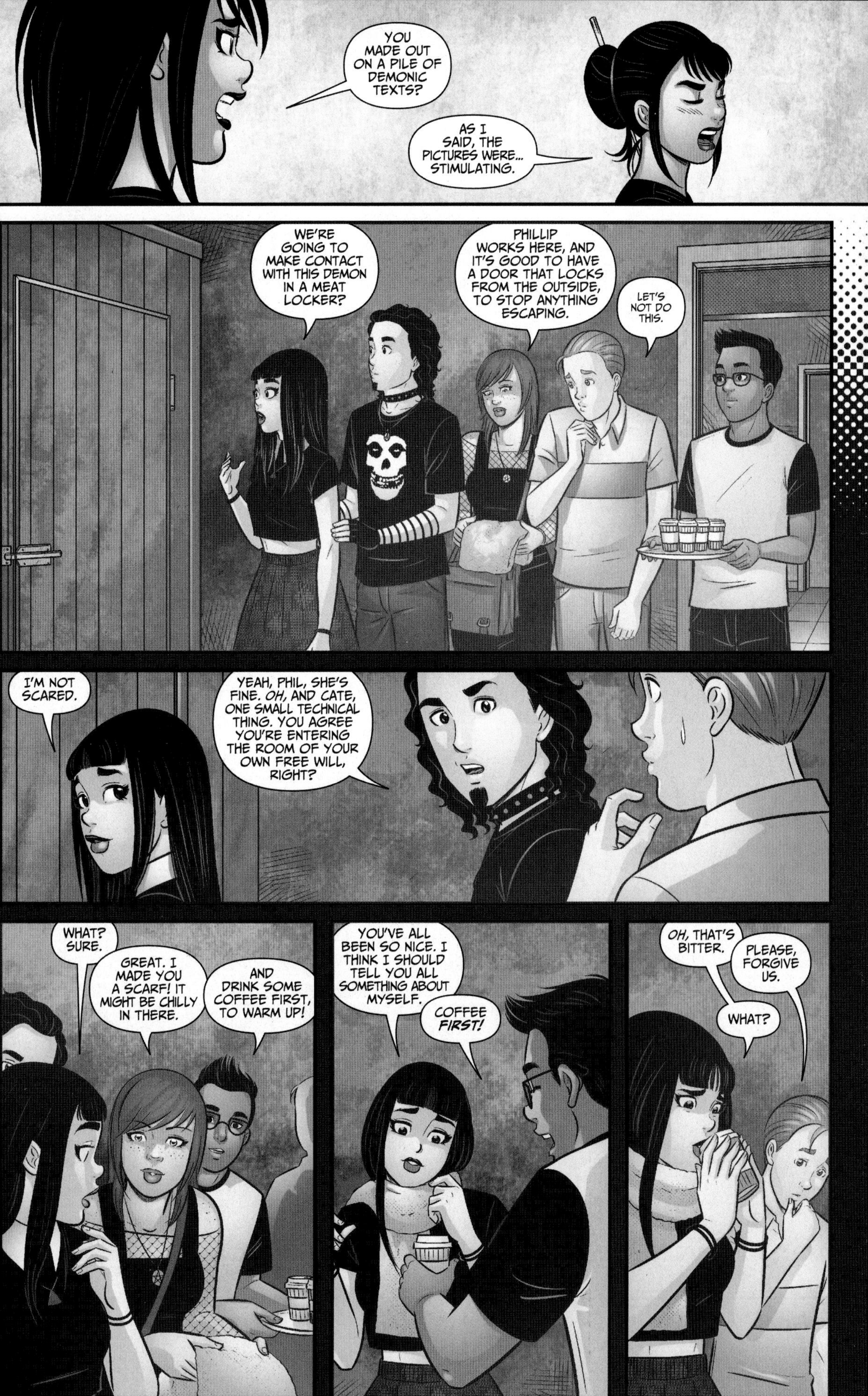
YOU MADE OUT ON A PILE OF DEMONIC TEXTS?
AS I SAID, THE PICTURES WERE... STIMULATING.
WE'RE GOING TO MAKE CONTACT WITH THIS DEMON IN A MEAT LOCKER?
PHILLIP WORKS HERE, AND IT'S GOOD TO HAVE A DOOR THAT LOCKS FROM THE OUTSIDE, TO STOP ANYTHING ESCAPING.
LET'S NOT DO THIS.
I'M NOT SCARED.
YEAH, PHIL, SHE'S FINE. *OH*, AND CATE, ONE SMALL TECHNICAL THING. YOU AGREE YOU'RE ENTERING THE ROOM OF YOUR OWN FREE WILL, RIGHT?
WHAT? SURE.
GREAT. I MADE YOU A SCARF! IT MIGHT BE CHILLY IN THERE.
AND DRINK SOME COFFEE FIRST, TO WARM UP!
YOU'VE ALL BEEN SO NICE. I THINK I SHOULD TELL YOU ALL SOMETHING ABOUT MYSELF.
COFFEE *FIRST!*
OH, THAT'S BITTER.
PLEASE, FORGIVE US.
WHAT?

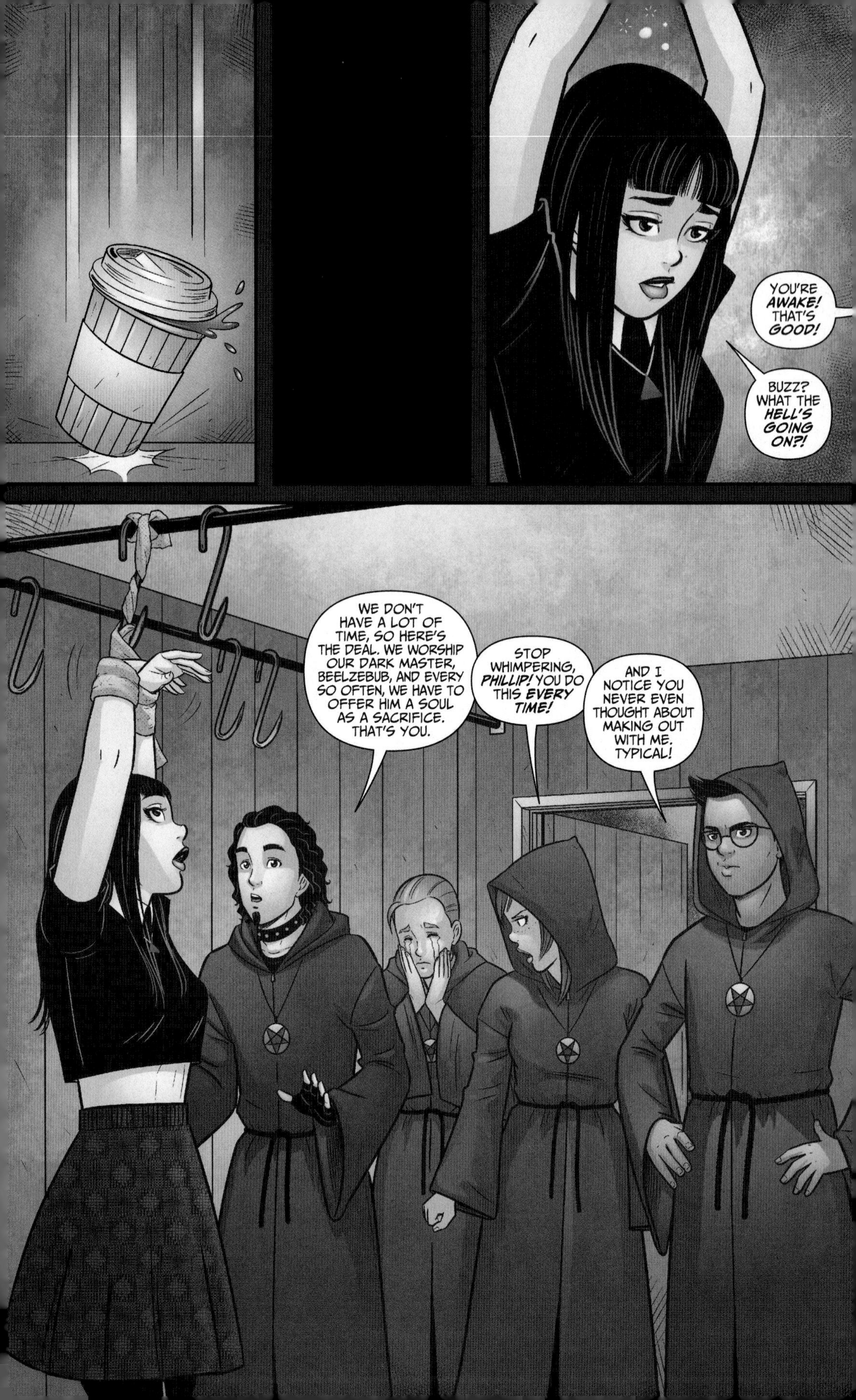
YOU'RE AWAKE! THAT'S GOOD!
BUZZ? WHAT THE HELL'S GOING ON?!
WE DON'T HAVE A LOT OF TIME, SO HERE'S THE DEAL. WE WORSHIP OUR DARK MASTER, BEELZEBUB, AND EVERY SO OFTEN, WE HAVE TO OFFER HIM A SOUL AS A SACRIFICE. THAT'S YOU.
STOP WHIMPERING, PHILLIP! YOU DO THIS EVERY TIME!
AND I NOTICE YOU NEVER EVEN THOUGHT ABOUT MAKING OUT WITH ME. TYPICAL!

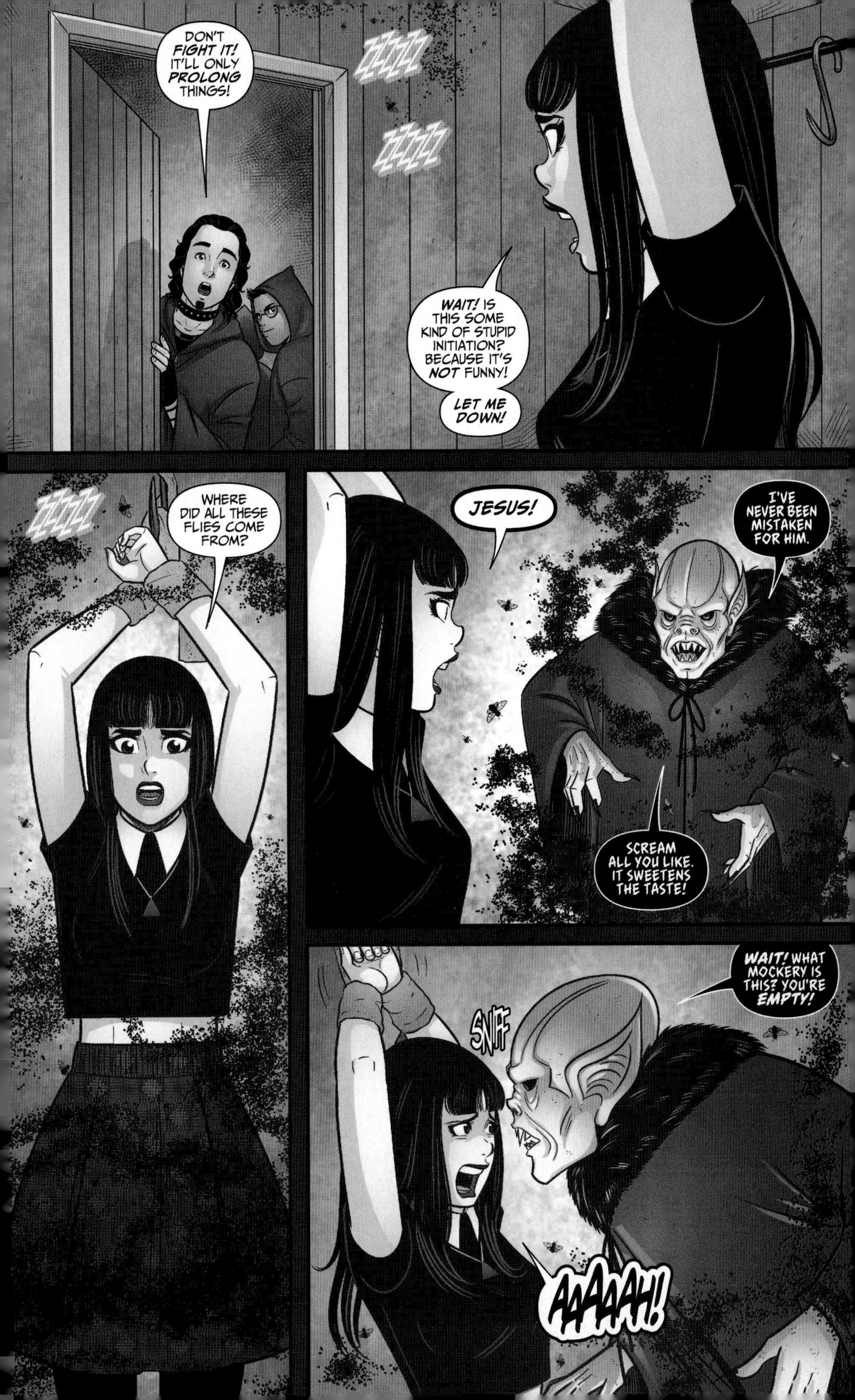
DON'T FIGHT IT! IT'LL ONLY PROLONG THINGS!
ZZZZZ
ZZZZZ
WAIT! IS THIS SOME KIND OF STUPID INITIATION? BECAUSE IT'S NOT FUNNY!
LET ME DOWN!
ZZZZZ
WHERE DID ALL THESE FLIES COME FROM?
JESUS!
I'VE NEVER BEEN MISTAKEN FOR HIM.
SCREAM ALL YOU LIKE. IT SWEETENS THE TASTE!
WAIT! WHAT MOCKERY IS THIS? YOU'RE EMPTY!
SNIFF
AAAAAH!

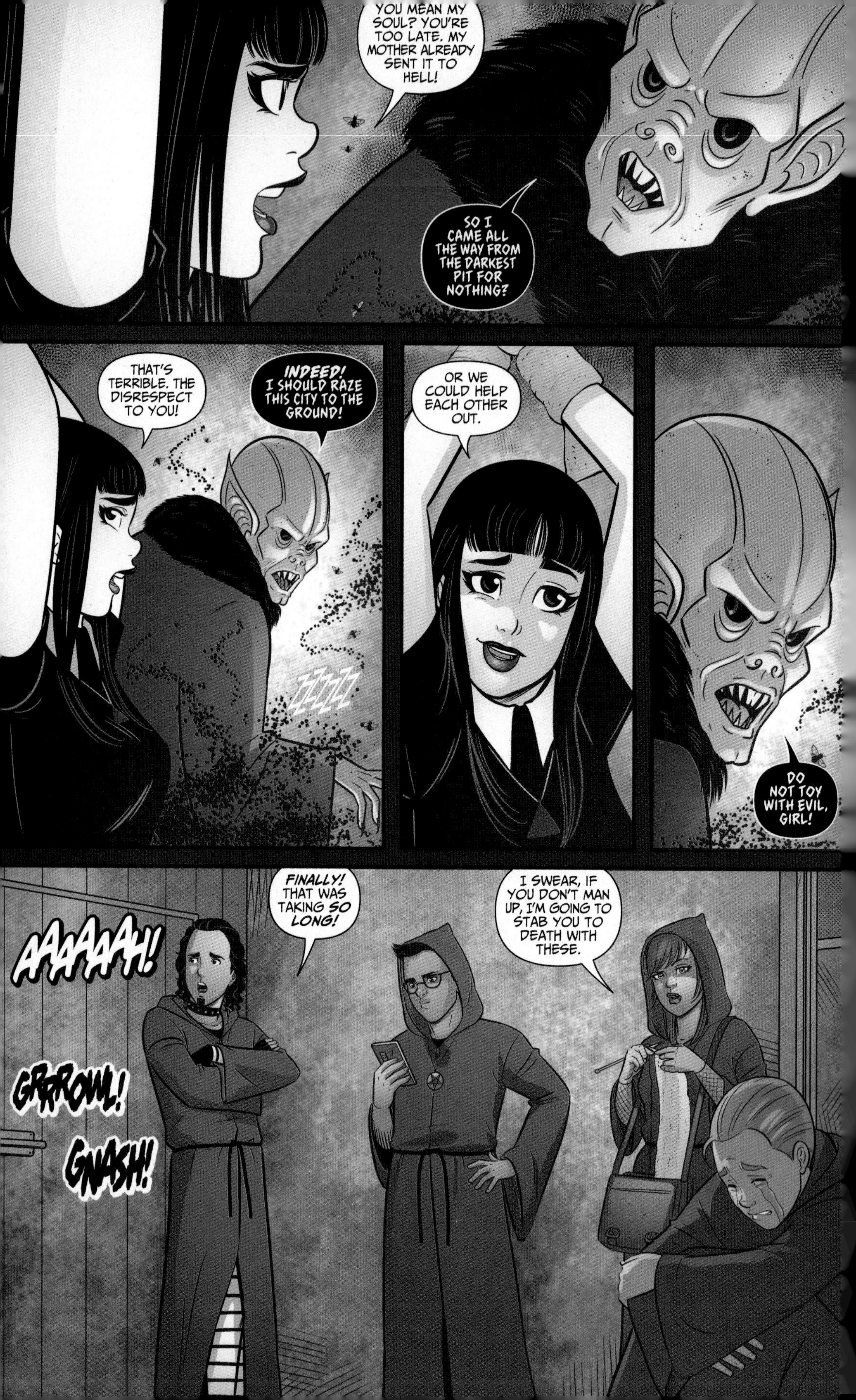

YOU MEAN MY SOUL? YOU'RE TOO LATE. MY MOTHER ALREADY SENT IT TO HELL!
SO I CAME ALL THE WAY FROM THE DARKEST PIT FOR NOTHING?
THAT'S TERRIBLE. THE DISRESPECT TO YOU!
INDEED! I SHOULD RAZE THIS CITY TO THE GROUND!
OR WE COULD HELP EACH OTHER OUT.
DO NOT TOY WITH EVIL, GIRL!
AAAAAAH!
FINALLY! THAT WAS TAKING SO LONG!
I SWEAR, IF YOU DON'T MAN UP, I'M GOING TO STAB YOU TO DEATH WITH THESE.
GRRROWL!
GNASH!

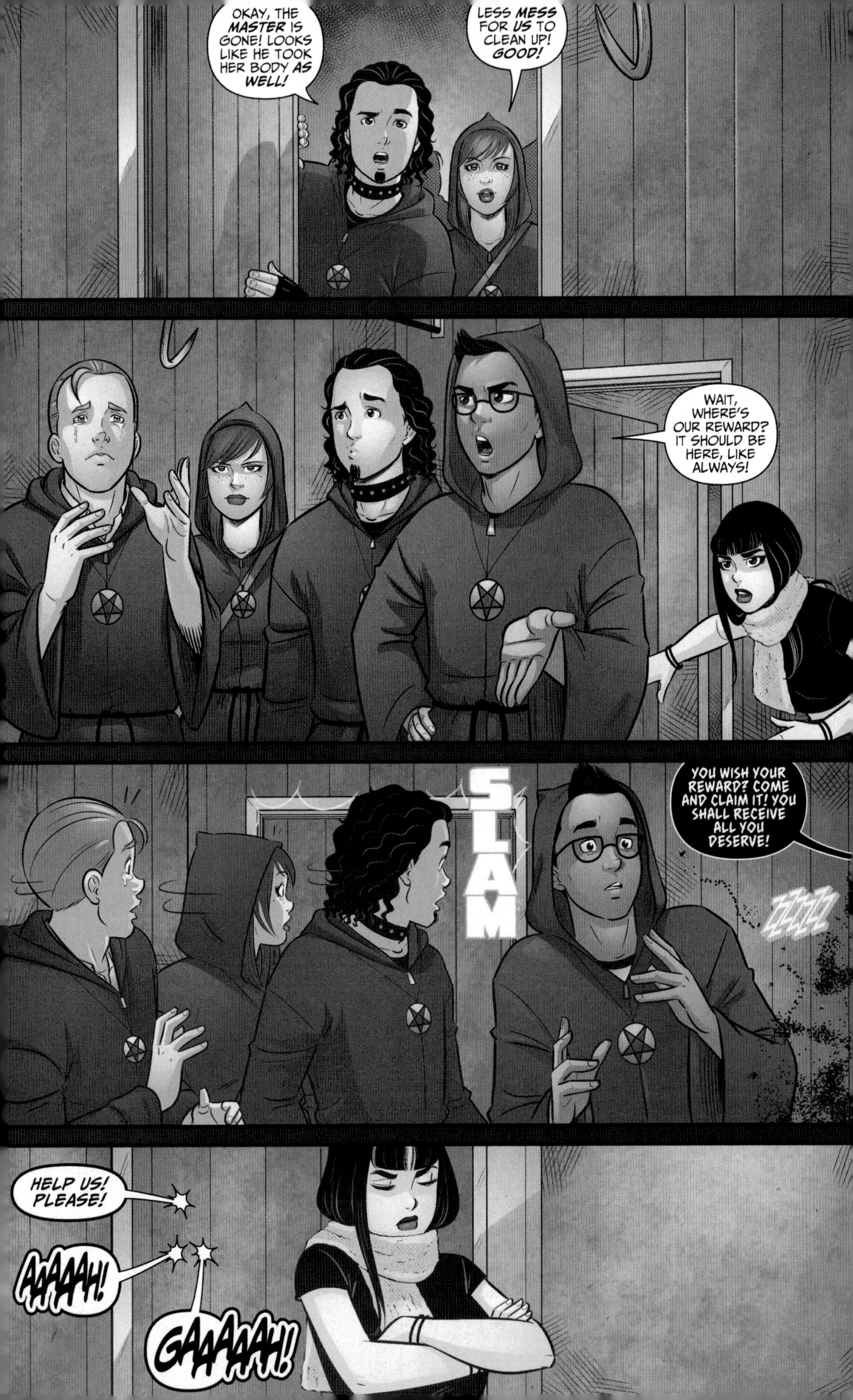

OKAY, THE MASTER IS GONE! LOOKS LIKE HE TOOK HER BODY AS WELL!
LESS MESS FOR US TO CLEAN UP! GOOD!
WAIT, WHERE'S OUR REWARD? IT SHOULD BE HERE, LIKE ALWAYS!
SLAM
YOU WISH YOUR REWARD? COME AND CLAIM IT! YOU SHALL RECEIVE ALL YOU DESERVE!
HELP US! PLEASE!
AAAAAH!
GAAAAAH!

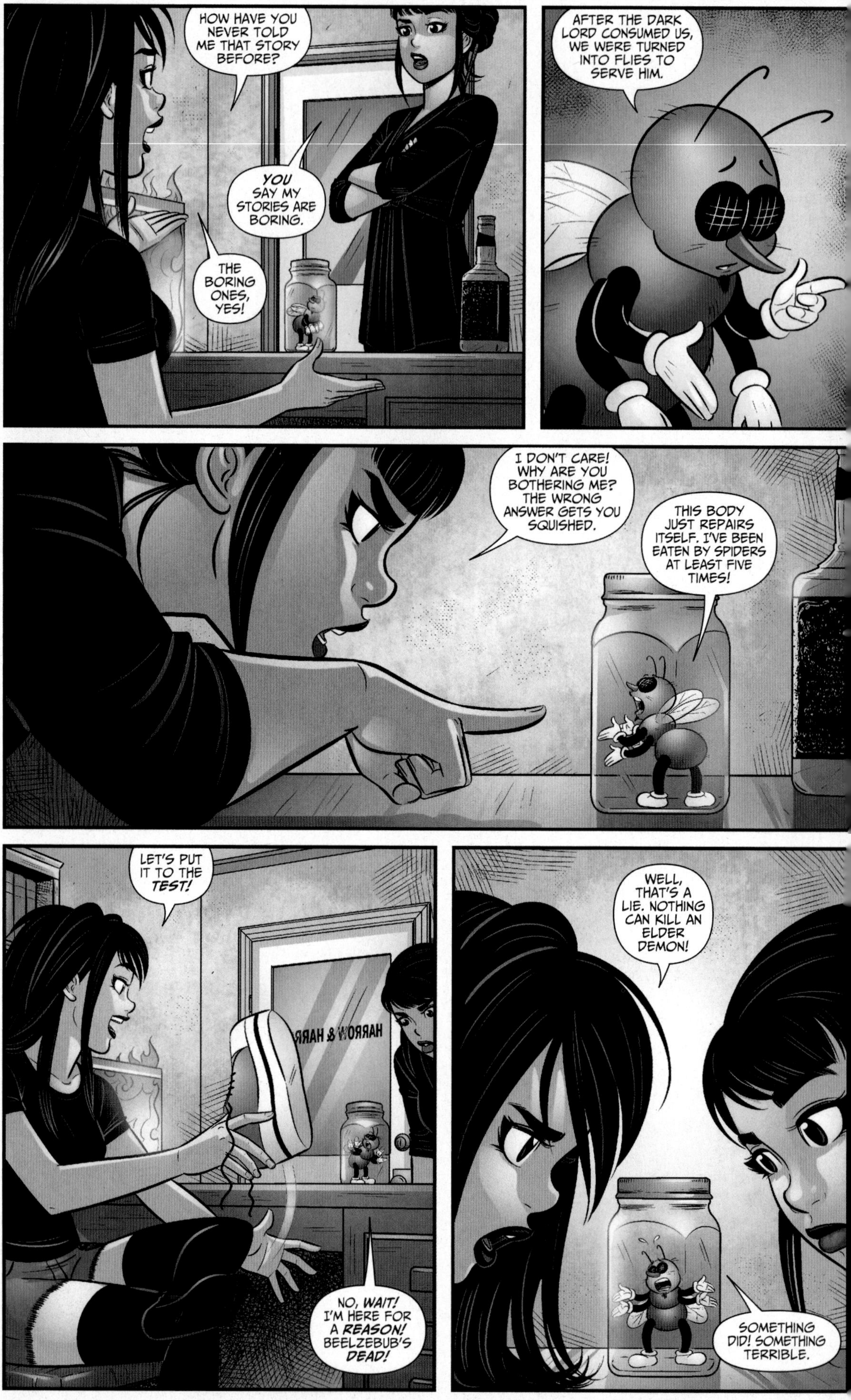
HOW HAVE YOU NEVER TOLD ME THAT STORY BEFORE?
YOU SAY MY STORIES ARE BORING.
THE BORING ONES, YES!
AFTER THE DARK LORD CONSUMED US, WE WERE TURNED INTO FLIES TO SERVE HIM.
I DON'T CARE! WHY ARE YOU BOTHERING ME? THE WRONG ANSWER GETS YOU SQUISHED.
THIS BODY JUST REPAIRS ITSELF. I'VE BEEN EATEN BY SPIDERS AT LEAST FIVE TIMES!
LET'S PUT IT TO THE TEST!
HARROW & HARR
NO, WAIT! I'M HERE FOR A REASON! BEELZEBUB'S DEAD!
WELL, THAT'S A LIE. NOTHING CAN KILL AN ELDER DEMON!
SOMETHING DID! SOMETHING TERRIBLE.

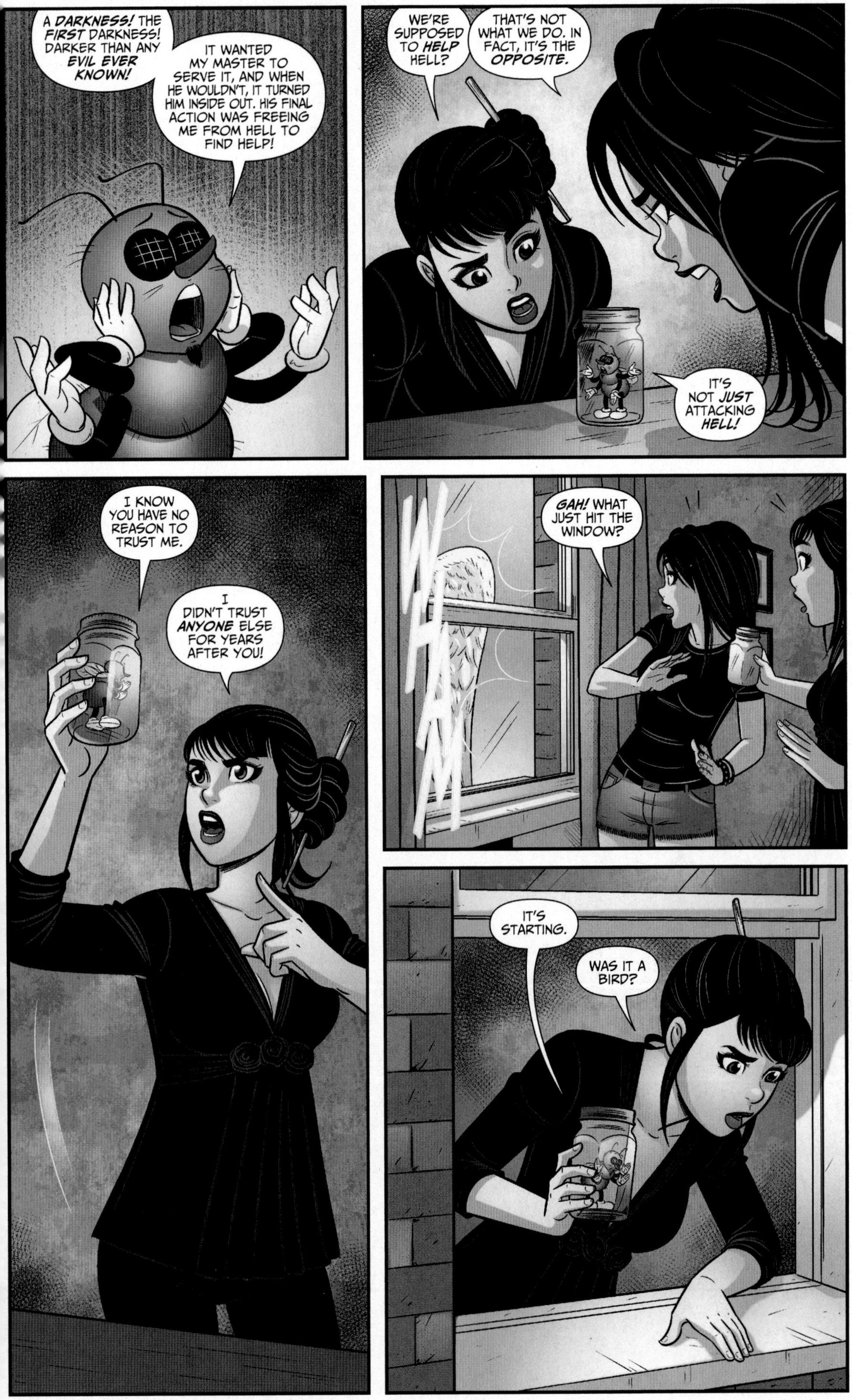
A DARKNESS! THE FIRST DARKNESS! DARKER THAN ANY EVIL EVER KNOWN!
IT WANTED MY MASTER TO SERVE IT, AND WHEN HE WOULDN'T, IT TURNED HIM INSIDE OUT. HIS FINAL ACTION WAS FREEING ME FROM HELL TO FIND HELP!
WE'RE SUPPOSED TO HELP HELL?
THAT'S NOT WHAT WE DO. IN FACT, IT'S THE OPPOSITE.
IT'S NOT JUST ATTACKING HELL!
I KNOW YOU HAVE NO REASON TO TRUST ME.
I DIDN'T TRUST ANYONE ELSE FOR YEARS AFTER YOU!
WHAM
GAH! WHAT JUST HIT THE WINDOW?
IT'S STARTING.
WAS IT A BIRD?

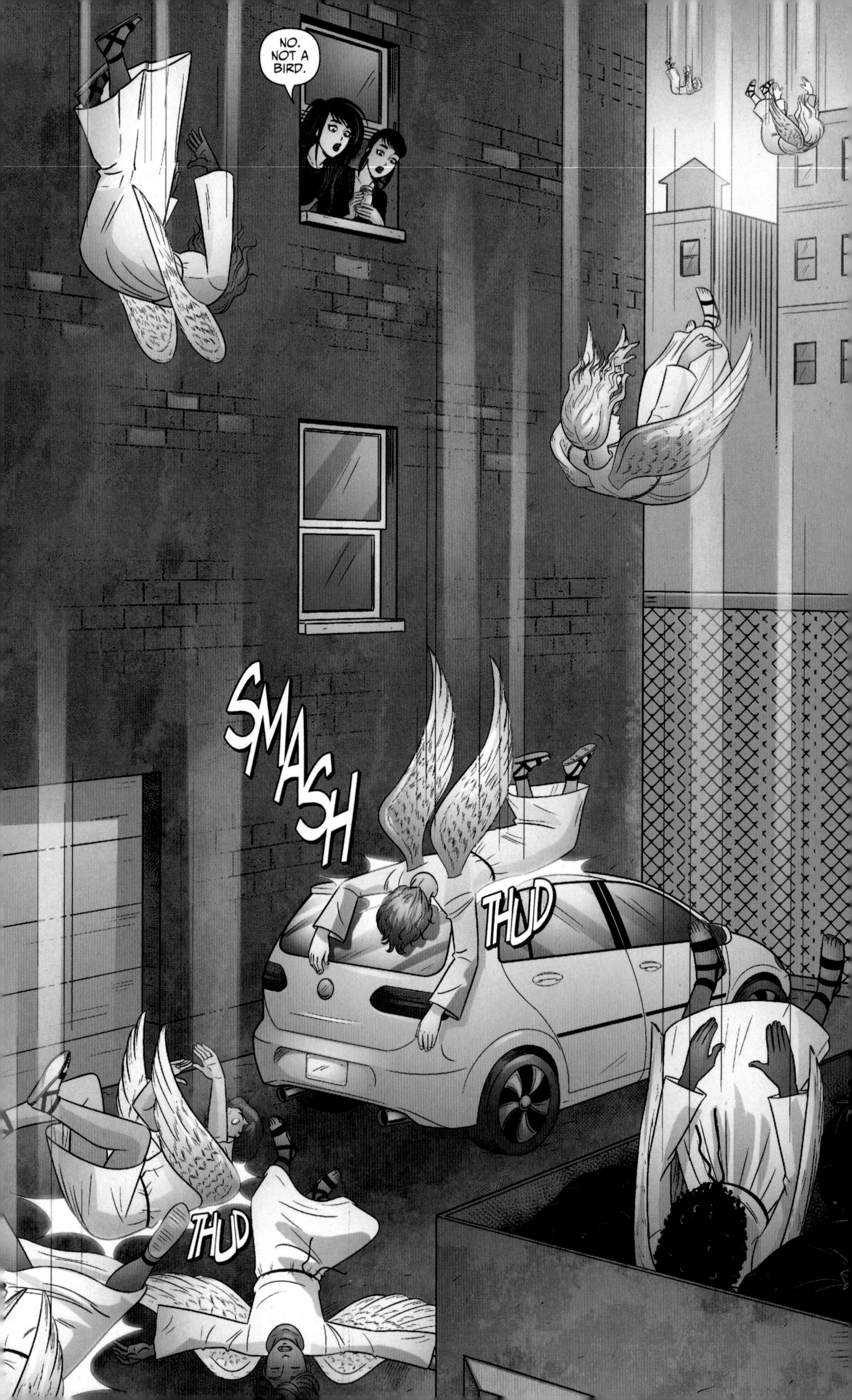
NO. NOT A BIRD.
SMASH
THUD
THUD

CHAPTER FOUR

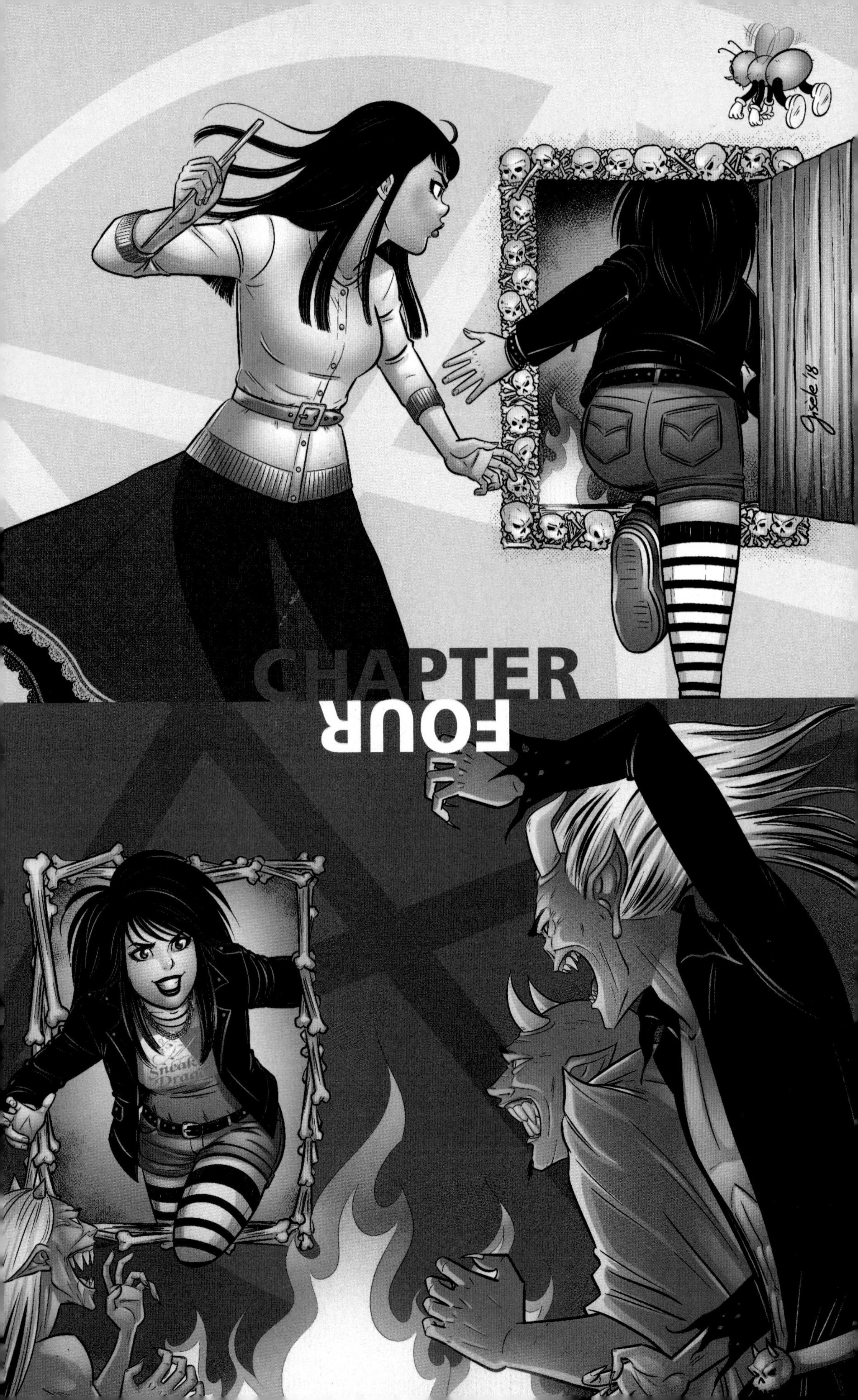

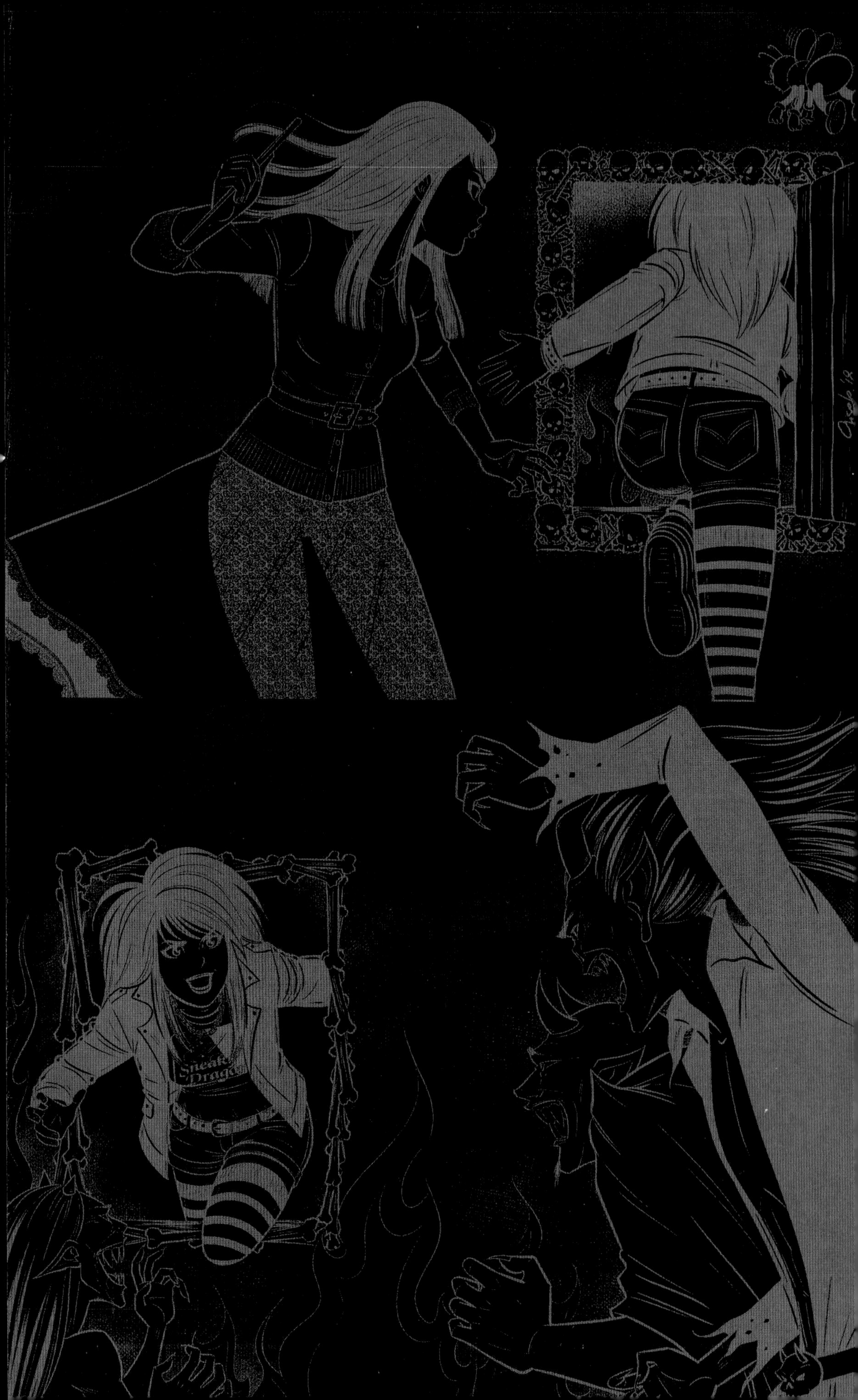

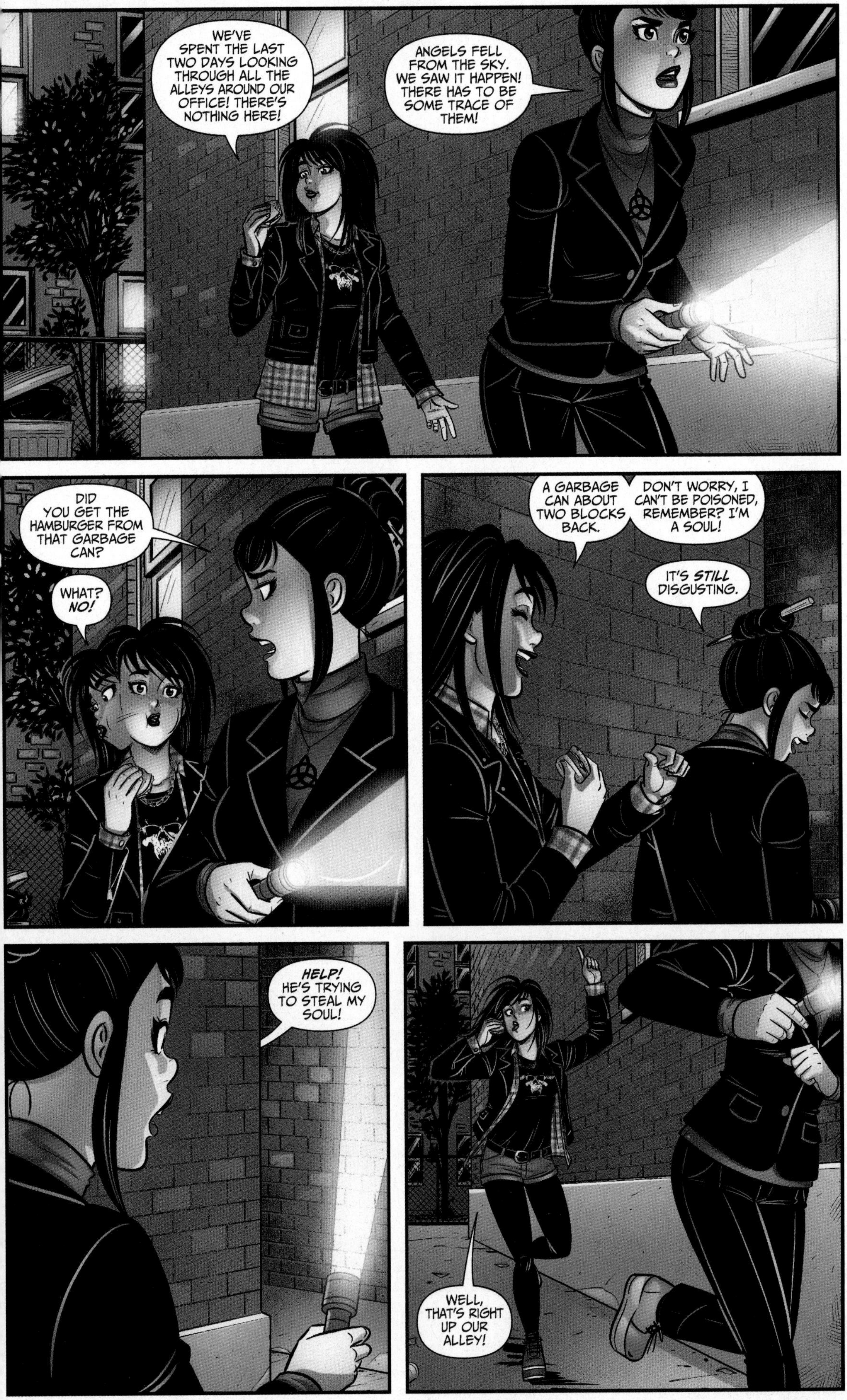
WE'VE SPENT THE LAST TWO DAYS LOOKING THROUGH ALL THE ALLEYS AROUND OUR OFFICE! THERE'S NOTHING HERE!
ANGELS FELL FROM THE SKY. WE SAW IT HAPPEN! THERE HAS TO BE SOME TRACE OF THEM!
DID YOU GET THE HAMBURGER FROM THAT GARBAGE CAN?
WHAT? NO!
A GARBAGE CAN ABOUT TWO BLOCKS BACK.
DON'T WORRY, I CAN'T BE POISONED, REMEMBER? I'M A SOUL!
IT'S STILL DISGUSTING.
HELP! HE'S TRYING TO STEAL MY SOUL!
WELL, THAT'S RIGHT UP OUR ALLEY!

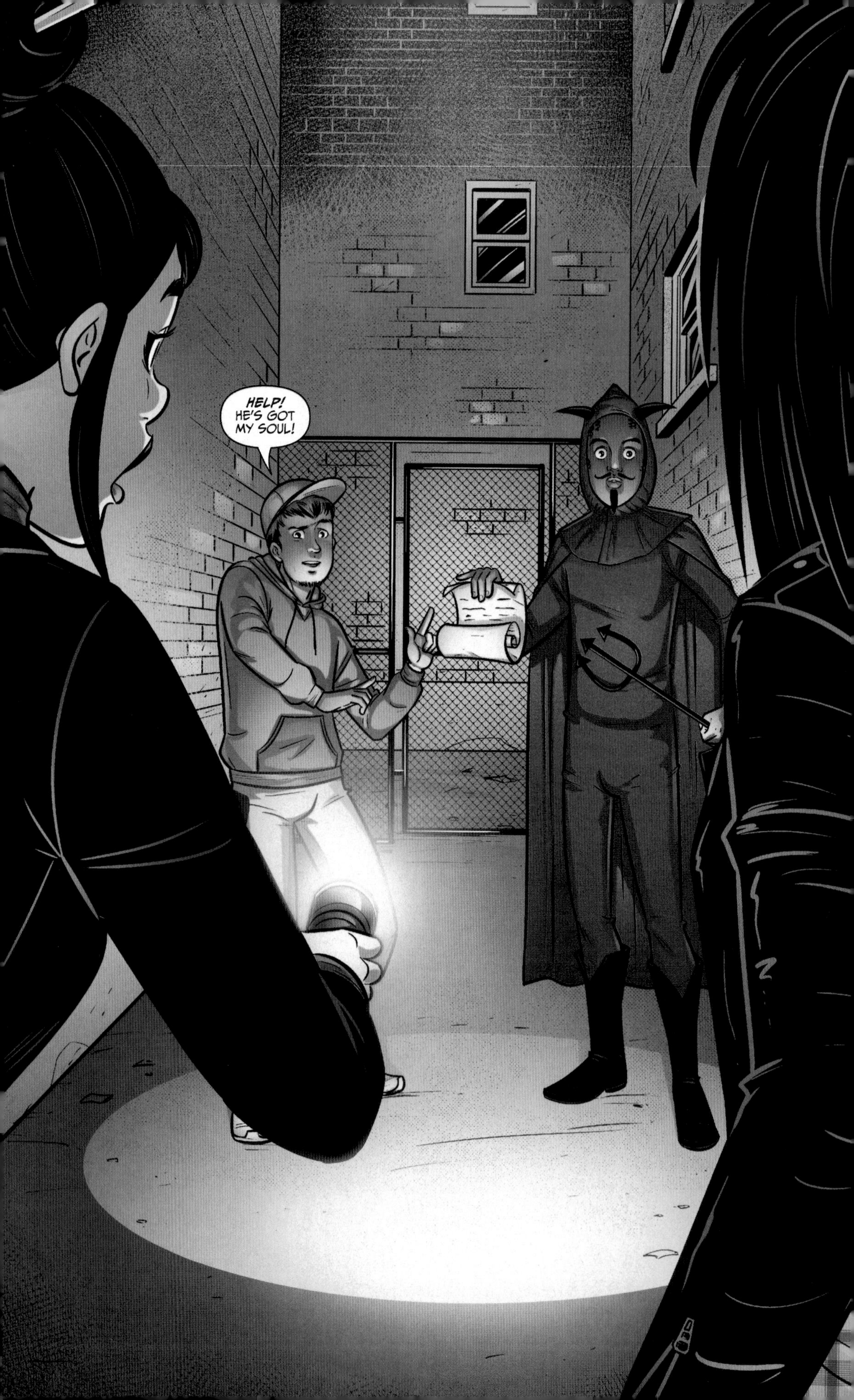
HELP! HE'S GOT MY SOUL!

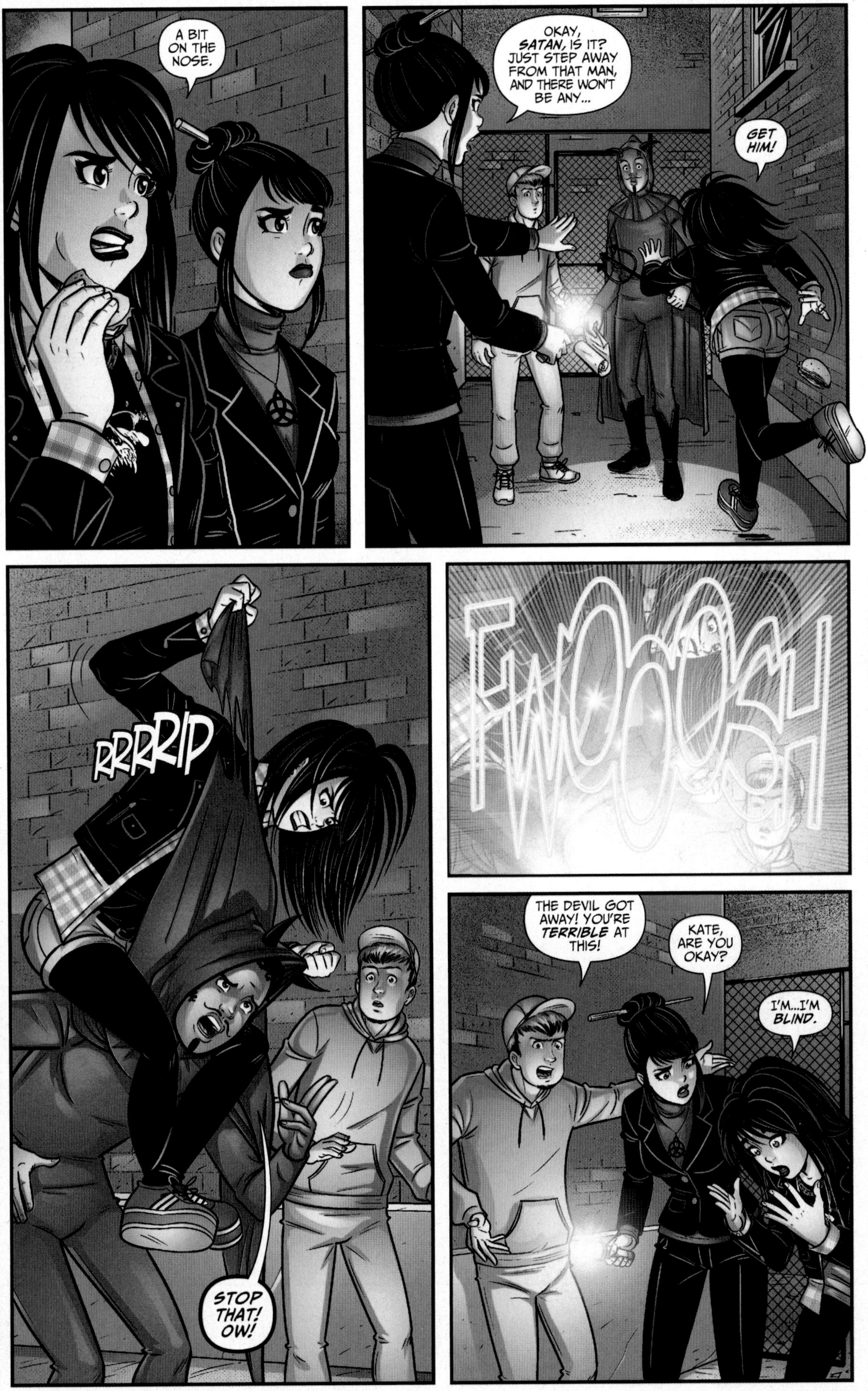
A BIT ON THE NOSE.
OKAY, SATAN, IS IT? JUST STEP AWAY FROM THAT MAN, AND THERE WON'T BE ANY...
GET HIM!
RRRRIP
STOP THAT! OW!
FWOOOOSH
THE DEVIL GOT AWAY! YOU'RE TERRIBLE AT THIS!
KATE, ARE YOU OKAY?
I'M...I'M BLIND.

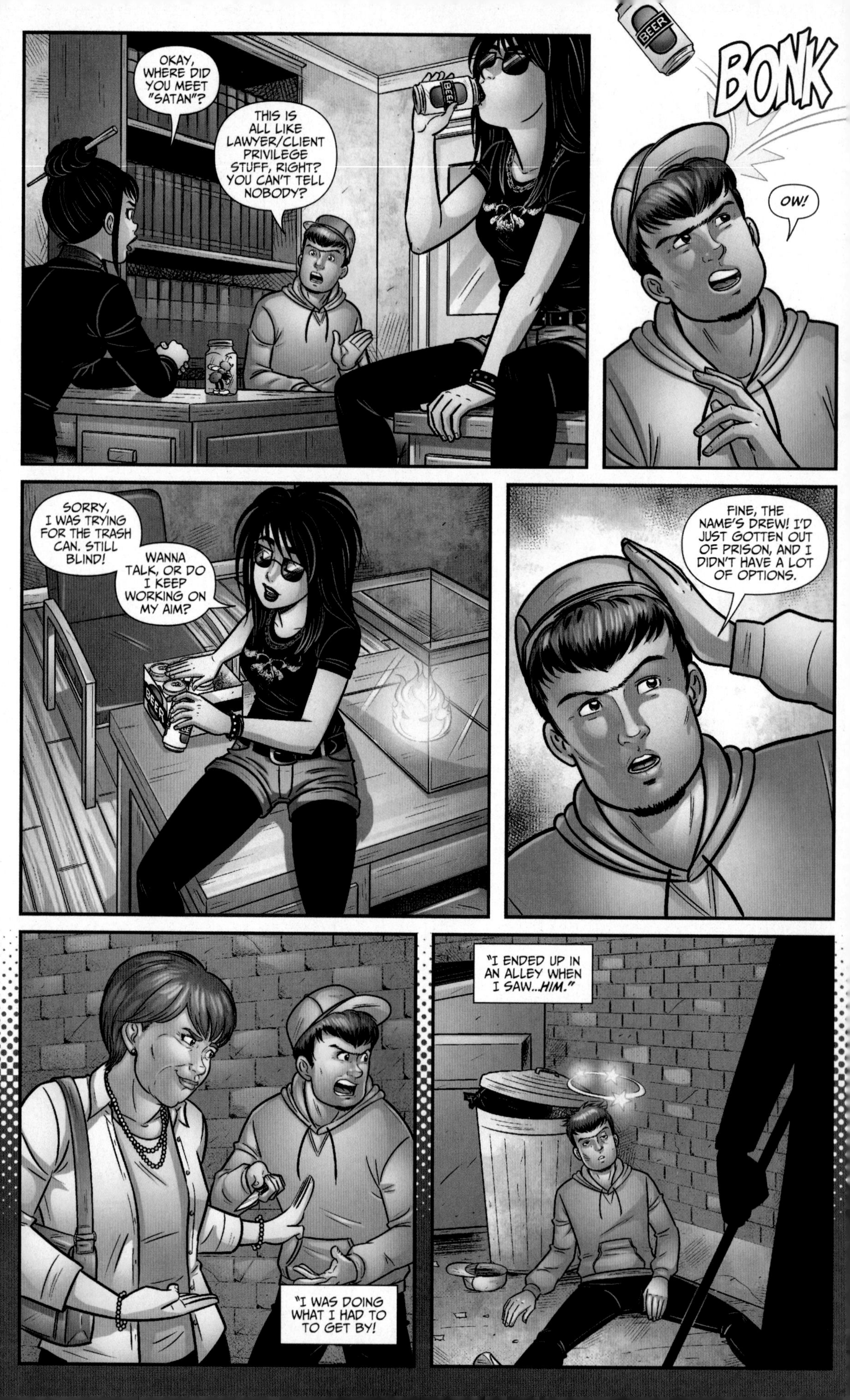
OKAY, WHERE DID YOU MEET "SATAN"?
THIS IS ALL LIKE LAWYER/CLIENT PRIVILEGE STUFF, RIGHT? YOU CAN'T TELL NOBODY?
BEER
BEER
BONK
OW!
SORRY, I WAS TRYING FOR THE TRASH CAN. STILL BLIND!
WANNA TALK, OR DO I KEEP WORKING ON MY AIM?
BEER
FINE, THE NAME'S DREW! I'D JUST GOTTEN OUT OF PRISON, AND I DIDN'T HAVE A LOT OF OPTIONS.
"I WAS DOING WHAT I HAD TO TO GET BY!
"I ENDED UP IN AN ALLEY WHEN I SAW...*HIM*."

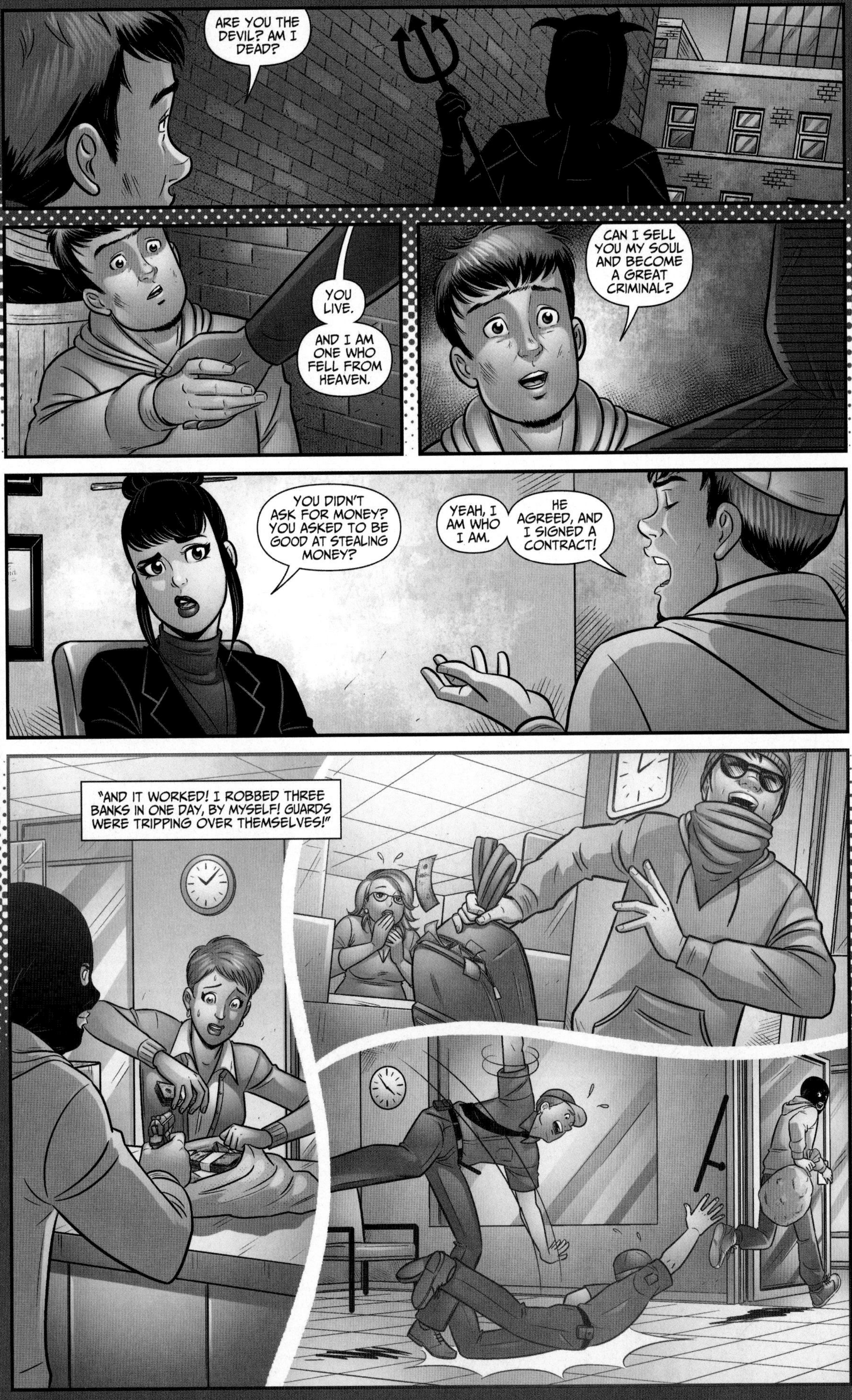
ARE YOU THE DEVIL? AM I DEAD?
YOU LIVE.
AND I AM ONE WHO FELL FROM HEAVEN.
CAN I SELL YOU MY SOUL AND BECOME A GREAT CRIMINAL?
YOU DIDN'T ASK FOR MONEY? YOU ASKED TO BE GOOD AT STEALING MONEY?
YEAH, I AM WHO I AM.
HE AGREED, AND I SIGNED A CONTRACT!
"AND IT WORKED! I ROBBED THREE BANKS IN ONE DAY, BY MYSELF! GUARDS WERE TRIPPING OVER THEMSELVES!"

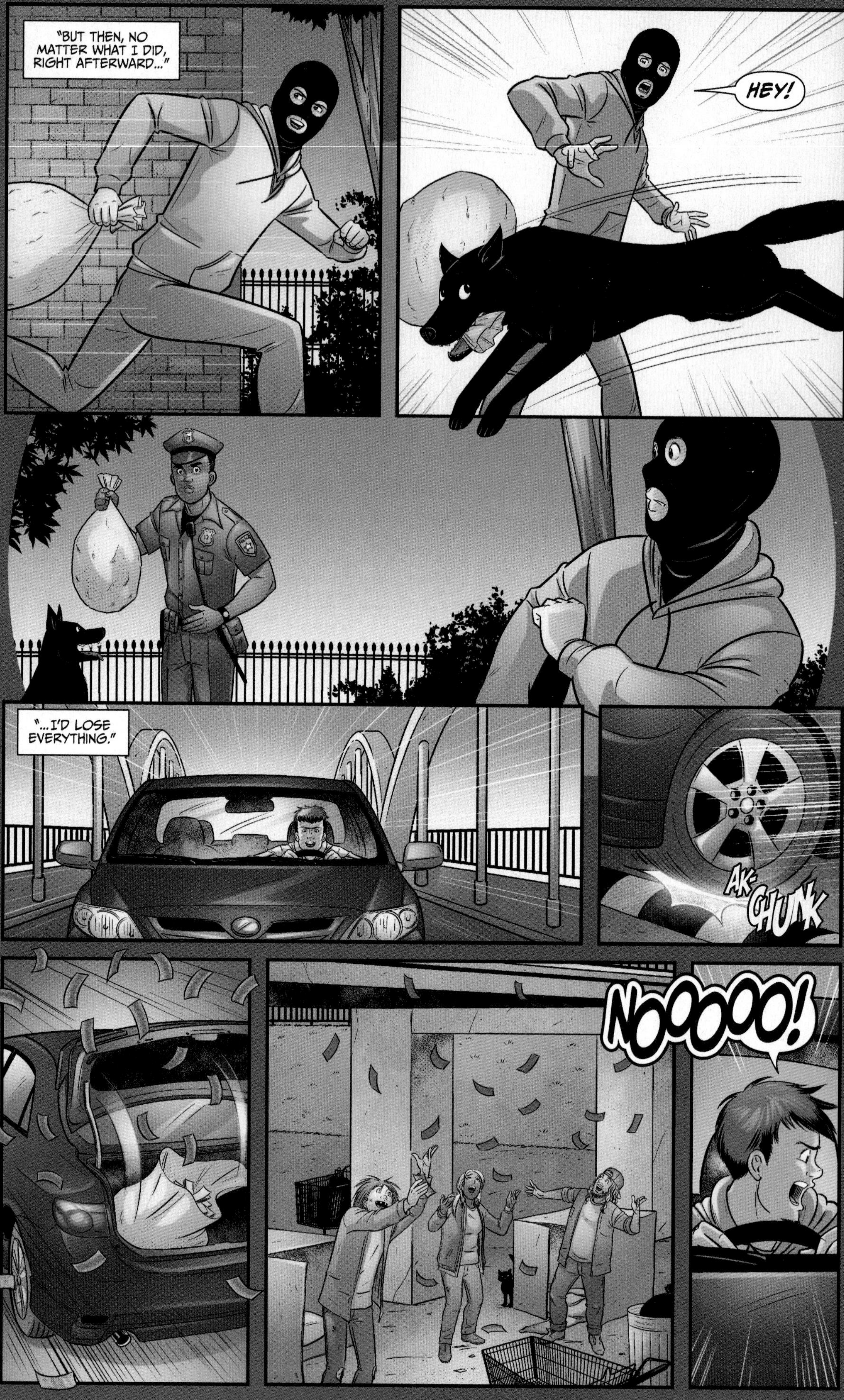

"BUT THEN, NO MATTER WHAT I DID, RIGHT AFTERWARD..."
HEY!
"...I'D LOSE EVERYTHING."
AK-CHUNK
NOOOOO!

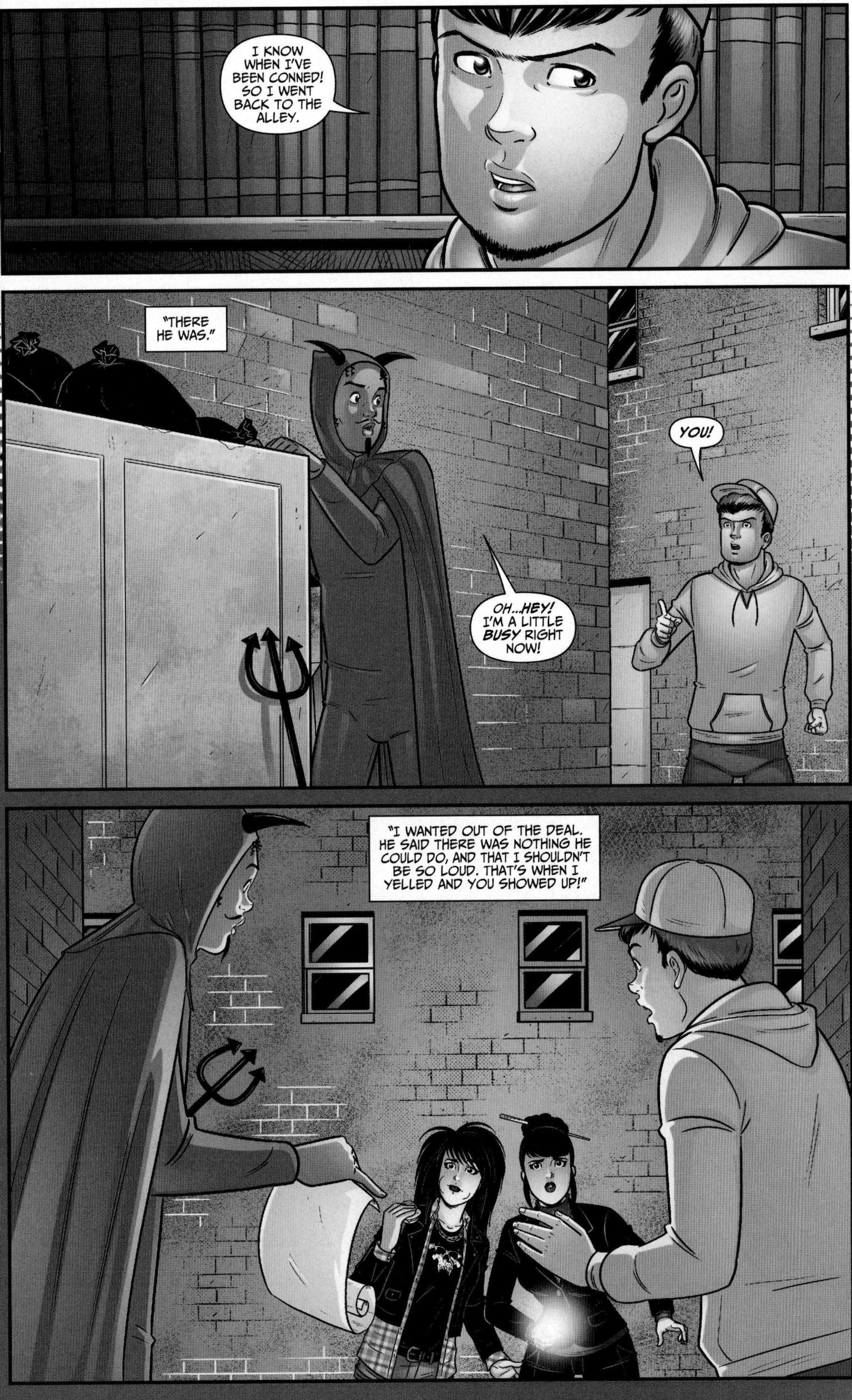
I KNOW WHEN I'VE BEEN CONNED! SO I WENT BACK TO THE ALLEY.
"THERE HE WAS."
YOU!
OH...HEY! I'M A LITTLE BUSY RIGHT NOW!
"I WANTED OUT OF THE DEAL. HE SAID THERE WAS NOTHING HE COULD DO, AND THAT I SHOULDN'T BE SO LOUD. THAT'S WHEN I YELLED AND YOU SHOWED UP!"

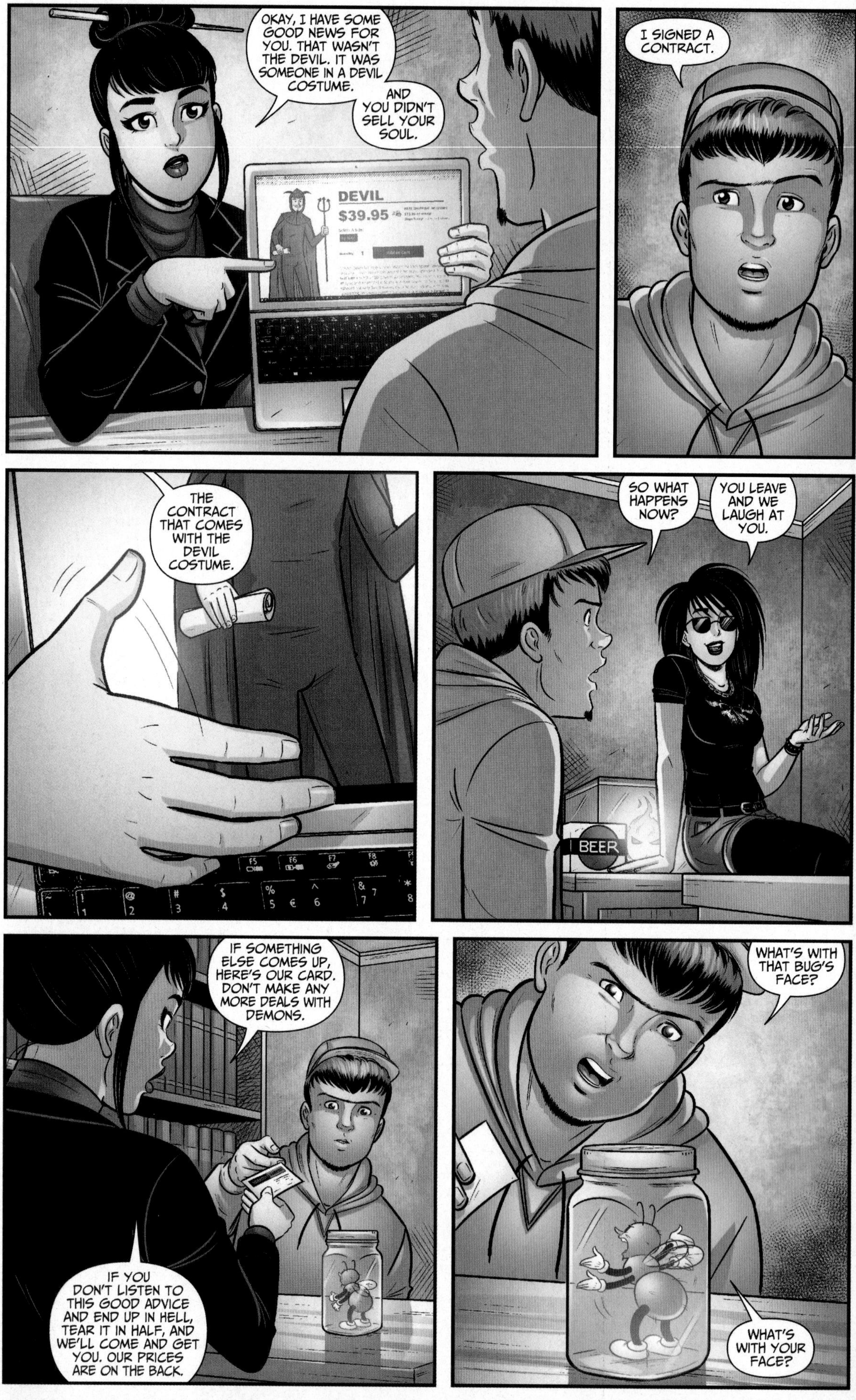
OKAY, I HAVE SOME GOOD NEWS FOR YOU. THAT WASN'T THE DEVIL. IT WAS SOMEONE IN A DEVIL COSTUME.
AND YOU DIDN'T SELL YOUR SOUL.
DEVIL
$39.95
I SIGNED A CONTRACT.
THE CONTRACT THAT COMES WITH THE DEVIL COSTUME.
SO WHAT HAPPENS NOW?
YOU LEAVE AND WE LAUGH AT YOU.
BEER
IF SOMETHING ELSE COMES UP, HERE'S OUR CARD. DON'T MAKE ANY MORE DEALS WITH DEMONS.
IF YOU DON'T LISTEN TO THIS GOOD ADVICE AND END UP IN HELL, TEAR IT IN HALF, AND WE'LL COME AND GET YOU. OUR PRICES ARE ON THE BACK.
WHAT'S WITH THAT BUG'S FACE?
WHAT'S WITH YOUR FACE?

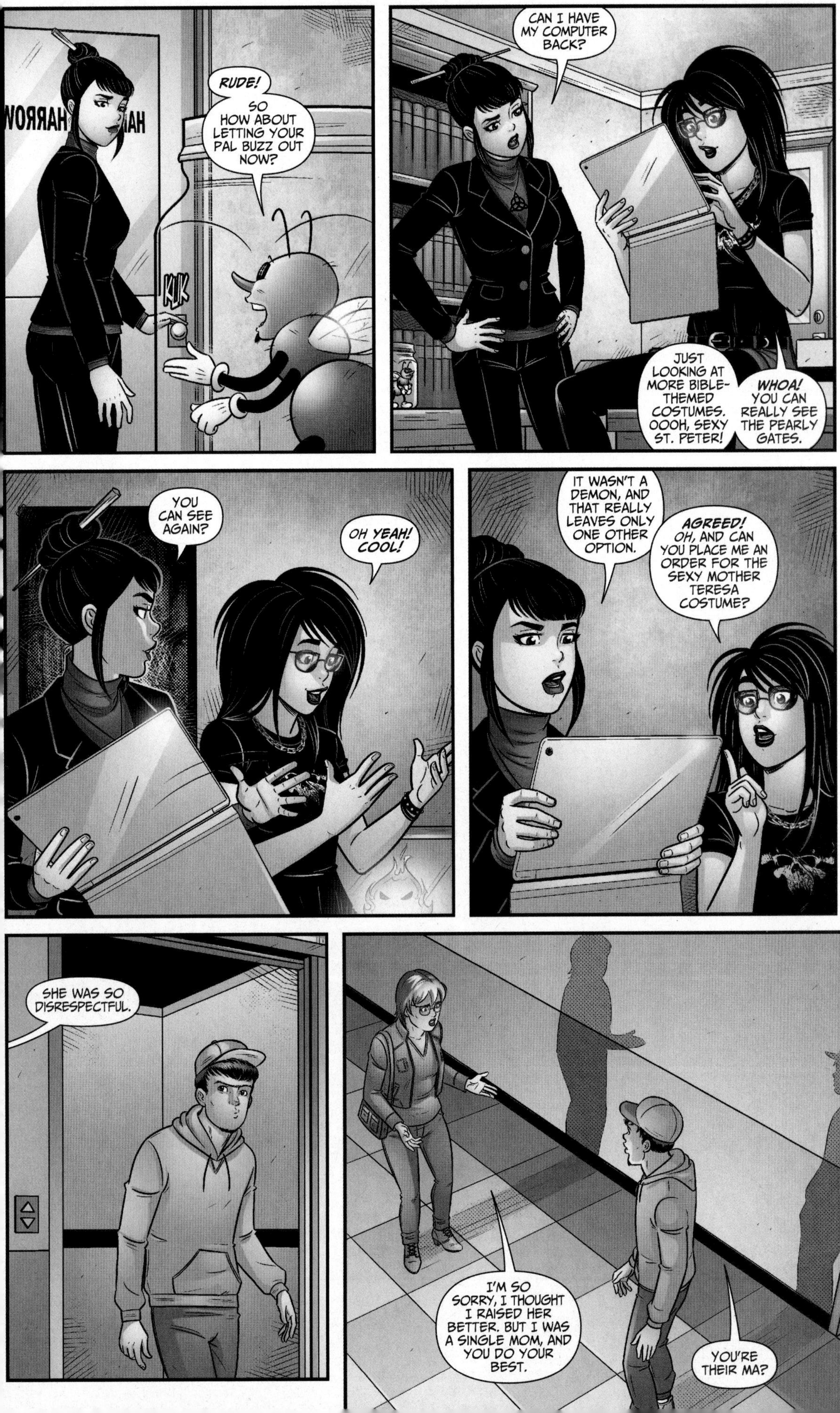
HARROW
RUDE!
SO HOW ABOUT LETTING YOUR PAL BUZZ OUT NOW?
KLIK
CAN I HAVE MY COMPUTER BACK?
JUST LOOKING AT MORE BIBLE-THEMED COSTUMES. OOOH, SEXY ST. PETER!
WHOA! YOU CAN REALLY SEE THE PEARLY GATES.
YOU CAN SEE AGAIN?
OH YEAH! COOL!
IT WASN'T A DEMON, AND THAT REALLY LEAVES ONLY ONE OTHER OPTION.
AGREED! OH, AND CAN YOU PLACE ME AN ORDER FOR THE SEXY MOTHER TERESA COSTUME?
SHE WAS SO DISRESPECTFUL.
I'M SO SORRY, I THOUGHT I RAISED HER BETTER. BUT I WAS A SINGLE MOM, AND YOU DO YOUR BEST.
YOU'RE THEIR MA?

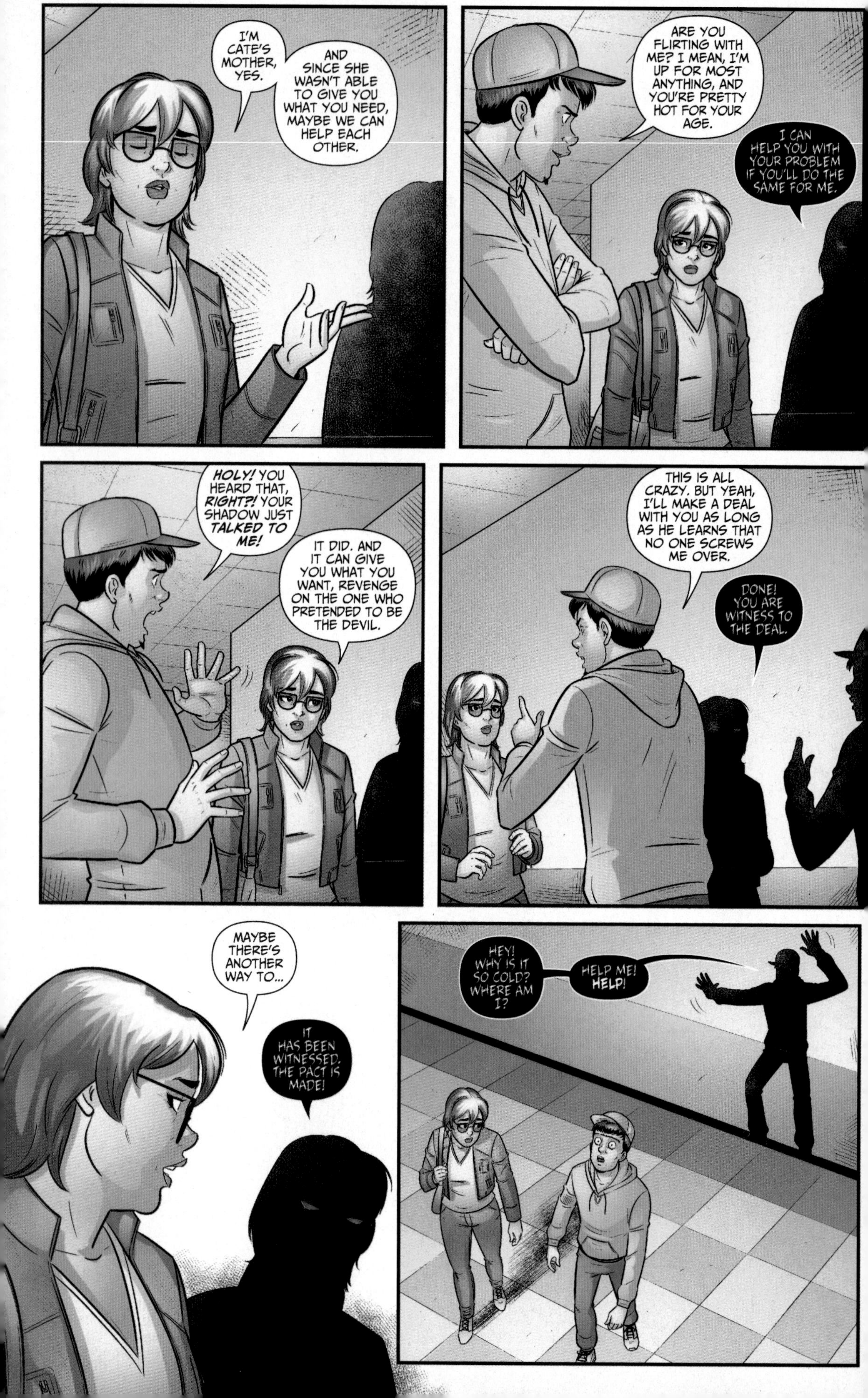
I'M CATE'S MOTHER, YES.
AND SINCE SHE WASN'T ABLE TO GIVE YOU WHAT YOU NEED, MAYBE WE CAN HELP EACH OTHER.
ARE YOU FLIRTING WITH ME? I MEAN, I'M UP FOR MOST ANYTHING, AND YOU'RE PRETTY HOT FOR YOUR AGE.
I CAN HELP YOU WITH YOUR PROBLEM IF YOU'LL DO THE SAME FOR ME.
HOLY! YOU HEARD THAT, RIGHT?! YOUR SHADOW JUST TALKED TO ME!
IT DID. AND IT CAN GIVE YOU WHAT YOU WANT, REVENGE ON THE ONE WHO PRETENDED TO BE THE DEVIL.
THIS IS ALL CRAZY. BUT YEAH, I'LL MAKE A DEAL WITH YOU AS LONG AS HE LEARNS THAT NO ONE SCREWS ME OVER.
DONE! YOU ARE WITNESS TO THE DEAL.
MAYBE THERE'S ANOTHER WAY TO...
IT HAS BEEN WITNESSED. THE PACT IS MADE!
HEY! WHY IS IT SO COLD? WHERE AM I?
HELP ME! HELP!

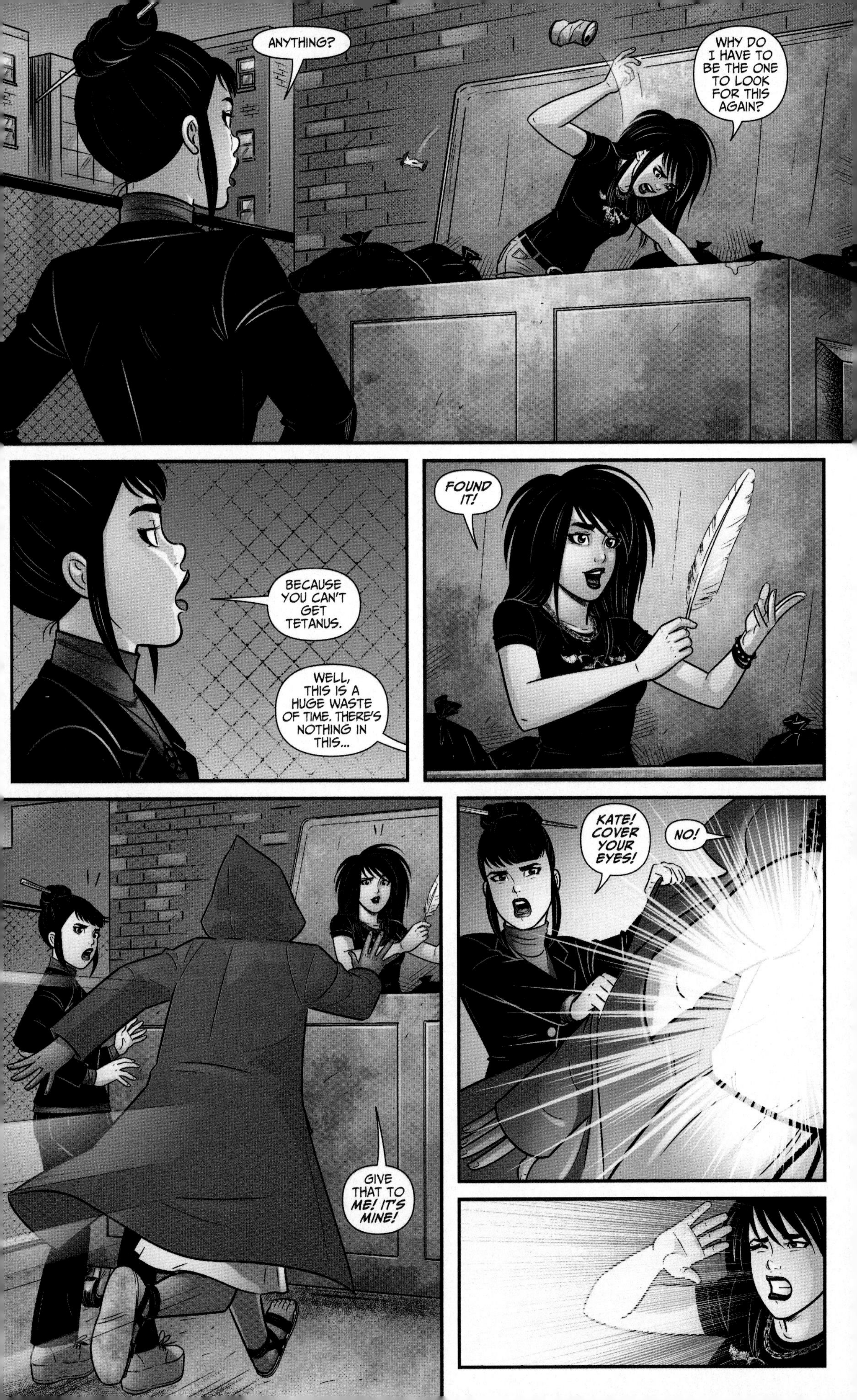
ANYTHING?
WHY DO I HAVE TO BE THE ONE TO LOOK FOR THIS AGAIN?
BECAUSE YOU CAN'T GET TETANUS.
WELL, THIS IS A HUGE WASTE OF TIME. THERE'S NOTHING IN THIS...
FOUND IT!
GIVE THAT TO ME! IT'S MINE!
KATE! COVER YOUR EYES!
NO!

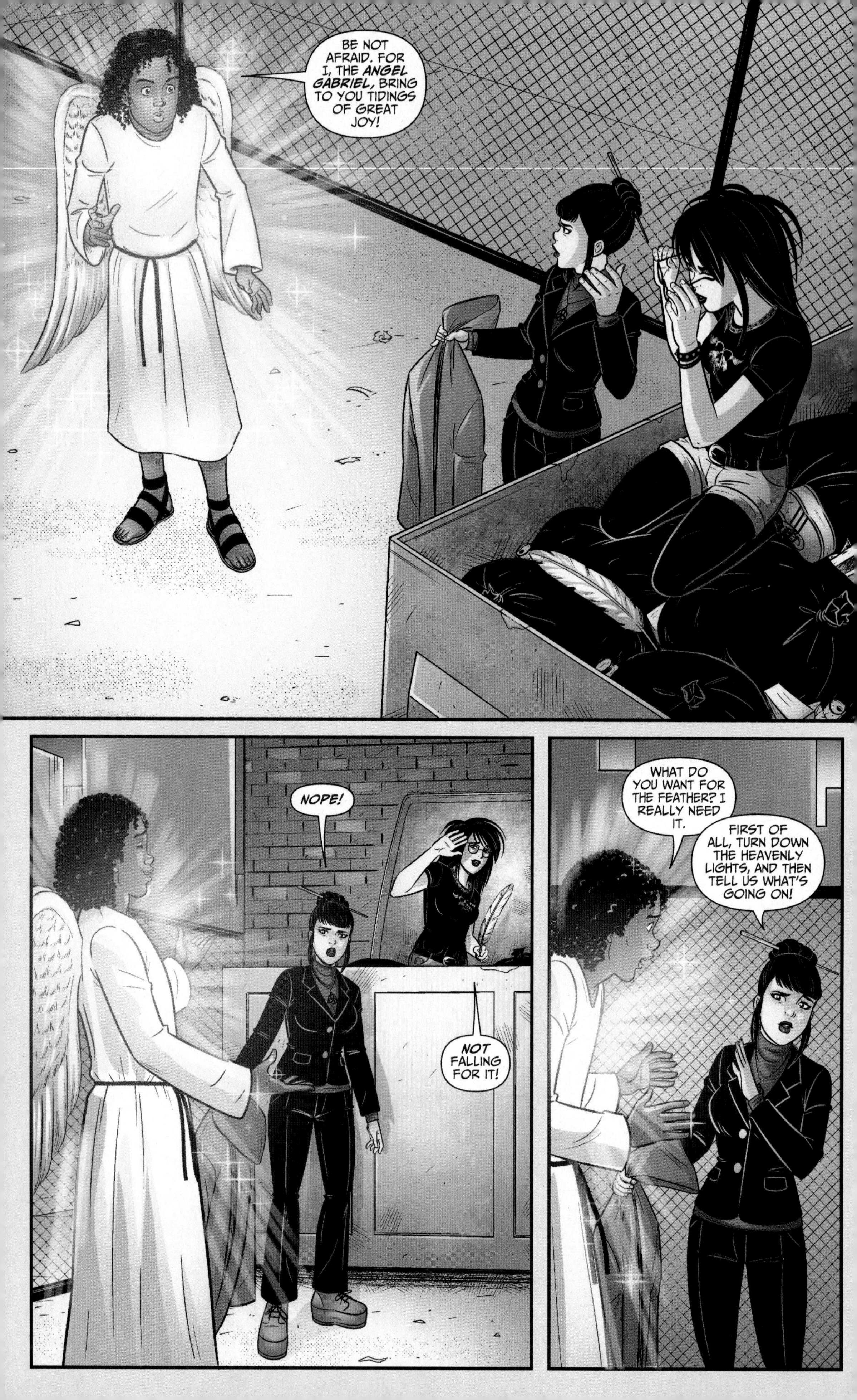
BE NOT AFRAID. FOR I, THE ANGEL GABRIEL, BRING TO YOU TIDINGS OF GREAT JOY!
NOPE!
NOT FALLING FOR IT!
WHAT DO YOU WANT FOR THE FEATHER? I REALLY NEED IT.
FIRST OF ALL, TURN DOWN THE HEAVENLY LIGHTS, AND THEN TELL US WHAT'S GOING ON!

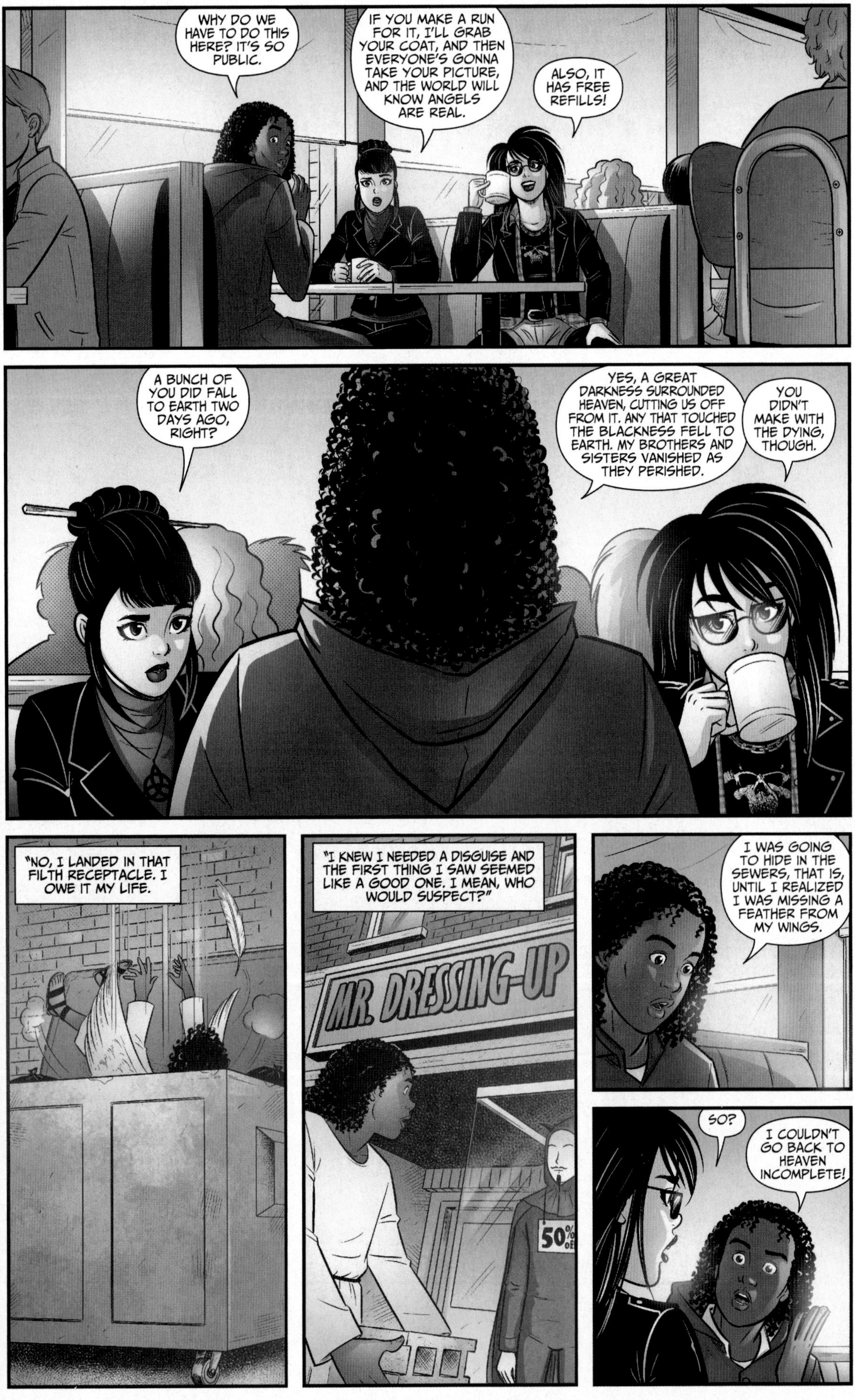
WHY DO WE HAVE TO DO THIS HERE? IT'S SO PUBLIC.
IF YOU MAKE A RUN FOR IT, I'LL GRAB YOUR COAT, AND THEN EVERYONE'S GONNA TAKE YOUR PICTURE, AND THE WORLD WILL KNOW ANGELS ARE REAL.
ALSO, IT HAS FREE REFILLS!
A BUNCH OF YOU DID FALL TO EARTH TWO DAYS AGO, RIGHT?
YES, A GREAT DARKNESS SURROUNDED HEAVEN, CUTTING US OFF FROM IT. ANY THAT TOUCHED THE BLACKNESS FELL TO EARTH. MY BROTHERS AND SISTERS VANISHED AS THEY PERISHED.
YOU DIDN'T MAKE WITH THE DYING, THOUGH.
"NO, I LANDED IN THAT FILTH RECEPTACLE. I OWE IT MY LIFE.
"I KNEW I NEEDED A DISGUISE AND THE FIRST THING I SAW SEEMED LIKE A GOOD ONE. I MEAN, WHO WOULD SUSPECT?"
MR. DRESSING-UP
50%
I WAS GOING TO HIDE IN THE SEWERS, THAT IS, UNTIL I REALIZED I WAS MISSING A FEATHER FROM MY WINGS.
SO?
I COULDN'T GO BACK TO HEAVEN INCOMPLETE!

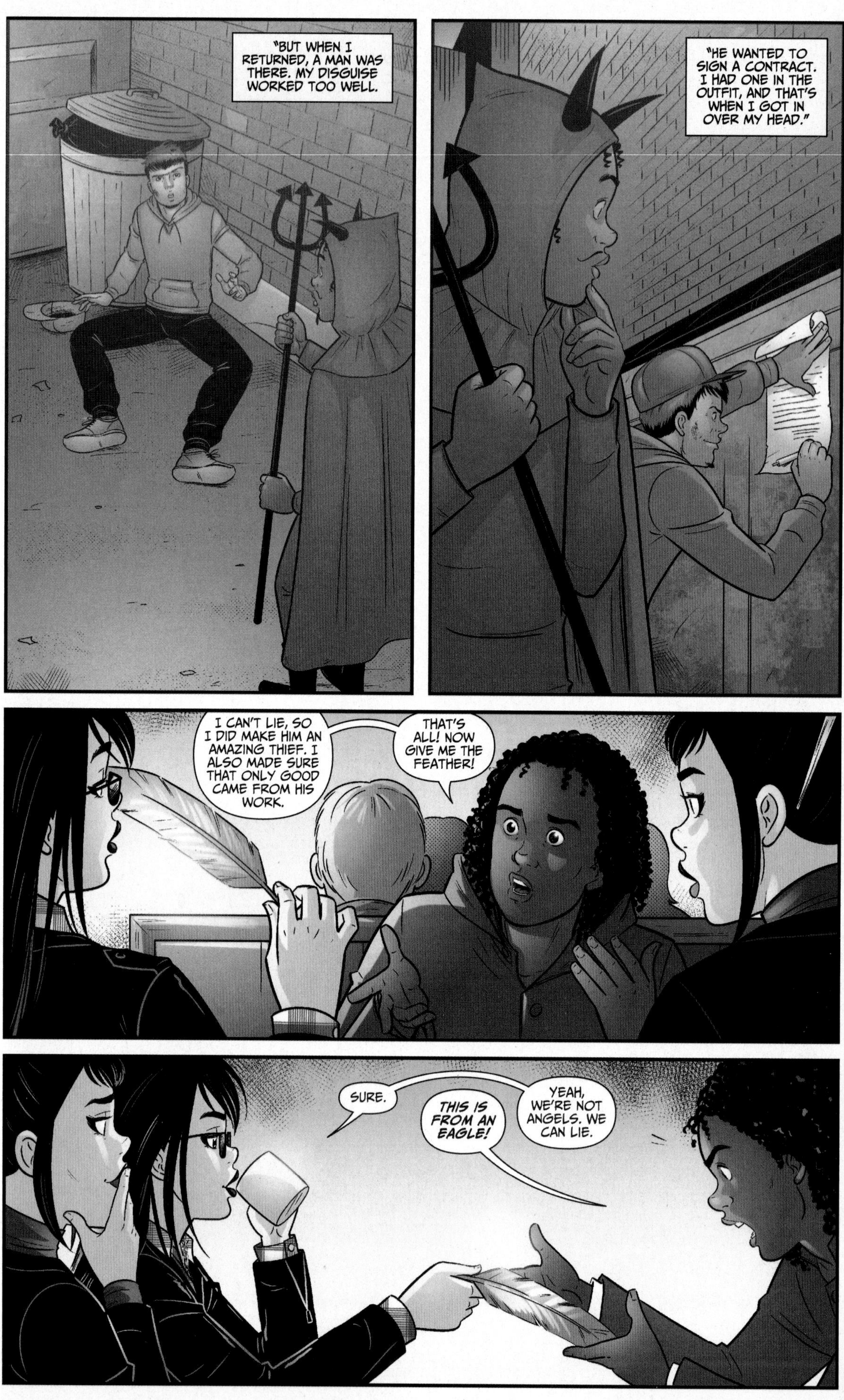
"BUT WHEN I RETURNED, A MAN WAS THERE. MY DISGUISE WORKED TOO WELL.
"HE WANTED TO SIGN A CONTRACT. I HAD ONE IN THE OUTFIT, AND THAT'S WHEN I GOT IN OVER MY HEAD."
I CAN'T LIE, SO I DID MAKE HIM AN AMAZING THIEF. I ALSO MADE SURE THAT ONLY GOOD CAME FROM HIS WORK.
THAT'S ALL! NOW GIVE ME THE FEATHER!
SURE.
YEAH, WE'RE NOT ANGELS. WE CAN LIE.
THIS IS FROM AN EAGLE!

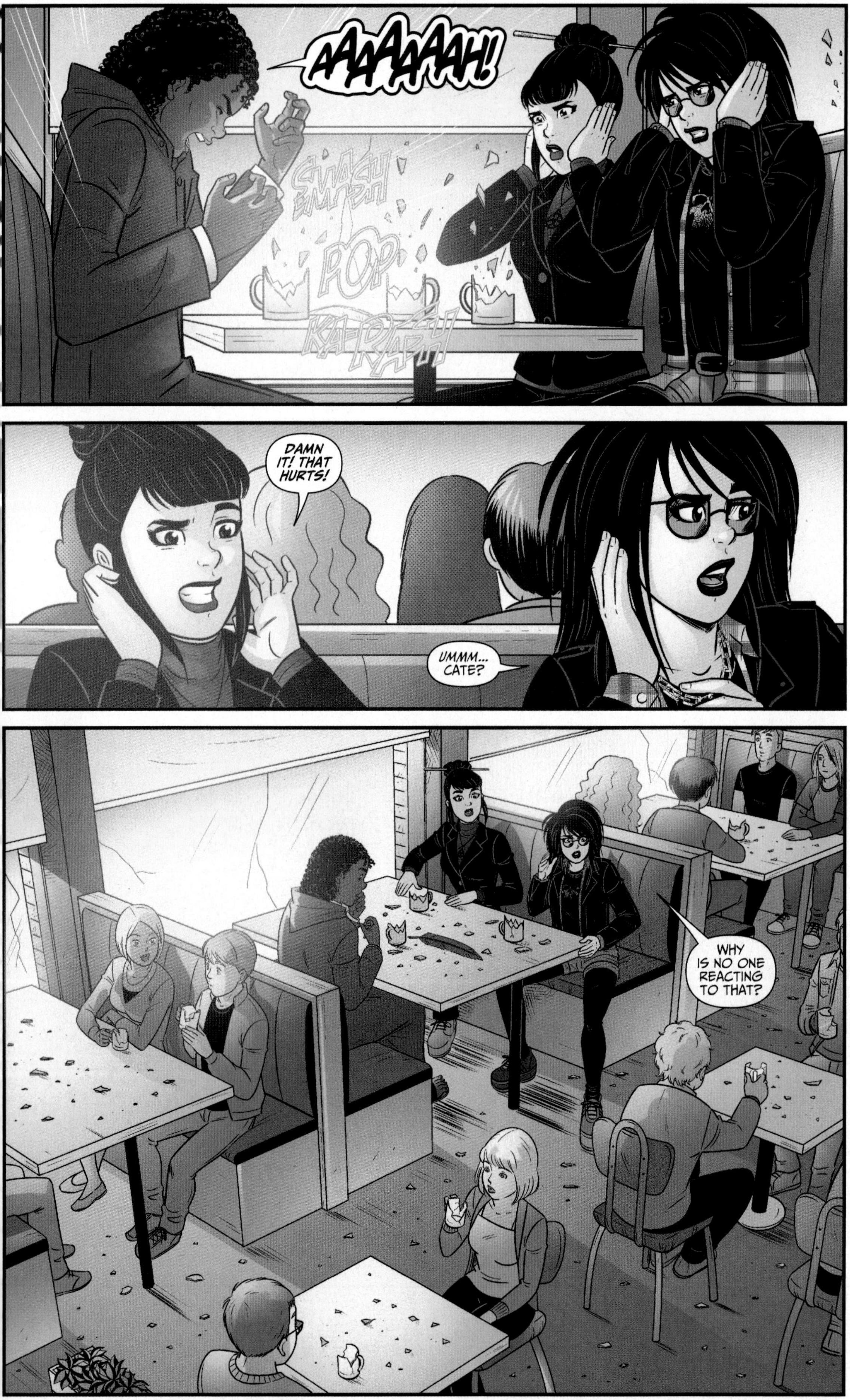
AAAAAAAH!
POP
DAMN IT! THAT HURTS!
UMMM... CATE?
WHY IS NO ONE REACTING TO THAT?

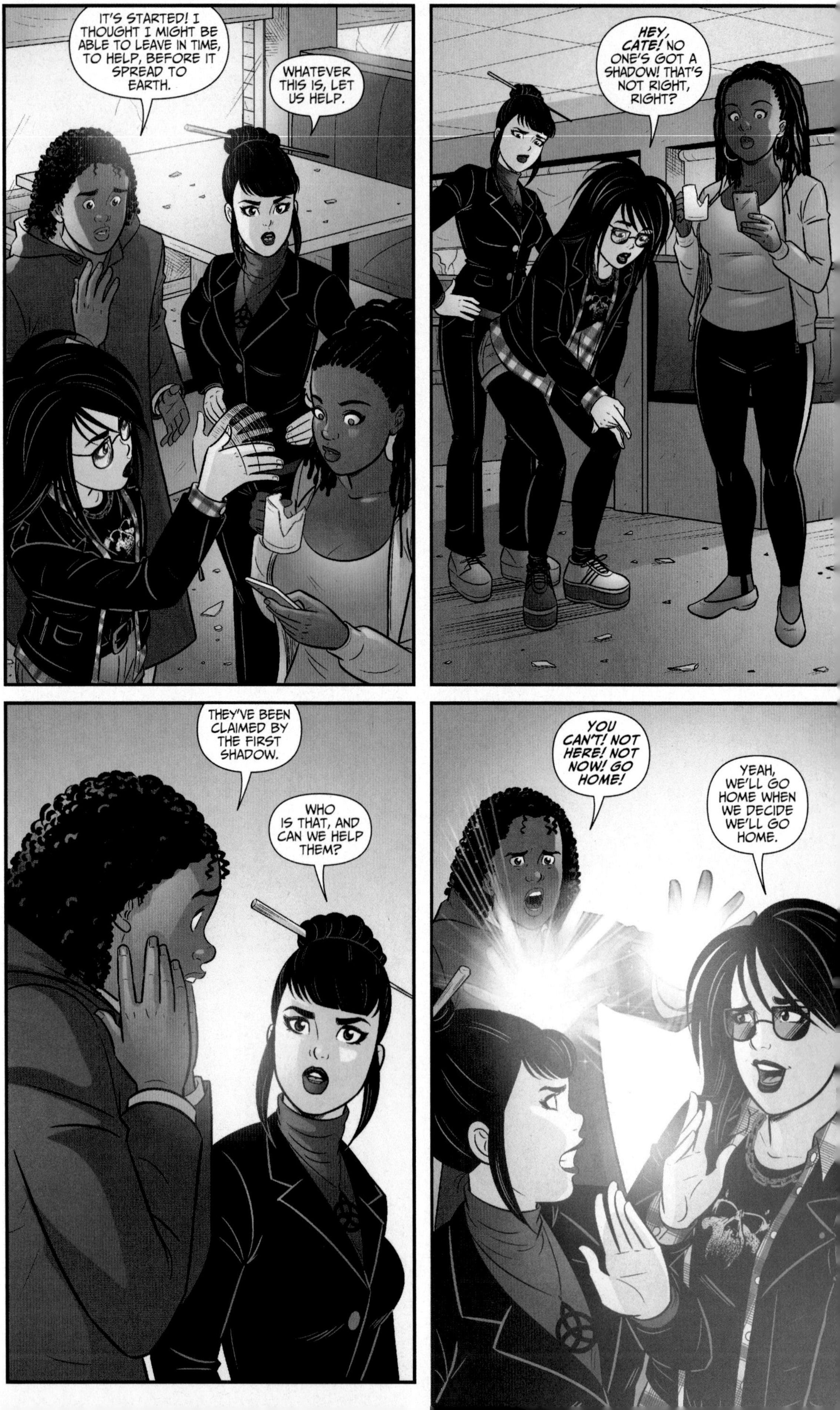
IT'S STARTED! I THOUGHT I MIGHT BE ABLE TO LEAVE IN TIME, TO HELP, BEFORE IT SPREAD TO EARTH.
WHATEVER THIS IS, LET US HELP.
HEY, CATE! NO ONE'S GOT A SHADOW! THAT'S NOT RIGHT, RIGHT?
THEY'VE BEEN CLAIMED BY THE FIRST SHADOW.
WHO IS THAT, AND CAN WE HELP THEM?
YOU CAN'T! NOT HERE! NOT NOW! GO HOME!
YEAH, WE'LL GO HOME WHEN WE DECIDE WE'LL GO HOME.

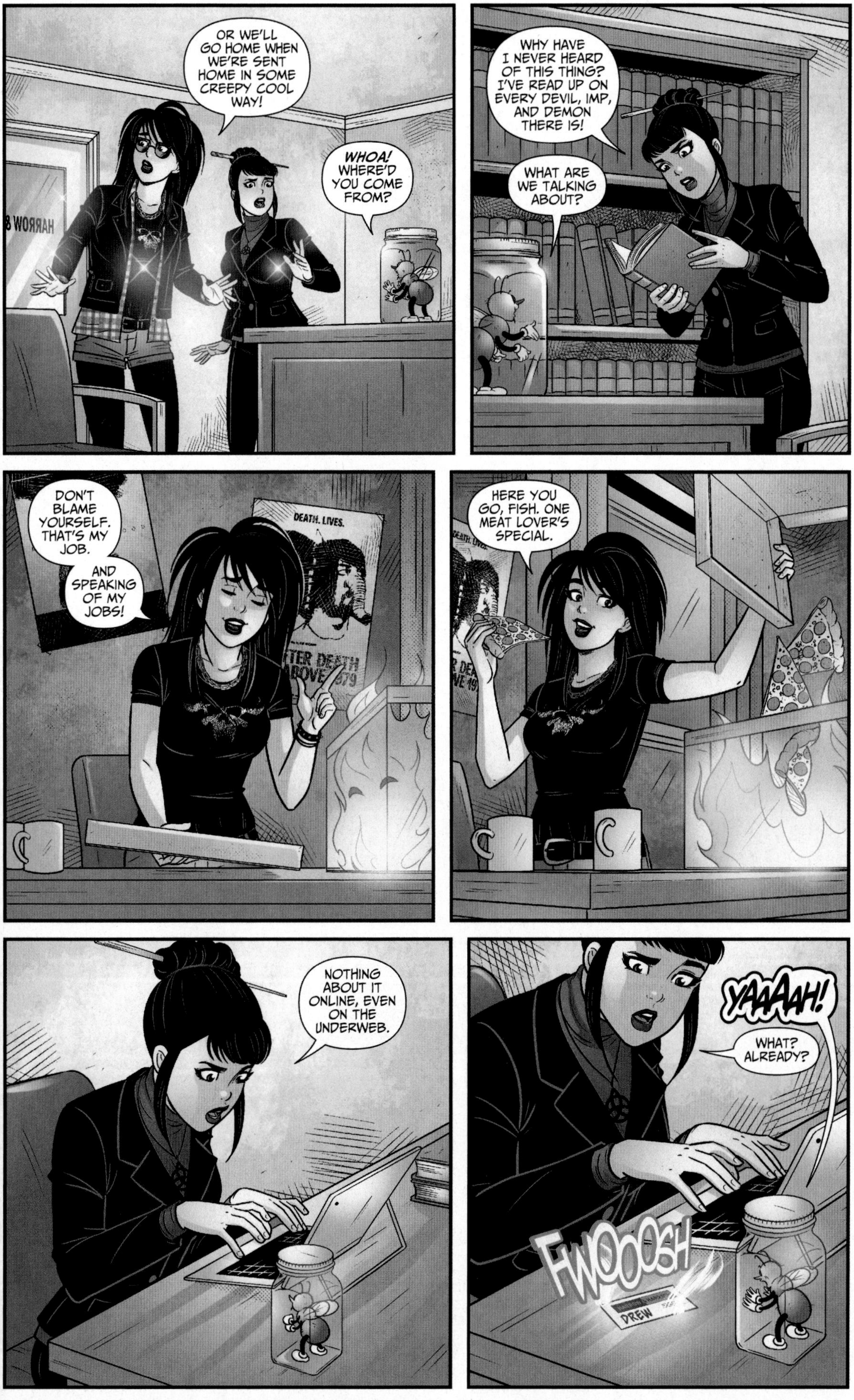
OR WE'LL GO HOME WHEN WE'RE SENT HOME IN SOME CREEPY COOL WAY!
WHOA! WHERE'D YOU COME FROM?
HARROW
WHY HAVE I NEVER HEARD OF THIS THING? I'VE READ UP ON EVERY DEVIL, IMP, AND DEMON THERE IS!
WHAT ARE WE TALKING ABOUT?
DON'T BLAME YOURSELF. THAT'S MY JOB.
AND SPEAKING OF MY JOBS!
DEATH. LIVES.
HERE YOU GO, FISH. ONE MEAT LOVER'S SPECIAL.
NOTHING ABOUT IT ONLINE, EVEN ON THE UNDERWEB.
YAAAAH!
WHAT? ALREADY?
FWOOOSH
DREW

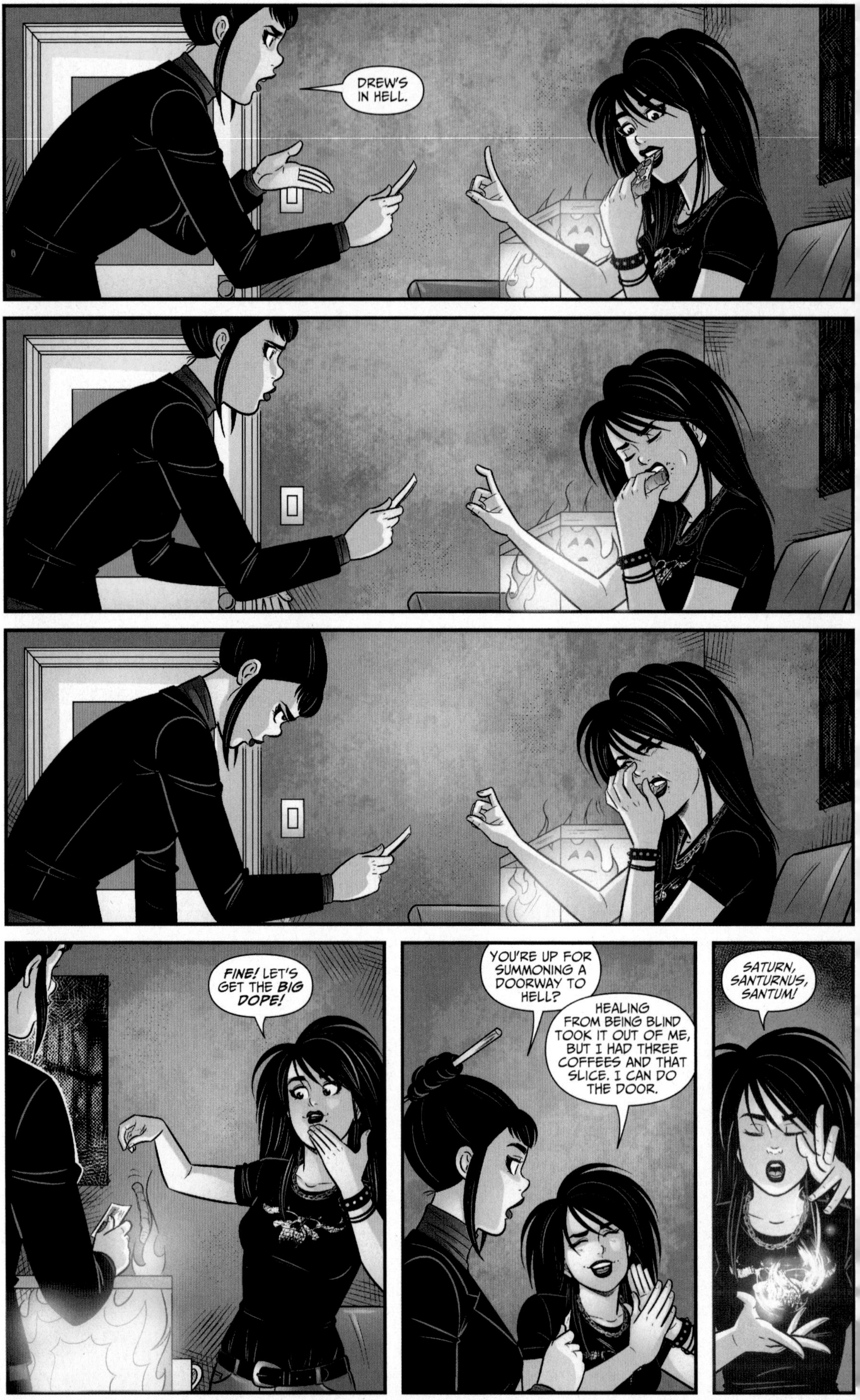
DREW'S IN HELL.
FINE! LET'S GET THE *BIG DOPE!*
YOU'RE UP FOR SUMMONING A DOORWAY TO HELL?
HEALING FROM BEING BLIND TOOK IT OUT OF ME, BUT I HAD THREE COFFEES AND THAT SLICE. I CAN DO THE DOOR.
SATURN, SANTURNUS, SANTUM!

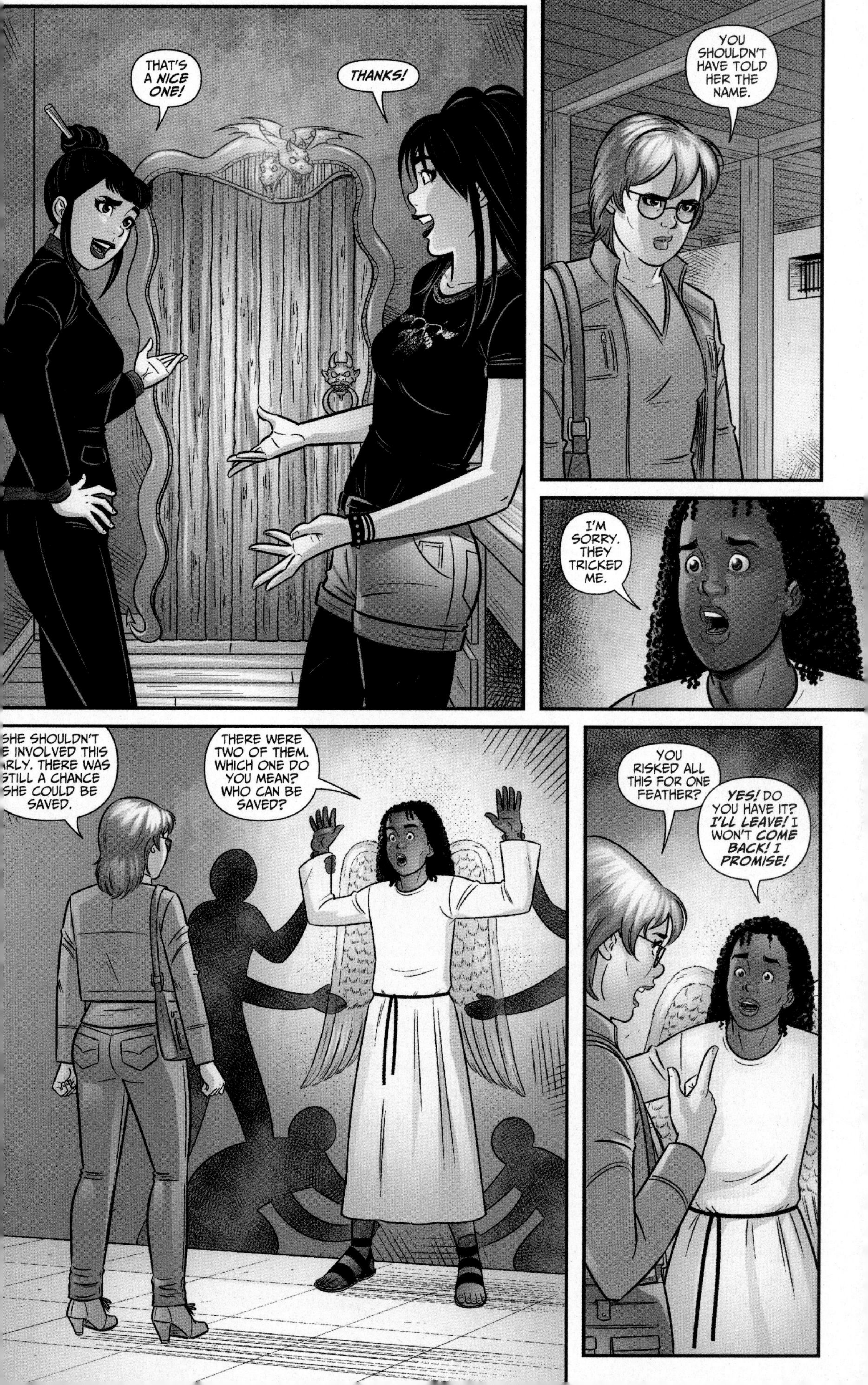
THAT'S A NICE ONE!
THANKS!
YOU SHOULDN'T HAVE TOLD HER THE NAME.
I'M SORRY. THEY TRICKED ME.
SHE SHOULDN'T BE INVOLVED THIS EARLY. THERE WAS STILL A CHANCE SHE COULD BE SAVED.
THERE WERE TWO OF THEM. WHICH ONE DO YOU MEAN? WHO CAN BE SAVED?
YOU RISKED ALL THIS FOR ONE FEATHER?
YES! DO YOU HAVE IT? I'LL LEAVE! I WON'T COME BACK! I PROMISE!

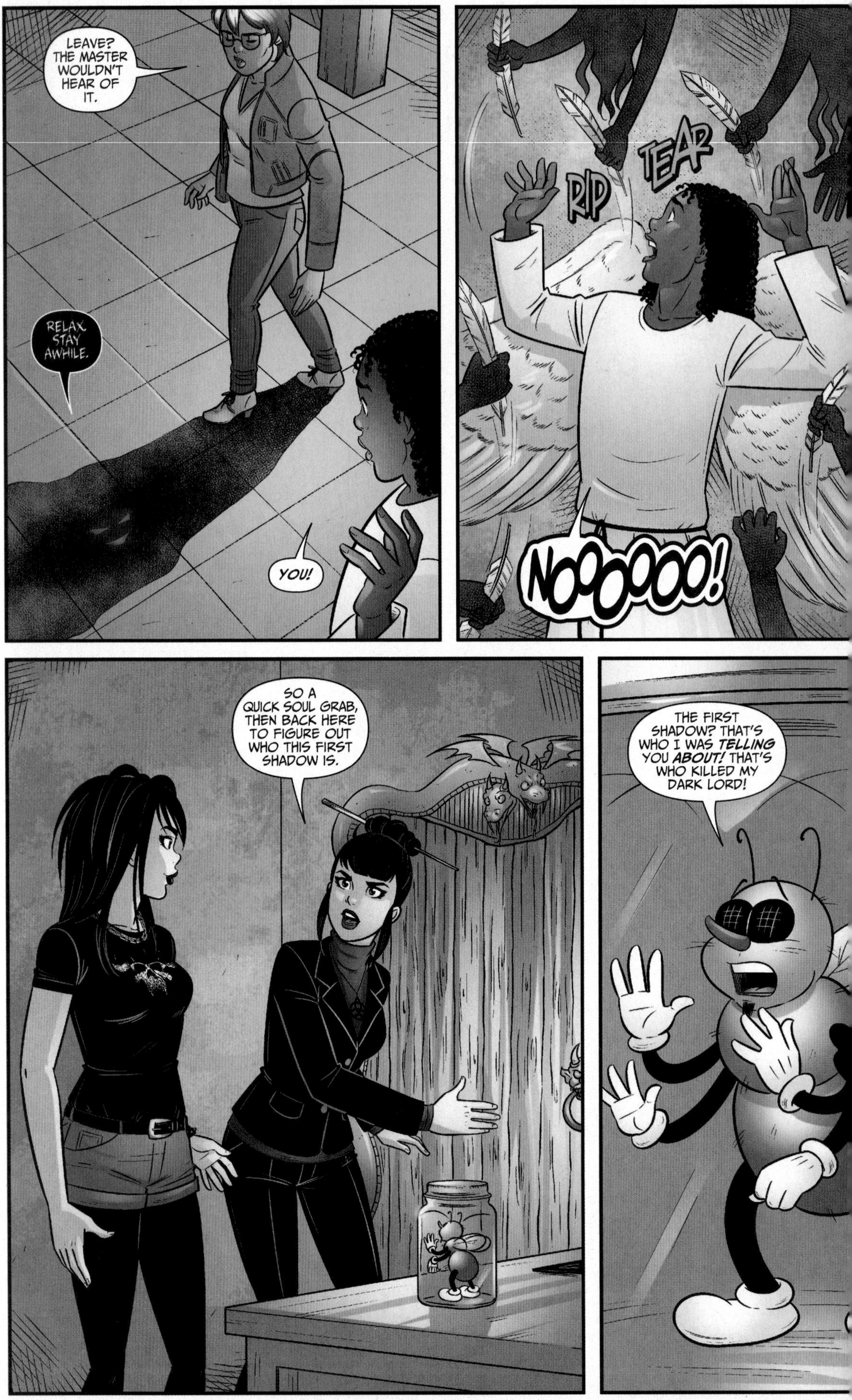
LEAVE? THE MASTER WOULDN'T HEAR OF IT.
RELAX. STAY AWHILE.
YOU!
RIP
TEAR
NOOOOOO!
SO A QUICK SOUL GRAB, THEN BACK HERE TO FIGURE OUT WHO THIS FIRST SHADOW IS.
THE FIRST SHADOW? THAT'S WHO I WAS TELLING YOU ABOUT! THAT'S WHO KILLED MY DARK LORD!

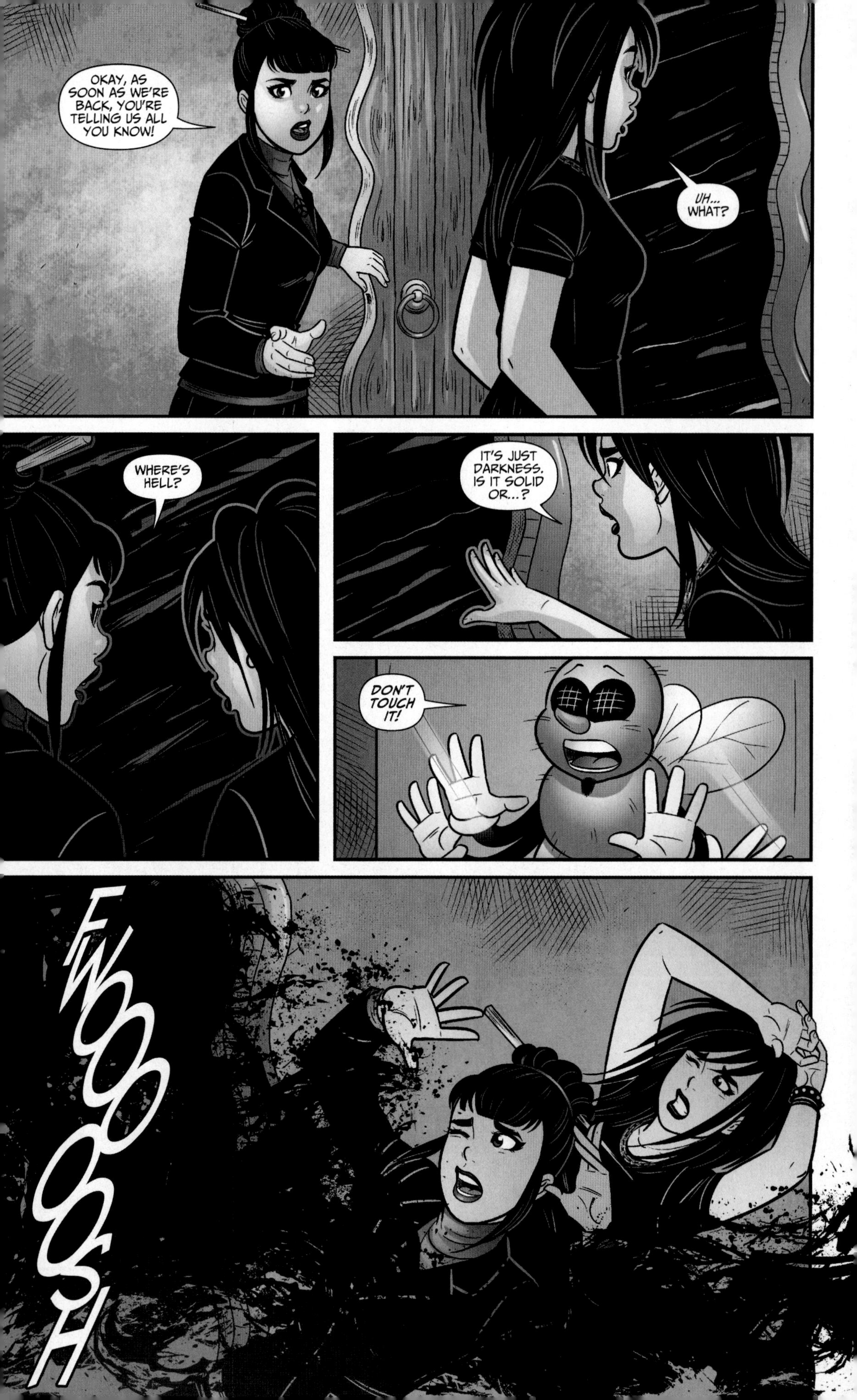

OKAY, AS SOON AS WE'RE BACK, YOU'RE TELLING US ALL YOU KNOW!
UH... WHAT?
WHERE'S HELL?
IT'S JUST DARKNESS. IS IT SOLID OR...?
DON'T TOUCH IT!
FWOOOOOSH

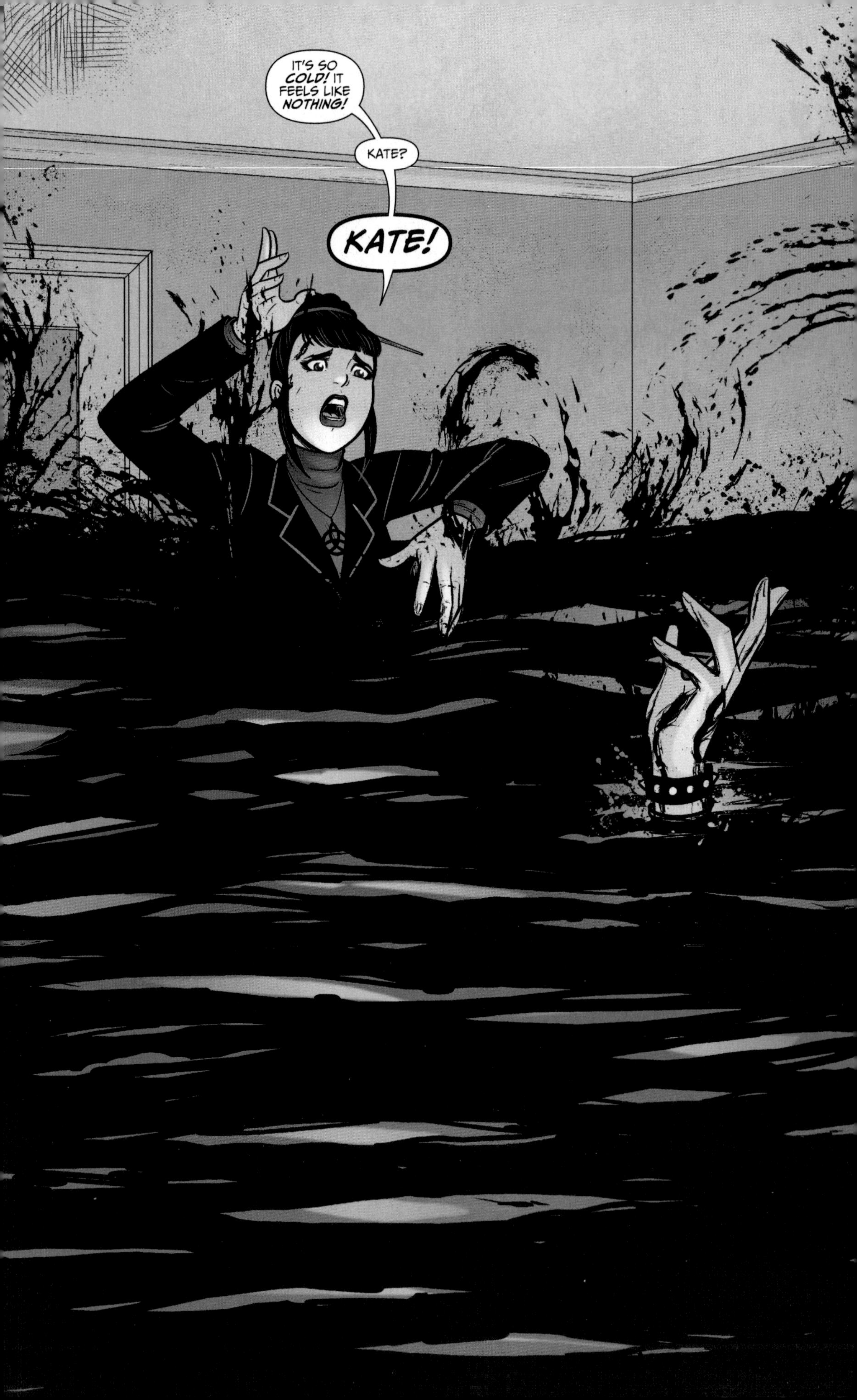
IT'S SO COLD! IT FEELS LIKE NOTHING!
KATE?
KATE!

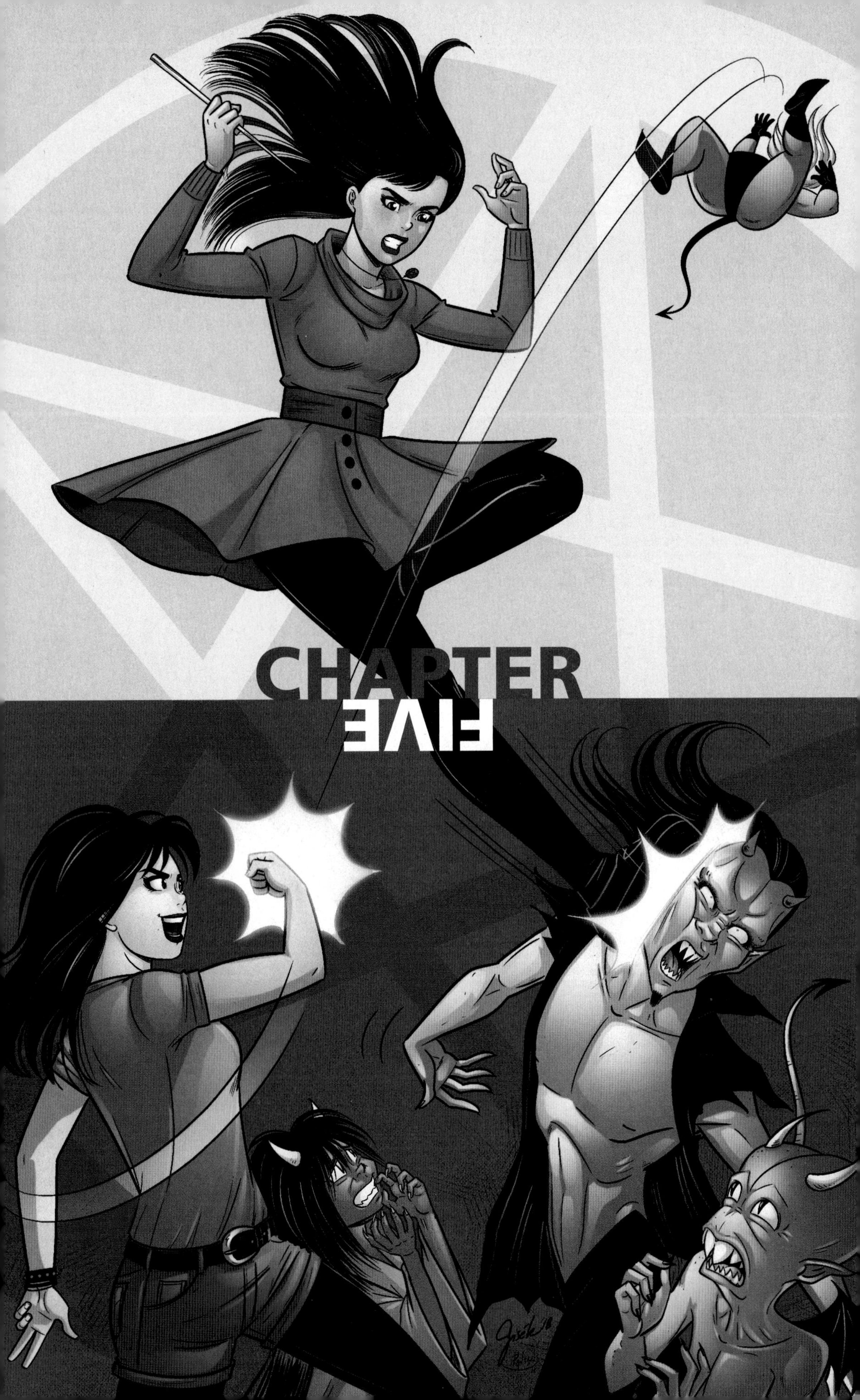
CHAPTER
FIVE

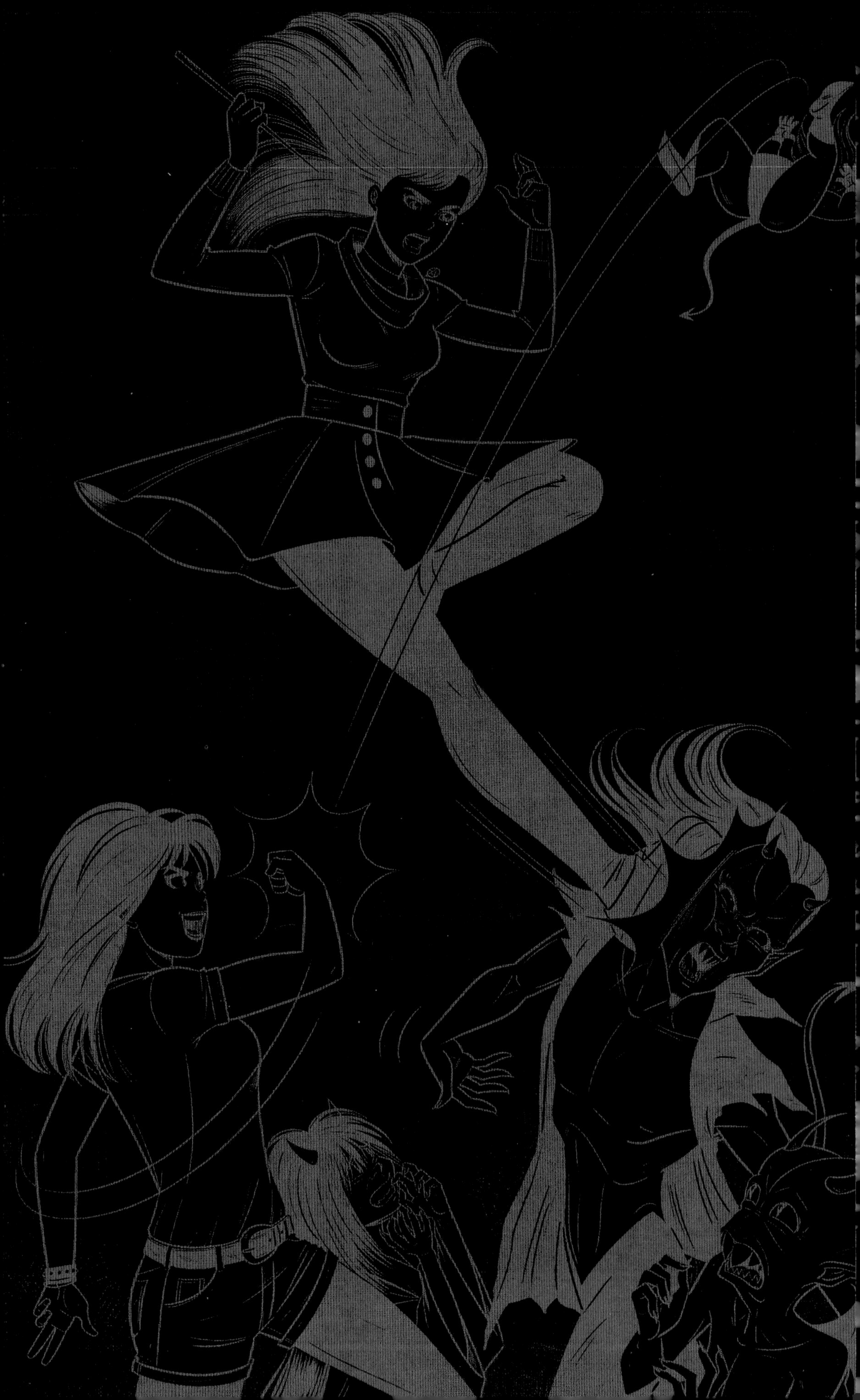

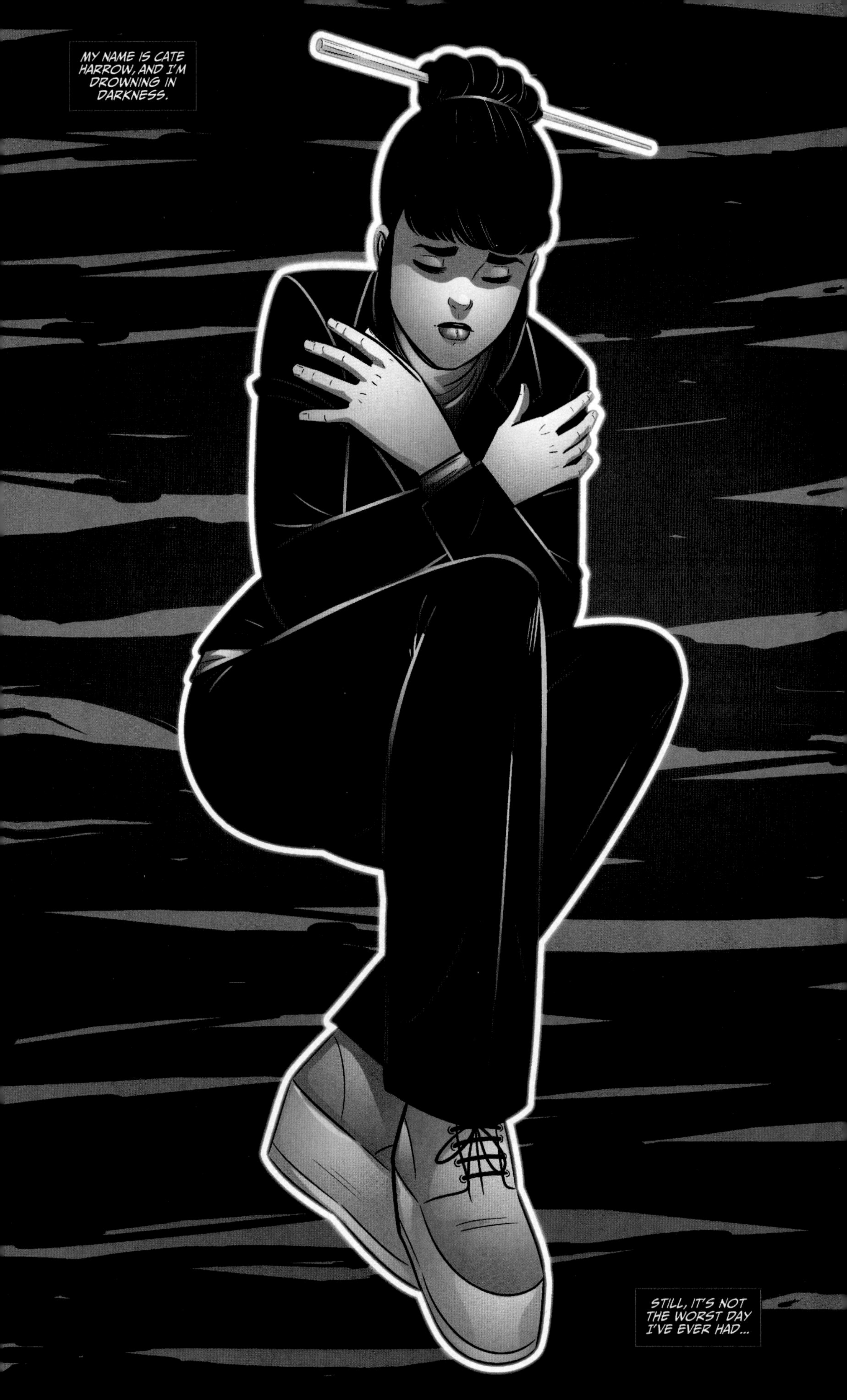
MY NAME IS CATE HARROW, AND I'M DROWNING IN DARKNESS.
STILL, IT'S NOT THE WORST DAY I'VE EVER HAD...

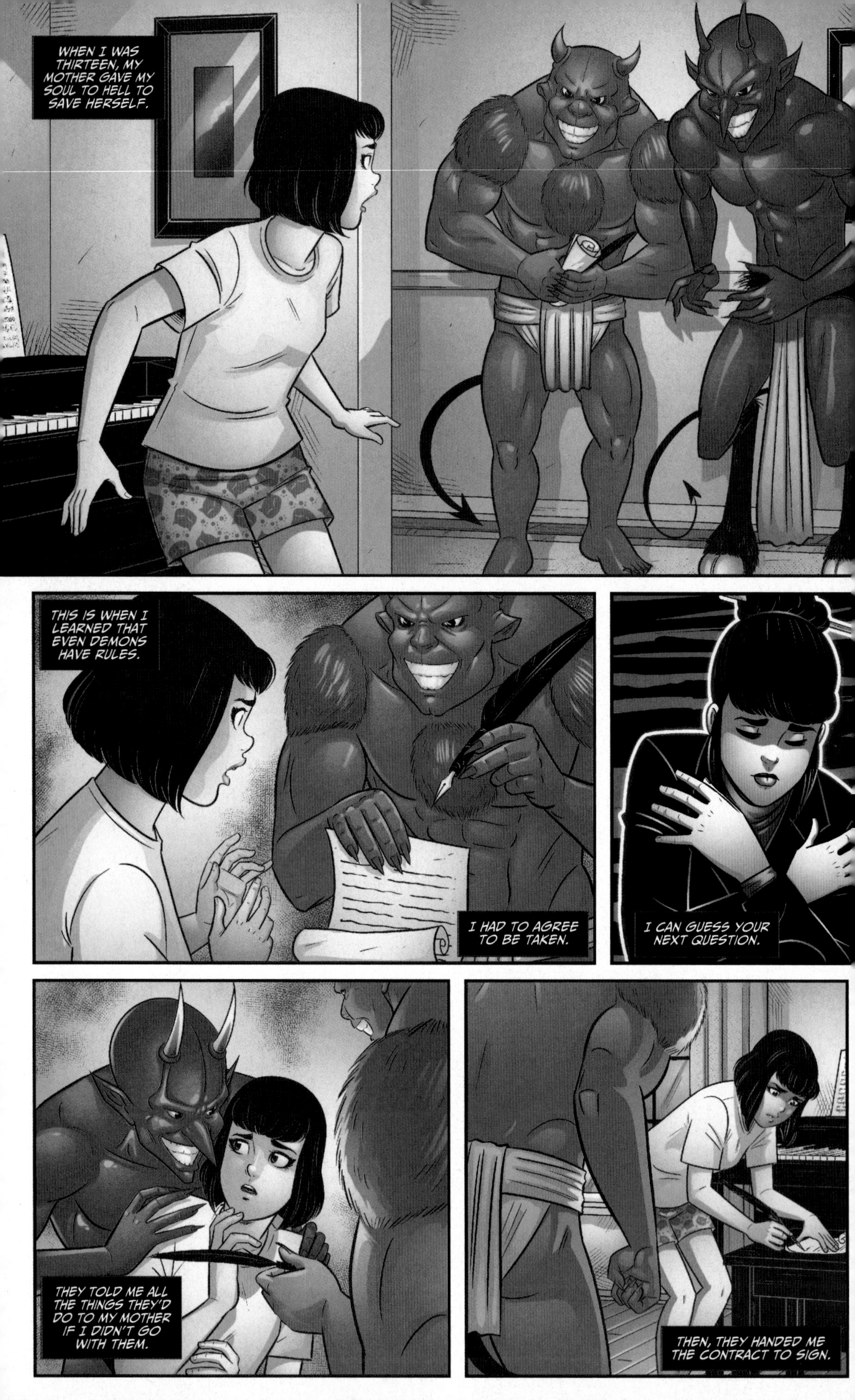
WHEN I WAS THIRTEEN, MY MOTHER GAVE MY SOUL TO HELL TO SAVE HERSELF.
THIS IS WHEN I LEARNED THAT EVEN DEMONS HAVE RULES.
I HAD TO AGREE TO BE TAKEN.
I CAN GUESS YOUR NEXT QUESTION.
THEY TOLD ME ALL THE THINGS THEY'D DO TO MY MOTHER IF I DIDN'T GO WITH THEM.
THEN, THEY HANDED ME THE CONTRACT TO SIGN.

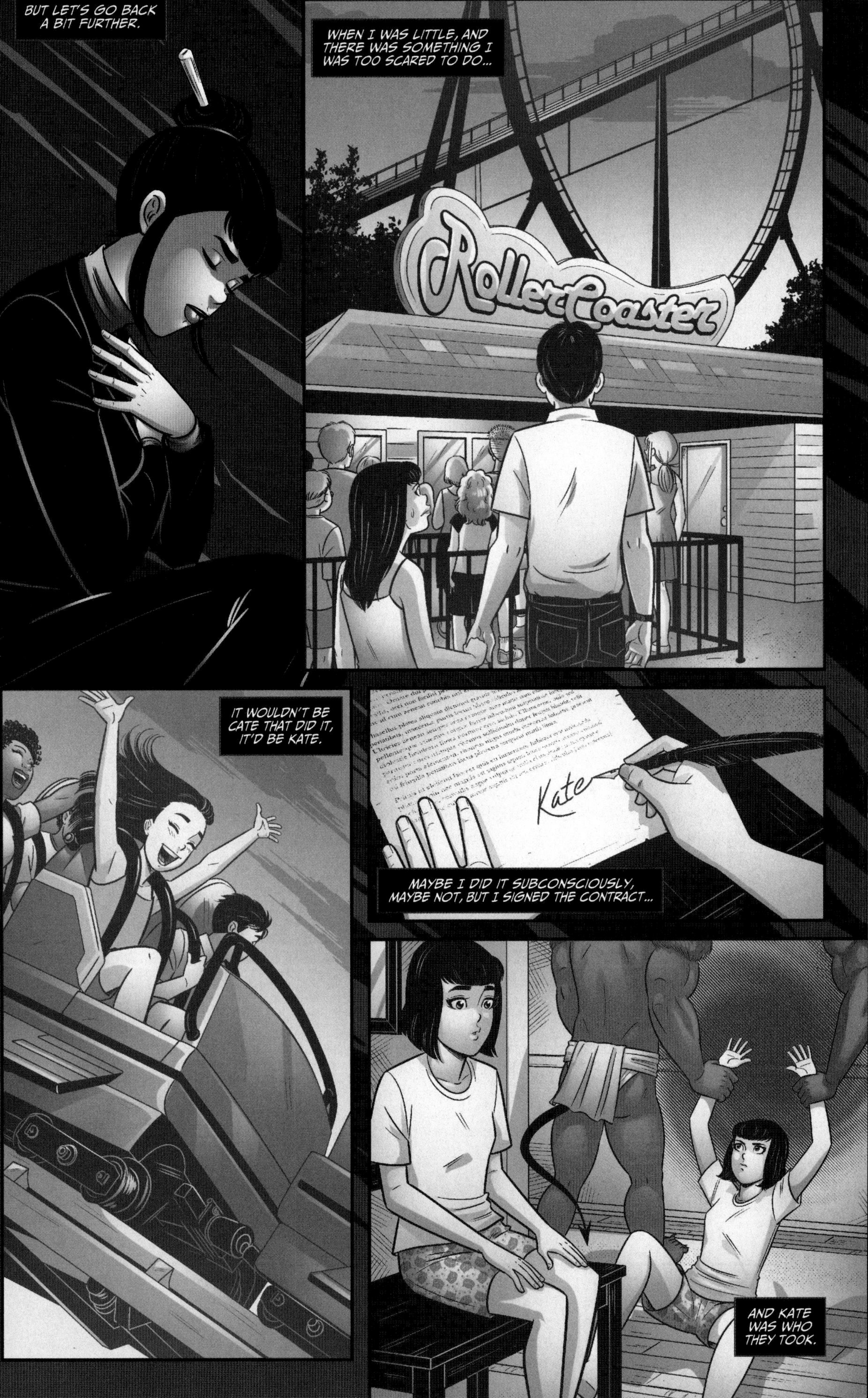
BUT LET'S GO BACK A BIT FURTHER.
WHEN I WAS LITTLE, AND THERE WAS SOMETHING I WAS TOO SCARED TO DO...
Roller Coaster
IT WOULDN'T BE CATE THAT DID IT, IT'D BE KATE.
Kate
MAYBE I DID IT SUBCONSCIOUSLY, MAYBE NOT, BUT I SIGNED THE CONTRACT...
AND KATE WAS WHO THEY TOOK.

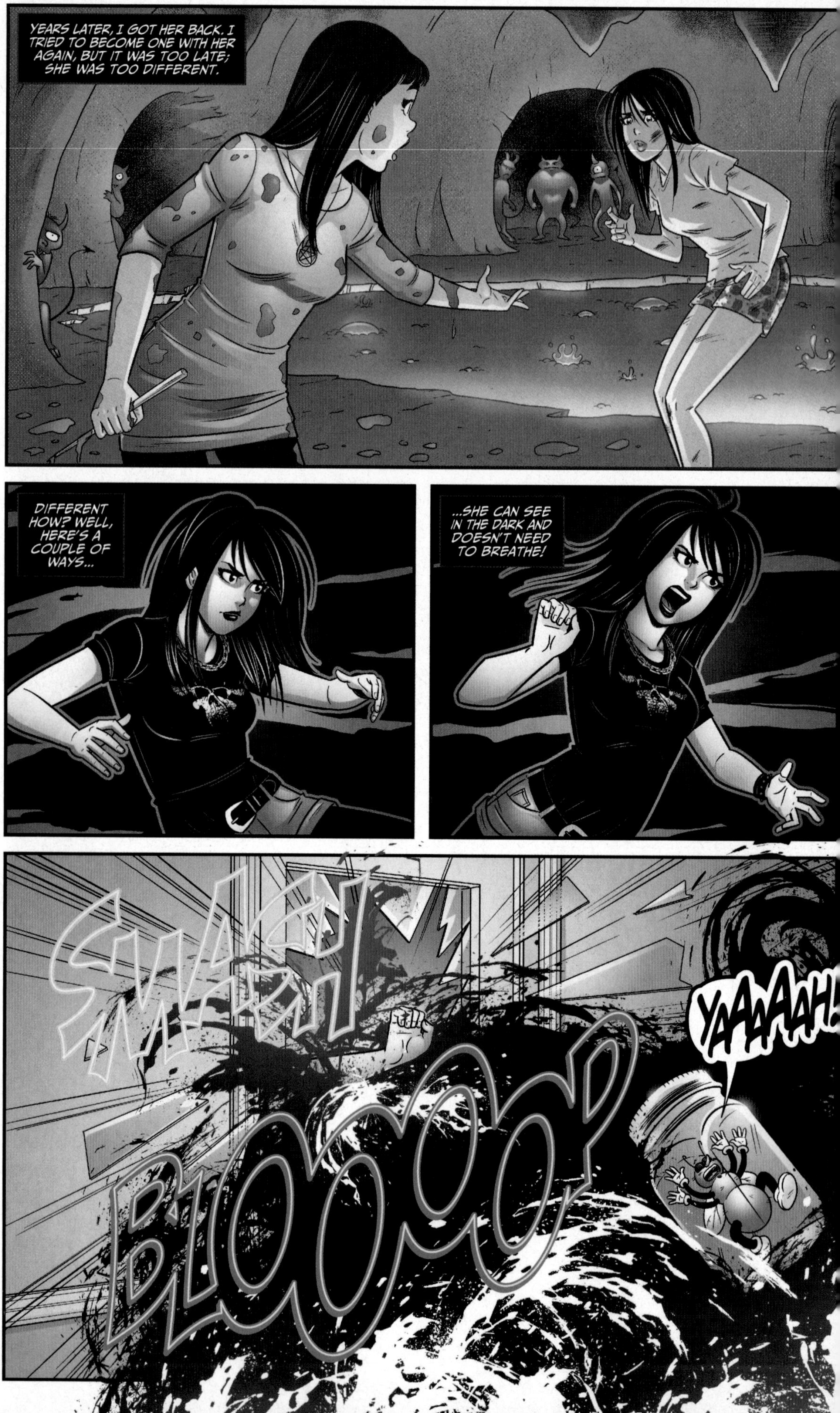
YEARS LATER, I GOT HER BACK. I TRIED TO BECOME ONE WITH HER AGAIN, BUT IT WAS TOO LATE; SHE WAS TOO DIFFERENT.
DIFFERENT HOW? WELL, HERE'S A COUPLE OF WAYS...
...SHE CAN SEE IN THE DARK AND DOESN'T NEED TO BREATHE!
SMASH
BLOOOOP
YAAAAAH!

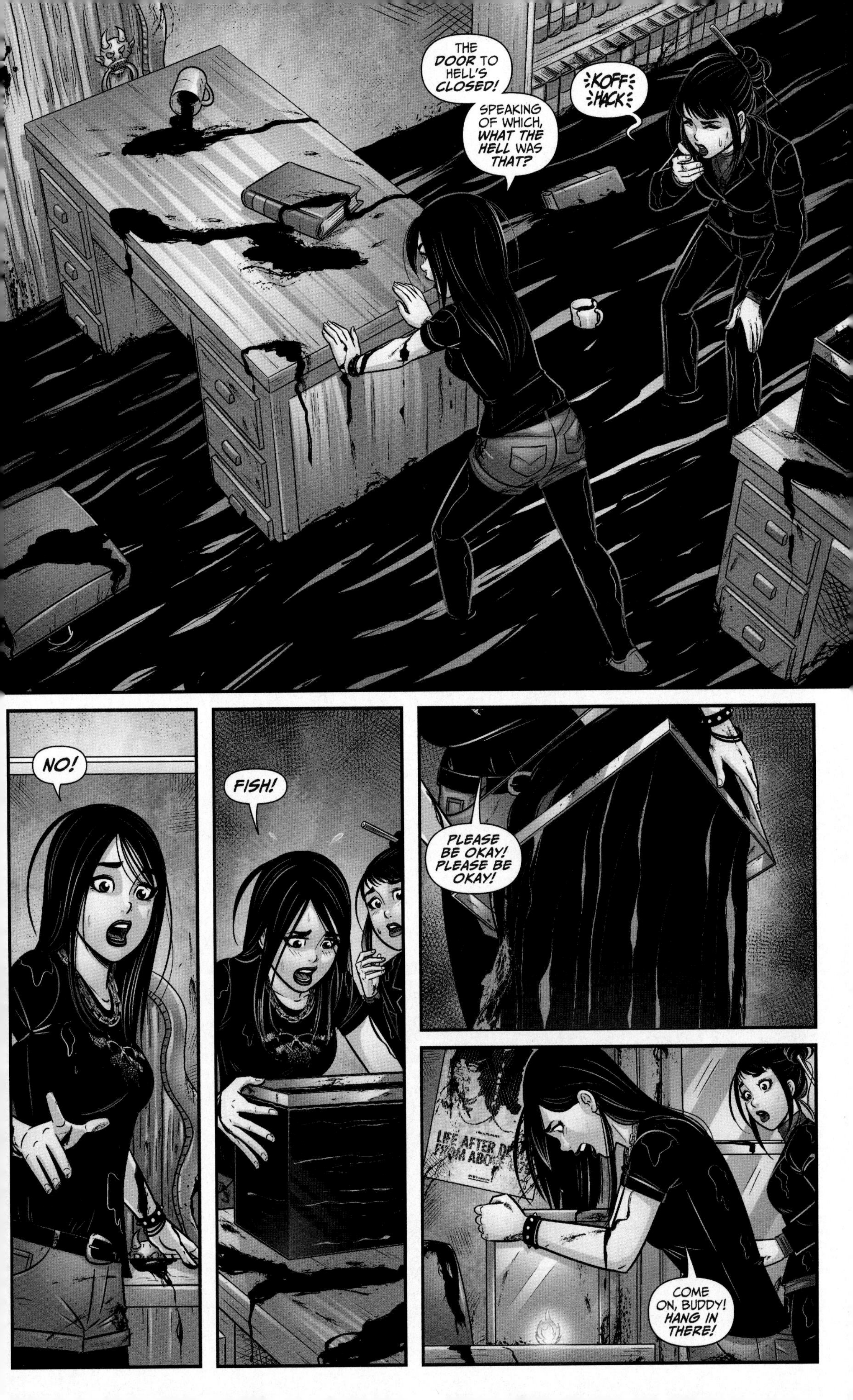
THE DOOR TO HELL'S CLOSED!
SPEAKING OF WHICH, WHAT THE HELL WAS THAT?
KOFF HACK
NO!
FISH!
PLEASE BE OKAY! PLEASE BE OKAY!
COME ON, BUDDY! HANG IN THERE!

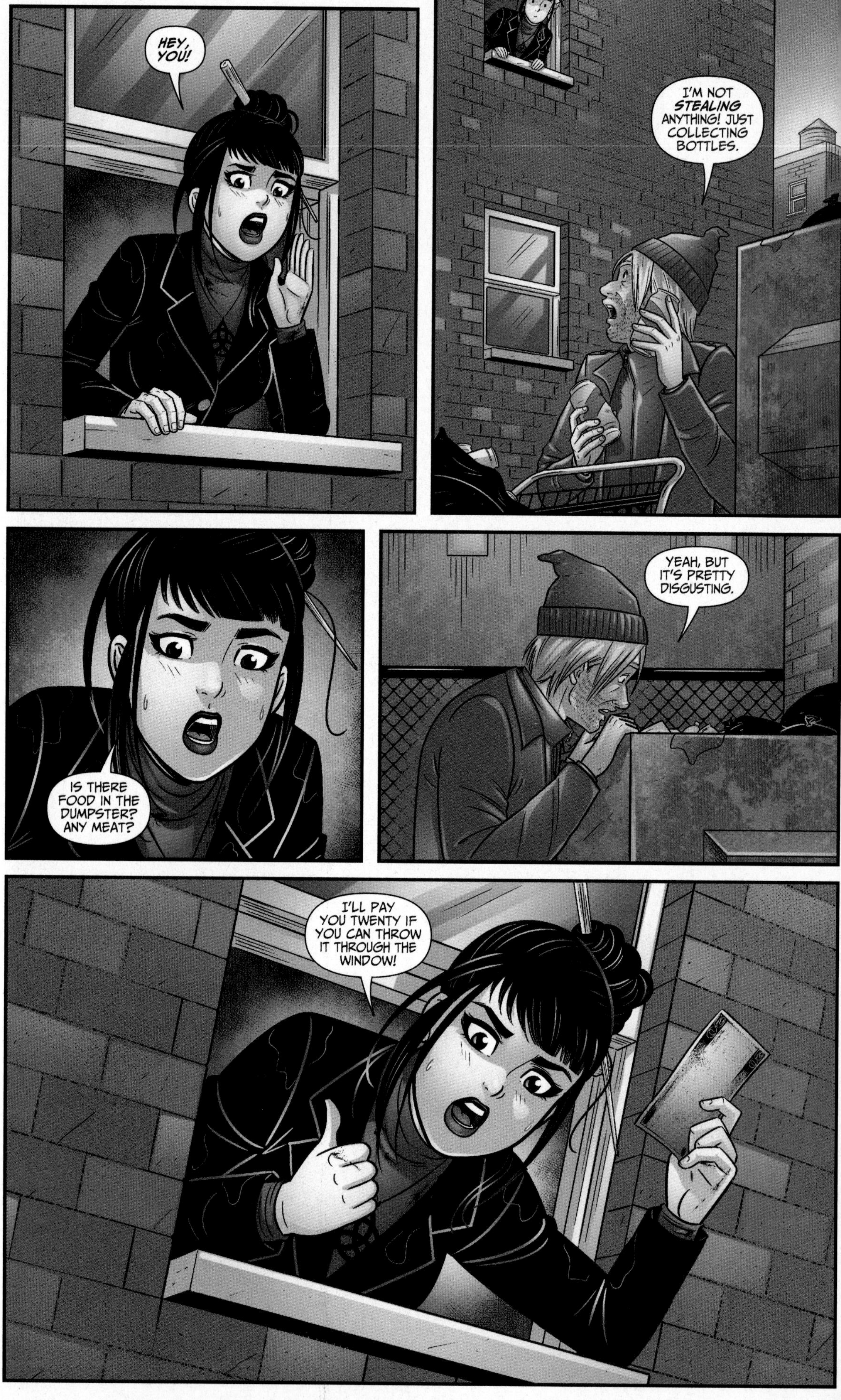
HEY, YOU!
I'M NOT STEALING ANYTHING! JUST COLLECTING BOTTLES.
IS THERE FOOD IN THE DUMPSTER? ANY MEAT?
YEAH, BUT IT'S PRETTY DISGUSTING.
I'LL PAY YOU TWENTY IF YOU CAN THROW IT THROUGH THE WINDOW!

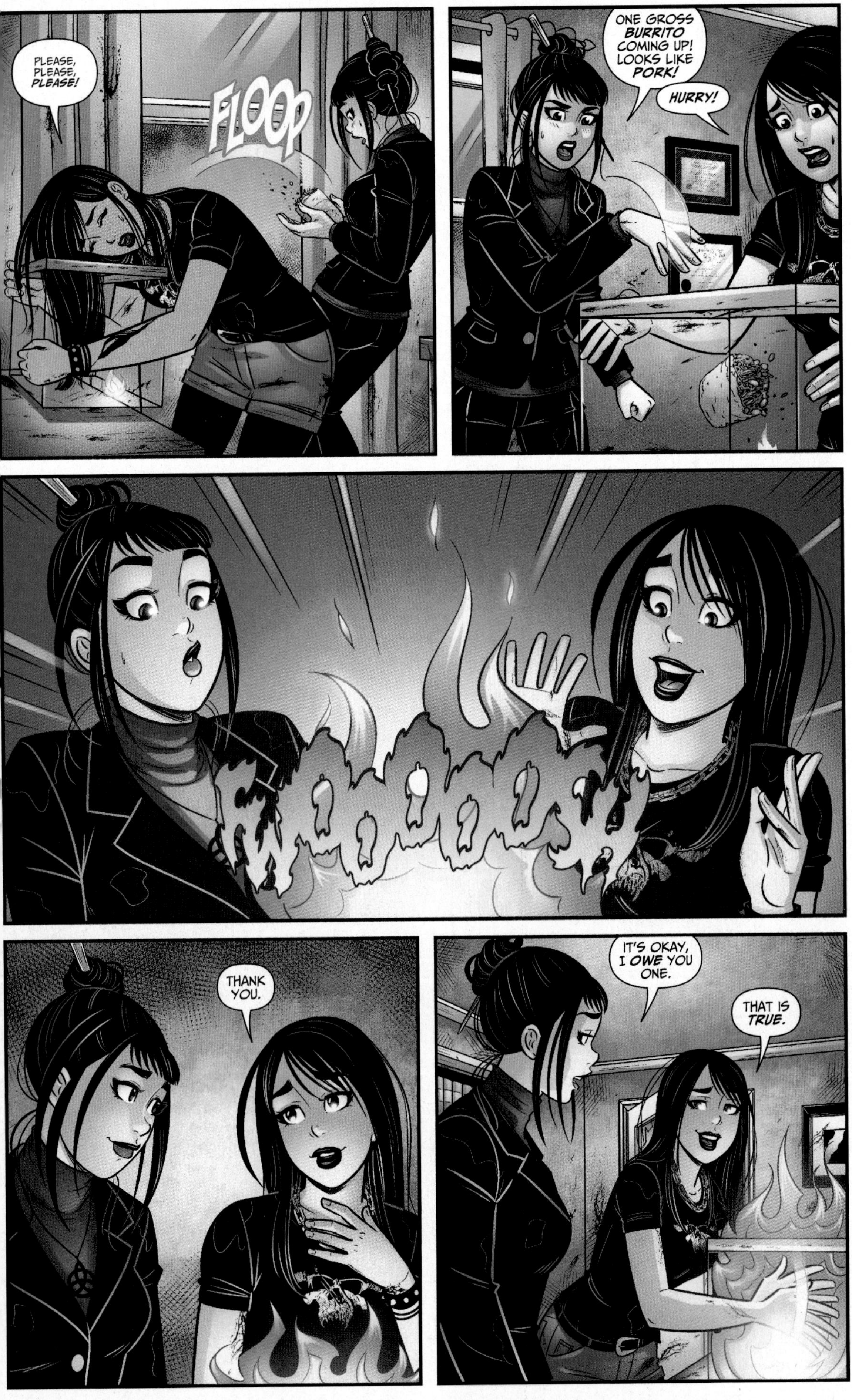
PLEASE, PLEASE, PLEASE!
FLOOP
ONE GROSS BURRITO COMING UP! LOOKS LIKE PORK!
HURRY!
THANK YOU.
IT'S OKAY, I OWE YOU ONE.
THAT IS TRUE.

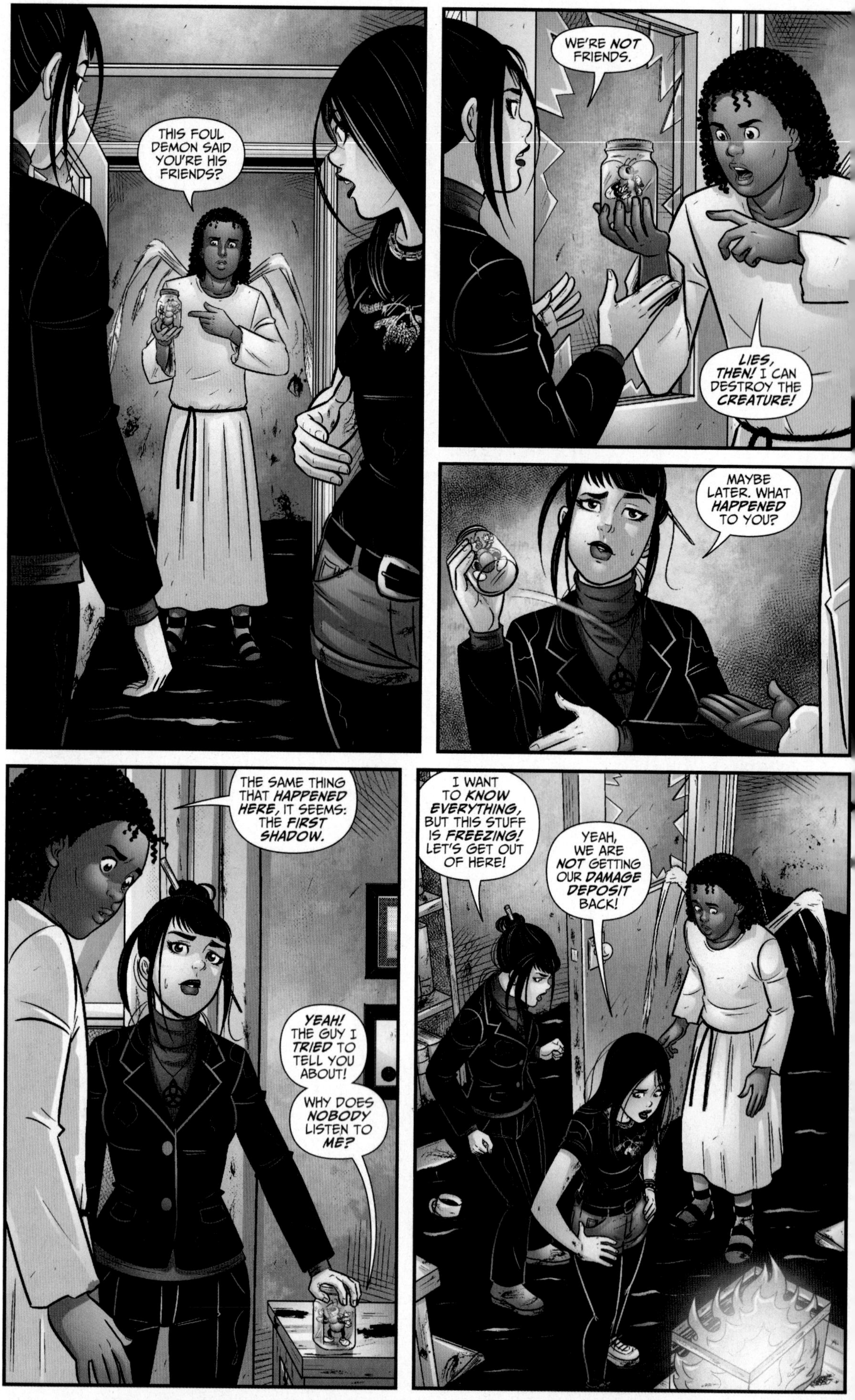
THIS FOUL DEMON SAID YOU'RE HIS FRIENDS?
WE'RE NOT FRIENDS.
LIES, THEN! I CAN DESTROY THE CREATURE!
MAYBE LATER. WHAT HAPPENED TO YOU?
THE SAME THING THAT HAPPENED HERE, IT SEEMS: THE FIRST SHADOW.
YEAH! THE GUY I TRIED TO TELL YOU ABOUT!
WHY DOES NOBODY LISTEN TO ME?
I WANT TO KNOW EVERYTHING, BUT THIS STUFF IS FREEZING! LET'S GET OUT OF HERE!
YEAH, WE ARE NOT GETTING OUR DAMAGE DEPOSIT BACK!

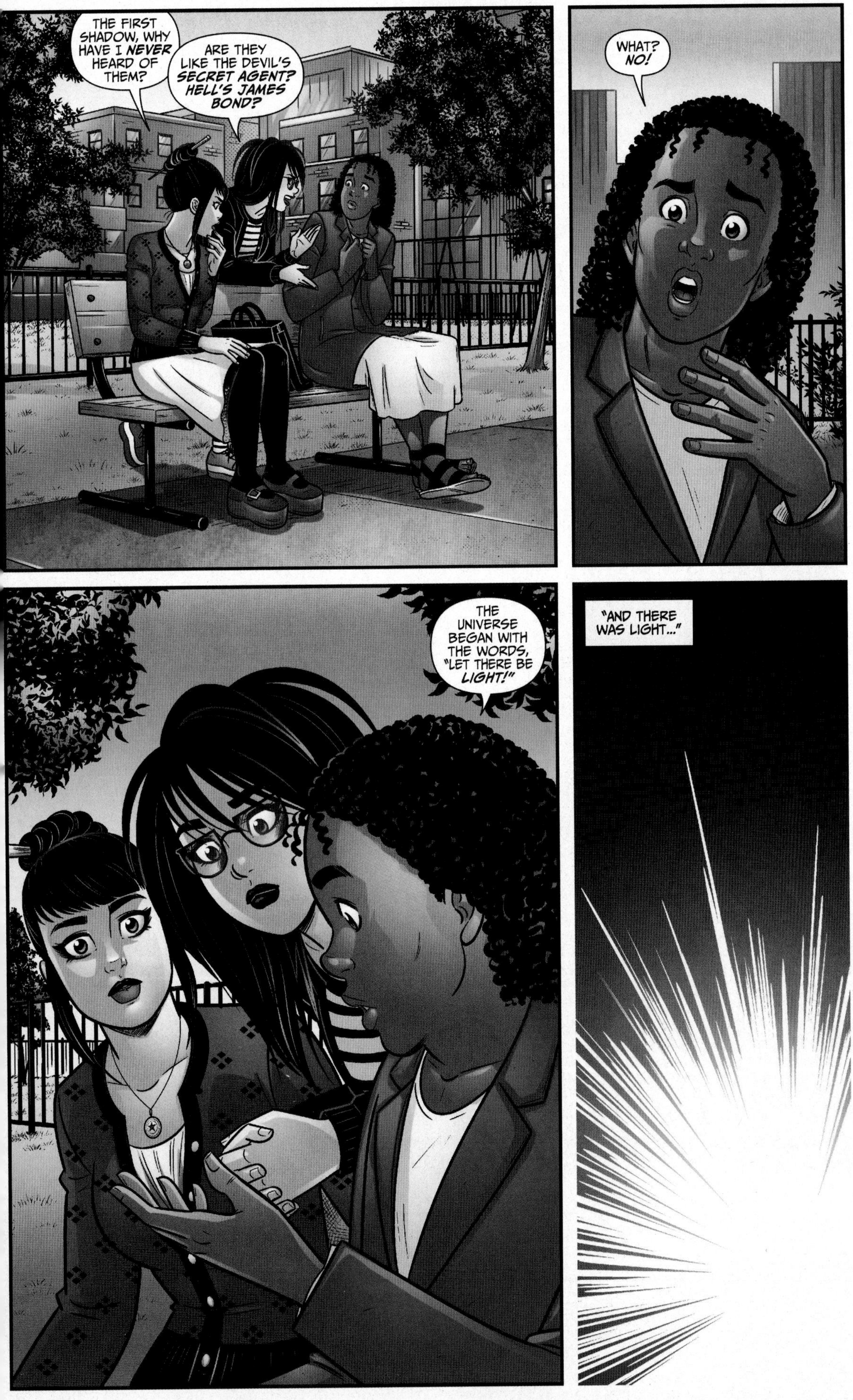
THE FIRST SHADOW, WHY HAVE I NEVER HEARD OF THEM?
ARE THEY LIKE THE DEVIL'S SECRET AGENT? HELL'S JAMES BOND?
WHAT? NO!
THE UNIVERSE BEGAN WITH THE WORDS, "LET THERE BE LIGHT!"
"AND THERE WAS LIGHT..."

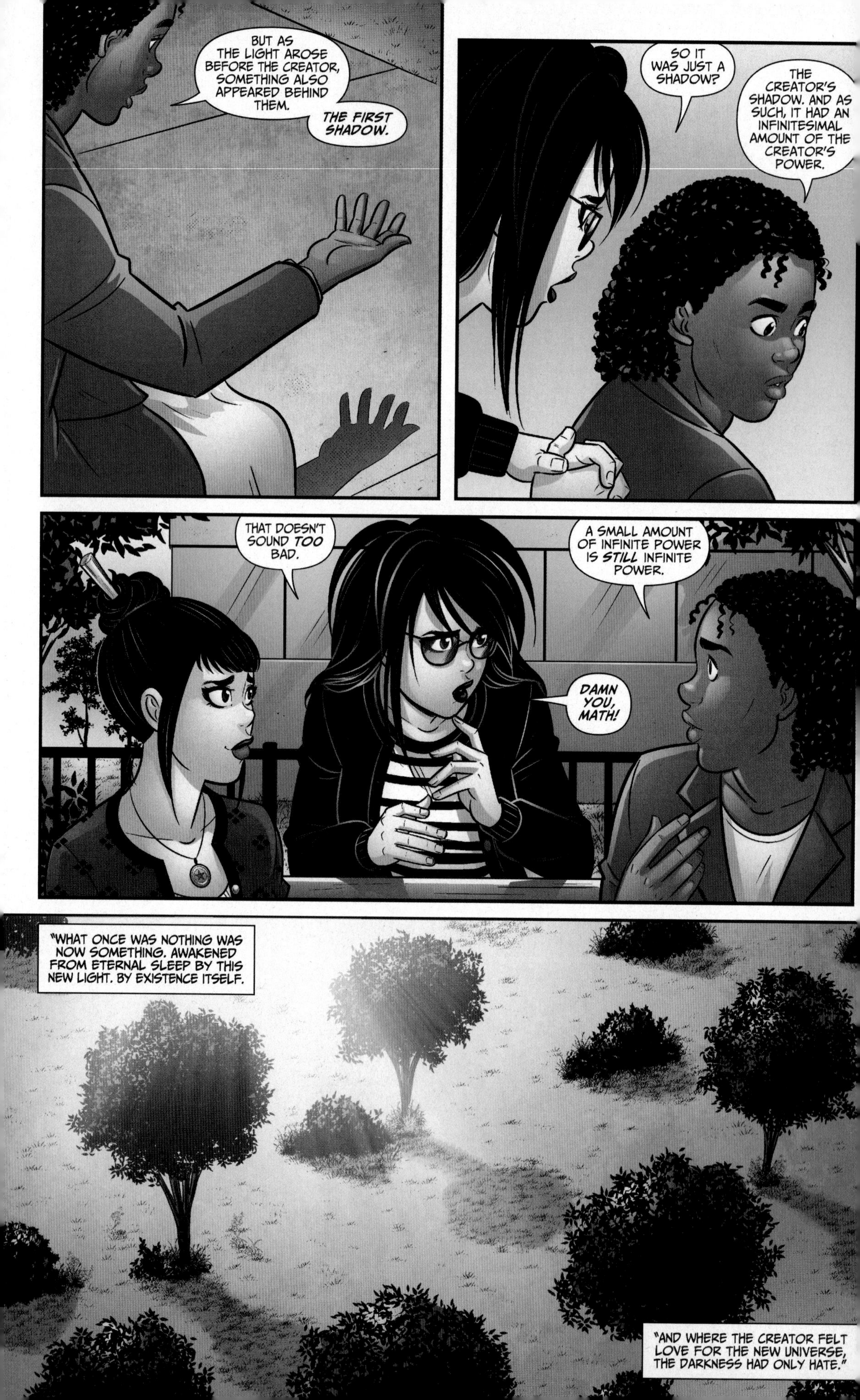
BUT AS THE LIGHT AROSE BEFORE THE CREATOR, SOMETHING ALSO APPEARED BEHIND THEM.
THE FIRST SHADOW.
SO IT WAS JUST A SHADOW?
THE CREATOR'S SHADOW. AND AS SUCH, IT HAD AN INFINITESIMAL AMOUNT OF THE CREATOR'S POWER.
THAT DOESN'T SOUND TOO BAD.
A SMALL AMOUNT OF INFINITE POWER IS STILL INFINITE POWER.
DAMN YOU, MATH!
"WHAT ONCE WAS NOTHING WAS NOW SOMETHING. AWAKENED FROM ETERNAL SLEEP BY THIS NEW LIGHT. BY EXISTENCE ITSELF.
"AND WHERE THE CREATOR FELT LOVE FOR THE NEW UNIVERSE, THE DARKNESS HAD ONLY HATE."

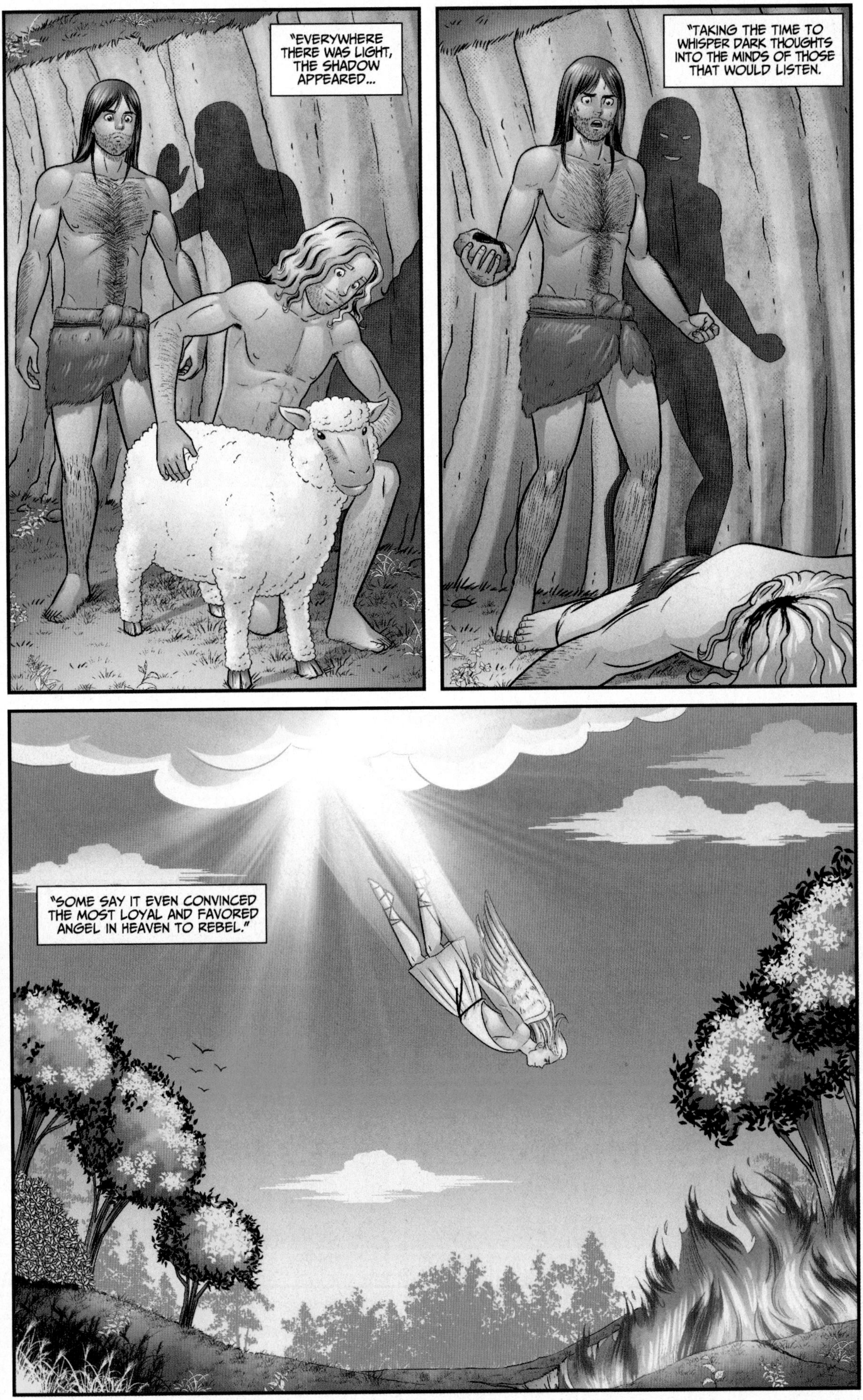
"EVERYWHERE THERE WAS LIGHT, THE SHADOW APPEARED...
"TAKING THE TIME TO WHISPER DARK THOUGHTS INTO THE MINDS OF THOSE THAT WOULD LISTEN.
"SOME SAY IT EVEN CONVINCED THE MOST LOYAL AND FAVORED ANGEL IN HEAVEN TO REBEL."

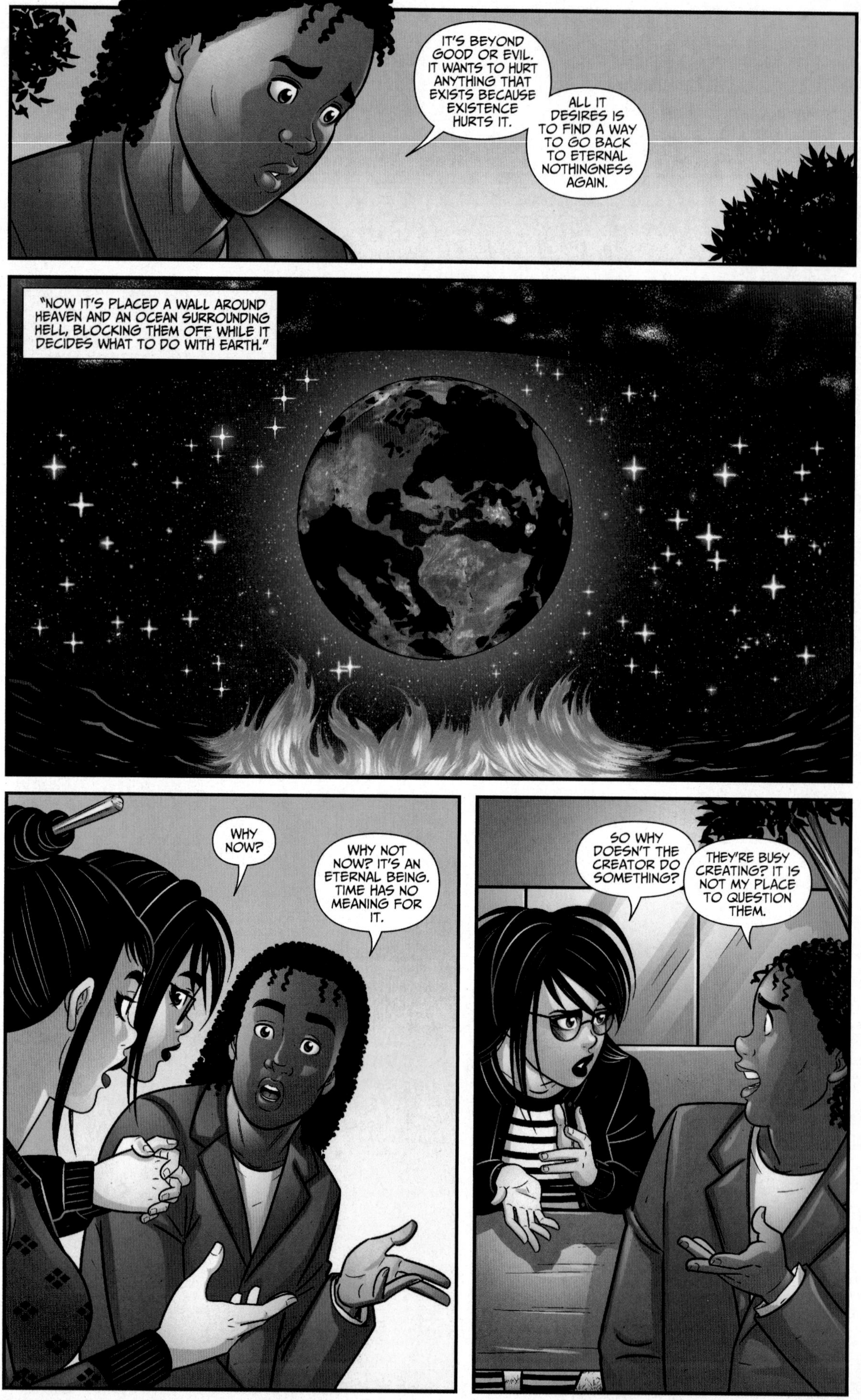
IT'S BEYOND GOOD OR EVIL. IT WANTS TO HURT ANYTHING THAT EXISTS BECAUSE EXISTENCE HURTS IT.
ALL IT DESIRES IS TO FIND A WAY TO GO BACK TO ETERNAL NOTHINGNESS AGAIN.
"NOW IT'S PLACED A WALL AROUND HEAVEN AND AN OCEAN SURROUNDING HELL, BLOCKING THEM OFF WHILE IT DECIDES WHAT TO DO WITH EARTH."
WHY NOW?
WHY NOT NOW? IT'S AN ETERNAL BEING. TIME HAS NO MEANING FOR IT.
SO WHY DOESN'T THE CREATOR DO SOMETHING?
THEY'RE BUSY CREATING? IT IS NOT MY PLACE TO QUESTION THEM.

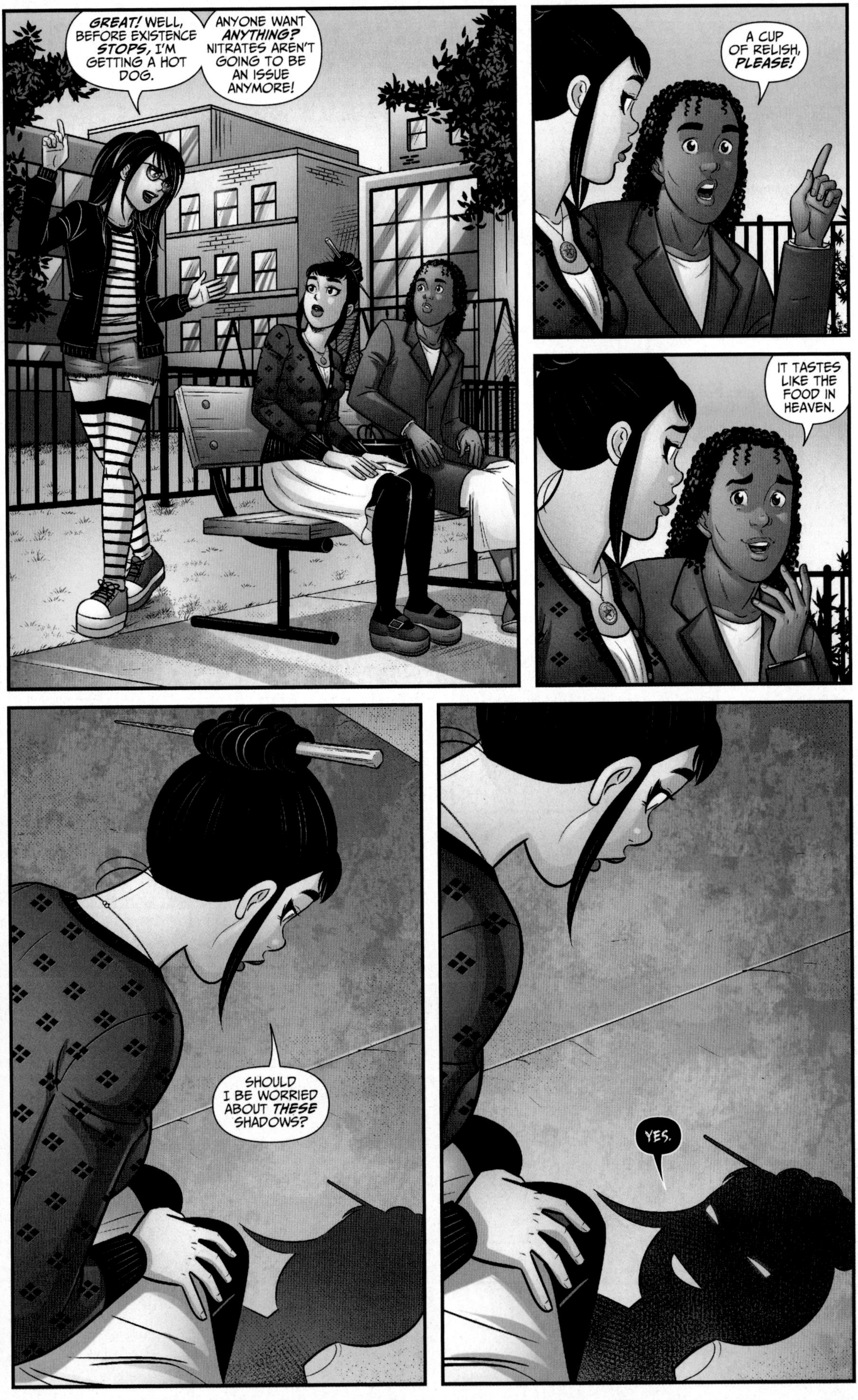
GREAT! WELL, BEFORE EXISTENCE STOPS, I'M GETTING A HOT DOG.
ANYONE WANT ANYTHING? NITRATES AREN'T GOING TO BE AN ISSUE ANYMORE!
A CUP OF RELISH, PLEASE!
IT TASTES LIKE THE FOOD IN HEAVEN.
SHOULD I BE WORRIED ABOUT THESE SHADOWS?
YES.

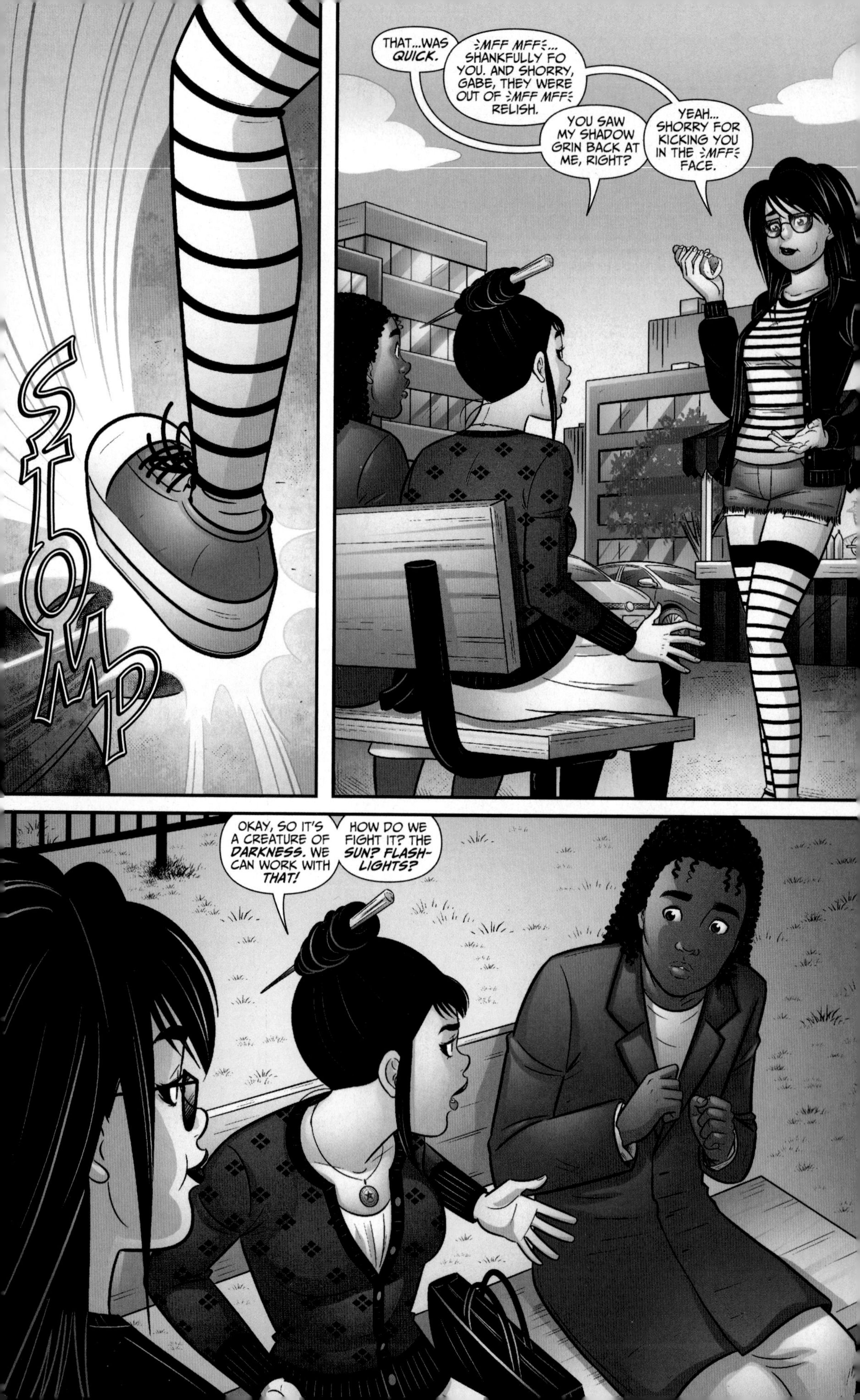
STOMP
THAT...WAS *QUICK.*
MFF MFF... SHANKFULLY FO YOU. AND SHORRY, GABE, THEY WERE OUT OF *MFF MFF* RELISH.
YOU SAW MY SHADOW GRIN BACK AT ME, RIGHT?
YEAH... SHORRY FOR KICKING YOU IN THE *MFF* FACE.
OKAY, SO IT'S A CREATURE OF *DARKNESS*. WE CAN WORK WITH *THAT!*
HOW DO WE FIGHT IT? THE *SUN? FLASH-LIGHTS?*

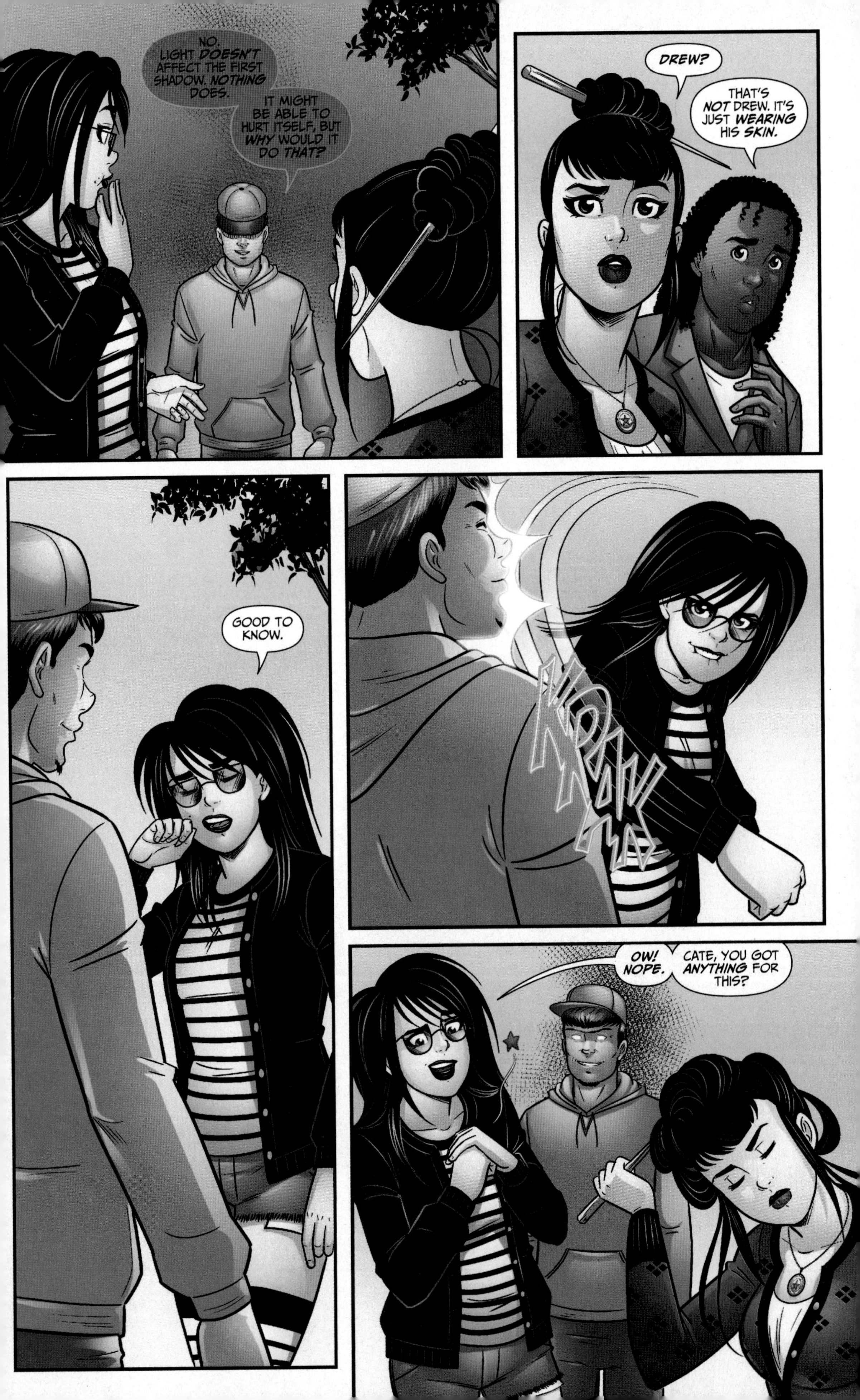
NO. LIGHT DOESN'T AFFECT THE FIRST SHADOW. NOTHING DOES.
IT MIGHT BE ABLE TO HURT ITSELF, BUT WHY WOULD IT DO THAT?
DREW?
THAT'S NOT DREW. IT'S JUST WEARING HIS SKIN.
GOOD TO KNOW.
KONK
OW! NOPE.
CATE, YOU GOT ANYTHING FOR THIS?

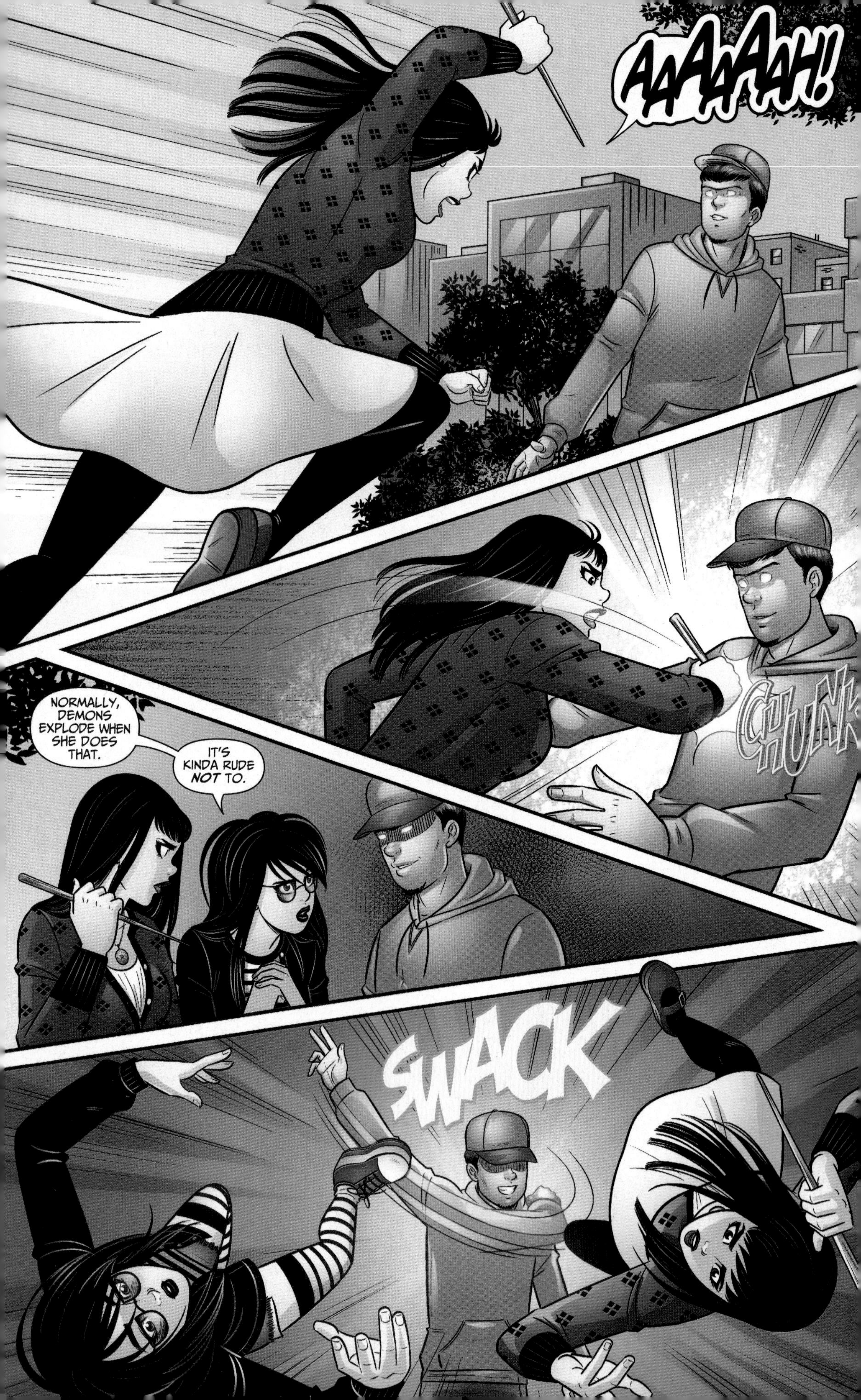
AAAAAAH!
CHUNK
NORMALLY, DEMONS EXPLODE WHEN SHE DOES THAT.
IT'S KINDA RUDE *NOT* TO.
SWACK

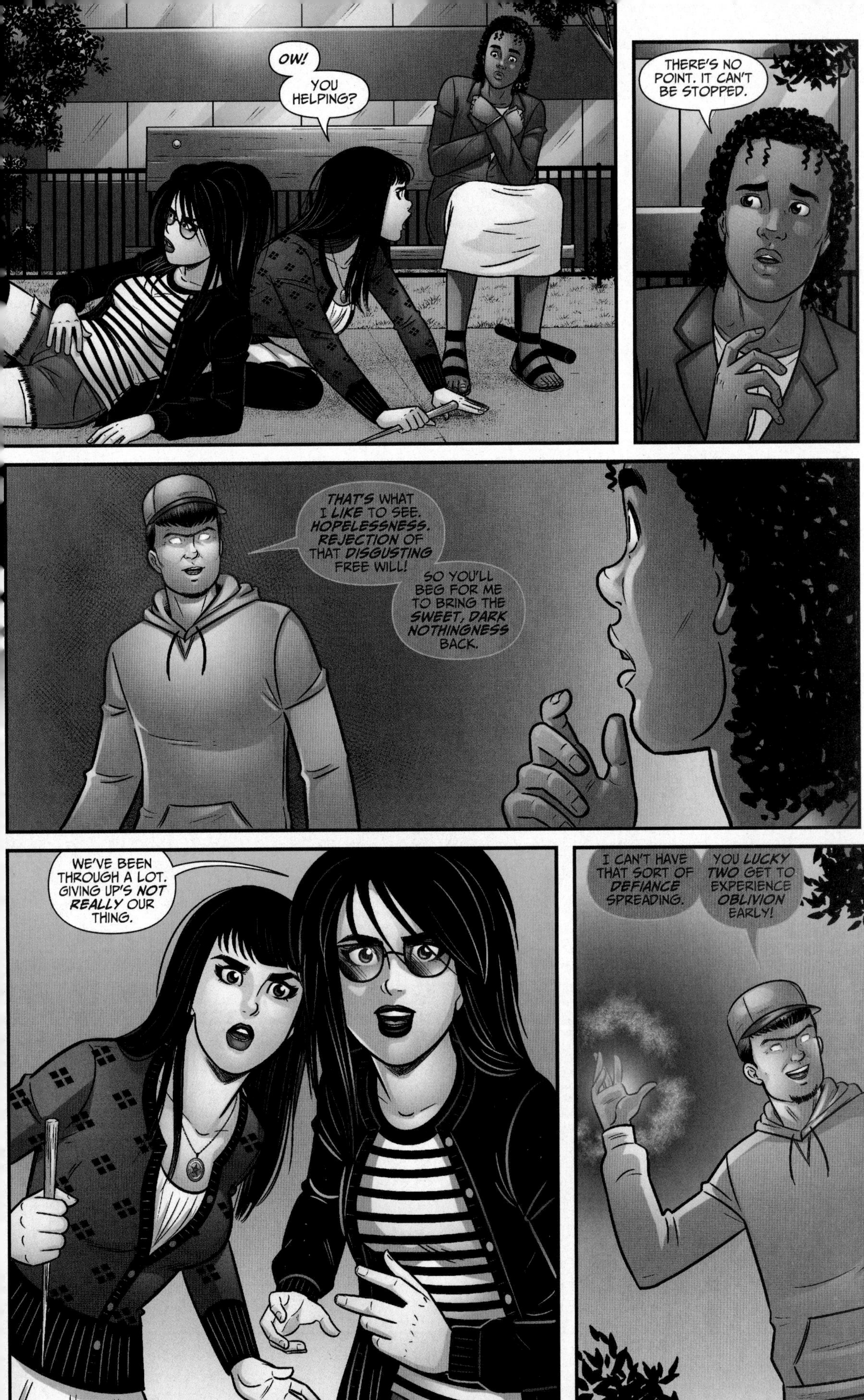
OW!
YOU HELPING?
THERE'S NO POINT. IT CAN'T BE STOPPED.
THAT'S WHAT I LIKE TO SEE. HOPELESSNESS. REJECTION OF THAT DISGUSTING FREE WILL!
SO YOU'LL BEG FOR ME TO BRING THE SWEET, DARK NOTHINGNESS BACK.
WE'VE BEEN THROUGH A LOT. GIVING UP'S NOT REALLY OUR THING.
I CAN'T HAVE THAT SORT OF DEFIANCE SPREADING.
YOU LUCKY TWO GET TO EXPERIENCE OBLIVION EARLY!

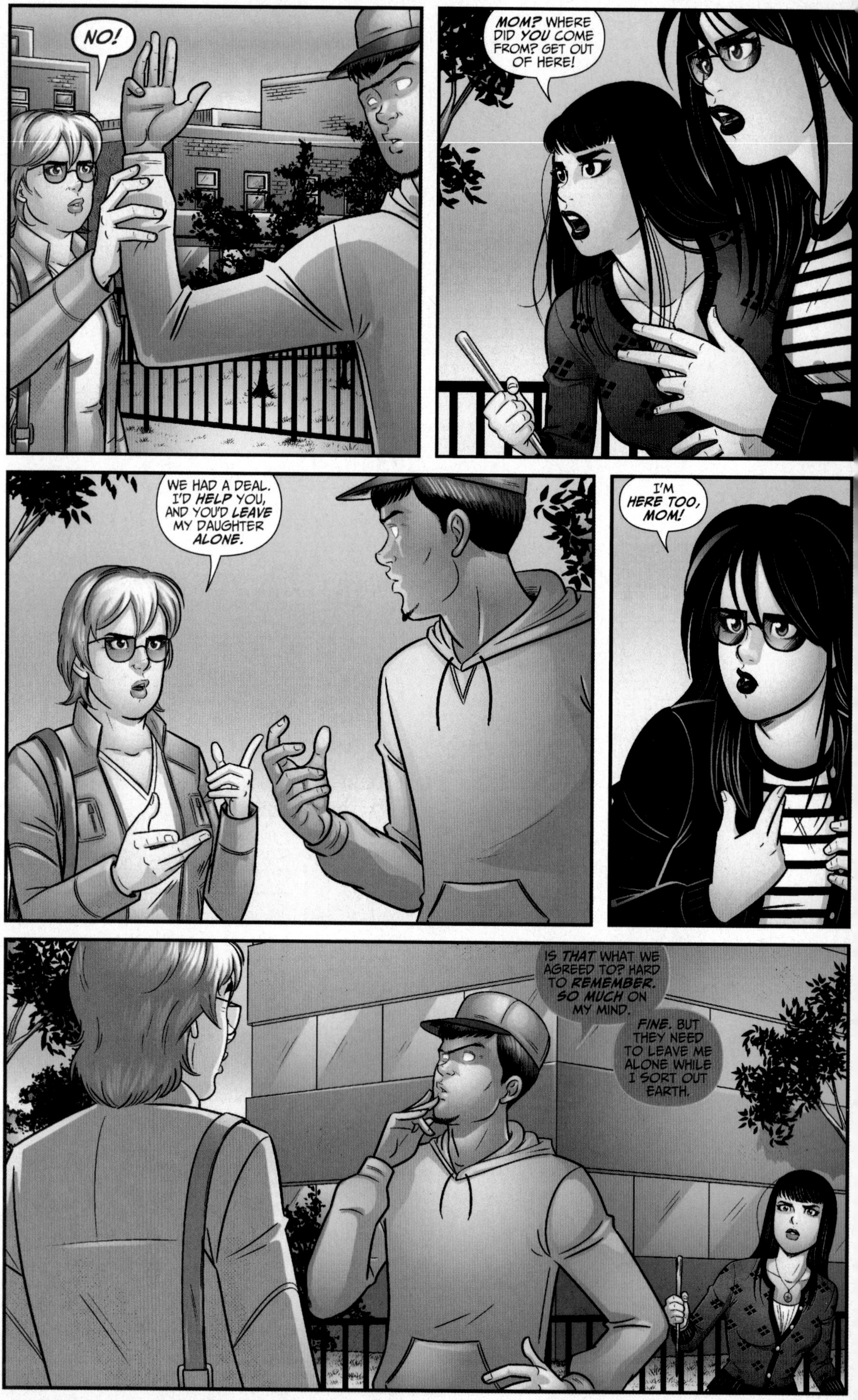
NO!
MOM? WHERE DID YOU COME FROM? GET OUT OF HERE!
WE HAD A DEAL. I'D HELP YOU, AND YOU'D LEAVE MY DAUGHTER ALONE.
I'M HERE TOO, MOM!
IS THAT WHAT WE AGREED TO? HARD TO REMEMBER. SO MUCH ON MY MIND.
FINE. BUT THEY NEED TO LEAVE ME ALONE WHILE I SORT OUT EARTH.

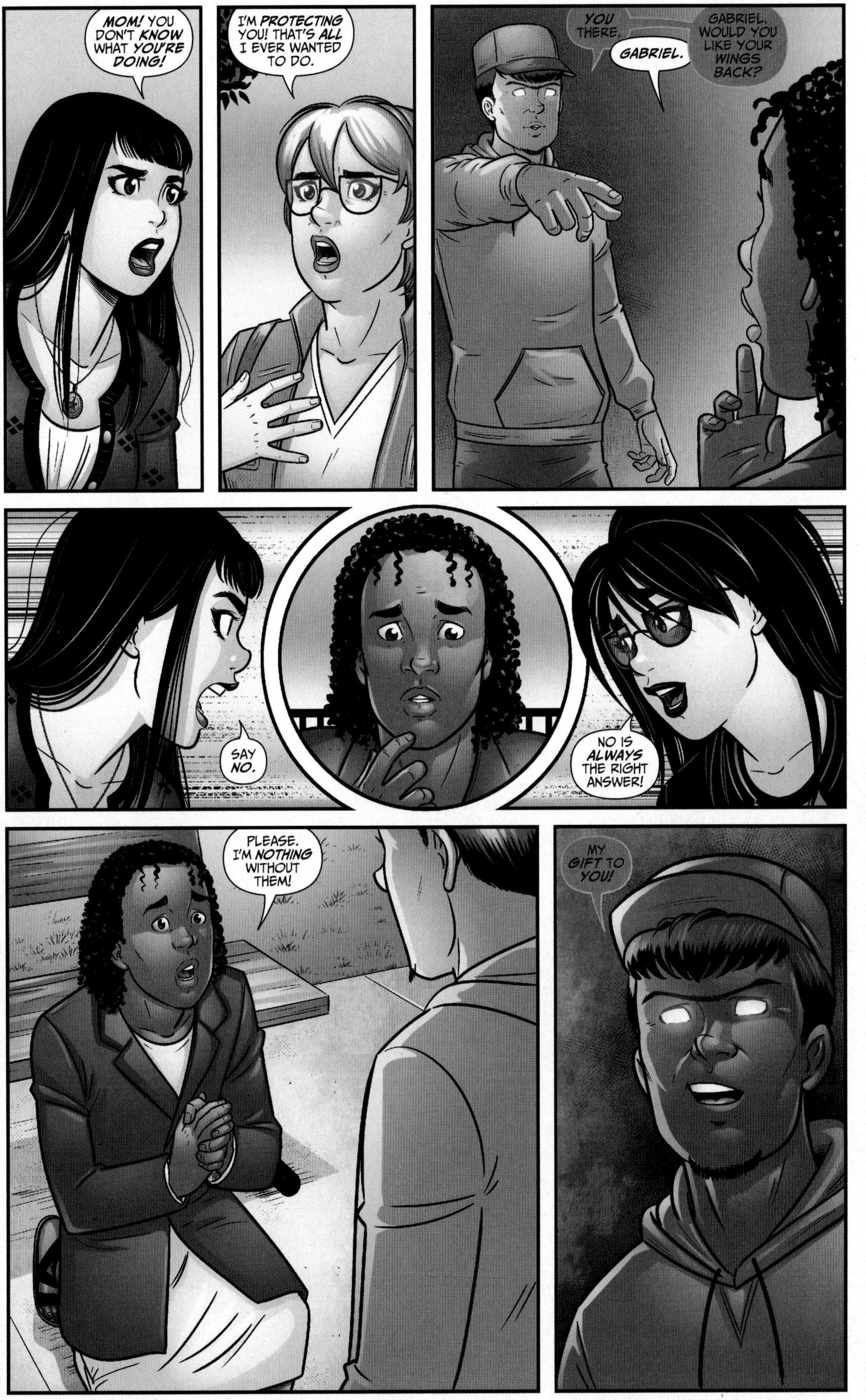
MOM! YOU DON'T KNOW WHAT YOU'RE DOING!
I'M PROTECTING YOU! THAT'S ALL I EVER WANTED TO DO.
YOU THERE.
GABRIEL.
GABRIEL. WOULD YOU LIKE YOUR WINGS BACK?
SAY NO.
NO IS ALWAYS THE RIGHT ANSWER!
PLEASE. I'M NOTHING WITHOUT THEM!
MY GIFT TO YOU!

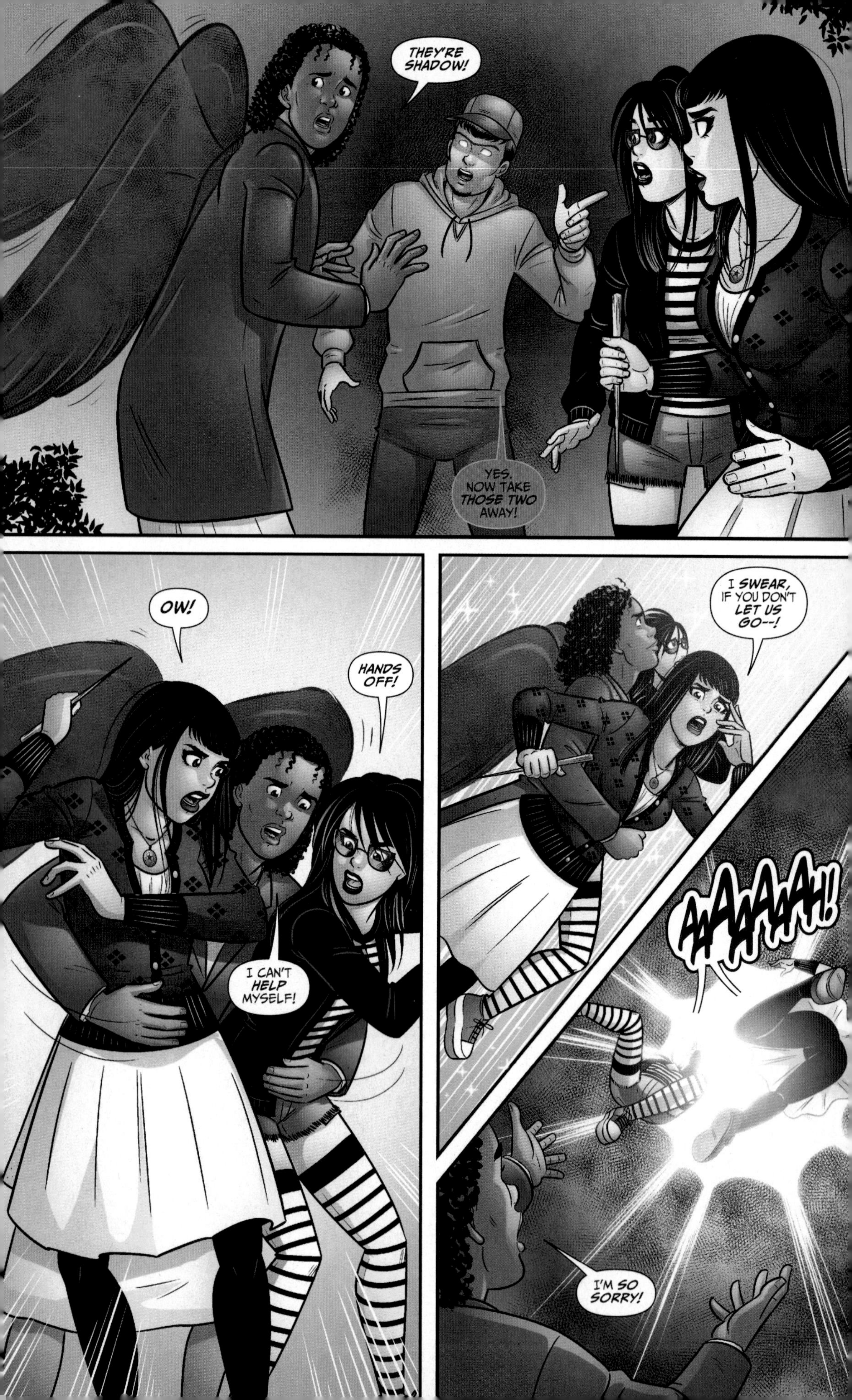
THEY'RE SHADOW!
YES. NOW TAKE THOSE TWO AWAY!
OW!
HANDS OFF!
I CAN'T HELP MYSELF!
I SWEAR, IF YOU DON'T LET US GO--!
AAAAAAH!
I'M SO SORRY!

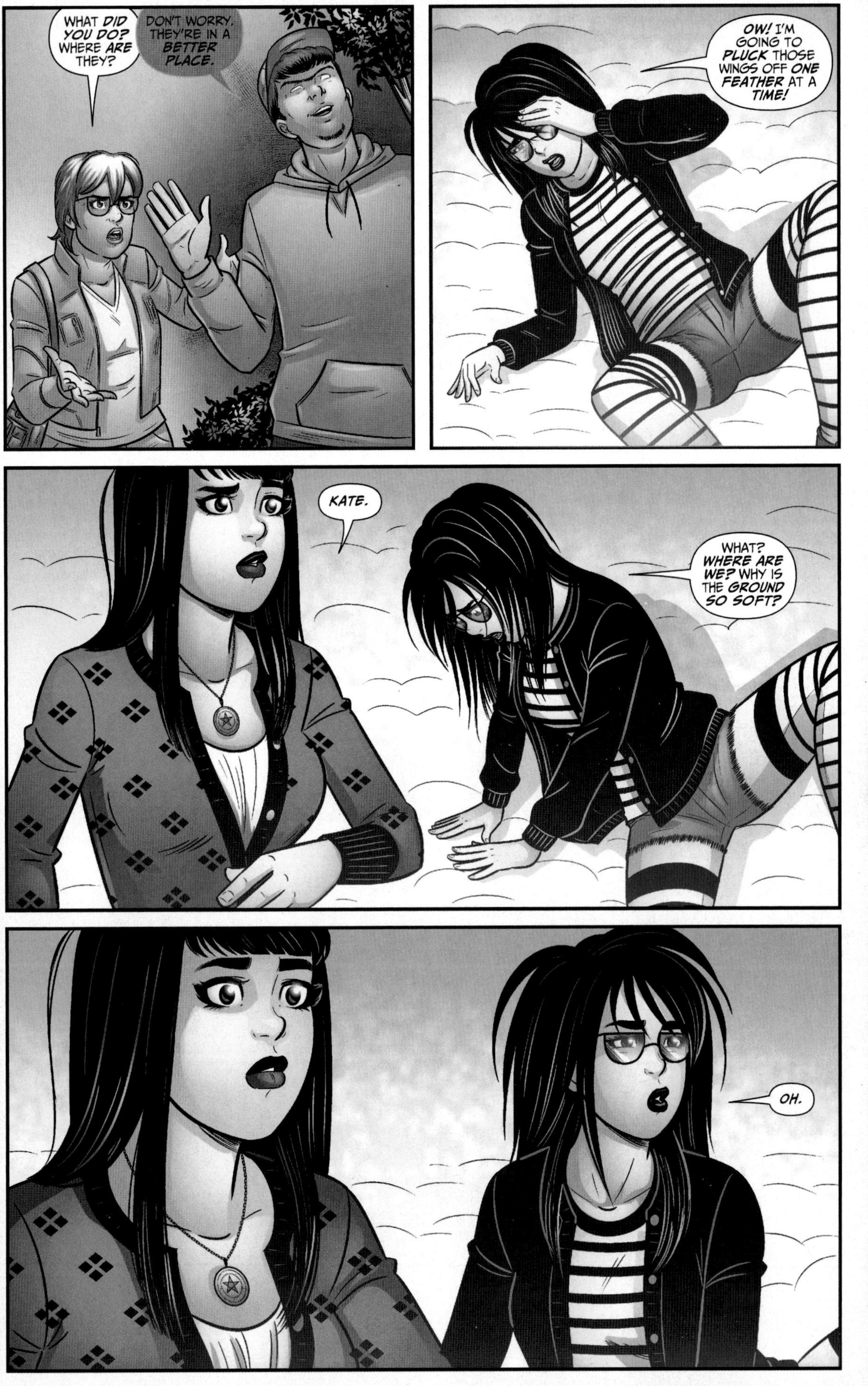
WHAT DID YOU DO? WHERE ARE THEY?
DON'T WORRY. THEY'RE IN A BETTER PLACE.
OW! I'M GOING TO PLUCK THOSE WINGS OFF ONE FEATHER AT A TIME!
KATE.
WHAT? WHERE ARE WE? WHY IS THE GROUND SO SOFT?
OH.

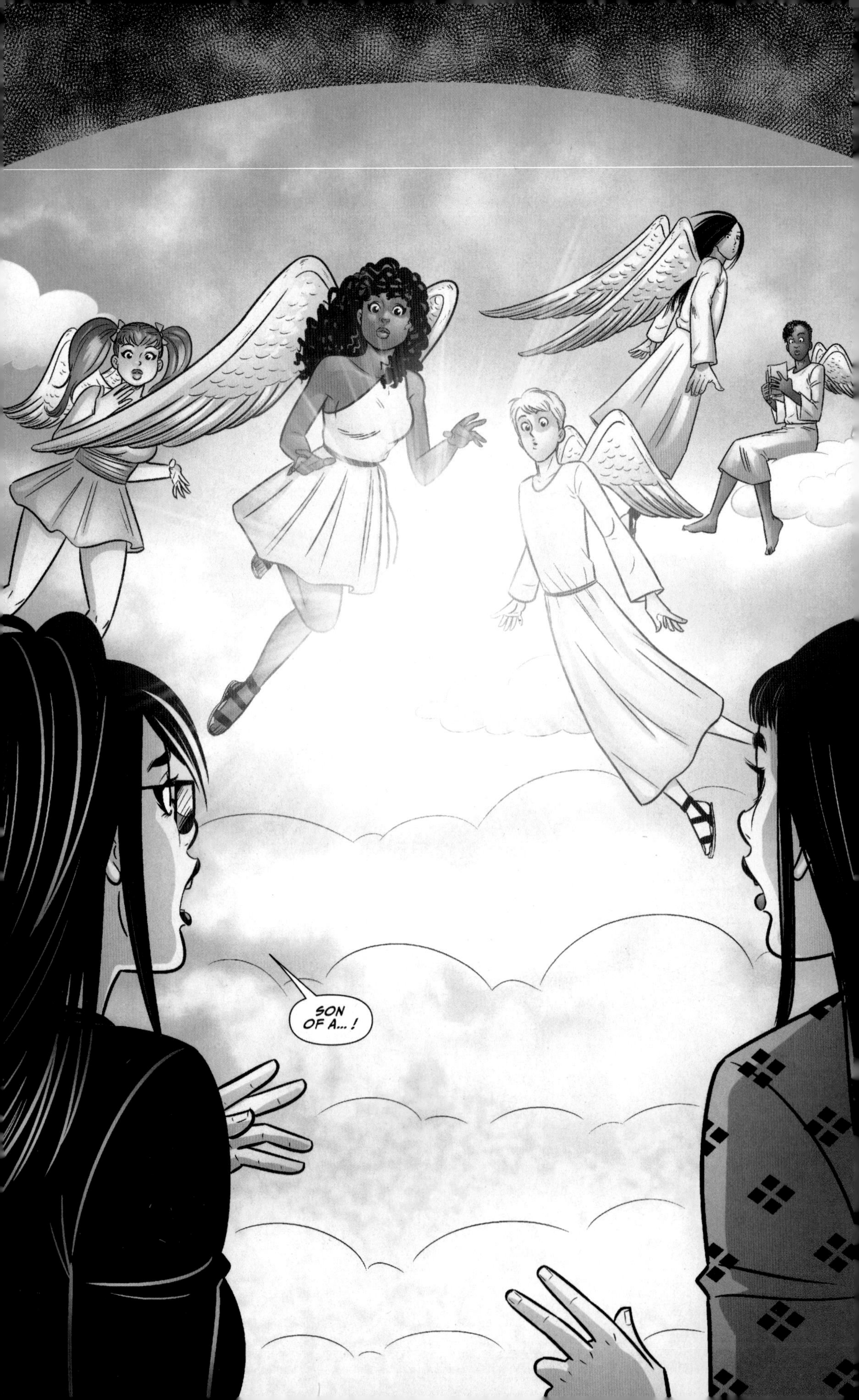
SON OF A...!

COVER GALLERY

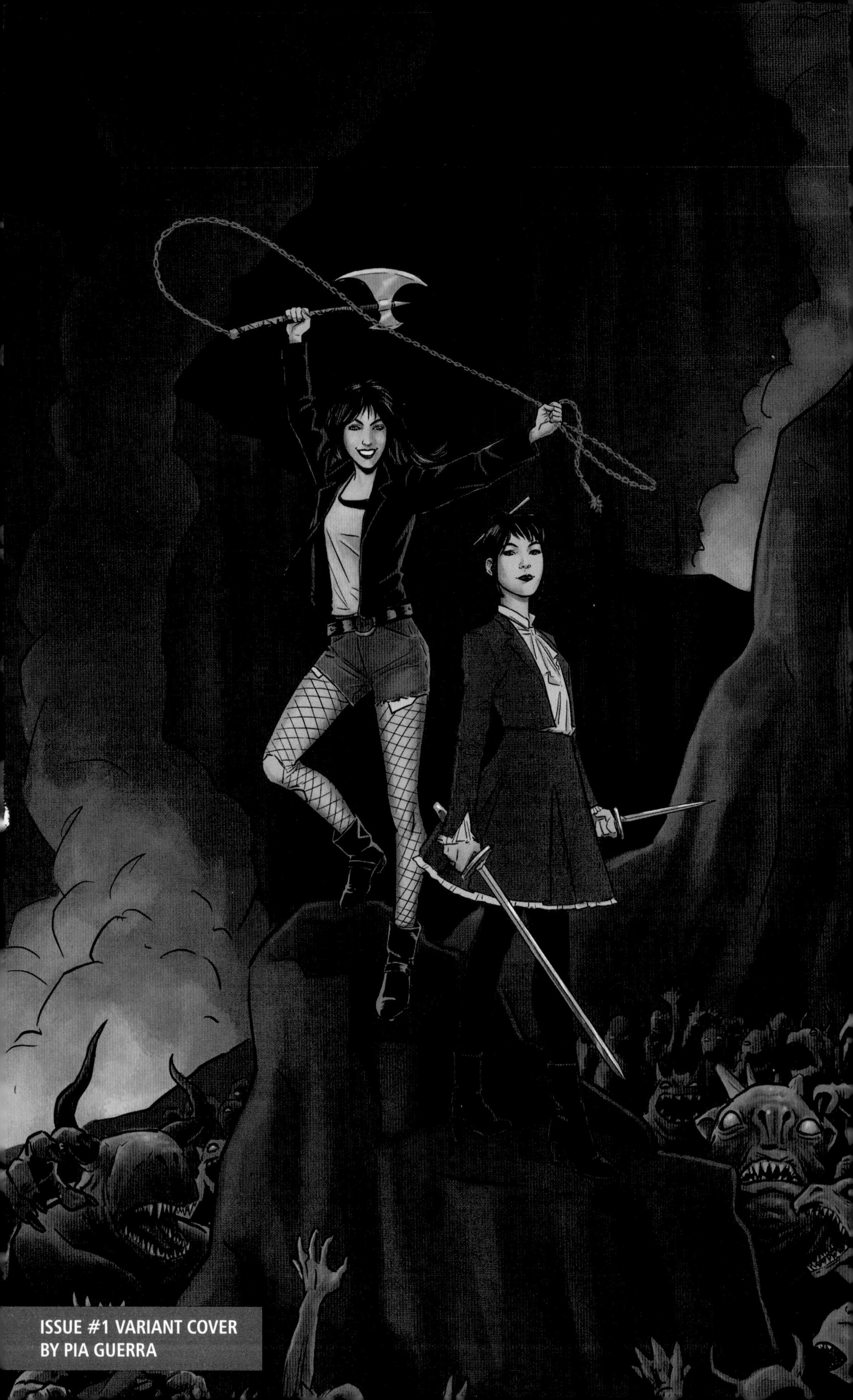

ISSUE #1 VARIANT COVER
BY PIA GUERRA

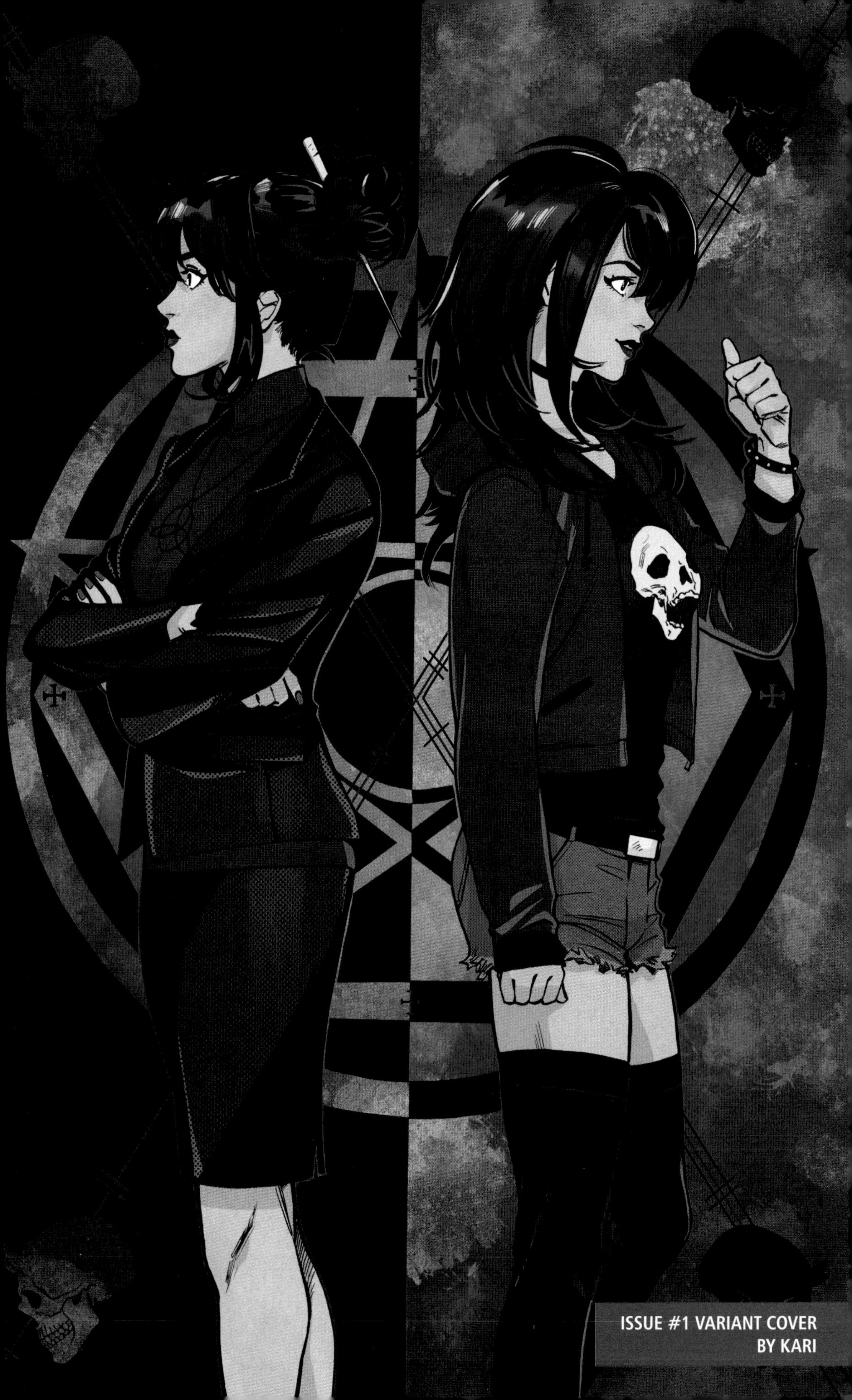

ISSUE #1 VARIANT COVER
BY KARI

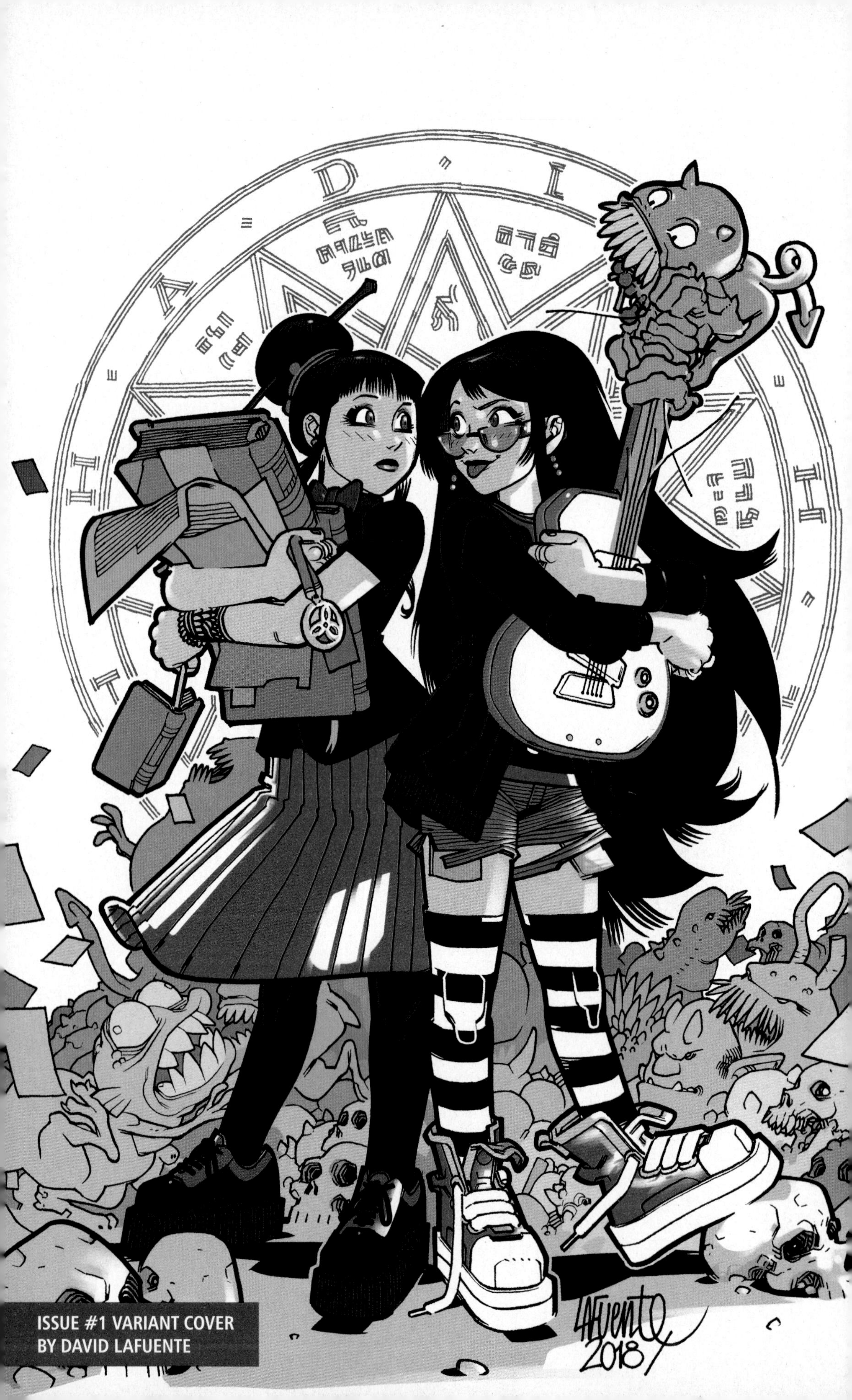
LAFUENTE
2018

ISSUE #1 VARIANT COVER
BY DAVID LAFUENTE

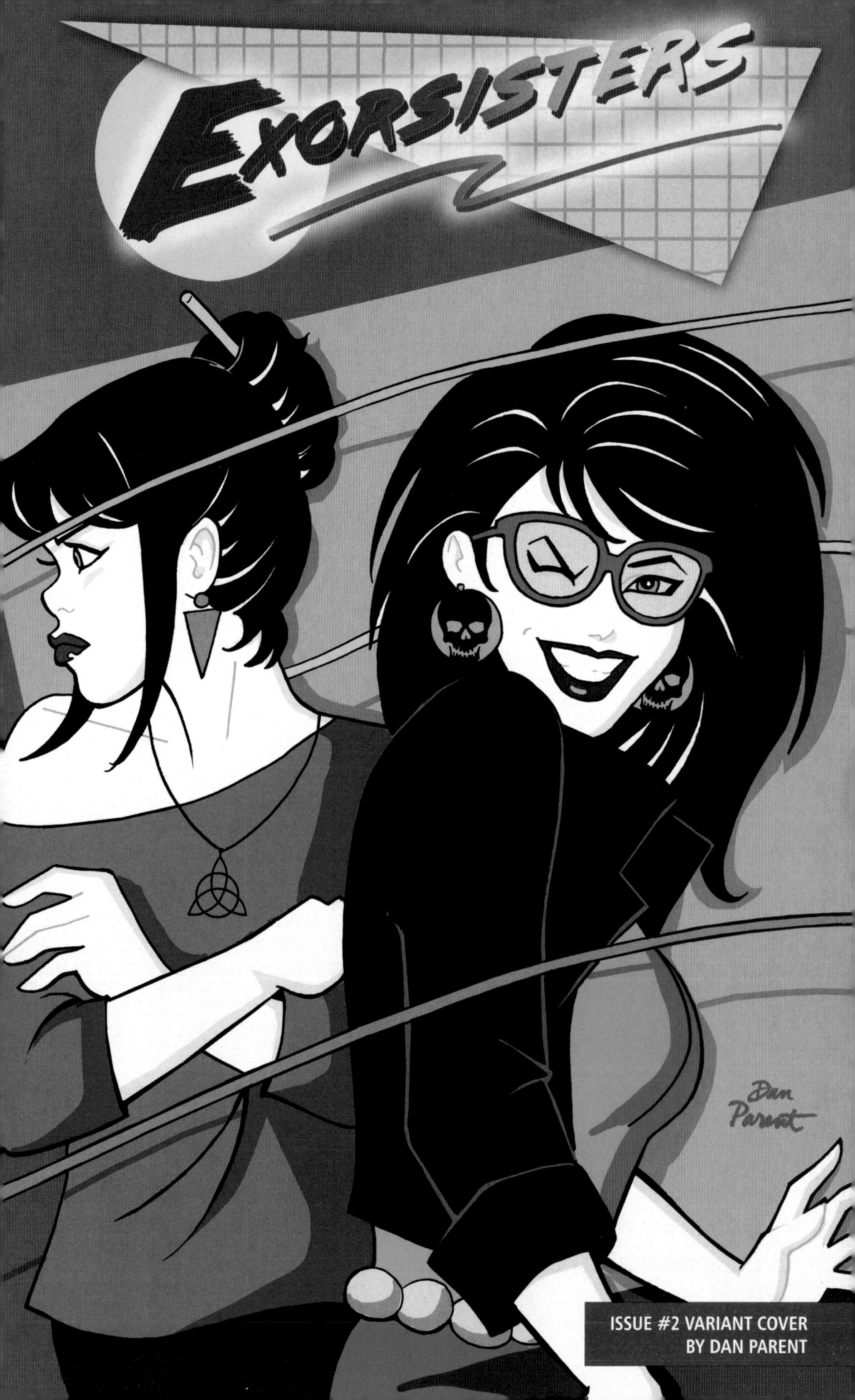
EXORSISTERS
Dan Parent

ISSUE #2 VARIANT COVER
BY DAN PARENT

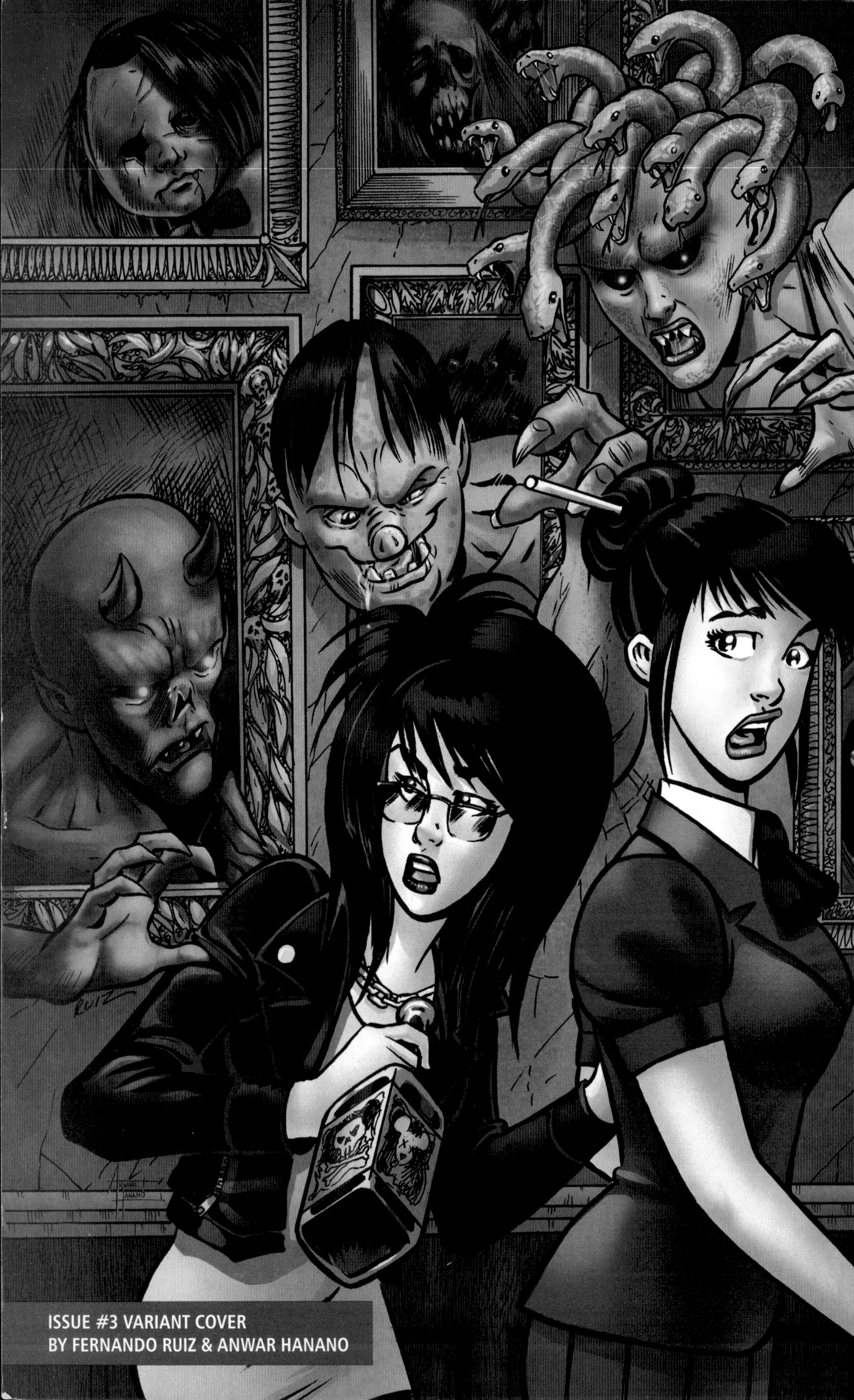

ISSUE #3 VARIANT COVER
BY FERNANDO RUIZ & ANWAR HANANO

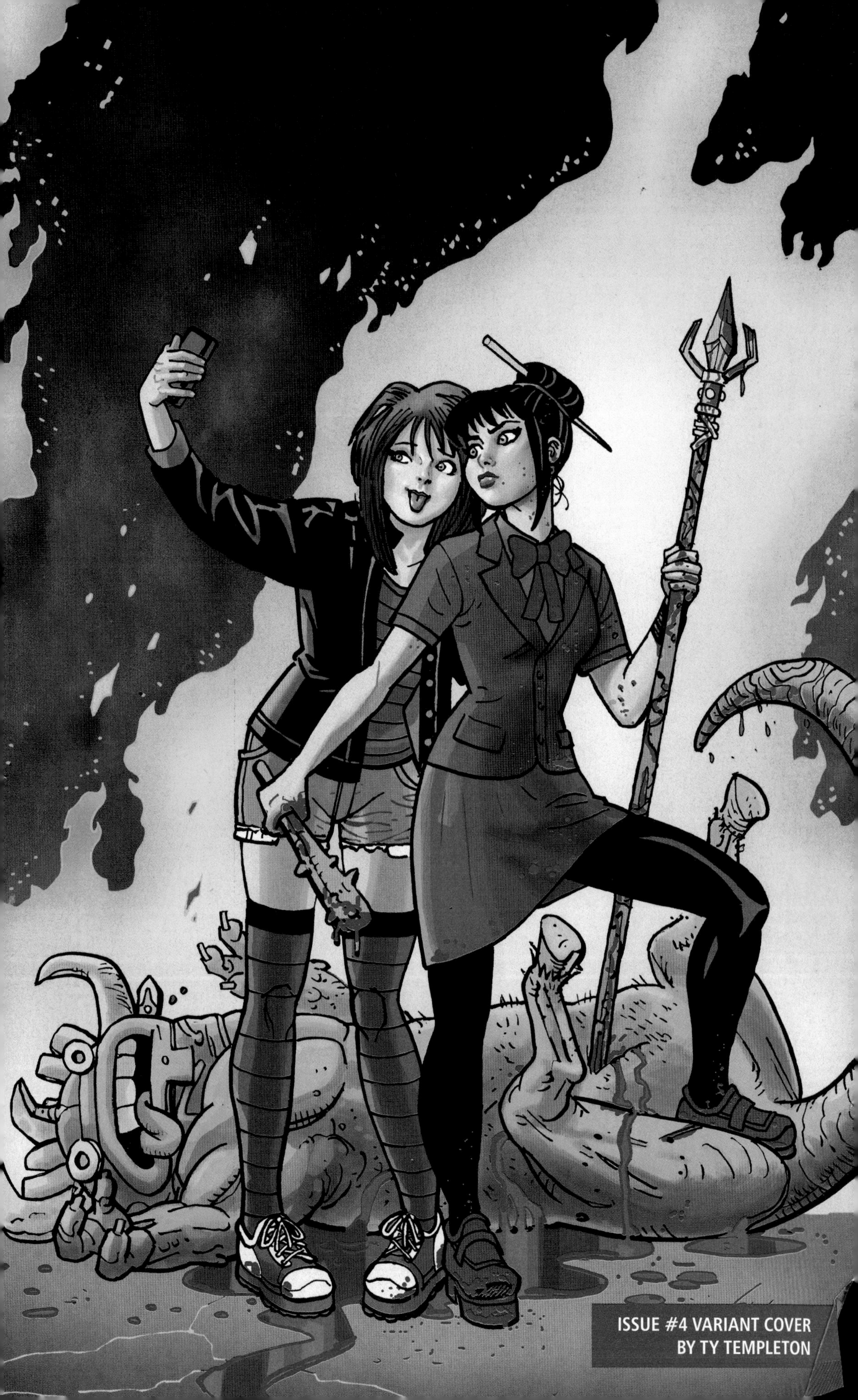

ISSUE #4 VARIANT COVER
BY TY TEMPLETON

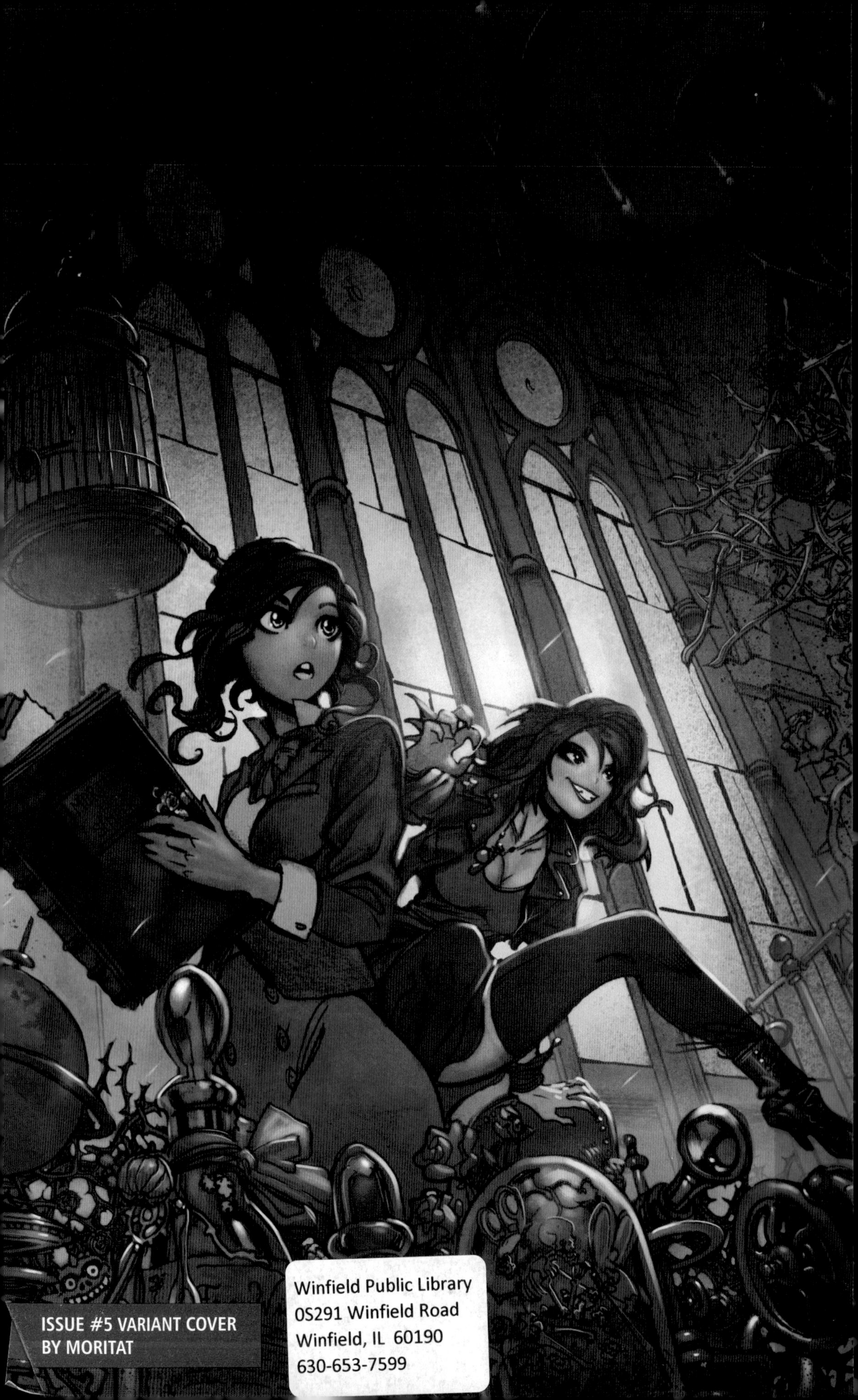

ISSUE #5 VARIANT COVER
BY MORITAT